CREATURES HERE BELOW

CREATURES HERE BELOW

A NOVEL

O.H. BENNETT

A BOLDEN BOOK
AGATE
CHICAGO

Printed in the United States of America.

Library of Congress Cataloging-in-Publication Data

Bennett, O. H. (Oscar H.), 1957-
Creatures here below / O.H. Bennett.
    p. cm.
Summary: "A black teenager and his mother create a makeshift family from their boarding house residents, but the son leaves home to confront his long-absent father"--Provided by publisher.
ISBN 978-1-932841-62-6 (pbk.) -- ISBN 978-1-57284-687-6 (ebook)
1. African American families--Fiction. I. Title.
PS3552.E54747C74 2011
813'.54--dc23
                        2011026352

10 9 8 7 6 5 4 3 2 1

Bolden is an imprint of Agate Publishing. Agate books are available in bulk at discount prices. For more information, go to agatepublishing.com.

for Pamela and Lillian,
for Bettina and Regina,
for mothers and daughters

MASON

Most of the blood was Mason's. It caused his ripped shirt sleeve to cling to his upper arm. Small drops landed on the white leather toe of his right sneaker. Mason turned the key and pushed the door open. He tried to do everything softly. He held his hand under his elbow to catch the drips and moved silently through the dark house. He slipped into the downstairs bathroom, easing the door shut with his shoulder before pulling the chain on the light over the sink. Instantly a face appeared in front of him, a dark, narrow, and closed face with brooding eyes, and tiny dots of blood sprayed from hairline to chin. That blood would belong to that brother who grinned too much, who talked too much.

Mason removed his shirt. The cut on his upper arm seeped vivid red, but it wasn't deep. He lowered his arm under the faucet and let water wash over it. He dabbed at the wound with a dry section of his balled-up shirt, dampened another part of the shirt and wiped the blood from his face. He avoided looking at his reflection except for the length of time it took to make certain his face was clean.

He couldn't recall how it had happened, exactly. They'd been behind Teddy's Billiards shooting craps, several men, old and young hunched in a circle passing bottles and dice. The brother who talked too much, a friend of Spider's, had made a joke. Mason couldn't remember the joke. He tried while wiping the blood from the toe of his shoe. Something about missing fathers and bastards. But the brother had eyed Mason specifically following the punch line. Mason guessed someone had told the brother the Pony story; after years and years, that still got laughs. Mason shoved the ru-ined shirt deep into the wastebasket beside the sink. The next thing he recalled was the crap shooters howling and cursing and the brother who talked too much scrambling up from their circle. The blade appeared in the brother's hand as quick as snap your fingers, but Mason moved in on him instantly, not giving him a moment to set. He drove his fists in with all his weight behind them, once, twice, and a glancing blow the third time. The faces around him were shocked at his speed. The upper arm cut had been inflicted on Mason's first stroke and he had not been aware of it until walking home. The brother who talked too much had a mouth of blood and torn lips and said from on his knees that he would be coming after Mason so he'd better watch his back. Mason said, "Bullshit talk got you in trouble in the first place."

The pain from the cut did not bother him, and now that he'd cleaned it, it no longer concerned him. The knuckles of both hands hurt a bit, but he dismissed that pain too. He reached up to pull the light's chain and hesitated. He regarded himself without comment, saw his bare, small, but muscular and virtually hairless chest. He had not enjoyed the fight but he was pumped up from it, as if on a slight buzz. It had all happened so fast, and had been so un-expected. Mason was embarrassed now, much more angry with himself than with a stranger who had made a dumb joke. His heart was just now settling behind his ribs. "Damn," he whispered and turned out the light.

He listened in the dark for the time it took his eyes to adjust. He listened for footsteps and voices just as when he was a boy craning an ear toward his door for the harsh whispers from his mother's and stepfather's bedroom. Mason felt glad for the silence and, in the darkness, relieved that for once his mother did not lie in wait for his return. No ambush, no flurry of questions asked too quickly to expect answers. And no lies from him. But Gail's presence still loomed in every corner of the big boarding house. She no longer had to confront him with her accusations; he knew everything she would say, just like he knew in the very heat of their arguing that they shared a common painful, unspoken agreement about the irrecoverable spiral that was his life.

Once adjusted to the shadows, Mason noticed a dim light from the baby's room. Sometimes Jackie left a lamp on all night for Cole, who'd shown signs of distrusting the dark. Mason crept by the stairwell that led to his bedroom and followed the light. The girl, Jackie, was in the nursery breastfeeding her baby, something Mason thought she'd given up. They sat in Gail's rocker within the yellow-shaded lamplight. Jackie had one leg up with the heel of her foot in the seat of the chair. The other leg stretched in front of her. Her right breast was only partially covered by her white terry cloth robe. Cole suckled the left. She sat, a disinterested, weary Madonna, gazing with fixed eyes not at her baby but at the wall a hand's length from her face. Mason stared from the doorway. Cole's light skin contrasted against Jackie's, which looked almost golden in that light.

"Does that taste good, ole King Cole?" Mason took a short step into the room.

Jackie's start registered only in her eyes and only briefly. She looked back at Mason without bothering to cover herself. "Did you come down here bare-chested to breastfeed my boy, Mase?"

Mason didn't say anything. He thought he smiled at her comment. He didn't take his eyes from her.

She said something about Cole, about how this was the only way she could get him to shut up. She certainly didn't seem to mind Mason's attention.

Mason told himself she was not all that sexy. She was such a tiny woman; even with a baby at her chest, she looked like a girl. But he found something alluring about her then, in the yellowish light, holding Cole, showing a smooth run of skin that rose with her breasts and flattened into the black spot of her navel.

Mason said, "Cover up."

"You cover up," she said. She leaned back, starting the rocker into motion. Cole's mouth came off her breast, then found it again. "God, hurry up, boy. Draining me dry every which way. Did he wake you up? Why did you come down?"

"I ain't been up yet. Just got in."

"Without a shirt? It ain't that hot out—" Then Jackie noticed the cut on his arm. "What happened to you?"

"She had long nails and a mean disposition."

"I guess so," Jackie said, evidently playing along. "She must have been a freak. Is that the type of girl you like? I never see you with nobody, Mase. What type of girl do you like?"

Mason sensed he should leave his mother's newest boarders be. He did not like Jackie, really. She was too loud and too fast, and she didn't seem to be much of a mother. Mason's mother had let everyone vote whether they wanted Jackie and the baby living there, inflicting all the noise and the smells and the hassles of an infant on them. Mason had voted yes. He believed that living in a nice home would be the first break Cole had ever received in his young life. But Jackie was always stepping out, roping everybody in the boardinghouse into babysitting at one time or another. Mason figured he spent more time with the baby than Jackie did, and he'd never seen Cole's father. Poor ole King Cole, he said to himself.

Jackie was saying, "—that's what the appeal is all about. Men like titty 'cause they remember back to when they was Cole's age, and they made chew toys outta their mamas. They feel all safe, and warm, and well fed. You ain't took your eyes off it once. You asked Cole what it taste like. Come find out for your own self." She stood long enough to return Cole to his crib, then leaned back in the rocker. She smiled at Mason while easing her robe off her shoulders. Her dark nipples pointed directly at him.

He felt heat rise in his chest, felt not the least bit the sting in his cut arm. He realized she was daring him, playing a game, but the ball was in his court and he couldn't move. He saw she was frowning at him now. He suddenly grew tight; the small room, not much bigger than a walk-in closet, seemed to be closing down around them. He smelled the odor from the plastic hamper near the crib, and from his own body; he smelled Jackie and the baby, a fleshy, sour, suffocating cloud.

He wanted to drop to his knees in front of her, push his face into her chest. He saw himself do it, how her arms would wrap about his head. But more than that, he wanted to breathe and found he couldn't.

Jackie straightened up in the rocker. Her feet came flat to the floor and she pulled her robe together, holding the lapels tightly in one hand. "What's wrong with you?" she asked. "Are you okay?"

"I can—" he began and stepped to her. He grabbed at her as she tried to pull away from him. The rocking chair lurched violently back, nearly spilling. Mason was trying to open her robe, not seeing that the moment had passed.

"Stop it, damn it," Jackie said.

He let go instantly. He slapped his hands down on the chair arms to stop the rocker from tipping over. Then he took a step back.

Jackie's angry frown turned into a grin. "You're wack," she said. "Didn't mean to rile you up so, Mase." She started laughing. She laughed at his confusion, his inability to take her dare, at the way he stood there stupidly in front of her.

He tried to think of something to say, but no quick retort came to mind. His hands closed into tight fists and Jackie stopped laughing.

"Hey, Mason," she said softly, "We're just teasin' with each other, right?"

He nodded almost imperceptibly and stepped out of the room. In the hallway, he found he could breathe again. For the second time within one hour, he was forced to puzzle out his reactions. First the fight and now this, and both had left him feeling much the same. As he climbed the stairs to his room, he thought he heard Jackie snickering behind him.

On his bed, he undressed to his shorts, kicking his sneakers across the room. He turned on the bed stand lamp, then turned it off. Thoughts of Jackie were brief, but the feeling of humiliation lingered. It was not Jackie's breasts he saw in his mind, but her wide mouth stretched open with laughter. Beside Jackie, he saw the grinning face of the brother who talked too much as he jabbered away to the circle of intent crap shooters. Mason's embarrassment heated his neck and the sides of his face. "Pony," he said and found it peculiar that the name had issued from his lips before it had formed in his brain. When he had thoughts of his father these days, every memory, every emotion they evoked surged in him as fresh and cutting as the day they were made. He slammed an elbow into the headboard behind him and jumped from the bed.

He went to the bathroom. Moonlight came through the translucent window and he relieved himself, not flushing to avoid waking anyone, and splashed cool water on his face without turning on a light. Just as he reached for the door to leave it opened and the light came on.

His mother, Gail, looked up at him from his chin level. Her eyes were partially lidded and she wore a black hair net. "Oh, I didn't know anyone was in here," she said.

Mason said, "Just finished."

"When did you get in?" This was asked reflexively; surely, they were both too tired for answers.

He did not want her to notice his cut. And he certainly didn't feel up to offering explanations, which she never listened to anyway. He said, "It's humid. Hard to sleep," hoping any sound from him would suffice.

Her eyes opened alertly. They roved over him while he waited for her to step aside. She said, "Uh, huh," without opening her mouth and went past him into the bathroom.

Mason shut and locked the door to his room. He flicked on the light then scooted under his bed. He slipped a hand into a rent in the thin cloth covering the underside of the box spring, then wormed himself back out from under the bed holding a small, brown sack. He found confidence in its weight in his hands, heavy for such a small, personal thing. He stuck his right hand in the wrinkled sack, then shook the sack away so that only the gun remained in his hand. He turned the gun over and over, held its barrel up near his left cheek, and looked one way and then the other like an assassin trying to determine which way his quarry had run. Then he held it straight out in front of him in both hands, elbows locked, aiming down the .38's sights at his closed door. He pressed his lips together and released them, making soft pow, pow sounds. The gun gave him a feeling of control in a way he did not understand. Already, visions formed in his mind: Pony in a room with him, and the gun hovering between them clutched in his hands, a bright spit of fire at the barrel's tip, and an end to the hate.

ANNIE

Miss Annie Gant woke gripped by pain in her left leg. The leg felt as if it was petrifying from her knee, hardening into a crooked column of stone beneath the sheets. The old woman clenched her teeth against the pain, digging with bony fingers into the blanket at her neck. She fought against the desire to cry out. A whimper escaped before she pushed her face into her pillow. She told herself to hold on. This pain had come before and she had fought through it. She wanted to ask God to help her be quiet, but feared removing her face from the safety of the pillow. She wanted to ask God for relief so she would not wake anyone, but Miss Annie was too afraid even to breathe. She wanted to disturb no one. No one must rush to her in the middle of the night as if she were the baby.

Long, tortuous moments passed and she silently struggled in the dark. She could feel blood finally begin to flow back into her limb, feel the relief of veins, once like the twisting hairs through marble, as they swelled again, returning life to her leg. She let out her breath and with lips moving against the fabric of the pillowcase, whispered thanks to God for allowing her to keep quiet. She heard her prayer answered with an inquisitive whine. A wet, black nose shoved toward her face.

"Shh, Sarrie girl, don't wake nobody. I'm all right now. Everything's all better. It's going away. I feel it letting go."

Annie considered Sarrie the most loyal of all her dogs and she was therefore her favorite. Annie could feel Sarrie's warm breath, see worry in the brow that dipped over large, opaque eyes. Behind her, she felt Digger jump up on the bed. She thought he too worried about her. But the terrier, being the most brazen of them all, probably just wanted the opportunity to obtain a soft resting place. He settled himself at her back. The others slept or waited patiently for their mistress to rise. They surrounded the bed, some huddled together, others quite independent, covering the floor like piles of clothes on laundry day.

Though the room was still dark, Annie could make out the hands of her bedroom clock. It was too early to climb from bed and start the day, yet she knew she would not go back to sleep. Death had showed her how he would take her: by locking up her joints, drying up her limbs until he reached her heart and she would turn into the ash she came from. While everyone else in the house slept, Annie waited for the first hint of morning to come through the blinds. Her pain slowly subsided and she hoped this morning she would be allowed to help fix breakfast. She held on to that thought for the rest of the dark hours remaining.

The house where Annie boarded was as old as she was, and it too had creaks and complaints. Upstairs in the hallway, and especially in Annie's room, the floor slanted noticeably, showing the uneven way the big house had settled through the long decades. The floorboards curved like an old woman's spine and they could tell her who walked over them by the pitch of their complaint.

In time, she heard the hallway floorboards and the shuffling of feet. She heard the toilet flush, then spray from the shower. That would be Tyler or Gail—probably Tyler from the way the boards creaked. Jackie rarely came upstairs and Mason did not get up this early. Mason would sleep til noon if Gail let him. But Mason was gone, she had to remind herself. How could she forget that?

On that early September morning, Annie had slipped down the stairs while the house remained full of shadows and every lamp and knick-knack on every end table and shelf sat perfectly still in the darkness. Everything sleeps except my dogs, she thought. Annie had heard them howling outside and had crept from bed to see what had disturbed them. She saw them on the floor and the chairs of the porch, curled into their sleep. When she turned from the window, she noticed the shapeless mass of the duffel bag by the front door. She eyed it for a moment but could arrive at no decision on it, so she dragged it to the meager light at the window. Men's clothes, briefs, T-shirts, a pair of jeans, and something else that startled her curious hands so that she first snatched them back out of the bag. Then she sent her hands back in, found the gun, and brought it out into the dim light, which gleamed on its nickel body. To Annie it seemed heavy, a somber weight appropriate for its ugly and sinister function. She dropped it back in the bag and wiped her hands on her nightgown as if something viral from it might cling to her skin. She knew instantly this would belong to Mason, not Tyler, and she whispered his name in the dark.

Annie headed toward the stairs, to go up to Mason's room, but then on a hunch went to the baby's room instead. He sat by pale yellow lamplight in the rocker, bouncing Cole on his lap and whispering nonsense to him. The baby would smile and reach toward Mason's face.

Annie said, "I didn't hear no crying. You didn't wake him this early just to play with him, did you?"

"Cole, tell Miss Annie you weren't asleep at all," Mason said turning the baby toward Annie. "'Miss Annie, I was just laying there,'" Mason said, adopting a baby voice. "'Eyes wide open, staring through them jailhouse crib bars, checking things out for my own self.'"

Annie remembered taking time that morning to look at the Mason no one else ever saw, the unhurried, unagitated Mason, smiling at Jackie's baby as if he were the proud father. He hugged the baby to his chest. To Annie, the teen appeared not too much older than the baby. Although momentarily subdued, flickers of his usual intensity showed in his pale brown eyes. He smiled up at her.

"I hope he goes to sleep now," he said.

"Is that why the duffel's in the front room?" Annie asked. "You going to check things out for your own self? I done looked in it already."

Mason came to his feet so quickly that Annie thought he'd drop the baby. She reached forward reflexively. But Mason handed Cole to her as he stormed by. She followed after him carrying the infant. Mason's right arm was submerged to the shoulder in the bag.

"It's still there," she whispered. "I wouldn't touch it, no Lord. Where did you get it? Where are you going? What do you need that for?"

"Always told you I'd go." He removed his arm from the bag and yanked the drawstring tight. "It wasn't just talk. I ain't just talk, you know."

"Where?" she asked, bending her face away from Cole's grabbing hands.

Mason shrugged. "I haven't made up my mind yet."

"You don't know. If that ain't the sorriest thing—"

"Keep quiet."

"If that ain't the sorriest plans I ever heard. You gonna just walk down the road in no direction at all? And what's the gun for? Where did you get it?"

"For protection, what else."

The baby was getting heavy for Annie. She wanted to sit down and she wanted Mason to quit this foolishness. She let the baby slip down to her out-thrust hip. "Is this because you and Gail had words last night?"

"Naw. I don't remember what words we had. I never know why Mama and me argue. We just do is all. Makes her feel better." He stepped close to Annie and Cole. "I'm the nothing nigger." He smiled the way Annie didn't like; only the right corner of his mouth turned up and only enough to suggest his impertinence.

"You promised your mama you'd go back and finish high school this summer. You're just two classes short!"

His response came under his breath and Annie did not catch it. But her words had no effect on him. He carried himself in a relaxed, sure way that said his mind was made up. Wherever he was going—and she felt he knew why if not where—he'd already set foot on the road.

The prospect of this house without Mason frightened Annie. She thought briefly she might move out too. But unlike Mason, Annie would have to answer the question of where before she set out. And she already knew there was nowhere to go. Who would let her bring all her dogs? "Sarrie will miss you, you know. She's become awful attached to you."

Cole gripped Mason's index finger, tried to bring it to his mouth.

Annie said, "I'm going to call Gail down. Let her talk some sense into you. I'll tell her about that gun, too."

Mason pressed his face an inch from Annie's. "You do and I'll shoot them dogs of yours, Annie. Shoot them dead."

Annie recoiled. Unable to reply in her shock, she ran away from him into the nursery and shut the door behind her. She leaned against the door, shaking. Cole began crying. She realized she was holding him too tightly. In the end, she was the only one to see Mason leave. And she was the only one who knew he had a gun.

Lying in bed, Annie sighed. Then more footsteps, quicker ones, Gail's certainly, sounded in the hallway then rapidly stamped down the stairs. Annie pushed herself from bed. It would be all right to get up now. She set her left foot on the floor and slowly stood on it, gingerly straightening the knee. Only a ghost of pain remained. Her curved toes pressed and spread against the worn rug of concentric ovals. Her feet never lifting above the worn nap of the rug, she moved across the room to her closet. She dressed and began moving with more confidence.

A knock came to Annie's bedroom door and Gail's head, helmeted in pink sponges, thrust inside. "You up, Annie? We're behind time already, and y'all ain't making me late this Sunday morning. This is a morning to be proud. I ain't working on CP time now and have heads turning when we run in all late."

"I've been up, slowpoke," Annie said. "I thought I'd go down and start some eggs and potatoes..."

"No, Annie, Jackie's already making gravy and biscuits. We're in a hurry. Tyler soloing in front of the Men's choir for the first time and I aim to be up front! Aren't you just so proud of him? Wait til I see Rachel Duncan; she's always making such a do over her George."

Annie bit off her disappointment at not being allowed to fix breakfast. Gail just did not trust her in the kitchen, she knew. "Ginger," she said harshly. "Get away from the door so Gail can come in."

Gail shook her head. The loose curlers wobbled. "That's all right, Annie. I ain't coming in. I've got to get these rollers down. Have you got all your mutts in here, Annie?"

Annie felt Sarrie brushing against her leg. "Well," she said looking down at the dogs, "The temperature dropped last night..."

"It's okay with me." Gail smiled. "You're the one who's got to live with the smell and vacuum up all the hair. Don't wear that dress, Annie. Wear your navy one with the jacket. We're going to be sitting up front; I want you to look nice."

Annie nodded. Pepper seemed to be walking with a limp, she noticed. She would have to take a look at him. "I could take the rollers out for you."

"No, I'll manage. Just wash up and get dressed."

Gail's head disappeared and Annie called out, "Gail?"

"Yes?" She poked her head around the door again.

"Pepper's not looking good. I think he's hurting."

"Well, you'll have to check him over when we get back. Isn't he the one you say eats whatever he finds?"

"But it's his leg."

Gail seemed to regard Annie for a moment. It was an assessing look Annie was very sensitive to. Gail made to close the door.

"Gail?" Annie called.

"What now, Annie?"

"You ain't said in awhile. Have you heard anything from Mason?"

Gail exhaled loudly while rolling her eyes and shut the door hard.

Annie said, "I got her mad, Sarrie." She began unbuttoning her dress. Mason had been gone for months; Annie realized she'd asked a fool question. Gail would've mentioned hearing from Mason. But she had not heard Gail speak his name in weeks, just Tyler this and Tyler that as if Gail's older son had already had the lid nailed on his box. Then Annie told herself that wasn't true. It was just that Annie missed Mason.

She washed her ancient face, which gazed back at her without blinking. The fleshy seams ran from all directions to the dark wells of her eyes. The wide, pronounced nose still remained, but the strong jaw had disappeared beneath loose skin. Where was the face Joseph Gant had kissed all over on her wedding day, the face he used to stare at until she would look down in embarrassment? She pulled on the stopper's chain and let the soapy water slowly drain away.

Nearly two months had passed since Mason left with his gun and no goodbyes. Dressed in her navy blue suit, her hair combed back into a small bun, Annie made her way downstairs, conscious of the multicolored stream of canine pelts that flowed around her legs. She first went to the windows in the living room, opened the blinds, and parted the curtains, allowing in the late October light. She looked out over the yard to the street. On Sundays and especially with winter coming early, the neighborhood was slow to awaken. Annie liked it best when the streets were teeming with people, children shouting and flashing by on their bicycles, little girls skipping rope, folk on their porches calling and pointing to their neighbors. The evidence of them could not be seen now, but Annie knew they would return. The people always came back.

Far down the street stood a pale green house, three stories tall with two yellow brick chimneys. Annie remembered when that house was the soft yellow of corn tassels and had a garden filled with blood-red roses. The neighborhood belonged to upper-middle-class whites then, mostly of German descent. Annie had come from the country to take a job as a maid, so fresh from the farm her new employer, Mrs. Buckler, had to buy Annie her first brand new pair of shoes. "Those won't do, Ann," Mrs. Buckler had said, pointing to the worn boots that had been Annie's mother's. "You'll ruin your feet. Ach! My guests will think me a penny-pinching ogre." So Mrs. Buckler took her by the hand to Camden's department store, where they would not serve her nor even let her in. Furious, Mrs. Buckler would select the shoes, bring them out to the sidewalk, and place the soles to the bottom of Annie's flat, leather-tough feet. "Maybe this scene in front of their window will shame them," Mrs. Buckler said. Annie loved the fierce-eyed woman right on the spot. She learned to prepare knockwurst and sauerkraut. The smell would fill that happy house, noisy with laughing blond children. She worked there twelve years until Joseph Gant took her away.

Annie smelled Jackie's biscuits and went into the warm kitchen. Cole sat near the table in his highchair drumming a spoon against the food tray. His mother snatched the spoon from Cole's hand. "You're playing on my last nerve, boy," she said.

Annie greeted them.

"Miss Annie, has Gail asked you for this month's rent yet?"

"No, she—"

"See, it's not due til the first, but come the last week of the month she gets all in my face, sweatin' about, 'rent day coming up'." Jackie rubbed a hand across her face. The tiny woman looked tired, Annie thought.

"Do you want me to make the breakfast for you?"

"Gail always think somebody's trying to pull something over on the rent." Jackie said, "Fuck the rent."

"I could run a stick of butter over the biscuits," Annie offered, but the young girl was not listening to her. Annie sat at the table next to Cole. She stroked his head, but he paid her no attention.

Jackie said softly, "Gail don't trust me."

"She doesn't trust me either," Annie said.

"I've got to get ready. I still haven't taken a bath. And if I don't go hear her precious Tyler sing, I'll never hear the end of it. She so much wants us to be one big, happy family—til rent day."

Annie allowed Cole to gum one of her knuckles.

"Would you watch Cole for me, Miss Annie? The biscuits come out in five minutes. I won't be long, but if I don't get in the tub now..."

Annie perked up. "Go on, girl. I'll take care of everything. Used to watch three babies at once back with the Bucklers."

Jackie disappeared.

Cole stretched from his high chair to reach one of his dimpled hands toward the spoon his mother had taken from him and placed on the table. Annie pushed him back down and told him to behave while wagging a finger at him. She went to the oven and checked on the biscuits. She hurried to the refrigerator for a stick of butter and daubed the tops of the biscuits. *I could put on some bacon right quick before Gail can say a thing about it,* Annie thought. She reached toward the back of the oven to butter the last biscuit when she heard a loud bang behind her. She turned her head. Cole and his high chair had toppled to the floor. Annie's arm went up and touched the heating element at the top of the oven. She heard her skin sizzle.

The baby began to cry as she ran to him, crooning "I'm sorry, baby. I'm sorry. You wanted that spoon didn't you?" She knelt and moved a hand over Cole's head and then his body, searching for injury. The baby wailed at the top of his lungs, his mouth wide, his face red and tears flowing. Annie felt a rising bump on the left side of his head. It was going to be a bad bruise. "Shh, Cole," Annie said.

"What's going on here?" Gail said, coming into the kitchen. "What happened?"

Annie looked up at her, feeling caught and helpless.

Gail ran over and took the baby from Annie. "Where the hell is Jackie?" Gail asked.

The baby's screams went unabated.

"There, there, big boy," Gail cooed to the infant, then hollered for Jackie, who came running still wet with a towel wrapped around her.

"What's a matter?"

Gail said, "You might try watching this poor child; he's yours. Look at the size of that bump already growing on the side of his head." Gail held the baby out to Jackie.

"But Miss Annie—"

"No. Don't give me no 'But Miss Annie was watching him.' You know you can't leave her alone with no baby."

Annie was still kneeling on the linoleum. She wanted to say something, to defend herself.

Jackie took the baby and inspected his injury. She told the baby to hush. Her towel fell away, staying up only where it was caught between her and Cole. "Shh, it's okay," she told him.

"Like you know," Gail said. "And if we got to take him to the doctor I suppose I'll have to be the one to pay for it again. You owe me from the last time. Here. Give him here. And cover yourself; Tyler's in the house." Gail took the baby back and began talking sweetly to him. He sniffed and continued crying, but his panic was gone.

Jackie covered herself and helped Annie to her feet. "Like Ty would mind," she whispered to Annie and winked. She glanced at the burn mark on Annie's sleeve and hissed, "Miss Annie—your arm!"

Gail went to the oven and turned it off. "There's an entire stick of butter with the wrapper melted on the biscuit tray. I told you, Jackie."

"I know, I know," Jackie said. Her eyes met Annie's.

Annie whispered, "I'm sorry."

"That don't help now, Miss Annie." She looked at the burn that had gone through the sleeve of Annie's dress. "Put something on that, okay?" She said to Gail, "Hand me my boy; I'm going to put some Bactine on that bump."

"Well, don't get any in his eyes," Gail said, taking in Annie with a glance as she passed Cole to Jackie. "And next time you'll listen to me," she added as Jackie retreated down the hallway. Gail turned to Annie, took her arm, and rolled up the sleeve. "What am I going to do with you, Annie?"

"I helped raise three of the Buckler babies. Cooked three meals a day for the entire family and the Mrs. used to just rave to her friends about how spotless I kept that house."

Gail stared Annie in the eyes.

Annie's dogs gathered at her feet.

"We'll put some butter on this," Gail said, "if there's any left."

GAIL

God is elusive. A preacher told Gail when she was still quite young that to live life right is to search for Him each and every day like a miner in the deepest hole looking for that vein of gold. Gail searches on her knees in her dark closet.

She is an old thirty-nine. She has borne three children: the first, the girl, Gail's mother took from her arms right after delivery. Gail could not find God then, though she called for Him. Gail's father, who would not stand for her mother's scheme, came back to help, but he was days late. He patted her hand while she remained bed-ridden and assured her he would find out where the child was sent and bring her back. But two days later he died of a heart attack and no one remained to champion Gail's cause. She called on God then too. But He did not come.

A preacher who found Gail in the last pew late one Sunday night told her God would not come when she called, but if she lived a Christian life, she could go to Him and He would always be there for her. So Gail began her search for God at every church and sanctuary she came across. There were sweet, sweet times when she came close or thought she'd found Him, when the music of the choir and the shouted word of the gospel seized her and she swayed and rocked, burned in the divine light. But the moments of communion were brief and rare. Now, when others hopped and flailed in the aisles and professed their love for Jesus, she too clapped hands and gave praise, but eyed them with skepticism.

Gail worked in various church missions, had attempted to tithe many times, and for a while sang in the church choir. She listened intently to the bellowing of Reverend Wilson for that one word, verse, or phrase that would make everything clear, that would allow her to give herself completely. Because no matter how often she placed her money in the silver tray, no matter how often she baked for the church sale, no matter how often she went to her dark closet, she could not overcome the anguish and resentment of her fourteen-year-old self who, exhausted from childbirth, had felt her daughter wrestled from her arms, and who had called upon a God who did not hear.

Gail wore the cream-colored dress with the pleats that showed she still had a figure. To hide her uncooperative hair, she shoved a wide-brimmed hat, also cream-colored, far down on her head. Her chin, with its shallow dimple, preceded her. Tyler walked beside her and she held on to his right arm. Annie and Jackie followed. This was the first time they'd gone to service as a group. But her boarders had expressed an interest in supporting Tyler on his big day. She wondered if Dan, her ex-husband, was coming; she had suggested Tyler call him. For a moment, while she dressed that morning, she had thought of Dan. It embarrassed her to think she still dressed with him in mind. She wanted to ask Tyler if his father would be there. She asked, "Are you nervous?"

He shook his head.

"Hey," she whispered to him. "I heard a new name for your list this morning. Ginger."

Tyler grinned, glancing over his shoulder at Annie. "Ginger? That is new. That makes an even dozen mutts, I think."

"We shouldn't make fun," Gail said and changed the subject. "Make sure you get a decent robe. Some are all frayed and the hems are coming down."

"It doesn't matter," Tyler said.

"What do you mean, it doesn't matter? Everybody is going to be watching you, honey. Course it matters."

"If I sound good then I sound good. If the robe is tattered people will say, Ty sounded good. They ain't gonna say, 'I sho felt uplifted til I saw that raggy robe!" Tyler laughed and Jackie must have been listening because Gail heard her laugh too. She gave Tyler a stern look that he, with a smile, absolutely ignored.

As they strolled into the churchyard of Calvary A.M.E. Gail could hear the organ already. "There better be seats," she said.

The boys with white gloves handed her a program. Gail liked seeing children dressed for church. It made her feel encouraged, as if clean, well-dressed children symbolized a social order that had escaped her, but thrived in other families in the congregation. She thanked the boys and waited just inside the door for Annie, Jackie, and Cole. Tyler kissed her on the cheek. This surprised her.

"If I embarrass us, it's your fault," he said, but he was smiling.

Gail was feeling proud, sensing his nervousness and bringing it on herself. "You're going to do just fine. All you have to do is feel it."

He said, "Yeah. I know."

Jackie went up to Tyler. She said, "Good luck, Ty." Gail saw her squeeze his hand.

"Hurry on," Gail said, pushing Tyler away.

The three women went down the aisle, Gail several steps in front of the usher. The front pews were full, but Gail made a space for them purely from the force of her will and the shove of her thighs. She managed to ignore the critical looks her pushiness gar-nered while waving to Rachel Duncan, who sat farther down the row. No sooner had everyone adjusted to the compressed intimacy of their new positions than they were instructed to stand by the assistant pastor.

The woman in a black robe behind the pulpit lifted her hands heavenward. She was a big woman with a square, mannish jaw and short, shiny hair. She smiled maternally at the congregation, who came to their feet and waited on her. "I know I have to thank God for waking me up this morning."

"Yes," some responded.

"Well," said a few.

"Praise Him."

"I know I have to thank God for setting my feet on solid ground and enabling me to worship in His house this morning," the minister said as she received more encouragement and scattered hand claps.

God's cheerleader, Gail thought, but she clapped her hands on this Sunday, eager to capture the spirit. Eager to see her son walk out in front of the choir. Eager for his voice to fill every ear.

"Do you want to thank God this morning, people?"

Now all responded and the organist touched his keys and the congregation sang on cue,

Praise God from whom all blessings flow.
Praise Him all creatures here below.
Praise Him above ye heavenly hosts.
Praise Father, Son, and Holy Ghost. Ah-men.

The pastor seemed to swell in her robe as she threw her arms out to her sides. "Please remain standing as the Calvary A.M.E. Voices of the Lord Gospel choir processes in. May their song be acceptable to You, oh Lord."

The choir marched in. They swayed from side to side with each step in unison and clapped.

Gail instantly spotted Tyler. He hadn't gotten a good robe, she noted, but was too full of pride to care. Jackie patted her hand. Gail nodded. She felt flushed with a mix of emotions and for a second almost dizzy. Just this one left, she thought. One snatched away, one ran away, and just the one left.

"Behave, be still," she heard Jackie say to Cole.

Gail said, "Cole, do you see Ty? Looky, Cole, there's Tyler." Gail was struck with a sudden, funny envy of Jackie. Not envy of Jackie's youth, for Gail would not have that again even if she could. Too many mistakes came with being young. Young people lived too easily, cooking up regrets they'd have to chew on in their old age. Jackie was young and made the same foolish mistakes Gail had made. But no one had come to take Jackie's first-born away. She had her baby and the chance to make something good from something bad. Gail knew Jackie did not realize how fortunate she was, and since Gail was in church, the word *blessed* came to mind. Yes, the girl did not realize how blessed she was. *One snatched away, one ran away, one left.*

Reverend Wilson was talking now, not delivering his sermon, but making announcements on weddings and funerals, and naming the shut-ins. Gail heard little of what he said, anticipating her son's singing debut. She allowed herself a quick second to look around for Dan. She knew where he stood when it came to attending church, but couldn't figure him missing Tyler's solo. Missing. She wondered about Mason. She felt her hands tighten. Mason and that easy anger that ignited with the thought of him.

"Put that back, Cole." Jackie took a dollar from the infant's hand and placed it back in the silver offering tray. "But don't you have the right idea." She smiled and held the tray out to Gail.

"Hold it a sec." Gail removed a neatly folded ten-dollar bill from her purse and placed it in the offering. Annie put in two dollars she could scarcely afford. "Annie, take that out. I was putting in for both of us," Gail whispered.

Annie smiled and passed the dish on.

Gail wondered if Annie had understood her. She looked from the old woman to the young one with her arms full of squirming baby. Appropriately, Gail sat in between the two of them. She was still thinking about Mason, seeing his lean face with the crooked smile, wondering what else she could do. She had told the police, but Mason was an adult now and though they assured her they'd keep an eye out for him, there was nothing they could really do. She called his friends once a week. "Jimmy, this is Mrs. Neighbors, Mason's mother. I'm calling—yes, hello. Then you've heard nothing? Sorry to bother you then." The boys were tired of her calls; she could hear it in their voices, which had changed from a sincere sympathy to curt politeness. But she would still take her list of names and sit by the phone every week for nearly an hour. She learned to change up the day she phoned so her call could not be predicted and ignored.

Now she had two lost children to fantasize about. Gail had these daydreams about the daughter she named Lillian. They begin with Lilly's age. She is ten and today she is jumping rope with her friends, and later they will go get ice cream. She is thirteen and this morning got her period for the first time, nervous and excited about becoming a woman. She is fifteen and tonight she is studying for a high school math test; she is good at figures, but English is her favorite subject. In the mornings mostly, Gail will sit at the kitchen table with her hands around a cup of coffee that will grow cold, and weave the intricate details of her lost daughter's life. She has dreamed her through her first kiss, on the back porch with a sweet boy while rain fell hard all around, and she has dreamed her to marriage, and now that Lilly is twenty-five, Gail has dreamed herself as a young grandmother.

Lilly is somewhere, and she is twenty-five.

She could not create such a world for Mason. Too much went with it, too much anger and regret she knew about. She knew the hyperactive boy who broke vases and cut his own little brother with one of the shards, and the teen who came home drunk and vomited on the stairs. She could not soothe herself with fantasies for Mason. Trouble attached itself to his heels like a shadow and followed him step for step. Wherever he had gone, this shadow would be there too.

They argued the last time she saw him. This one had been about the same things as the others, his promise to finish school, his staying out so late, his getting drunk. But the ending of the last one had been different.

The last argument was really about Gail stepping out on the porch to look down the street for him. It was about listening for his footsteps across the kitchen floor while pretending to watch the late night news. It was about his red eyes. This last argument took on a great significance. Gail brought it to mind often, trying to squeeze the details from it, searching for the evidence that he would leave her and clues to where he would go.

She had confronted Mason and his red, half-closed eyes at the kitchen door and followed his retreating back up the stairs to his bedroom.

"Why do you have to stay out so late, Mason? What is the fascination? I've lived in this town a long time and I know there is nothing going on out there worth seeing or doing."

Mason said, "Don't grief me. I'm beat. I gotta crash." Red veins netted his eyes. He dropped on his bed and kicked his sneakers off. He rubbed his eyes so violently with the balls of his palms Gail reached to pull his hands away, but then brought her hands down to her hips instead. "I'm an adult—"

"No. You're old enough to be an adult."

He snickered at that and his mouth dropped into a yawn.

"The woman you had the interview with called this evening wondering where you were. Did you think if you stayed out late enough I'd forget to ask you about it? Why don't you care about anything? School, something?"

"We're not doing this again. I ain't. Get off my back." He aimed an index finger at her face.

Gail didn't remember exactly what she said next. She recalled her anger though. Maybe she said nothing. He slowly curled the finger away. "I've had it with you. I'm full up with your shit," she told him.

"I don't blame you," he shouted back. "Kick me out. Kick me the fuck out." He came to his feet and glared down on her.

She was being dared. She thought so at the time, but now wondered if being kicked from the house wasn't exactly what he'd wanted. Then they were shouting at each other. All the old stuff spewed up like vomit. He was lazy, he hung out with hoodlums, he took money from her purse, he didn't help around the house. It was almost comfortable, as long as they stayed away from his dare.

Tyler stopped in the doorway in the middle of it. Darker than Mason or Gail, like his father, he wore only his briefs. "If you two would give each other and the rest of us a break..." he said. Gail told him to mind his own business, and he stomped away.

"I gotta work things out," Mason said. "All I ask from you these days is to leave me alone."

"You ain't turning out to be nothing," Gail said. "Not a damn thing. Just a nothing nigger."

Mason smiled at that, showing teeth on just one side of his mouth. "Nothin' comes from nothin'," he said.

She tried to slap him then, but he caught her wrist when her open hand was just inches from his face. He held her wrist even though she tried to pull it free. He still smiled crookedly and for a moment that grew longer each time she remembered it, Gail was afraid of her son. Jackie hollered something from downstairs about waking the baby.

Mother and son glared at each other and Gail hoped he could not see her fear. "I bet you better let me go, boy."

"I don't take hittin' so easy anymore. Do I?" He towered over her.

In that long second, she knew she no longer had any control of him. Gail ceased pulling against the strength of his grip, and he opened his hand. His fingertips left bruises on her wrist that were visible the next morning.

Mason let himself fall back across his bed. His feet still touched the floor. Gail could think of nothing to say to him. As she sat in church thinking of the last time she'd seen her eldest son, she absently rubbed her right wrist. Her last words to him had been spoken over her shoulder as she stood in his bedroom doorway. She heard Cole crying downstairs. She said, "You're just like Pony, just like him." He said nothing, but she heard him move, just a bit, on the bed; she had gotten her slap in. Pony Reed was Mason's father.

Now, months later, a new realization stole upon Gail. Her last words had not been news to him. They had just confirmed what he suspected and feared about himself all along. When he had said nothing comes from nothing, he had not been speaking of her but of Pony Reed. Gail pressed a hand over her eyes, but the tears came anyway. She had struck out at him with what scared him the most, the blood of his father.

"Look, Miss Annie, the proud mother is crying." Jackie patted Gail's leg.

"What?" Gail looked up. Tyler stood in front of the choir finishing his solo. His voice boomed off the stained glass windows filling the church wall to wall, but she had not heard him. He held the last note, expelling the last vestige of energy from his focused body, and pulled the young and old believers alike to their feet. Annie stood waving him on. A woman behind Gail said into her ear, "He's got the spirit, Sister Neighbors, he surely does."

Reverend Wilson came to stand next to Tyler just as he finished. "Praise the Lord." The reverend, so much bigger and rounder than Tyler, hugged him into the folds of his sweeping robe. "Y'all ain't been that spirited in a long time."

Jackie nudged Gail. "You were so nervous, you looked like you couldn't bear to watch. But he done real well. I didn't know Ty could sing like that."

Gail pulled a handkerchief from her purse and wiped at her tears.

Reverend Wilson was saying, "So many of our youth these days have no time for church. They're out on the streets, running loose with sin. Grabbing evil and injecting it into their veins. So I feel especially blessed when one of our young people comes before us and offers his gifts and talents to the Lord. I do believe Brother Neighbors deserves a hand. Amen!"

Gail rose to her feet, applauding along with the rest of the congregation. She saw Tyler become suddenly bashful and retreat to his spot in the choir. She tried to make eye contact with him, but he kept his head down. She kept trying to find his eyes, to let him know she had been with him, even though she hadn't. Her last argument with Mason replayed in her mind while she very carefully dissected it, missing altogether the rest of the service.

Outside, the women waited for Tyler to join them. Cole started whining and Annie said she thought he was getting a tooth. Gail eyed Cole without comment. The light-complexioned baby had been fathered by a white college boy. Jackie never spoke of him. Gail wondered who was the young fool who would miss that first tooth.

Dan Neighbors walked right up to Gail and she did not see him until Jackie nodded his way. "You look good," he said to Gail. He rested a large hand for a brief moment on her shoulder. "You always did know how to dress sharp. I like that."

Jackie said, "Hello, Daniel."

He grinned with his oversized, white teeth. He said, "Hello, Jaclyn. And good morning, Miss Annie."

"Did you hear your son, Mr. Neighbors?" Annie asked. "He was something."

"I made it just in time. That old Buick of mine, you know. Where is he? Putting away the robe?" Gail watched the way Dan's eyes took all three of them in. Why didn't he seem to ever change? Yet a few tight coils of white frosted his temples. "You know, his robe looked a might raggy around the bottom, Gail. Why didn't you tell him to pick out a nice one? Seeing as how he was going to be out in front and all."

"Maybe if you'd showed up on time you could have told him."

"Okay, okay." He held his palms up in surrender. "Don't start nothing on God's front yard now."

"You going to preach about God to me, Dan?"

"Wouldn't dream of it, Gail."

No one else spoke for a few uncomfortable moments. Dan pushed his hands into his pockets and pulled out the front of his pants. Gail pretended to be interested in Cole's shifting facial expressions. She always snapped at Dan whether he deserved it or not.

She considered apologizing. "I'm glad you came," she said.

He nodded and looked away.

To everyone's relief, Tyler came bounding from the church, keyed up from his success. Father and son hugged. Everyone told Tyler at once how well they thought he did.

"Could you see me in the back, Ty?" Dan asked.

"Dad was in the back waving and hopping the whole time I was singing," Tyler said. "I thought he was doing jumping jacks back there. Keeping the blood going so he could stay awake."

"Church does put me right under, but not today. You had everyone on their feet. You done good, boy." Tyler beamed. Dan continued, "I could show you some moves to go along with it." He began doing the twist, shaking his behind with exaggeration from side to side while trying to sing, "Jesus will never fail you. Oh, oh no. There's never been a time when he did not answer my call..."

Jackie laughed loudly. "He didn't get his singing talent from you, Dan."

Annie hid her smile with a hand.

Gail watched the frowns of other church members as they filed by to their cars. "Behave," she said.

Dan and Tyler laughed together. Ty slapped him five. He said, "Why don't you come back to the house today, Dad?"

"Oh, I can't, son." Gail noticed how Dan looked at her now. "Lavette is waiting for me in the car. I better get back before she takes my head off."

Tyler nodded and shrugged.

"Hurry," Gail said, "we don't want to disappoint her or anything."

"Gail..." Dan pressed his lips together and backed away a couple of steps.

"Leave him alone, Mama."

"Gotta go," he said and as he walked away, he began his singing again. Tyler and Jackie rewarded him with laughter.

"Mama, why do you have to be mad at him all the time?" Tyler asked.

"I'm not mad," she said. And after she'd walked a couple of blocks down the street, she forgot all about being snappish with

Dan Neighbors. She thought about Mason, and Pony Reed, and if stopping by the police station again would do any good at all.

MASON

Weeks before he left home, he had imagined how he would feel, what the morning would be like when he stepped onto the porch for the last time. His back would straighten as all the weight of the house tumbled from his shoulders. His lungs would inhale freedom like cool, morning air, and a giddy high would lift him as he eased the door shut behind him. No more of her rules, no more in by eleven or God's judgments, or that damn Dan Neighbors, or "Tyler manages to get up for Sunday service," or "Tyler finds work and brings a little money in," or trying to explain himself to her when he didn't know himself, or why is every little fun thing somehow wrong? The nothing nigger would just leave. The sun would be just coming up, still tucked behind roofs and chimneys. He'd sling his bag over his shoulder and march down the street aware that other early-morning risers along the way would spot him and wonder about his departure. He would ignore them, striding down the walk, never looking back.

It was still dark when he did slip from the house. He cursed Miss Annie in whispers, telling himself he was mad at her for being such a busybody and forcing him to leave hours before he'd planned. He responded to the guilt he felt at threatening her by trying to convince himself she had brought it on herself. She had been the only one who never hassled him, the only member of the Mason fan club, until he scared her by threatening to shoot her phantom dogs. She's just an old crazy woman who boards with Mama because no one else will have her, he thought. But he knew Miss Annie had more sense than others gave her credit for, and that they had been allies because they saw in each other qualities everyone else missed. He placed a hand back on the doorknob. The thought that the old lady would be glad he'd left bothered him.

One hand grasped the doorknob, the other the cinch of his duffel bag, and he did not move. To go back in would be wrong. His mind spun like a squirrel caught in the middle of traffic, frantically circling until hit. Write her, or maybe even call. Yes, that would do. His hand fell away from the door. He could write her later, tell her he was sorry. She might even like getting letters.

Mason went down the porch steps and walked across the lawn to the sidewalk. Children run away from home at night. Adults look you in the eye and say, "I'm not taking crap from you anymore; I'm out of here. I'm a history lesson, study that!" Mason walked down the street. No one witnessed his departure. *I should have said that to Mama's face,* he thought. This marked the first time he realized how immature it was, his leaving. Sneaking away like this made her seem even more right. Right about everything. That suggestion burned in him for blocks. He had to swallow down his frustration. "But this is so much less hassle," he finally said. "Let her wonder what happened. This is so much smoother."

He went several blocks in one direction before turning a few corners. A couple of backyard dogs barked at his passing. The freedom high he anticipated never surfaced. He labored instead to keep his thoughts as neutral as possible. His decision had been made and he did not want to waste effort rethinking it.

He arrived at Kenny Gamble's house. No lights shone. He was much too early. He circled the house. Everything was dark and locked up. He feared someone might think he was a prowler and call the police. They would search his bag and this entire adventure would be over. He didn't want to risk waking Gamble too early, either. He'd be the type to get pissed and Mason would lose his ride. He sat for a while on the porch steps, scratching at the sparse fuzz that grew under his chin and growing sleepy. He went over to Gamble's old Cutlass and tried the doors. The rear passenger-side door opened and he climbed in. He cleared the back seat of empty cigarette cartons and Styrofoam Big Mac containers, pushing the trash to the floor. The car smelled like cigarette smoke, damp cushions, and spilled beer. He propped his head up with the duffel bag and worked to get comfortable, which with his long legs was nearly impossible. He finally settled himself, wanting to sleep at least for a couple of hours, but he remained awake. He tried not to think backward to Mama and Tyler, and Dan. He allowed himself to think about Cole for a while until he wondered what the boy would grow up to be, then he cut that line of thought loose.

Mason fished the .38 from the duffel bag. He'd stolen the gun from the apartment of a guy whose girlfriend had let Mason in. He had flirted with and followed her for blocks. "Don't touch anything. This is my boyfriend's place," she'd said as soon as they were inside. That angered Mason. He began opening every cabinet, drawer, and cupboard in the place. It turned into a game, really. She followed directly behind him squealing protests and immediately slamming shut whatever he opened, permitting only quick glances inside. He made a note, though, of in which kitchen drawer he'd spotted a gun barrel. The girl was sexy, with braided hair and a very short skirt, and she lured him to the dark bedroom by unbuttoning her blouse. Her breasts bubbled from their cups. She placed one of his hands on them and asked his name.

Mason fought the impulse to snatch the hand away. He tried to relax. "Call me Pony," he told her. He snaked his fingers between her breasts, felt the dampness there, felt them grow into his palm when she breathed in. He wondered how she could be breathing at all when he could not, when he couldn't draw a single clean breath. *This is too easy,* he thought suddenly, *the boyfriend might come home or something.* Her hands pulled at his T-shirt. "It's too hot in here," he said. A hand tunneled under his shirt. "Back off!" Mason said and shoved her forcefully with the heels of his palms.

She fell against a nightstand. "Damn it, Pony," she yelled.

Mason was already retreating. "My name ain't Pony," he yelled back. He went straight to the kitchen drawer on his way out. She could not tell on him when the gun came up missing; she wasn't supposed to have him there in the first place.

Mason's fingers traced over the gun. He glanced at Gamble's back door, then settled back on his duffel bag pillow. The gun rested on his chest. He thought about the trip ahead to Washington, but mostly he entertained himself with half-formed visions of what he would do when he came face to face with Pony. What would Pony do? What could he possibly say? Mason did not know what he would do or say either. He saw his father's face and he saw the gun gripped tightly in his fist, and whatever room they were in was small and black. No sounds intruded. The confrontation remained vague, almost purposefully so. His emotions did not allow him the objectivity to define or question it. Just show him, he would tell himself. He would accuse Pony with the gun, the stubby barrel serving as a pointing finger.

He inspected the weapon one more time before putting it away. Certainly, it had helped commit some crime, had given one person dominion over another, made equals unequal. Only three rounds remained. Sitting in Gamble's car, he thought three bullets would do. More than do. His hate enfolded him, as if blinders had been affixed to his eyes, permitting him to see nothing except the blurred spot of space and time he ran toward. With Pony Reed's face before him, his mind spiraled from uncertain futures to a concrete past, and the first confrontation.

They met by accident the first time, father and son, late after a basketball game. Eleven-year-old Mason hung out with older boys because he was as tall as they were and could get a better game of B-ball. They were swift, shiny-skinned shadows under the hoops. Their hands were like webs and they could snare the ball in flight, spin and shoot graceful rainbows that jangled through the chain nets. Connie would shout, "Pick up your man!" and Spider would scream for the ball until he became hoarse. Rick Franklin, the tallest of them, could already dunk. Even though most of them were already teenagers, they let Mason play because he worked hard on the court, irritated anyone he defended, and passed the ball when told.

The best part about hanging out with them was the talk during timeouts and after the games. Invariably, they talked about girls, who put out and who claimed to be getting some. They screamed, ridiculed each other, and told lies. Mason felt privileged to be in their company. The boys played until the sun dropped and you couldn't see who was on your team and who wasn't, or even find the backboard.

Rick Franklin said, "Mason, we're going to get something to drink. You coming or you got to run home and get ready for bed?"

Maybe Rick had meant only to tease him, but Mason grinned at the invitation. This was the first time they'd acknowledged his presence after the game had ended. The camaraderie of the older boys thrilled him. He fell in with the swaggering group, remembering to pull his smile in, remembering to just chill.

One of the boys dribbled the ball the entire way from the schoolyard to Lincoln Avenue. Spider blasted Parliament on his boom box. The pulsing beat served to herald these new, young warriors fresh from blacktop triumphs. In the gathering darkness, the lights from the black-owned stores lining Lincoln Avenue came on. Red neon signs in front of Doc's Liquor Store and Fly's Teenage Club, which was nothing more than a pool hall, flashed their reflections in passing cars. The giant vanilla ice-cream cone glowed above Penny Cones. Lights from window displays at Camden's and Earl's Fashion Boutique sent the shadows of their iron security bars stretching across the sidewalk and into the street. The boys continued their slow-paced, arrogant strut, emulating their big brothers. They passed three bars, tried to peek into two of them, then laughed and scattered when someone came to chase them from the door.

Rick, Spider, and the rest finally stopped at the mouth of a narrow alleyway between Earl's and a barbershop, across the street from Doc's, where business thrived and cars constantly pulled in and out of his small lot. They sat on overturned garbage cans or leaned against the cement brick walls and listened to Spider's tunes. Mason grew disappointed; they did not seem interested in doing anything beyond watching the cars cruise by. He knew his mother would begin calling him in now, not knowing he was several blocks away. She would hit him for this, he knew, but the pressure to stay with the boys was too great. He had to show he could hang.

Jamal Jenkins exhibited the condoms he'd taken from his brother's room, and vowed he'd be putting them to use really soon. He lost credibility when he was unable to name the girl with whom he would use them.

"He'll use them to keep his pillowcase clean," Rick said, and made the jerking-off gesture in front of his groin.

Mason did not laugh with the rest of them, sensing Jamal would not take it from him as he would from the rest.

"Let's get a bottle," Spider said. "I'll go for it." They pooled their money, making note of who contributed how much and would therefore be entitled to shorter or longer sips. Mason donated fifty cents, assuring him of at least two good swigs. The people-watching began in earnest then, looking for that adult who wouldn't mind buying a bottle of Boone's Farm for them, someone who could be entrusted with their money, but not so uptight they'd make trouble, someone cool.

A man in his fifties, wearing a brown suit, stepped out of a station wagon. He stood beside his car lighting a cigarette.

"He looks okay to me. Let's ask him."

"No way," Rick said, "He's probably a principal or a parole officer or something. And he's too old. You gotta pick somebody still young enough to remember when he couldn't buy his own bottle."

A long-legged woman with a very short skirt slipped out of a Seville. She left her lights on when she went inside Doc's. Everyone said she'd definitely be someone to ask, but no one moved.

A tall, thin man with a fur-trimmed leather jacket and green beret sauntered down the street on the opposite side from the boys and paused under the red glow of Doc's sign. When the long-legged lady came out he went up to her. Mason couldn't hear what the man said, but in a few moments he heard the woman laugh. She opened the sack she held and allowed him to peek at her purchase.

Jamal said, "I know him. He bought us a six-pack last week..."

"Yeah, I know him too," Rick said. "Do you know him, Mason?"

Mason shook his head, not sure of what Rick wanted him to say. The man put his hand on the woman's waist and she quickly pushed it away. Some of the boys giggled.

"I'll go ask him," Spider said, but Rick grabbed the back of his shirt collar before he'd gotten two steps away.

"No, let the young 'un go. Give him the money."

Mason looked at Rick, certain that trouble was coming. Even then he knew the feeling, like falling into a river and letting the events carry him along, that loss of control. The subtle warning went off at the back of his head. "How come?" he asked.

"How come? How come? Initiation, boy. You want to hang with us or not? Damn, we ain't asking you to kill nobody." Rick kept grinning the whole time and Mason didn't think the others knew what Rick was up to.

Mason shrugged. "No problem."

Spider poured the change in Mason's front pocket. Mason felt the weight of it against his leg. It jingled as he started across the street.

The man stood very close to the woman now, almost pressing up against her. She wasn't laughing anymore. As Mason came up behind the man, he could see how uncomfortable she looked. The man had her pinned against the car door so that she could not open it.

"I'm just looking out for your health, baby." The woman had to hold her face back from his lips. "Surgeon General say a woman shouldn't be imbibing a whole bottle of malt liquor by herself."

"Ain't that nice of you. But if I can buy it, I can drink it. You better find your own." The woman looked around, but no one, except Mason, whom she didn't see, was paying any attention to them.

His hand was on her. His fingers extending over her belly. He didn't let her push his hand away. "Let's go for a ride. Where did you get such a fine car? You some kind of woman, ain't you?"

Mason looked back across the street to the alleyway and his friends. They were nearly invisible in the darkness there, but he felt their eyes nonetheless.

"Quit foolin' around now," the woman said. "Stop."

The man's head craned after the woman's. He was trying to whisper in her ear, or maybe even lick it.

"Quit foolin'," she repeated, her voice growing shrill.

"Mister," Mason said loudly and pulled on the man's arm at the elbow.

"Whoa!" Startled, the man jumped to the side.

The woman slid along the length of the car door, opened it, and quickly jumped inside. The door locks clicked, but then she rolled down the window and hissed, "I wouldn't make time with a slimy-tongued heap of black trash like you if my mama's life depended on it."

The man looked from the woman to Mason and back to the woman.

She tried to spit at him, but the spittle just ran down the door of her car. She backed into the street, her tires squealed, and the Seville roared away.

Mason thought he heard the boys laughing from across the street.

"Little brother, what did you do that for? Messed my rap all up. Damn it. She didn't spit on me, did she?"

Mason shook his head.

"You don't see no spit on me, do you?" The man brushed at the front of his jacket. "Bitch." He looked down the street. Only the receding tail lights could be seen. He turned on Mason, but his anger seemed to have instantly disappeared. "You spooked me good, sneaking up on me like that. That's five years less I'm gonna live." He resettled his beret over his short hair. He was tall, well over six foot, maybe six-two, but his back had a slight bow in it that kept his shoulders slumped forward. He had a narrow face and shared the same pecan-brown complexion Mason had. "She was looking hot though, huh?"

"Yeah," Mason said. The trouble warning still pulsed at the back of Mason's head.

"Well, what do you want? Costing me a sweet piece of tail. They all act like they ain't interested at first. That's how they hold on to their self respect, tell themselves they ain't easy. Five minutes later," he snapped his fingers, "they trying to climb up on you. You remember that, little man."

Mason nodded.

"Well, what did you want? Don't tell me, buy a six-pack for you right? You little brothers sure do start young these days. Nobody's listening to the Surgeon General." The man laughed; his teeth were very clean, very white.

"Boone's Farm," Mason said and dug in his pockets for the change, then held it out for the man.

"Hmm, like the fruit of the vine, do you?" He pulled a hand away from Mason's fistful of change. "I'm not going to go in there and dump a bunch of pennies and nickels on the counter. Man would run me out of his store."

Mason looked across the street again. He began to feel he may have been abandoned. He could not see anyone.

"Who's over there?" Now the man studied Mason intently, and the boy had to cut his eyes away from the man's hard gaze. Mason eyed the man's delicate, black leather loafers, which had tiny gold buckles and looked as soft as slippers. "I said, who's over there?"

"Just some friends waiting on me. You going to buy it for us or not?" Mason returned the man's stare. Countless times later, when Mason remembered this moment, he couldn't recall if he'd recognized anything familiar about the face. He came to believe he had, as the years went by, spotting some trait that resembled what he saw every day in the bathroom mirror. At the time, his impatience began to override his fear of the man and he'd just about made up his mind to return across the street without a bottle and take whatever teasing the boys wanted to dish out.

"So you're the gofer. What's your name?"

Mason answered, he thought quickly enough, "Rick, Rick Franklin."

"How old are you. You're tall... you about ten?"

"Eleven."

"Uh-huh, wine's going to kill you, boy. I seen guys go without eating, 'cause that wine makes 'em think their belly's full. Meanwhile they shrinking away to nothing. But I'll hook you up this time. Wait by the side of the door. And keep that nasty change for yourself. Don't go back over there and give it back to them boys who sent you to do their work."

The man went into the store. Mason waited where he'd been told; it seemed to take a long time. He thought about leaving since he still had the guys' money. He didn't like to wait. He started tapping his left hand against the knuckles of his fisted right.

When the man reappeared, Mason reached for the brown bag he carried.

"Not right in front of the door, fool. You want me to get popped for contributing to the delinquency of a minor? Come over here."

Mason smiled; he would have the money and he would bring back the bottle. He followed the man around the corner of Doc's, just outside the glow of the streetlamps and the neon.

"Come here!" The man grabbed Mason by the shirt and slammed him against the liquor store wall. The impact jarred the air from his lungs. His face was pressed into the peeling paint and cracks in the concrete block wall. He tasted blood in his mouth. Mason couldn't breathe. "Now, boy, listen up," the man whispered. Mason felt the man's lips moving against his ear. "You ever interrupt me while I'm scoring on a fine piece of tail like that again and they going to need a spatula to scrape you from this wall. You understand?"

He let go. Mason dropped to his knees heaving, trying to get his burning lungs to reopen. When they finally did, it hurt to inhale. He couldn't stop coughing.

"You're okay," he heard the man say two or three times. The man squatted down to face level with Mason and gently wiped the dust from the wall off his face. The lines of fury in the man's face melted away. "You're a good-looking kid," he said. He set the bottle down beside Mason. The man stood, and Mason glared up at him. "Straighten yourself up before you go across the street. Don't let them know you've been in a tussle." Then the man just walked away.

"Jesus, Mason," Spider said. "We didn't say you had to blow the man's cock in order to get a bottle. What took you so long?"

Mason still fought to keep his composure. He'd been rattled bad. He didn't answer, and allowed someone to snatch the bottle from his hand.

"Least he got the job done," one of them said.

"Shh, shh, listen up, guys," Rick said. "Mason and that brother were probably having a long talk, huh Mason? Do you know who he is?"

Mason wanted to go home. He shook his head.

The boys went to a cleared lot of gravel and weeds behind Gaines Funeral Parlor, the gate through which most blacks in town journeyed to heaven, and the last business on Lincoln Avenue before the residential section began. They sat in a circle on the ground and circulated the bottle. A yellow light near the parlor's back doorway illuminated the dark faces in the circle, and Mason eyed each in turn as he received the wine and tilted the bottle up. Dancing moths harassed the yellow bulb at the door. In a fenced-in lot, long hearses reflected the moon in their gleaming sides.

Connie said, "I wonder if there is any dead people in there now. Waitin' to go to hell or something."

Mason sipped the wine; it burned the cut in his mouth. The next time it came around, he only pretended to drink, stopping the flow with his tongue.

The boys grew louder and sillier, more from imagination than alcohol.

"I went to a funeral once for this granduncle of mine," Spider said. "He went to the hospital for some simple surgery to remove something from his throat."

Jamal interrupted, "Is this a spooky story?" He looked nervous.

"Only if you get scared, spook," Spider said. "Anyway he dies on the table and my aunt is suing the doctor 'cause that weren't supposed to happen. They take him to Gaines here. And at the funeral she kisses him goodbye and his right eye just pops open. My aunt just sees that big eyeball just staring right up at her and she screams and falls down trying to get away."

"Bullshit," Rick said. The boys laughed, and Mason, now much calmer, allowed himself to laugh too.

"Anyway, she wouldn't let them close the coffin until they closed his eye first. Everybody had to wait nearly an hour." Spider looked around. "They say it happened because my uncle's wishing he'd kept an eye on that doctor in the operating room."

They laughed and snorted. Jamal threw the empty wine bottle against the funeral parlor wall. It shattered and everyone laughed at that too.

"Hey, guys, I got something funny too, dig this," Rick said, "Mason, do you know who that dude was who bought our bottle?"

He studied Rick's dark face and dark eyes and wide grin. At that moment, Mason knew positively who the man was. It came to him clearly and definitely, as irrefutable as courthouse evidence, as forceful as a Baptist sermon. He knew that had been the man his mother rarely ever mentioned—who, when asked, she described as a free spirit, not a man for settling down, who she reckoned still had growing of his own to do, who left town when Mason was hardly one year old. This was the man Mason had imagined to be a romantic drifter, a loner, larger than life, moving from city to city, even around the world. He knew that man was his daddy. But he said a nearly silent, "No."

"My old man knows him," Rick said, visibly struggling to contain himself, about to burst with his announcement. "He came back in town two weeks ago. That's Willie Pony Reed, that's your daddy!"

The howls of laughter were immediate.

"No, he ain't!" Mason shouted and jumped to his feet.

The boys were rolling on the ground, holding their sides.

"Damn, Mason, you had a family reunion and didn't even know it," Spider said.

"He ain't my daddy," Mason said and kicked at Rick's legs. But the older boy was laughing too hard to care.

One boy controlled his laughter long enough to say, "What'd he do, Mason? Leave your mama and take all his pictures with him too?"

"Fuck you guys, that ain't funny," but Mason knew he was about to cry and he ran away from them.

The taunts chased after him. "Now y'all can go to father and son night at the PTA." "Who'd your Mama say it was? The mailman?"

Mason ran the entire way home, nearly oblivious to the frowns of the people he brushed by or the blaring horns of the cars he darted past. When his eyes welled, he wiped them immediately, sucked in air, and blew it out forcefully. He heard his name coming at him when he arrived back on his block.

"Maa-sonn," Mama was calling him in.

As he came down the street, moving inchworm slow now, he saw her leaning over the wooden railing at the end of the porch, which ran the width of the house. "Maa-sonn!"

His hurt turned to anger aimed at the woman calling his name. She had not warned him. She had not told him what Pony Reed was like. He should have been able to recognize his own father. She should have told him. Something. "Don't let them see you been in a tussle," the man, his father, had said. At the front gate, Mason took a deep breath. His hand rested on the cool metal gate latch. He exhaled slowly and again wiped his eyes. "Right here," he said and repeated himself as he opened the gate.

Mama came to the edge of the front porch steps. Her fists poised on her hips; the right hand dangled a dishtowel. Her head eclipsed the porch light at the door and Mason could see all the hair on her back-lit head sprung wildly in every direction; she looked like the Moses of her stories having descended from the mountain and discovered the idolaters. "You're going to make me have to go down to the schoolyard and yank you by the ear in front of your friends, aren't you?" She was always threatening to embarrass him that way when he came home late. That night, he felt she already had.

Mason's body trembled. He fought to contain the anger vibrating just beneath his skin. His anger strengthened him. He was not afraid of her. He climbed the first step and saw she had that tight-faced look; her eyes hardened to glass and her lips thinned out when she was frustrated with him.

"What happened to the side of your face? You've been fighting."

The guys hadn't noticed. She had noticed immediately.

"No, I ain't." He went up the steps, braced for the hit, and it came, a hard slap over his right ear.

"Don't you start lying to me, boy. Don't you carry a lie into this house."

Mason did not wince at the slap, did not bring his hand up to touch his smarting earlobe. He denied his mother the satisfaction of knowing she'd hurt him. Her eyes showed surprise over his cool reaction. He liked that. "Don't let them know..." his father had said. Mason discovered a new weapon.

He quietly said, "I ain't been fighting."

"Then what happened?" Mama asked. "Tell me."

He tried to think of reasons why he shouldn't tell her. She'd be mad that he'd gone up to Lincoln Avenue, but that didn't matter now. He'd suddenly realized she could no longer hurt him. Not really. Neither spankings nor her quick hand would hurt anymore, because he wouldn't let it show. "I met my daddy. I saw him. I met him."

Mama's mouth opened a bit. The tightness dropped from her face. Her eyes flicked back and forth, scanning his. She brought a hand up. Mason again braced himself, but she only gripped his shoulder. "Where?" she asked. "Did he do this to you? Did he hit you?"

"No. I fell." he lied, just the first of the many lies he would tell for Pony Reed. "No, *he* didn't hit me." He emphasized "he," but Mama seemed to miss the accusation.

Mama's hand gently rubbed the right side of Mason's head as if her tenderness could smooth away the slap. She did this absently as she looked down the front walk, expecting, Mason figured, to see her old boyfriend come strutting into the porch light's glow. She did not look afraid, exactly, at that moment. If his mother was ever afraid, Mason could only guess what that would look like. Instead, she seemed wary, and alert. Her mind was sorting through the fact of Pony's return at high speed. Mason could see this. She wondered what it meant. Would he come by here? What did he want? She asked, "What did he say to you, baby?"

Mason shrugged and pulled his head to the side to get away from her touch. "Nothing, he—"

"We've gotta watch him, baby," she interrupted. "He'll start coming around. He says things. He'll start asking for whatever crumb you got."

Mason could still feel the weight of the change in his pocket. Pony had given it to him. "You never told me about him."

"I did." Then she hesitated. "Never thought he'd show up again, sweetheart." She was eyeing him hard now, bending over slightly to close the small difference in their heights. "I think, maybe, you found out something about him tonight. Hmm?"

Mason did not reply.

"Go wash your face good, hands too. Your plate is in the oven."

He pulled the screen door halfway open and turned back to Mama. "He won't be coming around," he said. "He didn't even know who I was."

"Oh," he thought he heard her say.

He went inside, closing only the screen door, and walked down the hall before glancing back at his mother standing on the porch, still in the same spot, both hands gripping the dishtowel.

At their next meeting, Pony insisted he'd known all along it was Mason he'd put up against the wall that night. "I just wanted to check you out before I told you I was your old man," he maintained. "Besides, you said you was Rick, and I knew the Franklin boy already."

While lying in the back seat of Kenny Gamble's Oldsmobile, Mason wondered for the millionth time if that were true. And he asked himself, again, what the hell would it matter if it was. Pony was the master at making lies feel true, and making the truth ring like lies. Mason knew this all too well.

Too restless to try to sleep any longer, he sat up in the car. The sky lightened. He could distinguish the details of the Gambles' backyard: the sagging stockade fence, old sycamores, and a crumbling brick fire pit, no longer lawful to use for open trash burning. Mama had one in her backyard too, near the alley. Tyler and he had used it as a hiding place. His watch read six-fifteen, still too early to wake Gamble. Mason propped his head against the rear passenger-side window, allowing his legs to stretch across the back seat. He said, "Everything takes too goddamn long."

At seven o'clock, he knocked on Gamble's back door, waited, then knocked again harder. He waited only a few seconds and then banged steadily on the screen door with a fist until the inner door opened a crack.

A bleary-eyed woman peeked through the screen. "Somebody's house better be on fire," she said.

"I'm here to see Kenny. We're going—"

"You're gonna pay him for the gas, right?"

"Half." Mason asked, "Can I come in?"

The woman flipped the hook on the screen door and walked away yawning.

Mason stepped in, immediately crinkling his nose at the stale, spoiled-food smell of the kitchen.

The woman, in a thin pink gown that clung to the tires of fat around her waist, slipped barefoot across the floor. "Everybody is still sleeping. You just gonna have ta sit tight."

"Just tell him I'm here, all right?" Mason said.

She did not answer, disappearing down a short hallway into what should have been the dining room, judging by the glass chandelier hanging from the middle of the ceiling, but which now passed as a bedroom. Mason could see her climb back into her bed. Light in that room made it brighter than the dark kitchen he stood in. He could see the woman cover herself with the sheet. Someone mumbled, and Mason realized she wasn't alone in the bed. He thought he heard the woman answer, "Gamble's rider."

The kitchen was a mess. He could tell that even in the dark. Uncovered pots and leaning towers of plates blocked every inch of counter space. Mason saw something rather large with a sleek, polished body streak from a skillet to underneath a plate. And it was big enough to make the plate move just a bit. No chairs were in the kitchen, so Mason sat on the floor with his back against the refrigerator. The refrigerator steadily hummed in his ear.

Snoring came from the bedroom. The big woman had fallen back asleep and the other shifted restlessly. Mason could see the other sleeper was a woman too, when she turned onto her back and the sheet settled over her breasts. One smooth arm lay outside the sheets. This woman was light-complected or maybe even white.

He didn't know who she could be, didn't know anyone who lived here except Kenny Gamble. And Mason knew Gamble only well enough to know he didn't like him. Gamble was loud and dumb, and masked his ignorance with an aggressiveness that made others uncomfortable around him. He might quickly strike out at you to see you flinch, and consider that funny. But today he was Mason's cheapest ticket out of town.

The next moment, Mason forgot about his trip. The light-skinned girl swung her legs out of the bed. Just her toes touched the carpet at first. Mason could see one of her thighs all the way up to the hip bone. She sat up, then stretched to her full arm span. She wore only a large, sloppy T-shirt that read *Nike*. As she stretched, he could see her nipples thrust against the shirt. She had long, thick, dark hair that fell in crinkled waves past her shoulders. When she stood, he glimpsed her bikini panties before the T-shirt fell into place.

Mason smiled to himself and wondered again who she might be, and why she slept with the fat woman. But he'd visited a lot of households packed with family: big brothers who never seemed to move out, and single daughters who returned with a brood of their own so that every room in the house became a bedroom come nightfall. If the towers of dishes were any indication, this house was loaded wall to wall.

The woman yawned and padded directly toward Mason. He grinned but didn't move. She scratched absently under one breast and came to stand directly over him. She had smooth, well-muscled legs. Mason liked that; he didn't care for women who let their legs get fly-leg hairy.

He said, "Hi."

"Whoa, shit!" She leapt straight up in the air, and then landed with a fly-swatter in her hand, snatched from the top of the refrigerator. She began dealing Mason loud, stinging blows.

Laughing all the while, he crawled away from her assault. "Ouch, ouch, what did I do?"

The attack ended when she turned on the kitchen light, though by now it wasn't so dark anymore. "Who are you? Some lazy burglar who fell asleep on the job?"

Mason was still laughing. He was a little disappointed by the girl's rather plain face. She showed traces of being pockmarked.

The last blow of the swatter came down on the arm he held up defensively.

"Hey, chill," he said, "I'm Mason. I'm waiting on Kenny."

"Yeah? Me too, really. What're you doing here? How long you been sitting in here? You scared me, you goofy. I almost peed on you."

"What's all that screamin' in there?" Mason heard the fat woman ask from the bed.

"Just me beating up some burglar, old woman."

"Well, leave that boy alone. Come in here and give me some morning sugar."

The light-skinned woman shook the fly-swatter at Mason as if to warn him against any further tricks, then darted back into the dining room/bedroom. This time a blanket fell across the doorway.

Still on the floor, Mason rubbed the back of his neck, staring at the concealing blanket.

Heavy thumping came down the stairs and in a moment Kenny Gamble appeared in the kitchen, scratching himself in a place that made Mason hope he wouldn't offer to shake hands anytime soon. "Damn, Mason, was that you laughin' and carryin' on down here?" He cleared his throat. His heavy-lidded eyes blinked lazily. Mason noticed he'd shaven his head completely since last they'd talked. It made him look even more reckless. "What's the time?"

"Nearly eight," Mason answered.

Gamble opened the refrigerator and hung on its door. He seemed as if he was having trouble focusing his eyes. "God damn it! Who drank all my Diet Cokes?" He hollered so that the entire house would hear him. "Who drank all my fuckin' diet Cokes! See why I'm leavin', Mason? Bought a six-pack last night, just last night, and drank one. One. These niggers will clean you out."

"We can pick some up on the road," Mason said.

"You don't see me drinkin' their goddamned coffee." He continued to look into the refrigerator, the light shining on his face. "Nothin'." He slammed the door in disgust.

Mason stood with his arms crossed. He was tired of being in the filthy kitchen, and he felt as if his journey wouldn't really begin until he left town. "It'll be good if we got an early start. Less traffic and all."

"Hell, Mase, you gonna let me take a bath first?" Gamble let a hand glide over his bald head; it looked like a giant malted milk ball. "You like my new look, Mase? I couldn't find my comb yesterday, so I said, what the hell."

Mason smiled.

"And we gotta wait for Gina anyway. She's goin' as far as Ohio or West Virginia or some hick place with us."

"The high-yella woman with the thick hair?"

"Yep."

Mason whispered now, stepping close to Gamble and deciding quickly he could wait for him to take a bath. "She's the one who was screaming a moment ago. She uh, went in there to give that woman some, uh, morning sugar."

Gamble's disgusted look mirrored Mason's. "Yeah? I knew it. I been tryin to crack on that ever since she got here. Some sick shit, ain't it?"

Mason nodded, but he found it all amusing somehow.

Gamble started down the short hallway, then turned around. "Mason, you carryin'?"

Mason shook his head.

Gamble again sent a hand over his skull. "Well, it is gonna be a long drive..."

Mason agreed with that. He realized it was going to be a very long drive.

Almost eleven o'clock and Mason was actually closer to home than he had been four hours earlier. In fact, his mother might spot him if she decided to go grocery shopping at Piggly Wiggly that morning. That thought kept him scooted far down in the seat with only his eyes and forehead at window level. Gina sat next to him in the front seat because the back had been filled with suitcases and a set of TV tables. They waited for Gamble, parked not far from Doc's Liquor Store.

"I don't know why he needs that stuff on a trip." Gina drummed her fingers on the dash. "Considering the errand we're on here. Don't you think you look a mite suspicious?"

Having discovered the woman's preferences, Mason had little interest in her. He did sit up a bit more, but covered a side of his face with one hand.

"Big-time drug courier, are you?"

"That ain't it."

Gina said, "You're not running from the law, are you? Oh, geez, what have I gotten mixed up in now."

Mason didn't look her way. She and the fat woman had shared a tearful goodbye, featuring a lot of hugging. Gamble and Mason just rolled their eyes, not even helping the women load the car. Apparently, she had intended to stay in town awhile but had changed her mind.

"I could've taken the bus," Mason said.

"I hear you. I have a feeling we're going to be saying that a lot before long."

Mason felt annoyed. He didn't want to be allies with this woman and was in no mood to be in agreement with her. He had foreseen the trip's beginning and envisioned its end, but nothing of the middle. And certainly not this.

The driver's side door opened and Gamble hustled in, grinning. "Score," he said and patted his pocket.

"Just don't take any while you're driving," Gina said.

"Hey, don't you worry about it." Gamble started the engine.

"I'm in this car; I have the right to worry about it."

"Shut up, you dyke."

"What did you call me, you bald turd?"

"Mase, I need gas money."

"Christmas," Mason said.

GAIL

Gail was a city girl, fourteen years old, and did not like the country. She missed her friends. She sat at the bedroom attic window of Mrs. Alice Durkee's house on an evening of watered-down purple sky, and watched her mother talk to a man who had driven up in an old Ford. Gail did not know the man. Yet she was certain the conversation was about her. Everything that had happened, all the wheels her mother had set in motion over the past four months were about her, pulling her from school and bringing her here, to the outskirts of nowhere to "visit a family friend" her mother had never mentioned before.

Gail missed Sundays at the New Life Baptist Church Sunday school, not because of those tired Bible lessons Deacon Simmons used to dance around the tables about, but because afterward she and her friends would take the offering money they held back and buy cold Cokes in the little glass bottles and hot tamales in tight plastic wrapping from a street vendor, then rush over to Anita's house and spin Motown on her phonograph and talk about the latest dances and the cutest boys. The girls practiced slow dancing together, holding each other's waists and talking in affected voices. There was always a lot of giggling.

Gail would always be in the center of all the talk. She was one of the first girls to have a steady guy—sweet, sweet Pony Reed, a quiet boy, good in school and on the basketball team. The girls always wanted to hear where she and Pony had gone and what they did, and how far did they go. Gail could tell they were all jealous and she didn't mean to brag. Pony was just the coolest! And they were in love.

He did not know where she had been taken or else he would've come for her. She believed that. Like a young princess in a dark tower, she waited at the attic window, feeling the now-familiar yet still funny rolling movement in her belly. Frightened by what the movement meant, and frightened by her surroundings, she waited for rescue.

Gail could not tell Pony where she was even if she could get in touch with him. Somewhere in the Missouri countryside, Alice Durkee's place wasn't quite a farm. There was a long backyard, probably a hundred yards long, where grapevines grew this way and that over obscured wooden frames, making them look like shaggy, green huts all in a row. It was a cool, too-sweet smelling walk under the vines that Gail and her mother took every day. But there were no animals, and no fields. And almost no front yard. A narrow, black tar highway went within scant yards of the house's front porch. It seemed cars did not travel it much. Yet along it stretched Gail's only hope.

A long-haired white boy had twice tipped his hat to her where she sat on the porch as he drove by in a pickup with pink and blue peace signs all over it. He would be her salvation. He had grinned at her and seemed friendly, and better, he could not be someone her mother knew. He must've lived somewhere down the road because he drove by regularly, in the mornings and again in the evenings, probably going to and from work. Through the thin trees that lined the road just past Alice Durkee's property, Gail could spot his silly-looking truck coming from more than a half-mile off.

Her mother still talked to the man in the Ford. Gail couldn't tell who he might be. For a moment she thought about calling to him. She could show him her stomach even from the window. Someone else besides Mama and Alice should know that she was there, and that she was pregnant. But in the next moment, Gail saw her mother shaking hands with the man. She knew then that he was in on it too.

Gail's mother, Nora Wallington, was the youngest member of the Mothers' Board in New Life Baptist Church's history. At thirty-two, and despite being divorced, she garnered much respect from the rest of the congregation. Gail had watched as her mother became more and more wrapped up in the church. The more involved Nora grew, the more strict she became with Gail at home. Gail discovered, too, that worshipping Jesus in fellowship was not the only reason for her mother's zeal. She and the Reverend Hammond had spotted one another in Bible study.

Gail had never heard her mother called beautiful or pretty. Other women mostly used words such as attractive or handsome to describe Nora. She used too much mascara, Gail thought, with which she tried to give herself larger-looking eyes. The thick, Egyptian-looking lines she drew on herself would have looked comical on anyone else, but Nora's serious face made them seem less obtrusive. Or perhaps it was simply that others were usually kept on the defensive with Nora Wallington, and had little opportunity to critique her. Except Clay Hammond: he had found time to examine Gail's mother, and, apparently, liked what he saw very much.

Reverend Hammond embodied everything that a young preacher should be. New Life was his first church. Three years younger than Nora, he had plenty of fire and conviction. He gave his sermons with a rhythmic cadence that was very appealing, even though most of the time he was telling his faithful that they were on the path to iniquity and hellfire. His smile was disarming, and he would joke after the service while everyone filed out as if he'd forgotten how he'd proclaimed them all weak, willful, and wicked.

Gail had noticed the way her mother looked at the reverend. Gail would squeeze her mother's hand right there in the pews and be very happy for her. After all, Reverend Hammond appeared to be a nice man, and her mother seemed to like him so much.

Their romance was above public reproach, conducted as it was under the scrutiny of the deacons and the Mothers' Board. The reverend, who retained his job at the sanction of the congregation, could not afford a scandal. If the preacher came over for dinner, he'd leave early. If they went on walks—and they did often—they'd take Gail with them. They were the picture of Christian propriety.

Finally, it was Gail provided the scandal. One evening while his parents were away, she and Pony stumbled, groped, and bumped their way toward parenthood. Gail had gotten her first period just a few months before, so when the cycle stopped she was at first grateful, before becoming more worried than she'd ever been in her young life. She confided in two of her closest friends. They were astonished, awed, and of no help whatsoever. She prayed for the monthlies to return, but they didn't. It took her weeks of sleepless worry and spontaneous tears before she could tighten up the courage to tell Nora.

Gail finally told her mother she was pregnant while Nora sat at the table in the dining room of the small house alimony and thrift had gotten her. She was admiring the shine her just-completed wax job had brought out of the table. Gail sat in a chair next to her mother and unburdened herself. She gave the news in the form of a confession. She said she was sorry, really sorry. She sniffed and wiped her tears with a flat hand.

Her mother jumped up and stepped quickly away from her then turned about, arms crossed. "Gail, what are you saying! Why, the reverend and I haven't even... I didn't even think you were kissing Pony yet. You slutty... You little, little slut." Her mother covered her own mouth with both hands then let her hands slide down to her neck as if she were choking herself. "God, Clay." Her widened eyes looked more scared than angry. "You're going to ruin your life and embarrass me right out of the church. Is that it? Is that what you wanted?" She said nothing for a moment, not waiting on an answer, but trying to think. "Was it the Reed boy?"

Gail nodded.

"How could I raise a slut? How? Where did you lie down for him? How many times? Huh?" Her mother grabbed her blouse with lightning speed. She pulled; it tore and the buttons popped. "What did you do for him? What do you even know how to do?" She tore at Gail's blouse and Gail tried to push her away. She grabbed Gail's bra too and yanked it down. Nora seemed startled to see developed breasts nearly as large as her own.

Backing beyond her mother's reach, Gail knocked over one of the chairs. She re-covered herself.

"Who else have you told? Does he know?"

She could taste the salty tears on her lips. She shook her head. "I told Nancy and Patty. I told them I thought I was."

"Well you're going to go back and untell them. Tell them it was a false alarm. No. Tell them you made the whole thing up. You just wanted to fool them for awhile. You hear me? You do it."

Later the same day, from her room, Gail heard Nora making phone call after phone call. Her plans were already underway. She stepped briefly into Gail's room near bedtime, still looking as if she wanted to grab Gail again. "We're going to take care of this, Miss. No one is going to know, you hear me? We're going to take care of this and get right back to our lives."

Within a few weeks, her mother pulled her out of school. Nora told the story that a bedridden aunt in Chicago needed her and so she and Gail would be gone for some time. As far as Gail knew, she told this story to Clay Hammond too.

They left one evening when Gail was more than three months along, and just beginning to show. They went nowhere near Chicago, but south into the countryside. Mother and daughter had never been so far apart, never had so little to say to one another. While Nora drove in silence, with only the sound of the wind and the oncoming cars passing by, Gail began to think. Until now she had been more than willing to have her mother handle her problem, but the secrecy and the false stories, together with their clandestine exit from town, scared her badly. The feeling she didn't want to admit to was that she was submitting to something terribly wrong. She counted the headlights on the highway. She stayed pressed against the passenger-side door and risked puzzled, sidelong glances at Nora, trying to read her future in her mother's face.

Mrs. Durkee's house glowed in the moonlight. It looked like one of hundreds of houses Gail had seen situated just off the highway, so close that the trucks flung dust and rocks on the front steps. Her front step was maybe twenty feet from the road. But this road was quiet as Nora pulled the station wagon into the bald front yard. Gail had spotted no other traffic for several miles and this added to her feelings of isolation.

"She's going to help us," Nora said.

The porch roof sagged on thin, yellowed columns, under which two chairs rocked on metal slides beside a card table. As soon as Nora cut the engine, Gail heard crickets, thousands and more, giving the nighttime everything they had. No one came out to greet them. Even Nora seemed hesitant.

"Grab a suitcase, miss," she finally said, "We're going to be here until the baby comes."

Mrs. Durkee waited inside for them, in her nightgown. She was a big, squat woman with drooping skin at her elbows and straightened gray hair that projected stiffly from her head. Her lips looked always wet; Gail thought they had the same kind of shine as earthworms. Gail hated this co-conspirator instantly.

Alice Durkee looked at Gail as if she was appraising a plucked chicken about to go into the kettle. She said to Nora, "She be young like you say, but the body all growed is the problem. Head didn't catch up. Never mind that now. I'll show y'all to y'all room." She led them to a big, hot, and stuffy room that mother and daughter would share for the next several months.

They were slow months filled with hot days. Mostly, the women did nothing but watch Gail grow. "She gains little weight," Alice once said, "which is good. She looks like a thief with a melon under her shirt. You'll be able to return home soon after she delivers."

Alice and Nora played cards on the porch. Gail and Nora took walks under the grapevines where the shade was coolest. Many times, Gail wanted to tell her mother that she had changed her mind and wanted to keep the baby, that to give it away would be to give away a piece of herself. To lose it forever. The very idea began to scare her more and more. She and her mother could raise the baby together. Why not? They could raise it together until Pony and she got old enough to go on their own. What would be the matter with that? But she knew Nora would never listen, and the courage to make her listen never came to Gail.

Well into her last trimester, Gail began taking notice of the brightly colored truck passing by twice a day dependably. She would eat quickly, then tell her mother the house was too hot and slip out to the porch to see the pickup drive by in the evening. She had waved to him, once or twice, and he had tipped his straw cowboy hat in return. Stroking her enlarged stomach there on the porch, she devised her simple plan of escape. The problem became one of timing. Either Nora or Alice was always with her when the pickup came by. But it turned out the problem of timing was taken out of her hands completely.

Alice, who claimed to have delivered enough babies to stock her own town, had told Gail what it would feel like, but the fierceness of the first contraction took her breath away. She was in a porch chair when it happened, thinking this would be another failed attempt because Nora stood at the kitchen sink doing the dishes. She covered her face in her hands and rocked rapidly back and forth in the chair. The hurt faded as if it had never been, so amazingly abrupt was its retreat. But Gail knew she'd been warned. Her escape would have to be today. She waited, hoping Nora would finish the dishes and walk away. And she hoped the truck would come back before the pain returned.

Sluggish minutes passed and yet suddenly Gail spotted pink and blue flashes through the trees, quick flits of color between leafy branches, presently joined by the rough burping of the pickup now scarcely a half mile away. She would have to make her move to the road now, even though she could hear dishes rattling behind her head and she knew Nora stood at the window. She stepped off the porch stairs. Water whined in the faucet. She could hear the truck engine grind, slipping into a lower gear. It would be leaning into the hairpin turn, up a slight incline that aimed it in a straight line to shoot past Alice's. Gail took an angle to the road that could be interpreted as a walk to the vineyards. She wanted to know if Nora watched, but did not dare to turn around. Her face would give her away in an instant. Her heartbeat doubled and tripled with each step. Now she heard the truck gain speed. Sunlight reflecting off the windshield showed intermittently between the tree trunks. She could no longer maintain her feint toward the vineyards. Now she'd strike directly for the road, praying she'd get there before the truck, praying the white boy with the hat would see her, praying her mother would be looking down at dishes and suds, praying her rescuer would stop. Just as she made her move toward the road, the pain returned, a broad, clawing pain that seized her in mid-step and almost caused her to fold up on the spot.

"Oh, no..." she whispered. "Not now, please not now." She gritted her teeth, letting the tears roll. The truck came into full sight. Each step across the powdery dirt of Alice's brief front yard was excruciating. She felt herself weakening rapidly. The truck bore down on her. Only three yards from the road, she wanted to flag him down, wave her arms, but the pain would not let her. She nearly doubled over her swollen belly. One arm slung under it to hold it in place.

The truck came on too quickly. On the shoulder of the road, she managed to extend one arm, showing one white palm to the driver.

"Oh, please, Jesus." She cried now from pain, and from her hope so near to breaking. "Please, stop."

The tires squealed, but the truck went by, hot wind and its loud music swept after it. Then she heard a whine and turned to see the pickup reverse itself.

"Hey, gal, what's wrong?" the long-haired boy asked. He was older than she'd first thought, but he was within her touch, her deliverer. "What's a matter?"

She gazed into his face. He seemed kind, concerned, and yet somehow cheerful too. The music blared. She found she couldn't speak. She managed to nod as she leaned against the truck door, still staring into the man's eyes. She needed only a second to catch her breath.

"What's wrong with her?"

Gail felt hands clamp down on her shoulders. She was jerked backward.

"Nothing's wrong with her that minding your own business won't fix," her mother said. Nora's face flared into a snarl.

Gail cried out, "Help me, Jesus."

"Shut up, girl." Alice Durkee was there too and they each had one of Gail's arms. They pulled her away from the truck as she wailed and cried for help. She did not have the strength to resist them. She tried to sit down where she was, but they bore all her weight, dragging her across the dusty yard.

Her mother's nails cut into her upper arm. "Come on, Gail, damn it!"

Weak as she was, Gail tried to fight. She twisted her head around and spotted the idling pickup. The man had opened his door. He'd placed a booted foot on the ground, but froze right there, half in, half out of his shaking truck surrounded by the loud music. She kept calling for his help, then shouted, "Get my daddy! Get my daddy! Charlie Wallington! Charlie Wallington in St. Louis."

The man said nothing. She didn't know if he'd heard her.

Her mother cuffed her in the mouth.

"You stay out of our business, boy!" Alice shouted.

The pain intensified. The baby was coming. They dragged her up the porch steps. She looked back again for her rescuer. Gone, already.

JACKIE

The October sky had not brightened in the two hours they had spent inside the church to hear Tyler. It was such an even, pale gray that it looked as if the crooked chimneys and flaking shingle rooftops had been set before a blank movie screen. The group headed home. Gail walked quickly with Tyler bouncing next to her, still excited from his solo performance. Burdened with Cole, Jackie and Annie followed far behind. Jackie did not like the looks of the washed-out sky, wondering if it meant rain and what she would wear that night if it did.

Beside her, Annie began limping. Jackie heard a quick, soft gasp slip from the old woman. She could tell from Annie's face that the old woman was in pain.

"What's wrong, Miss Annie? Your leg?" Jackie asked.

Annie bit at her lower lip. She shook her head, Jackie's only evidence that she had been heard. Annie stared down the street, past the backs of Gail and Tyler a block ahead, as if trying to gauge the remaining distance against her ability to cover it.

Cole began wailing as if he'd fallen on his head again. He had been whining since the end of service, but now started up a prolonged screeching. Jackie forgot all about Miss Annie's struggles right next to her. She spoke sharply to the baby boy and held him away from her so his tears and strings of spittle would not soak her dress.

"I'm going to leave you right here at the curb for the garbage men, boy."

The crying continued unabated at a pitch that knifed right into her. He'd practiced this kind of marathon crying before. It amazed

Jackie that his tiny lungs could sustain the intensity so long. In the beginning, she used to answer his loud summons immediately, feed him, or check to see if he was dry, or touch his forehead to see if he was warm, or just hug him to her while he nuzzled against her as if wanting to return to the womb. Later, she began to think she spoiled him by promptly responding to his beckoning and would wait a few moments before picking him up. Still later, it became a contest, a test of wills. She would attempt to ignore him to see if he would cry himself out. He rarely did.

The other day he'd stood up in his crib crying for all he was worth, his tiny, sand-colored hands grasping the crib slats. Jackie waited in the doorway beyond his sight. When she entered, a pudgy, wet hand reached for her, but she ignored it. She sat in the chair a yard away and eyed him while he bawled and reached between the bars of the crib for his mother. Still she made no move toward him. She observed him in all his red-faced, open-mouthed, infant fury and moved not a muscle. She figured he had to be taught he was not the one in control. Her eyes bored into Cole's drowning eyes. Jackie sat impassively until she heard Gail's quick steps approaching, then jumped to pick up the baby. "I pick him up; he wants down. I put him down; he wants back up," Jackie explained in response to Gail's frown.

Now, still a couple of blocks from home, he battered her again. His pants were dry. It wasn't time for feeding. What did he want? What did he want this time? She knew if he didn't shut up he'd spoil everything. She had gone to Tyler's debut to get on Gail's good side. She wanted Gail to sit for Cole again, though the older woman had told her she would not. Also, going to hear Ty sing spared Jackie the ordeal of having to listen to Gail tell her about it fifty to a thousand times. But if Cole didn't behave there would be no hope of talking Gail into watching him. Her hands pinned the baby's arms to his sides. He would spoil everything. She very badly needed to see Perry. "Please, shut up, boy," she said. The sharp screeching filled her head with razor blades. Without a thought, she shook him. His head rocked violently back and forward.

"No, child. No." Miss Annie had fallen behind, but now hurried forward as best she could despite her pain. She came forward, reaching out with an ancient, knotty hand. "Stop that, girl."

Cole's breath momentarily caught in his throat, which made a clucking, choking sound, scaring Jackie. She held him still against her then.

His crying continued with more rage than ever, and even Gail stopped and looked back with her hands on her hips and her wide hat obscuring the top half of her face.

"That ain't the way," Miss Annie said, now next to Jackie and placing a hand to the side of the infant's face. "We told you he was teethin'. That really hurts. Don't it, Cole?"

"He won't stop crying," Jackie said. "He doesn't mind me."

"Put your finger in his mouth, honey," Miss Annie said. "Gentle like. Rub his gums. I used to dip my finger in the sugar bowl for the Buckler babies. Worked sometime if the pain wasn't too, too bad."

Jackie let Cole gum a finger. In a few seconds he quieted to a more tolerable whine.

Miss Annie smiled.

"Yeah, but it won't last," Jackie said.

Ahead, Gail pivoted about and continued her march home, but Tyler waited on the sidewalk for them to catch up.

"It won't last," Jackie said again.

Jackie had let her dark brown hair grow down to her shoulders where the ends curled stiffly inward. The bangs she teased into a frothy nest that obscured her forehead. Her eyes were large, dark, and pretty, and she knew how to look at a man in a way that made him uncomfortable, if she wanted to, as if she saw all of him at once. Before Perry came along, she would flirt with almost any male. She found it a natural way to interact with men; it made a man your friend quickly. Sometimes all it took was a smile, or a look, or leaning close during a conversation.

She was a small woman, a size three, which made her look a few years younger than the twenty she had achieved. People therefore treated her as though she were younger, and more often than not,

Jackie acted the part enthusiastically. She had the figure and breasts of a little girl, though the latter swelled some during pregnancy.

She graduated from high school having learned very little and went to a secretarial school for four months. Her first full-time job taught her a bit about computers. It was at the headquarters of a local men's clothier, Burton and Son's, and it seemed like a promising job. But her chronic tardiness and then the pregnancy put an end to it. Now she tenuously held on to a data-entry job for a kitchen-supply wholesaler in a windowless office that drove her crazy. The people there acted as if shipping out a case of salt-shakers on time meant life or death. After a long night staying up with Cole, she would track toothpicks, plastic catsup bottles, and literally the kitchen sink on her computer screen while she fought to stay awake. Sometimes she lost the fight and received a nudge in the back by the office manager, who suggested she skip the late-night talk shows and get to bed earlier, and also warned Jackie of the limits of her patience.

The job at Burton had been better. But back then it was the never-ending parties that caused Jackie to show up late. She met Perry there. A business major at Purdue, he interned in the office one summer for college credit. She didn't like him at first. He was one of those white boys who carried himself as if he knew the world existed for his benefit, and did not hesitate to take advantage of this fact. His first day, he went straight to the coffeepot, picked out a mug (which happened to be Jackie's), and helped himself. She waited until he'd added the Cremora and stirred in the sugar before taking it away from him just as he brought it to his lips.

"Thanks, but less sugar next time," she said and walked back to her desk. She'd wanted to see his reaction, but didn't want him to think her interested enough to even turn around.

The next morning a hot cup of coffee was steaming on her desk when she got in, made just the way she liked. He earned a smile for that.

He had dirty blond-colored hair, which he wore tight on the sides, long on the top, and swept back with a dab more grease than necessary. Still, he managed to look professional at work and wore very crisp shirts and stylish ties with tiny knots.

Jackie did not flirt with Perry. But he invited himself along when a group from the office decided to meet for happy hour. This happy hour became happy evening as Jackie and a couple of her friends lingered while chatting. Perry had stayed too, and after a while he returned and asked Jackie to dance. Jackie looked at the nearly empty dance floor. It was still too early. Only an older, obviously inebriated couple was dancing. She shook her head.

"Hey," he said and touched her briefly right under the chin to get her to look his way. "I promise I won't embarrass you." Holding on to just two of her fingers, he led her to the dance floor.

"Go for the strange, girl," one of Jackie's friends called.

She grinned at her friends, allowed herself to be led away, and behind Perry's back rolled her eyes.

They danced to three songs. He danced well, and they had fun. Jackie must have looked surprised because somewhere in the middle of the second song he said, "What's the matter? Didn't you know some white boys have rhythm?"

"Oh? Where?" she answered coolly.

She wondered where Perry must be now. She knew he had finally graduated and must have been back in town for weeks. She put Cole on the floor as she stepped into her bedroom. Her baby seemed to have calmed down now.

"Mama thanks you for stressing her out, boy," she said. "Go read the newspaper or something."

Cole looked up at her as if he understood and was mulling over the suggestion. She left him there and went upstairs to Gail's room.

The big master bedroom at the back of the house was cluttered with newspapers and discarded clothes. The sheets and bedspread lay in a restless twist streaming to the floor. Gail would normally never tolerate this sloppiness, Jackie noted, but did not stop to consider what it might mean. Gail sat on the edge of the bed, one high heel in her hand, and rubbed at calluses on the pads of her right foot. "I could tap dance barefoot," she said without looking up at Jackie. "It's like having pebbles in your shoes. And tomorrow Mrs. Hirsch is going to have the entire staff scurrying around to put up

Christmas decorations. In October, can you believe that? That's going to wear these feet out."

Jackie tried to show interest. "Maybe you should soak them," she said. "I could get that little tub we used to wash Cole in."

Gail let her foot slip to the floor then rubbed a hand over her face. Small bags were beginning to form under her eyes. Her face looked puffy and her usually pronounced cheekbones didn't show so well just now. She picked up the hat she'd worn from beside her on the bed. "What's a matter with him? Maybe that fall hurt him worse than we thought."

"No. No, he's all right. He's fine now. Just teething."

"Where's it coming in at? The top or the bottom?"

"What, the tooth? I don't know." Jackie reminded herself not to lose patience. "I mean, I can't tell. You want that tub?"

Gail looked up at her now with a tired smile on her face.

Jackie did not understand. She thought her landlady would be in a better mood after hearing her son sing. "What do you want, girl? Are you going to be late with the rent again?"

"No," Jackie answered quickly. "You'll get the rent."

"I will, will I?" Gail went to her closet, and stood on tiptoes in order to place the hat on the highest shelf. "Then you must want me to babysit," she said, facing around again.

"Not for the whole night, Gail. I need to talk to someone. I'm not going out to go out."

"On a Sunday night, too. Knowing you ain't going to wake up on time Monday and you won't be worth nothing all day. That woman warned you about nodding off before, Jackie."

"I just said I wasn't going to be out late. He'll be asleep by the time I leave. You won't really have to do anything. Come on, Gail. I need to find—there's someone I need to talk to."

"Where's he now? Who's watching him now?"

"I am," Jackie shrugged. "He's in my room."

Gail shook her head. She reached around to get the zipper at the back of her dress.

Jackie stepped behind her, unhooked the fastener, and zipped the dress down. "Come on, Gail," she said.

"Where's all these friends you say you have? Why don't they ever want to come over and help you out?"

Jackie shrugged again. "They're always out doing something or another. And I can't get a hold of them. They have plans. Excuses, you know. Besides," Jackie added with a smile. "I want to leave the boy with someone I trust to take proper care of him."

Gail laughed loudly, and said, "Girl, get away from me."

Jackie did not see what Gail had found funny. "The boy likes you, Gail."

The older woman made no reply. She stepped out of her dress and laid it across her bed. Jackie stood there anyway, not wanting to give up on her only chance. But Gail moved from bed to bureau, pulling off her earrings and ignoring Jackie's presence.

"Thanks a lot, Gail," Jackie finally said. She kicked at an open sheet of newspaper lying near her feet, causing a loud smack. She walked out of the room.

Just outside the bedroom doorway, she heard Gail say, "Well, you know, Miss, you're very welcome. How many times have I watched that boy of yours and never asked a nickel for it?"

Jackie turned around but did not re-enter the room.

Gail faced her bureau now, her back toward Jackie. They eyed each other's reflection in the large, unframed mirror above the bureau. "Maybe I have plans. Like your friends, maybe I have something to do. I could take a bath, do something with this hair besides hide it under a hat." Gail pulled her fingers through her hair, which had been pressed down by her hat. "...Fix my face and go around and see some of my friends, maybe have a drink or two. Maybe I planned to forget everything and do something like that. Would that be wrong?

"What were your plans? Don't tell me. I'll guess. Goes like this: You want to go see Cole's father. He ain't come by or called, but you know it's just because he's a little scared. You want to give him the time he needs, but you still wonder, why doesn't he come around and see his boy? Might tell him that you don't want to put any pressure on him, but if he would stop by he might see that things could work out. Am I close?

"Then you got to ask him for a little money. After all, the boy is his too. And don't worry, Jackie, he'll give you some money. For a while at least, helps absolve them of all these guilty feelings they have. Lets them tell themselves they are handling the situation.

"How was my guess? I know you look down your nose at me, Miss, but all the time you're running around like your backside is on fire to get just where I am."

Jackie said, "I don't want to get where you are."

"I know. I didn't say you did." Gail began picking up the clothes from the floor. "I guess you've got to try, right? He might fool us. But in the meantime, start working on another plan."

Jackie leaned, arms crossed, against the doorjamb. She wanted to defend Perry but nothing she could say that would faze Gail came to mind.

"I think Dan Neighbors still has a thing for you," she tried.

Gail straightened up and tossed an armload of clothes upon her bed. "You going to tell me how well you know men?"

Jackie smiled. She knew when she'd scored a direct hit with Gail. "No, I mean it. I bet he does. And see, that's why I ain't running to be just like you. 'Cause I ain't going to give up."

Gail stood beside the bed in her slip looking at the tumble of clothes. "I have piles of laundry and I want to vacuum all the upstairs, and get that chicken thawed for dinner."

One more try, Jackie thought; the older woman seemed calmer now. "Gail, please, won't you watch the boy for me? Just a couple of hours, okay?"

"No," Gail said.

Nothing went right. She made a few phone calls. Her friends were out, sick, or busy. No one wanted to sit for Cole when Jackie couldn't offer them any money. She lay across the bed with the phone on her chest. She fed Cole and changed Cole and when the boy crawled under the bed and got stuck, she called Tyler to extricate him. Tyler left for the mall after that with some friends before Jackie could consider asking him to babysit, which she already knew he'd never do anyway. She used to be able to get Mason to watch Cole easily. He would practically volunteer, though he'd act like he was really being put out by the whole thing. Too bad he had left.

Mostly she lay there and thought of Perry. She rocked her crossed legs. Gail was wrong about Perry. He loved her and he would love Cole too. Before he'd gone back to Lafayette for his last semester, they had worked everything out. They would find a little apartment together at first. He would start his career. Perry would introduce his parents to their new grandson, Cole. That would be something to see; Perry always spoke of his mother as something of a control freak and his old man as a very starched shirt. But they would love Cole too.

"No promises," Perry had said, "they break too easily anyway. But we'll try. We'll work toward it." He'd held her in his arms while he spoke, making her feel reassured and protected.

If Perry would just talk to her, and not just on the phone, and not with his friends around. She knew his friends talked against her. They were probably telling him to leave her alone, her and Cole.

God, what if Cole had scared Perry away?

She jumped up. The phone fell to the floor and she stared at it until the recording told her to hang up and try again. The urgent, annoying beeps that followed attracted Cole, who came crawling from around the end of the bed. He grasped the coiled cord for a second before Jackie snatched it from him and returned the phone to her nightstand.

Cole began to cry.

Ignoring him, she went to her closet. Before Cole, and before she had left home, most of her money had gone into her wardrobe. She parted the hangers and found a short, backless, burgundy dress. She held the dress in front of her for a moment, studying the reflection in the full-length closet door mirror. Perry loved her in this.

"What do you think, boy?" Jackie asked.

From his spot on the floor, Cole quieted, and murmured approval while reaching out with his damp hands.

Jackie draped the dress across the bed and placed a pair of black pumps next to it. She dashed into the bathroom for a quick shower and dried herself in front of the steamed bathroom mirror. Her figure had snapped back tight and firm after Cole. In fact, one might see her diminutive body and believe her incapable of bearing children. If she arched her back, the lines of her ribs would show and her breasts would altogether disappear. Her androgynous form long ago ceased to concern her; she had learned appeal lay not in what you uncovered but in how you covered what you had. She prided herself on knowing how to dress. Imagination was more powerful than reality and her clothes suggested rather than revealed. She styled her hair meticulously, then put on lipstick a shade lighter than the dress she'd picked. Her confidence grew. She would find Perry; they would straighten everything out.

Cole had been playing, she discovered, while Mama was in the bathroom. He'd found the pretty dress she'd shown him and dragged it from the bed down to the floor.

"Damn it, boy!" She snatched him up and away from the dress in swift motion. She raised him level to her face. She shouted, "You little shit" in his frightened face.

Her harsh voice startled Cole. His eyes popped open, then shut tight. He shrieked.

Jackie could see the wrinkles his little fists had squeezed into her dress and a dark circle of drool. She raised him a bit higher. "Damn," she repeated. "Perry, look what you did," and felt the rage suddenly rising within her like a geyser.

The baby wailed.

Jackie did not move, did not breathe. The only movement in the room came from Cole's squirming legs. Her muscles had tensed for action, but froze only a split second from responding to the horrifying signal sent by her brain. She could see the baby flung from her, slamming against the bed's headboard. Cole would lie shattered, as lifeless as one of his stuffed animals. And the wall between that vision and the reality of Cole still in her hands was tissue-paper thin. In the space of a terrible second, she had nearly done it. Her control fought to resurface through her anger. She breathed again. She saw her frightened son held roughly before her, felt again his weight, and the vulnerable softness caught between her fingers. She pressed him to her chest, wrapping him in a tender hug. She kissed the top of his head, feeling his warm skin and silky hair against her lips. While gently rocking, she whispered, "My baby shhh. Shhh, my baby boy." His tears ran down her breasts. She hugged him for a very long time, absorbing his warmth and surrendering hers. She held him well past the time when he had stopped crying and she had started.

A damp rag and ironing salvaged the dress. Cole finally fell asleep in his crib. Along with a bottle filled with grape-flavored drink, she placed his favorite toy, a ragged, one-eyed dog, in the crib's corner. She listened to his soft, rapid breathing.

"Boy, you just want me to hurt you, don't you? That's right, lay there all innocent-like now. You can't fool Mama."

She left the door to his room open. The others would hear him if he awakened. But he would sleep through, no problem.

At her closet-door mirror, she adjusted a shoulder pad before putting on her white leather biker jacket. She licked her right pinky finger and stroked up her eye lashes with it. Her tongue moistened her lipstick and she smiled.

This early Sunday evening grew cooler and quieter with each passing minute. Jackie's heels struck loudly on the sidewalk. Her friend Kei—he dropped the "th" from "Keith"—would not be at home long. He had agreed to drive her over to Perry's. Holding Kei to an agreement could be difficult at times; his attention span was short. But Jackie considered him one of her best friends. They gossiped together relentlessly, talked clothes, and because they shared the same sexual preference, she could talk to him about men. He'd stuck by her during the pregnancy. Well, at least, he didn't point a finger at her like so many had while she grew bigger and bigger with a white baby.

Kei had advised her to move out of town, to Chicago or San Francisco. "You and me don't belong in this smallville, Jaclyn. We are individuals. We like to express ourselves as individuals. The rest of these rednecked hicks and small-time niggers don't like that. They always worrying about what's in. You notice that? In clothes and cars and dancing, you name it. You know what 'what's in' means? Means how have we agreed to dress now? What will you accept? How have we agreed to dance now? What won't you laugh at? They scrapping and scraping to look as alike as ants. We should all be wearing Levi Docker pants and polo shirts.

"They don't want to know anything about a stylish fag, or a pretty black girl who hunts white snake."

Jackie had insisted that she didn't go for white men in general, just Perry—and his skin color just didn't matter to her.

He'd said okay and shrugged too quickly. Kei just didn't care what people were into. Though he figured everyone was into something. He maintained he could tolerate anything.

A block from the house where Kei rented a studio apartment in the attic, Jackie spotted his old red Volvo driving toward her. She waved him down and he pulled over. She got in and gave him a look of obviously feigned anger.

"Now see," he said showing his teeth. "I was coming to get you. Didn't want you to have to walk."

"Like a rug you lie."

"I know." He pulled the car away from the curb. "I like your hair," he said.

Kei wore his hair short on the sides and top, but straightened and moussed until it resembled black turf cut as evenly as a golf course green. In back, he had let it grow to a six-inch plait, which he tied off usually with a yellow or red ribbon that dangled to the small of his back. He sported gold loop earrings and the shadow of a scruffy beard. The total effect of his appearance might have suggested a pirate or a rogue, but his manner dispelled such notions quickly.

"How's that little butterball boy of yours?"

"Oh, hell, he's just fine. Could use a father and a much better mama though."

"Well, you're not a natural mom type, but you're going to do a good job."

She almost asked him what he meant by that—how he knew what kind of "mom type" she was—but she didn't want to get into it with him now. "Thanks for the ride, Kei," she said.

"There's a party going on at Phil's."

"Sunday night?"

"Spontaneous, naturally occurring, the best kind. Planned festivities always have something wooden about them."

"That's where you were headed?"

"I thought I said I was coming to get you?"

"You did."

"Well, I'd like to stick to that story."

She could tell Kei really wanted to make the party. "We can drop by after we find Perry. It won't take long. You can probably drop me off and Perry will bring me back."

"Maybe he'll want to go to Phil's too." Kei laughed; Jackie did not. "You're sweating him an awful lot, girlfriend."

Jackie began chewing a thumbnail then quickly pulled it from her mouth, not wanting to ruin the polish. "I just need to talk to him face to face. Let's just find the fool."

Kei followed Jackie's directions. They drove north on Highway 41 to a suburban hamlet that lay along the slopes of gentle hills and was connected by curving, tree-lined lanes. On the way out, Kei asked about Mason. Had they heard anything?

"No," Jackie said and gazed at her friend. "He is not your type. At least, I don't think he is."

"The ones I like most never are."

Many of the huge homes could not be seen from the street and they had to drive by slowly while Jackie tried to remember which one belonged to Perry's family. She finally spotted it, explaining to Kei that she'd been there only a couple of times before when his parents weren't home.

"He's that ashamed of you?"

Jackie shook her head. "He says it's them who'd embarrass him. He said his dad is stiff. That's the word Perry uses, stiff. I guess he's a bigoted old bastard."

"Not ready to send his grandson to Howard instead of Harvard, huh?"

They made a U-turn and cruised slowly by the house again. It sat far back from the street. It was dark now. The shadowy elms out front obscured their vision. Some lights were on, and the long walkway to the front door was lit by small yellow lights. A low brick wall clothed in thick, dark ivy ran the width of the front lawn parallel to the sidewalk.

Kei said, "It's like a damn fort."

"Turn around again."

He shook his head but did as he was told. "This is a definite low point, Jaclyn. We can't get any more high school than driving by the house of the boy you have a crush on. Don't tell anyone we did this."

"You're the one who doesn't care what people think."

"The police are going to come and arrest two niggers for casing this neighborhood. You tell me what their names are."

"Shush."

"Jaclyn and Kei." He stopped the car in front of the house on the third drive-by and turned off his headlights. "You can't tell if he's home from here. You've got to go knock on the door, girlfriend."

"No, Perry wouldn't want that. I'm trying to see if his car's here."

"What's he drive?"

"A white Supra."

"Nice."

Jackie climbed out of the car. "I've got to peek in the garage. Unless you want to?" Kei gave her a stony look. "I didn't think so. Don't go nowhere."

He said something else about the police beating people, but Jackie was already scurrying down the long, winding driveway, trying to tiptoe in her high heels. Finally she stopped and took them off. The pavement was cold on her feet and she regretted taking her shoes off immediately, but didn't put them back on. She wrapped her jacket tighter around herself, but couldn't zip it up on the run with a shoe in each hand.

A Cadillac sat in the driveway in front of the garage. Jackie slipped around it. Her feet were freezing. Her toes began to hurt.

She crept up to the small windows on the garage door. She nosed the glass and held her shoes to either side of her face to block outside light. Except for a golf cart in the rear, the garage was empty.

A bright light came on almost directly over her head.

"Can I help you? Who's there?"

The voice came from the house—a woman's, but Jackie could not see her. She faced that direction anyway, spotlighted, and tried to peer into the shadows around the house. She shuffled from one cold foot to the other.

"Who's there?" the woman asked. It sounded more like a demand. "What do you want?"

"Hey, hi," Jackie answered. "I was looking for Perry. Um, I didn't want to bother nobody if he was out, so I was just looking for his car." And she added again, "I didn't want to bother nobody."

The woman didn't say anything. Jackie wondered if she should try explaining bare feet in late October, but decided to let the woman guess for herself. She stood under the light for a few more moments, feeling embarrassed and stupid, and silently thanking Perry for putting her in this position. Finally, she slipped her pumps back on and turned to leave. She said, "Good night."

"Perry's not here," she heard and footsteps followed.

A woman came into view just within the lamplight's glow. She was tall, blond with traces of silver, and to Jackie's eyes looked fiftyish. She wore a shaker knit sweater and had a deep frown on her face as she eyed Jackie. Jackie knew she must be Cole's grandmother and that seemed very strange. She definitely could see traces of Perry in this woman's face, around the nose and mouth, and similarities to Cole too.

"Perry went out earlier with his friends."

Jackie nodded. She suddenly wished she'd worn a different outfit, maybe something she'd usually wear to the office. She crossed her arms. The creaky, scratchy noise her leather jacket made sounded loud. She wanted to walk away from this woman, continue down the driveway, but knew it wouldn't be right. She felt like she needed to stand her ground, even though no one had challenged her to back down from anything.

"I don't know when we expect him back."

Jackie was well aware she was being examined. The woman clearly wanted a close look. "It's okay, I was just out this way," Jackie said.

Mrs. Sullivan asked, "Who may I say came by?"

The question set Jackie to wondering how much this woman might know about her. Would Perry have said anything? She really did not want Perry to know she had been searching for him. She didn't want him to know she'd become desperate enough to start a chase. "Yes, please tell him Jaclyn came by. It isn't urgent. Good night."

"Good night," Mrs. Sullivan said, smiling politely.

Back in the car at last, Jackie kicked her shoes off and tucked her feet under her to warm them up. It felt like sitting on two blocks of ice. "They're numb. Turn up the heat."

"I'm not going to be the wheel man if that's the best burglary you can do. Who caught you?"

"His mother. Turn up the heat."

"Oh? And how is Mom?"

"Scary. Let's try his friend Dennis's place. I think I know where it is."

Jackie took a pack of cigarettes from the top of the dash and lit one. She wasn't much of a smoker and took only a few drags before rolling the window down a crack and tossing it out. She gave Kei directions while he talked about some guy from out of town he hoped would be at Phil's. She did not pay him much attention.

They ended up driving by three different houses, each of which she believed Dennis might live in. But none had Perry's car parked nearby.

"You want to tell me again why you couldn't just call him?" Kei asked without his usual humor.

"Hang with me, Kei," Jackie said reaching over to give his shoulder a squeeze. "I have to see his face. You can't see if people mean what they say over the phone. Hell, I can't tell anyway. They could be picking their nose and saying, 'but sweetheart, I love you'."

Kei laughed.

"Let's go back in town. I know a couple of places he hangs out. Then we'll hit the party."

She sat arms crossed and quiet in the car during the return trip. Kei kept trying to start conversation, but Jackie was preoccupied. She'd been certain she would find him home on a Sunday night. She had rehearsed in her mind how it would go. They wouldn't talk much at first, and they'd both feel awkward, but they would look into each other's eyes. She would see the truth there: that he was so in love with her. Then he'd grab her up in his arms and kiss her. He'd say some bull about how crazy things have been but that he missed her and hadn't really realized how much until now. But she wouldn't make it too easy. Maybe she'd guilt him a bit about not visiting Cole. He'd nod and promise to change. They'd kiss again, and maybe he could find a place they could go to for just a little while. After all, she'd have to get back to Cole.

But she hadn't even found his car—just a middle-aged woman, a complete stranger to her, whose nose and the way her lips pressed together looked just like Cole's.

They drove up and down the parking lots around two night-clubs and found one white sports car that could have been Perry's, though she didn't think so. Jackie went into that night club and stood at the entrance way, peeking around at the small Sunday night crowd until the doorman insisted she pay the cover charge. She left, finally prepared to call it an evening.

"Maybe you'd better take me home," Jackie said to Kei. "Between Perry and Cole and Gail Neighbors..."

"You need some uplifting. We're going to Phil's and get us a drink or two. Next time, you call this cracker and have him come to you."

Jackie did not protest. She realized she ought to get home to Cole; it was just that she didn't care what she did just then. It had been a long day. The thought of Monday morning, getting Cole to the babysitter's, and heading to that closed-in office to count boxes of toothpicks made her even more weary. She decided she didn't care where Perry was or what he did. She could forget him as easily as he'd forgotten her.

They went to Phil's. The house lay along a crumbling street without sidewalks. The cars in front had been parked at every angle in the drive and front yard. Kei and Jackie walked around to the side, entering through the packed kitchen. The stereo could be heard from outside, but inside it could be felt. The bass boomed through the floor and up the soles of Jackie's feet.

Only a few new faces hovered amongst the familiar ones, who paused from loud conversations and laughter long enough to smile Jackie's way. Already nodding her head to the beat, she squeezed her way through, shoulder height to most everyone. Friends reached out to touch her as she went by or squeeze her hand.

"Girl, where you been?"

"Where you been hiding, Little J?"

Girlfriends asked about Cole. When he was very young, Jackie used to bring him with her to parties. She was determined not to miss a beat of her old lifestyle, and that meant parties and friends. She would place him in the host's back bedroom on a bed along with the guests' coats and jackets. That did not work out so well. He would cry and she could not hear him above the music. And it was no fun to quit dancing in order to check up on him or to change a diaper. The girls used to coo around Cole, and tell Jackie how cute he was. She would pretend to ignore the snickers about his complexion and straight hair. She stopped going to the parties after awhile. The crowd wasn't the same, didn't react to her in the same way. More guys, none that she was interested in now that she'd found Perry, came on to her, thinking the single mother easier prey. Some of the girls were great. They had kids too. They understood. But that didn't change the fact that her clique had been pulled in various directions by their new responsibilities, and had much less time for each other.

Iced-down beer filled a plastic trash barrel. Kei popped one open, took a sip, and gave it to her. He was in his element now. Jackie watched him grin from ear to ear as he surveyed the premises.

"There goes Angela Banks stumbling out of the living room with her fingers still halfway up her nose. Don't waste a crumb,

Angie," he said, though not loud enough for the girl to hear. "Coming?" he asked Jackie while pushing his way through the doorway Angela had come from, not waiting for a reply.

She'd decided to leave the coke alone while pregnant with Cole and felt good about that. She saw no reason to go back to it. It cost too much. And if guys gave you some, they always expected something else in return. Jackie stayed in the kitchen, half listening to the gossip her friends laughed and squealed about. She accepted another beer someone handed her, and then a strong drink from a paper cup. She wasn't sure what it was, but she chased its clammy aftertaste away with another beer. Before long she was dancing in a tight tangle of elbows and legs.

A cute boy with a fade-cut hair style, maybe two or three years younger than her, showed her a lot of attention. Younger guys always thought she was their age. She danced with him and allowed him to take off her jacket and run his hands up and down her bare back while they danced, until she roughly pushed his hands away. This in no way deterred him.

Jackie ducked away from him for a while, talked and laughed with friends and realized she'd missed socializing. She and her friends watched Kei rapping hard to some guy, who looked uninterested, except for a moment when he played with Kei's ponytail. The girls were betting he'd strike out. But by the time the gathering showed signs of winding down, Kei and his new friend were long gone. Her ride home had disappeared with them.

She could have asked the young guy with the fast hands for a ride, but that would have been more trouble than it was worth. Besides, she felt just high enough—and definitely lonely enough—not to trust herself to say no when the time came. She found a ride with some girls who rented a house together. She knew only one of them well.

"Jackie, we need another roommate," her friend said during the ride home. "The rent is cheap and we're having a lot of fun. You're fly enough to hang with us. Debbie is leaving in January."

"No bambinos," the driver said quickly. "You understand?"

Jackie said, "Oh, yeah, I understand."

They dropped her off in front of the huge boardinghouse. All the lights were off, and most of the house lay hidden by the trees and their shadows. Jackie was cold. She went around back, but instead of hurrying up the back porch steps, sat down on them. She leaned against the porch's edge, conscious that it probably dirtied her white jacket. The beer had made her feel thick-headed and witless. And the loud hip-hop had left her ears buzzing. Beyond that irritating hiss, she heard cars passing by out front and the blurred voices of a man and woman maybe three houses down. Still, she felt quiet. Her frustration at not finding Perry slipped from her; she was too exhausted to hold onto it. The first calm minutes of the day held her there. Then came the sound of crying from inside. Cole. Gail had undoubtedly discovered that she'd left him alone by now and she would have to hear her say, "How dare you leave him alone?" She would threaten her with social workers again. Cole's cry was almost a scream. He wasn't hurt, she knew. He was not in trouble, nor was he scared. The cry was for her; it was a demand. Her entire body tightened as if braced for a blow. She had to go inside. She had to return to that.

MASON

Somewhere in Ohio they'd come to another stop. He waited in the car at a gas station, one with a tall Sohio sign that could be spotted from miles away. He listened to the growing and then receding swoosh of cars streaming by, and felt the heavier labored rush of the big rigs pushing the air in front of them, radiating with the heat from the highway. The noise and the heat so mingled that Mason would always associate them.

Mason clenched and unclenched a fist. The door with the stick symbol for "Men" remained shut. He'd envisioned the journey as quicker than this. He would confront his father and then, afterward, he would be free to go anywhere he wanted. After the payback. But all this took too long.

"Gamble is driving me crazy. He's supposed to be driving me home, but so far—just crazy," Gina said.

The girl, Gina, looked more exasperated than Mason, if that was possible. She pulled her hair back, lifted it off her neck, and exhaled loudly, then reached over and hit the car horn, two sustained blasts that caused the gas station attendant in the little glass booth to scowl.

She wore black Lycra tights that came to her knees, a shorter blue skirt, and a sloppy, light blue T-shirt she lifted up every now and then to let air under it. During the trip, Mason would slouch low in the seat beside Gina with his knees pressed against the glove compartment and gaze up at her every now and then. The traces of scars on her face actually weren't as bad outside in direct sunlight as they were inside, which didn't make much sense. Mile after mile he'd noticed, or maybe he imagined, that she'd scooted closer and closer to him.

Gina leaned across Mason to stick her head out the passenger-side window. "We're melting out here," she shouted.

He could smell her sweat and feel the extra heat her body brought with her. "Do you mind?" he asked. The picture of her giving that big woman "morning sugar" wouldn't quite shake loose from his mind. The idea fascinated him; the image repulsed him. If that's what she liked, at least she could have better taste. He found a pun in that thought and briefly smiled.

"When Captain Butthole of Rust Bucket Airlines finally comes out of there, you and me are changing places. He's been running his fingers along my leg and pressing against me the entire trip."

Mason heard her but didn't answer. Sitting in the middle would be too hot—better to stay by a window and get the breeze even though it was warm. Besides, the cramped conditions were her fault: her suitcases, lamps, TV, and tables filled the back seat and the trunk.

Cars pulled into the station, fueled up, and left. Other men went into the restroom and came out. A boy went in and came out immediately, shooting bewildered glances over his shoulder. Three station wagons in a row had pulled in, each loaded with family. Mothers yelled for their kids to simmer down, took the youngest ones by the hand, and led them to the ladies room. Fathers pumped gas and fished in their pockets for change on request for the soda machines. The scene, reenacted three times in a row with but minor variations, struck Mason as comical, though he didn't allow himself to smile. The coincidence did not amuse him so much as the families themselves, father, mother, kids, dog, like the casts of television sitcoms. The people seemed absurd, playing as though they were on TV, their real lives and secrets packed away as tightly as their suitcases.

Gina chatted away, something about stopping to get a bite to eat and then something about the number of miles between Columbus and Wheeling.

Mason climbed out of the car and shut the door without looking behind.

"...and drag his black ass out of there if you have to," he heard her say.

The strong odor of urine hung just beyond the door, overcoming the disinfectant smell of the white cakes placed in the urinals. The floor was puddled. Graffiti had been scribbled over the walls. A pair of dirty white Reeboks protruded just beyond the closed door of the farthest of two stalls. Mason shoved the door open. Gamble sat on the floor with the back of his head resting on the filthy lip of the toilet bowl.

"Occupied. Damn it!" he said. He glanced up at Mason but there was no recognition in his eyes. "Had to get even," he said drowsily, "so I can drive."

Mason squatted next to Gamble, drew back his right fist, then slammed a hard jab into Gamble's face. Gamble's head banged off the bowl's porcelain edge and bounced back into a second punch. He slid unconscious to the floor.

"Damn," Mason said. The second punch had caught teeth, leaving a deep cut on Mason's pinky knuckle. His entire hand hurt and he shook it to dispel the pain. He then rummaged in Gamble's pockets and fished out a set of car keys with a coke spoon attached, as well as a Ziploc bag containing coke, and several shiny red and blue capsules.

He pocketed everything and then pulled Gamble to his feet, almost slipping in a puddle in the process. Gamble easily outweighed Mason by thirty pounds and getting him upright was a feat. Mason leaned against him in a corner of the stall. The smell closed in, filling his nose and lungs. He wrapped one of Gamble's arms about his neck and half-dragged, half-carried him out. He saw Gina emerge from the car and start moving toward them.

"Well, help me before I drop the son of a bitch," Mason said. He allowed himself a deep breath of air.

Gina ran like a man. "Jesus, what did you do?" She stooped under Gamble's other arm. They managed to get him to the car.

Mason said, "You told me to drag him out if I had to."

"Shit! You gonna do everything I tell you? Let me know now." They folded him into the car.

Gina softly slapped at Gamble's cheeks, generating no response. "What did you do to him?"

Mason stepped close to her. "I didn't do anything to him," he said. He pulled the baggy of drugs from his pocket, holding it close to shield it from any onlookers. "This did it to him. Get in. Let's go."

Mason got behind the wheel with Gamble propped in the middle. "We should just throw his little kit away," Gina said. She held her hand for a moment just under Gamble's nose.

Mason rolled his eyes and started the car. What did she think, that Gamble was dead? "I'll trash it down the road. But you can't tell him we ever had it. Gamble gets weird."

"I know. Hey…his face looks a little puffy."

Mason shrugged. "Maybe he fell down."

They drove away from the station and back onto the highway. Mason had never owned a car and had little driving experience. He stayed in the right lane, doing only a bit over 55. For several miles, he gripped the wheel with both hands. The number of cars on the highway surprised him. The vast openness of the Ohio countryside surprised him too. He was glad to be driving and in control. "You've got to watch for the signs, so don't take a nap or anything," he said to Gina. He adjusted the rearview mirror. It framed Gamble's large, dark nostrils. "I'm going to tell him we think he got rolled while he was in the john."

"Shit. He's going to be pissed."

Gamble's slick, smooth head rolled back with the bump of his Adam's apple protruding. Hopefully, he would not be coming to anytime soon.

"He's been anointed with the Holy Ghost," Mason said, then laughed, ignoring Gina's frown for the moment. The violence he'd done against Gamble exhilarated him. Pony would be next. "Someone laid holy hands on our boy."

"What the hell are you talking about?" Gina asked.

"Ain't you ever seen preachers anoint their flock with the Holy Ghost power?"

She shook her head. "My religious upbringing was limited."

"The holy rollers do it, and the A.M.E. and some Baptists. The preachers slap people on the forehead and they faint, fall back like a domino. It's all bullshit, really. But the people think some bit of God's spirit is being put in them. You can see how that'd make you pass out."

Mason smiled without realizing it. The memory of one of his favorite days returned to him as fresh as the sunrise that began it. He remembered the butter-soft sun rising between the houses and alleyways on those Sunday mornings his mother herded the family to church. That was when they lived in the little apartment, when Dan Neighbors lived with them. Tyler and Mason slept in bunk beds and his mother would shake them awake with a hand on each. Mason remembered the dark and the cold, and trying to hide beneath his blanket as long as he could get away with it, until she returned to snatch the covers away, exposing his curled body to the chill.

Funny, Mason thought, only the cold mornings come to mind, but we went to church all year round.

He said, "Back in the days when my mama searched for God, she used to drag the whole family up before sunup to get us to some sunrise service. Seems like it was a different church every week. Believe so. She couldn't find one that would quite suit."

Mason recalled tiptoeing quickly over the cold tile floor to the bathroom door to wait his turn. The boys brushed their teeth and washed their faces at the kitchen sink while Gail got ready in the bathroom. The tiny apartment never seemed smaller than when all four of them dressed to go out at the same time.

Sometimes quick whispering came from Dan and his mother's room, words over whether or not they'd sleep in on one particular Sunday. Mason couldn't recall Dan winning any of these discussions. His stepfather would stumble from the bedroom in his twisted boxers, scratching, and following an out-thrust hand blindly to the john.

Big Dan Neighbors was always laughing about something or other, except on those Sunday mornings when he'd grumble, bitch, and moan. At the time, Mason would worry that Dan would complain too much and begin another argument with Gail. He and his little brother would freeze at the sink, each with foamy white toothpaste lips, listening to the voices. He'd see the fear on Tyler's face and certainly, Tyler saw the same open-eyed look when he gazed at Mason.

But even if there were shouts and harsh, snapped words from behind that bedroom door, Dan would get up anyway. He did it for Gail, those Sunday mornings, they all did. Dan and the boys never mentioned it to each other; it wasn't a plan they had devised, but they all knew that Sundays and church were important to their mother in an urgent, maybe secret way. She cleaned and looked after her men all week and then on Sunday mornings the bill came due. She'd hear about a new church or new pastor and off they'd go. Baptist, Sanctified, A.M.E., holy roller, didn't matter. Gail had to try them all.

Mason saw the highway through Ohio stretch out almost perfectly straight in front of him. At the same time he saw his family in their Sunday best, walking down the street to a church that looked more like a corner grocery store. The big, plate-glass windows said, "The Holy Ghost True Redeemer Church, Come Save Your Soul." How old was I then, he tried to remember, nine? Ten?

Mason described it all for Gina, though he didn't check to see how his story was received, as he didn't really care whether she listened or not.

This particular storefront church had a line of people waiting to get in, mostly women and children. Women in hats. Ugly hats too, Mason thought, with fish nets and fruit sprouting from them.

On that frosty morning, the Neighbors family stood in the slowly creeping line. Mason followed behind Gail, Dan, and Tyler. Tyler leaned against his father's leg, almost falling asleep after each step. A big hand of Dan's stroked the top of Tyler's head. Mason remembered that distinctly because he realized at that moment that Dan Neighbors never touched him that way, with natural, unpremeditated, comfortable affection.

Gail shook hands with the grinning man who stood in the doorway. He wore a full-length tan leather coat with fur trim at the cuffs and collar. Heavy gold rings circled most of his fingers, which caught the available morning light and reflected it in a spray of directions as his hands moved to envelope the hand of the next member of his flock. His expressive face smiled easily and his hair had been sculpted into a too-perfectly round Afro.

He covered one of Mason's hands with both of his and held it. To those remaining in line he said, "This is what I like to see. The people in line for the Lord and not the liquor store." The cold metal of the preacher's rings pressed into Mason skin. Mason snatched his hand back.

The pastor glared at him for that. Mason returned the look without fear. "He looks like a pimp," Mason whispered to Dan when they were safely past the pastor. Dan's face soured when he glanced back at the man and he nodded to Mason.

When everyone found seats the service got started. A round, delicate-looking man played the organ. The preacher appeared wearing a red, silky robe as bright as fire. He shouted the same brimstone lesson Mason had already taught himself not to fear. After all, none of it bothered Dan.

Dan sat there with his arms locked tight across his chest, and his neck bulged over his collar and his tie knot. He looked made of iron. Tyler, still young enough to get away with it, had fallen asleep. Eagerness shone from Gail's face. Mason would look across Dan's chest and arms at his mother, who leaned forward with her mouth partly open.

"Seems kind of sad to me in a way." Mason said to Gina. He kept his eyes focused down the highway. "Like Mama, they all seem to be looking for something, a little desperate, sitting there in their best dresses and hats. A bunch of desperate niggers. They all running away from something or looking for something and they're afraid cause they don't have a clue. No one's clued them in. They're so afraid of themselves and their lives. Scared shitless. They got to find something else. God will do nicely. I don't believe many come there to praise Him cause life is so wonderful. Some want a new Lincoln, some want their husbands to stop doing crack and fucking around. Some want jobs. Some," Mason added, "just want to know who they are."

Gina asked, "Do you believe in God, Mason?"

He didn't answer right away, yet finally said, "Every now and then."

He'd thought he was going to face God on that day, or some portion of him. Mason listened to the same messages that were already very familiar to him, even at that young age, when, with no warning, the pastor started speaking in tongues. Mason's mouth dropped open and he grabbed the sleeve of Dan's coat. Even Dan sparked up. The words didn't sound like a foreign language; they sounded more guttural, more animal than that. They sounded old and dusty. The preacher's voice had changed too, growing heavier, as if coarse sand had been poured in his throat.

The plump organist stepped up to the preacher and asked to be anointed with the Holy Ghost. The preacher's hand came up and slapped him on the forehead. The organist stiffened and fell over like a plank. Smack. Dan said, "Jesus." Mason and he both looked at Gail, wanting to ask, what have you got us into this time? But she did not look their way. Her hands waved in the air and she cried, "Yes, Jesus," along with everyone else.

Others started going forward. They circled the preacher, whose hand came down on their foreheads with loud slaps. Skirts flew up. Hats rolled off heads. The anointed fell away from the preacher. Attendants caught them from behind and lowered them gently to the floor. Some lay still and others twitched their limbs and moaned. Mason asked Dan how the preacher was doing it, but Dan didn't say anything. Then Gail stood and Mason was scared for her. He remembered calling out to her, but she ignored him. Mason thought she'd been entranced. Hypnotized, he feared. By then, the preacher had surrounded himself with supine bodies resembling the pictures of Jonestown Mason had seen on TV. Gail's turn came. The old words, as Mason came to think of them, were pronounced over her and, at the touch of a palm, she fell blissfully away. Her dress floated up as she fell back.

Mason looked to Dan. At least he wasn't buying any of this Holy Ghost stuff. Dan was a rock, a bulwark, unmoved—unsaved—and safe.

Then Dan got up too.

He had to yank his arm away from Mason, who sat dumbfounded for a moment before jumping up to follow his stepfather. They stood on either side of Gail, whose eyes were closed. The preacher spoke over Dan in tongues, and his palm came down on the big man's forehead, pressing gently and firmly. The two men's eyes flashed at one another and Dan, like an axed tree, fell to the floor beside his wife.

Mason could not believe his eyes. Suddenly, with Dan lying there he knew everything he'd heard in church was true: the Ghost, the Son, hell, heaven, the coat of many colors, animals on the gangplank two by two, Eve's fig leaf, all hit him between the eyes because Dan—who never bought any of it, not even Christmas—lay on the floor of a corner grocery store, laid low by the power of the Holy Ghost.

Then the glowing red robe stretched up and away right in front of Mason, who gaped at the angry face of the pastor. The voice gave him chills. The preacher's perfect Afro hung a little wilted now and sweat made his face shine, and he held his anointing hand high over his head and reared back as if pulling the divine power directly from heaven.

Mason did not remember how he managed it, but he saw the open palm of God descending toward him from above, and from below he saw Dan Neighbors wink at him—a telling, everything-is-the-same wink—then Dan reached down and quickly straightened out Gail's dress, covering her legs. That had been his sole purpose for getting anointed, Mason later learned. The preacher's hand made a soft smack as it landed on Mason's forehead. Mason did not move, only stared past the billowy sleeve of the robe at the preacher. The man pushed at Mason's head, but still Mason would not move. The preacher stepped closer. "Don't mess up my perfect record this morning, my brother," he said in a voice not so old at all. He pressed on Mason's head again. Mason crossed his arms. The preacher said, "Some cannot be saved," and moved down the line to anoint the next soul waiting.

But it had been a good day, as Mason recalled. Dan and he shared a secret. "Weren't going to have no damn flim-flam preacher and everybody spying up my wife's skirt," he subsequently confided to Mason.

Gail had been delighted that Dan had allowed himself to be anointed with the Holy Spirit. She kissed him on the cheek on the way home, then dabbed the lipstick from his face with her handkerchief. Husband and wife walked home with their arms tightly about each other so no space showed between them. Mason and Tyler followed, relieved and reveling in the freedom that came with the end of another service. Mason enjoyed seeing Gail and Dan hold on to one another. Their love made him feel secure; Dan would not disappear down the highway as his father had. He didn't think about it that way just then, just simply felt good seeing them get along. It made him happy for his mother too. Dan had done more than fulfill his basic Sunday obligation to Gail, as far as she knew, he had participated in it with her. She would be content. She would sing off-key hymns in the kitchen while preparing the biggest meal of the week. Following the anointed couple home that cool morning, Mason watched their vaporous breath mingle and float toward him from over their heads like the ethereal body of a ghost.

Mason told Gina bits of that recollection, or maybe all of it, though a few hours later he couldn't say how much talking he'd done. He shut up abruptly, feeling inexplicably embarrassed. Gina then began to fill the silence he'd left. She talked non-stop now. She said something about putting Gamble in the trunk. She was joking, but Mason wished it was possible. She chatted incessantly, and Mason figured she was relieved that Gamble, for a while, didn't call the shots. She mentioned wheelchairs, or some kind of wheels, and Mason heard something about her home. Otherwise, he listened to her not at all.

Mason avoided mom and pop diners as a matter of course. It just felt safer to go to a Mickey D's or a Burger King. They were the same everywhere and seemed to treat everyone the same too. The next in line always got served next, and the counter girl had little to say to anyone except maybe, "Is this for here or to go?" In the small diners and grills, he never knew. As a boy he'd gone into a grill back home called the Tennessean. Stone-faced white men eyed him from around their newspapers, and a big, sweaty white woman with two kids glared at him. Only whites were in there. Instantly aware that he'd intruded, he sat at the counter anyway, more afraid to leave than to stay, and ordered his cheeseburger and milkshake to go. The waitress didn't say a word. She took his order then went down the counter and joked with other customers a bit before giving it to the cook. Mason waited, growing angry but doing his damnedest not to show it. He played with a plastic straw, twisting and untwisting it, pretending to ignore the slight that people who'd ordered after him were already eating. Finally, the waitress slid his cheeseburger in front of him. He thanked her loudly so everyone could hear, then walked out. He heard, "nigger" in a high, squeaky voice as he went through the door—one of the big woman's children. He didn't turn around at the sound of laughter behind his back.

Of course, Gina insisted on stopping at a tiny mom and pop operation in the middle of nowhere, bringing back that little memory, which at the time had seemed like such a big deal, one of the only times he could remember directly feeling racial prejudice. He'd told Dan Neighbors about it, who said Mason must've imagined the episode.

"I go there all the time," Dan told him. "They ain't been nothing but friendly to me. I know a lot of people who eat there."

Still, maybe one black boy alone was a different story. They wouldn't have to disguise themselves then.

"Mase, you know how impatient you get. Then you get all huffy and get to frowning. That puts people off to you, son."

So somehow the entire incident had been his fault, his construction. He had imagined it or brought it on himself with his attitude. After talking with Dan, he no longer trusted the facts as he had perceived them, and he never mentioned the incident to anyone else. But he never went into restaurants he didn't know about alone. The experience of being made to feel small returned to Mason while sitting in the booth across from Gina. A flash of anger heated the back of his neck. This further delay annoyed him; he didn't want to be in this redneck joint with this girl. His fingers drummed the flimsy table hard enough to make the flatware rattle.

They were the only blacks in the restaurant. Besides two waitresses, Gina was the only woman. Three other tables were occupied. Three men, looking like farmers, sat in the opposite booth. One man with a big, red nose sat alone with an untouched slice of apple pie, studying a Rand McNally. Two others—Mason saw only one, but the man in the John Deere cap must've been talking to someone across him—sat in a booth farther up the row from the one Gina and he were in.

"Relax, will you?" she said. "What are you doing? Sizing up the room?" Her hair, thick as wire, fell on both sides of her face. They sat at a window and Mason could see the soft, late afternoon sun reflected in her light eyes. "I've been here before. They have the fattest burgers in the business."

He could see Gamble's Oldsmobile from where he sat. Gamble was still sleeping it off in the front seat. Mason thought they should have done more miles before Gamble woke up.

Gina asked, "Where are you going? What are your plans?"

He shrugged, avoided looking into her eyes again by gazing out the window at the broad Ohio sky. Across the road, flat fields of dusty crops hugged to the curve of the earth. "Just want to get out of that backwards town. Tired of small towns."

"I don't mind small towns. Less crime—"

"How're you guys today?" A curly-haired brunette waitress appeared at their table. The front of her legs pressed against the table's edge at mid-thigh as she leaned over the table.

Gina smiled, "Super."

"Oh, please tell me you're from Utah." The waitress looked to Mason. "Are you from Utah?"

He frowned. "Indiana."

"God, we get Hoosiers all the time. I need a Utahite? A Utahoan?" Her hand briefly rested on Mason's shoulder as she giggled. "What do you call someone from Utah anyway?"

"A Utahini?" Gina offered. Both girls laughed.

They're both screwy, Mason thought.

"See, me and the other waitress, Louisa, got a pool going. We put in a dollar a day each, and the first one to serve somebody from Utah gets it all. It's up to eighty-four dollars!"

"Well, we'll say we're from Utah if you want," Gina said.

The waitress grinned, then wrinkled her nose. "No, Louisa would run out and check your license plates." She took their orders and said she'd be back in a jiffy. "Must be a great state," she added, "no one ever leaves the damn place."

"She's dizzy," Mason said.

Gina said, "She's great." She leaned over the table closer to Mason. "But where were we? You were telling me why you're in such a hurry."

"Who said I was in a hurry?"

"You did, kind of. The way you act. Are you running to something or away from something? I'm just starting to realize a person has to be going toward something." Her eyes lit up; she seemed pleased with this observation. "That's where directions come from, isn't it? What we head toward? If you're running away, then you could end up anywhere, and you're still looking back, aren't you? Think about it. You're being driven by what you left behind. It's still in control."

"I'm not running from anything," Mason said defensively, believing her words were meant for him. He exhaled heavily, suddenly tired out by her, and the road, and Gamble.

"Well, who is she?"

Mason frowned.

"Who's the girl you're sweating to see so badly?"

"Not a girl."

"A boy?"

"No," he answered quickly. This girl seemed to keep him perpetually agitated. "My father—" he said and bit off the rest. Maybe she noticed then that he didn't want to talk about it, but he felt stupid about the slip. He told himself he'd have to be a lot smarter than that.

"I hurried away from Hagerstown," Gina said. "Packed one bag, forgot my shampoo and toothbrush and the clothes in the dirty laundry hamper and shot out of there so quick I was a mile down the road before I heard the door bang shut. Now I'm heading back almost as fast. Shit. Starting to think getting away doesn't have a lot to do with distance."

Her smile had faded. She didn't say anything else.

Mason didn't think he had anything to say to her. Only for a moment did he wonder what she had decided to run from and then run back to. He looked out at the car again—no sign of life there yet. The sun had softened and turned color as if perhaps it had shined too brightly that day and had burnt out. He rarely took notice of such things as the color of the sun or the sky. The cheeseburgers came. The waitress said, "Enjoy your meal."

Gina arranged the lettuce and tomato on her bun, then looked up at him. He took a bite of his cheeseburger; it was as good as Gina had promised.

"I feel bad about leaving Maxine. She doesn't have anybody right now."

"Maxine? That's the big woman you stayed with at Gamble's house?"

"Yeah. She's not so big. Maybe around the middle. I warn her about all that greasy food she eats. She still strains bacon grease to cook with. She's a darling. A genuine good soul, you know, if there is such a thing. You have to get to know her though; she has all these walls. Protective barriers. She can be tough."

"First thing she said to me was did I have the gas money."

Gina smiled. "See, she's just looking out for me. Maxy didn't trust Gamble not to blow all his money on coke and beer. Which, as it turns out, is exactly what the fool did."

Morning sugar, Mason thought and grinned at Gina.

"What?" she asked.

"Morning sugar."

"Yeah. That's how she used to wake me up in the morning when I was a little girl. I'd pretend to still be asleep until she kissed me, then I'd pop right up and kiss her back."

"Oh, she raised you?" Mason frowned.

"What did you think?"

He shrugged, tried unsuccessfully not to grin.

"What did you think? Oh, you're sick!" She shook a finger at him.

"Hey, you were in bed with her. What would you think?"

"Sick," she said again, but didn't really seem angry or insulted. "Maxine was a friend of my mom's. She took care of me after my mom died. I mean, my pop did too. He paid the bills. But he was a salesman and very busy and not around a lot. After Mom died, I don't think he saw any reason to hang around for too long at a time. He was a nice man, don't get me wrong, quiet for a salesman; he just had to handle his grief his own way and that meant getting on the road. That's how Maxine explained him to me."

"Don't believe her. They always tell kids some nice shit about their old men. And that's what it is, shit. He probably just wanted to get the hell..." Mason let the rest of his thought die, seeing in her face that his words had stung.

"No, he's okay," she said. "He sent money all the time. We still write. But Maxine and I are the tightest. She looked after me when I felt alone and didn't think I'd ever get over my Mom, and when kids at school used to tease me because of my skin."

"Tease you? I know plenty of brothers who get off on light skin."

"Not like mine. I was a sight. Acne all over," her finger traced lines over her pockmarked face. "My cheeks, around my nose, on my nose, in my scalp, eyebrows, you name it. They called me everything you can think of: moonface, pizza-to-go, volcano, pus-bomb..."

"You can't hardly tell it now," Mason said, but that was a lie and he didn't think he'd said it convincingly.

"I got picked on harder because of my skin color. They were jealous. Can you believe it? 'Black is beautiful. Say it loud, I'm black and I'm proud.' What about all that? Do you remember all that chanting we used to do, or are you too young? I barely remember myself. It's gone now. Now we ain't even black, we're 'African-American.' That's 'PC.' Doesn't matter anyway if they can be jealous over one yellow girl with a fucked-up face. The girls especially. I used to know half a dozen ways home from school and I used to change up which way I'd go because these girls would be waiting to beat me up. LaTanya Speakes. LaTanya Speakes said my sores were what you get when you try to put white skin on a nigger. Her friends and she guessed right one afternoon on which way I walked home. They chased me down an alleyway—this was seventh grade, I think—and when I tried to climb a fence to get away from them, they grabbed my legs and my hair." Gina dug her fingers into her hair. "I yelled, 'Max! Max!' I was shouting and cussin' and fighting. They pinned me on my back in the alley right in a pile of garbage, right behind neighbors' houses, but I guess no one heard me because no one came to help.

"LaTanya kneeled on my chest and held a square piece of mirror with no frame around it, you know, just the glass, right to my face. She goes, see what we gots to look at every day in class? Yo nasty face. Why don't you fix yourself up? You don't think nothin' of yourself. Get rid of these Sno-Caps. Have some pride.' Then she pressed the edge of the mirror tight against my face like a barber does a straight razor and dragged it down, one side then the other, ripping the acne sores and most of my skin too. I cried. Blood was everywhere, flowed down my neck, soaked the collar of my blouse. I don't remember it hurting—just the blood. I think it scared LaTanya. She ran off and they all followed her except one girl, who felt so bad she helped me home. Good thing, I was crying so much, I couldn't find my way."

Gina snickered. The soft laugh surprised Mason.

She nodded her head from side to side. "We're even. You told me a story and I told you one."

Mason had finished his cheeseburger. While she had talked, he'd twisted his napkin until it resembled a short piece of rope. He became conscious of the passing of time again. "We'd better get back on the road," he said.

Gina placed her big carpetbag purse on the table in front of her. "What's the damage?"

Mason reached for his wallet.

"Aw, shit!" Gina said.

"No money, right?" But she was looking outside, and then Mason did likewise, surveying the parking lot. It didn't quite sink in at first. Gamble and the car were gone.

Mason ran out of the restaurant and to the edge of the parking lot. Both directions down the road stretched long and vacant. He pressed his hands along the sides of his head and clasped them in back. Gina stood beside him. Then came the waitress holding the unpaid check. He glanced at Gina, who with one hand covering her face, peeked between her fingers at the road in front of them.

"But wait a minute," she said, "I thought you had the keys."

"It's been a long time since Gamble needed keys to start a car," Mason said.

"What's wrong?" the waitress asked. No one responded to her. "You two have to take care of this bill." She held out the slip of paper.

The sun was gone. The sky seemed to get dark all of a sudden. Mason kicked at the space in front of him. "That bald, fucking bastard coke head."

"I just don't believe this," Gina said. "I had everything in the back of that car." She told the waitress, "Our ride has left us."

"She doesn't give a shit, Gina. She just wants us to pay the damn bill. If we were from Utah, then maybe she'd give a shit."

The waitress looked truly hurt and at a loss for what to say.

"Mase, why did you pick now to show us how stupid you can be? She didn't know." Gina found her wallet in her bag and paid the girl. "I'm sorry for my goofy friend here," she said.

"Don't apologize for me," Mason said. But he did feel stupid, and now he was angry with himself as well as Gamble. It was acting just like his father to jump down the throat of whoever was closest when something went wrong. Mama had said it: "You're just like your father."

Gina glared at him and he walked away from her.

He remembered his gun. Now it was gone too. He gazed down the road again while trying to convince himself he didn't need it. But he wanted the gun. He wanted it badly. He wanted that look on Pony's face, the look he knew the gun would give him. The gun would have put him in control.

Gina walked up to him. "You owe me four dollars. That's including the tip."

From down the vacant road rolled the murmur of the highway not a half mile away. The parking lot lights flickered on.

"Can you niggers see me now?"

They both spun about at the sound of Gamble's voice. The car had been parked on the side of the restaurant next to stacks of cardboard boxes and a Dempsey Dumpster. Mason could make out the shape of Gamble sitting on the hood of the car.

Mason strode toward Gamble.

Gina said, "Now, just be cool Mason. I mean it."

Gamble leaped off his car and came at Mason. They closed the distance quickly until only an inch separated their noses. Gamble's breath was stale. Mason locked eyes with him and did not blink.

"Come on guys, be cool," Gina said.

"Where's my shit, Mase? You took it, you little fuck. I woulda really left you if it weren't for Gina. But don't sweat it. You're going to get to DC cause I'm going to kick your ass all the way there."

Mason was very much aware of Gamble's bigger size and his reputation for being a vicious fighter. But Mason was known to be a tough fight too. And he figured if Gamble had really wanted to fight he would have led with a fist instead of a question. In street fights, the dude who threw the first punch won almost all the time. Mason was peripherally aware that two men had stepped from the diner and were watching them all the way to their pickup.

"Just what the fuck are you talking about, Gamble? You want something from me? Take it."

Gina was talking, a frenetic buzz around them, and stepping closer and closer to where he and Gamble squared off.

"I want my blow, Mase."

"I don't have it, fool. I found your raggy ass on the floor in the men's room. Somebody must have ripped off your blow."

"You hit me."

"Not yet." Mason waited for Gamble to move, a twitch of the shoulders. His skin tightened over his knuckles.

"Well, somebody hit me."

"Hey, you two!" The silhouette of a man stood in the light of the restaurant doorway. "Take your trouble away from my place before I call the cops."

Gamble turned to look at him. It was an excuse to break the eye contact.

Gina pushed her way between the two of them then, and Mason stepped back. "Both you guys chill before we all get into trouble. Ken, Mase found you passed out. Someone else took your little goodies. All we found on you was your keys."

"Word, Gina?"

She looked him straight in the eyes. "Yeah, word," she said.

Gamble headed toward the diner. "I'm gonna get something to eat," he said and laughed, "Don't leave without me. And Mason, payback is a real bitch. Watch for it."

"I don't think he believed you," Mason said to Gina. He hurried to the car and to his duffle bag. He rummaged through the bag until his hand felt the gun's rigid shape. Turning his back toward Gina, he quickly inspected it. Half the chambers showed light through them. "Okay," he whispered and secreted the gun back into his bag. He smiled when Gina came near. "Guess I'd better throw this away."

He pulled Gamble's baggy of drugs from his pocket and tossed it over his shoulder into the dumpster.

Mason had wanted to stay awake, but far down the highway he must have drifted off. Awareness returned slowly. His head rolled heavily and pain stabbed between his shoulder blades, lancing up to his neck.

The windows were glossy black. Nothing of the landscape could be seen and he imagined the sensation resembled hurtling through space rather than driving down a highway. Lights from billboards or windows streaked behind them, abandoning them to plummet ahead on their own. The car ate up the miles mindlessly. It seemed as if the road was being created just beyond the reach of the head-lights, only to race beneath them and disappear again.

Gina's face rested against his shoulder. Some dampness soaked his shirt sleeve there, but he did not mind. Her left hand rested on his lap. The right lay buried somewhere between them. Without thinking, he touched her hand, allowing his fingers to caress hers, and marveled at her softness, not so different than Cole's. Gently, he squeezed the hand, hoping not to wake her, but simply enjoying the contact of skin and the press of her body against him. He felt a mild stirring, then suddenly remembered Gamble. He let go of Gina's hand. Gamble stared straight ahead. The green dashboard light illumined his features, exaggerated his bottom lip, highlighted the circles of his nostrils, and reflected wetly from his eyes. The rest of him blended from green into the blackness. Gamble had been watching Mason touch Gina. Mason was sure at first, but the longer he looked at him the less certain he became.

Gamble's fat hands locked on the steering wheel. Mason experienced a disturbing uneasiness, realizing his safety and well being rested in those hands. Gamble was flaky, and he'd let Mason off the hook much too easily. A twitch from Gamble would send the speeding car into a tumble, or rocketing off into trees. But Gamble wasn't crazy enough to hurt himself, and an accident was unlikely; he seemed fresh. After all, he'd slept the entire day.

Besides, what would it matter if the nothing nigger was found spread along the highway? Mason turned back to the passenger-side glass, a black mirror now, except for random comets of light.

GAIL

Reverend Carter Wilson stood on the other side of the screen. Gail, who'd been right by the front door dusting when she heard his knock, opened the door so quickly that he hadn't had time to put his pastor's face on. She caught a brief glimpse of him in the porch light that she hadn't seen before. He'd looked pensive and troubled, or maybe just tired. His head hung down. The fleshy half-moons under his eyes were more pronounced. His forehead wrinkled in waves that pushed his eyebrows down over his deep-set eyes. His brown-black lips were small and pinched. In that moment, he had seemed wholly human and vulnerable, plagued by the same doubts and ambiguities of spirit and nature that assailed everyone else. Not, it seemed to Gail, the man so certain of his link in the chain between God and man. Not the man who plucked verses from the Bible as readily as a farmer would peas from a pod. Not the man whose every strutting, jumping, spinning move radiated his supreme confidence in the supreme being. Who could clasp hands in prayer with the same surety of getting a connection as when dialing a phone.

"Reverend Wilson." And Gail thought it sounded more as if she'd asked a question than offered a greeting.

He looked up. The familiar pastor's face magically reappeared. The same face he used to cajole, embarrass, flatter, and tactfully rebuke the members of his flock. It wasn't a salesman's smile— nothing so phony or self-aggrandizing as that. And if his smiling, confident face was something less than earnest, she didn't see it as a deception, or at least not as a cruel one. In that second, Gail saw perhaps the pressure he placed on himself to be the sure, wise, and happy steward. The face, like the robe and Bible, was a tool of his trade.

She felt closer to him, to the man she'd spied for that moment through the screen.

She said again, "Reverend Wilson, please come in. Aren't you putting in a full day."

"Sister Neighbors," he grinned, "why do they call it a day of rest?" He exhaled with exaggeration to feign exhaustion, smiling to show he joked, but Gail suspected it neared the truth.

She let him in and motioned him toward the big recliner, the one left by Dan.

He went to sit down, then straightened back up. "I just want to say again how wonderful, what a blessing, truly, to hear Tyler sing today. I believe every soul at Calvary would agree to that."

Gail thanked him for his words, silently reprimanding herself for being the only member of the congregation who'd missed Tyler's debut.

"Is he here?"

"Should be back any minute. He's with friends. Can I get you some coffee, Reverend? Iced tea?"

He said yes to the tea and followed Gail into the kitchen. "Does he have plans for college?"

"Yes, we're applying for scholarships now. He has a good chance."

"You must be proud. And the other boy? You've heard nothing?"

Gail shook her head. When she told Carter Wilson that Mason had left without word, he had unexpectedly announced it to the congregation at Wednesday night's intercessory prayer meeting, the last one she would attend. At those meetings, the truly devout prayed for each other and for those who, for one reason or another, could not attend church or pray for themselves. Hands were clutched to form human chains from pew to pew.

Gail had stiffened with embarrassment at first as Wilson informed everyone of her wayward son, and as the wide, dark faces of overweight women turned their sympathetic eyes in her direction. She stared toward somewhere in the space beyond the pulpit and would not make eye contact with them. The praying and loud pleading began. Wailing voices lifted as if baying at the moon. "Dear Father God, we beseech thee to return Sister Neighbors's son to her loving, mother arms. Help him to know the way home. Keep him safe on his long and twisting road, and let him know the straight and narrow path leads to you, oh God in heaven..."

Blood had flowed to her face. Gail had burst into tears, crying "Please, Jesus," and fallen into the arms of the big-bosomed woman next to her. Strange hands squeezed her shoulders and patted her back. Whispered consolations were breathed into her ear.

Searching Wilson's weathered face there in her kitchen, she wondered if all those well-performed prayers would work if she didn't believe in their power. Was it enough that those who'd prayed believed? Would that do? Could Mason come home then? Could Lilly? She wanted to ask her pastor.

He was saying, "I've been visiting the sick and shut-ins ever since service ended today. We do need a bigger ministerial staff. I've written to the bishop about it. Twice in fact. Everything is numbers-driven, never mind that we have such a great many elderly who need particular attention."

Gail handed Carter Wilson his tea. He seemed to want some response from her. "I imagine you must stay very busy," she finally said. She felt awkward standing in the kitchen with him, but he would not move.

"I came to see Sister Anna."

"Annie," Gail corrected. "It's always been just Annie."

"You are not related, isn't that right?"

"She boards here."

"On social security?"

"Yes."

"Any relatives?"

"None I know of."

"How is Sister's health?" he asked.

Gail wondered what Wilson wanted. He asked questions, but they were perfunctory. He didn't seem too interested in the answers. "You could visit with her, but she usually turns in at nine, so..."

"Is she provided for, Sister Neighbors? When the time comes?"

Gail had not thought about that—about who would pay for Annie's funeral. It seemed morbid to talk about. Practical, yes. But morbid.

"The church will try to help if we can."

Maybe he wanted Gail to volunteer to take care of the expense herself. She supposed it would probably come to that, but she didn't wish to commit to anything just yet. "I don't know her finances completely. You'll have to get with her sometime."

"I have a counterpart at a Lutheran church on the east side." He sipped his tea, managing to nod his appreciation while continuing to speak. "When he visits the elderly of his congregation, it's not to find out if they can pay their doctor or the undertaker, or to make sure they have a way to the pharmacy, but to ask that his church be remembered in their wills."

Pouring herself the dregs from the tea pitcher, Gail heard the reverend, but she was thinking that she hadn't given Annie Gant much time or thought lately. They used to watch TV together on Friday nights.

"Well, on to topic two, which is, Gail," the switch from Sister Neighbors to Gail was not lost on her, "we miss you down at Calvary. Now, I know you haven't missed a Sunday since I can't remember when. Some people I can just count on seeing when I look out from the pulpit at all them brown, yellow, and black faces. Yours is one of them, Gail. Good weather or no. Might be late sometime but that's okay. Now I am alarmed. You've quit the Gospel choir, the Sunday School Board, and I'm told you haven't baked any of those delicious pecan pies for the building committee fund drives in a long time."

Cole was crying.

"I never could hold a tune," Gail said under her breath, thinking about having quit the choir, feeling suddenly uncomfortable. She listened for the sounds of Jackie going to Cole's aid.

"I feel this has to do with your missing young man. Always headstrong, you said." He peered over Gail's shoulder in the direction of the crying, then returned his eyes to hers. "You mustn't close yourself off, Sister...not in your hour of need. Remember, 'Delight thyself also in the Lord and he will give thee the desires of thine heart—'"

"Psalms. Yes, I know." She looked down the hall toward the unabated crying.

Years of Sundays had been spent in her search for the right church and the right pastor, visiting every denomination from sedate Methodist to energetic Sanctified, listening intently for answers, for a truth she could believe. Why was Lilly taken from her? Why couldn't they be reunited? Why did Jesus answer some people's prayers and ignore others? Every church had promised her "the desires of her heart." She finally joined Wilson's church not because he impressed her with his speaking, or because she found the congregation friendlier or the message clearer. In the final analysis, what she loathed to admit to herself was that she'd chosen Calvary because it was within walking distance. Simple.

"Sister?"

Her hand came up between them asking for a moment. "The baby's mother must be asleep," she said.

At Jackie's doorway, Gail flicked on the light and stared at the vacant bed in disbelief. "She didn't!" She immediately went to Cole's room, where the baby stood in a corner of his crib, wet-faced, slapping at the headboard in frustration.

"Where's that scrawny, silly, boy-hungry mama of yours, Cole, huh?" She hefted the baby into her arms with a faked groan. "Oh, you stink, yes, you do. Now hush—the way you smell, I'm the one who should be crying." She placed her anger at Jackie on a back burner. Rather, she felt grateful for this distraction, a chance to get away from Reverend Wilson and his nosiness. She was not in the mood for religion, had not been so inclined for a long time now, even before Mason went his own way. She lay Cole on the floor on his back, making quick work of changing him, talking to him all the while, "What does that pastor think he can tell me I don't already know, huh?" She thought she spotted a rash beginning high up on the boy's fat thighs, but Jackie had no ointment in the room.

Cole quit crying, even seemed to gurgle a thanks to Gail.

"Well, you're welcome," she said, pushing to her feet and holding him closely. He had that much nicer baby smell now. "Much better, sugar pie." He tried grabbing her nose, but she kept it just out of reach. "Sugar pie, honey bunch," she sang and whirled around. He beamed a toothless pink grin. She danced back into the kitchen with Cole, prepared to handle the pastor's prying, but Wilson was not there. Voices came from the front room.

Gail recognized the heavier voice immediately, before she even stepped into the living room and saw him leaning on the opened screen door. Something flushed around her heart at the sound of him, an involuntary, quick-spreading, warm sensation, as if a flash bulb had gone off in her chest. A response she wished neither to name nor analyze.

"Hey, Gail," Dan said, not waiting for an invitation to step inside. "Getting chilly out there. Can't scold me today, padre, I was at service this morning. Wasn't I Gail?"

"I saw him outside, after service."

Reverend Wilson raised an eyebrow in Dan's direction.

"Aw, Gail, now you know I was there. How'd you like my boy, padre?" Dan's obvious pride widened his face. "He's something, don't you think?"

Reverend Wilson nodded. "Well, Sister, you've got company, and definitely have your hands full, so I'll be moving along. We'll chat again soon."

"Yes." She smiled after him, walking with him to the edge of the porch.

Wilson stood on the bottom step for a moment as if unsure of where to go next or if he should be leaving at all. He had not had time to drive home his point, Gail realized, and pastors usually don't give up until they're completely talked out. Certainly she hadn't been as involved in church as she used to, yet somehow she didn't think anyone had noticed. She hadn't noticed herself.

The night air was thin and cold. Bad for the baby. Dan's presence behind her concerned her more than Reverend Wilson's. The two of them had trapped her for the moment. She turned her back on Carter Wilson before he walked away. When she stepped inside, she cut the artificial smile she had worn for the pastor. "He's over Marky's. Studying for a test."

Dan said, "Came to see you."

She did not look at him but pretended to be involved with Cole, running a hand over his soft down hair. "How come you ain't sleepy?" she asked the baby.

Dan, still physically imposing, was only half illuminated, with the dim lamplight striking just one side of him. That lit side of his face shined, and Gail saw, finally allowing her eyes to linger, a seriousness that she had missed while Wilson was still here. When he looked this way, Gail almost always felt diminished, smaller, weaker, a feeling she fought against on a deep level. She could surrender to him still.

He used to come back at night, later than this, after they had first separated eight years ago. Just eight? His knock at the door would awaken her and she would pull on her robe, clutch it to her breasts and rush to the door even while chiding herself for moving so fast.

With just the lights of the kitchen on, they would talk, sitting at the hard metal kitchen table she used to have. If he was hungry she would fix him a little something, not asking him if he got along without her easily, or how he could possibly get to his job on time without her to nudge him awake in the mornings, or if the word was true that he was seeing other women. She did not ask any of those questions. Aloud. They talked, though. She remembered once he'd said timidly, staring into his coffee mug as if it were a bottomless well, "I left because you don't love me." That one had stunned her into muteness, while he shoved his chair back and walked out. She thought she had heard him crying.

Other times they would talk in whispers that roared into shouts and woke the boys. She would talk until her jaw hurt and they'd stabbed each other with their anger and frustration, and after that, she would take him to bed. They would end up there somehow, with his weight above and between her, his darkness drowning her, her hands desperately grasping the muscles of his back and shoulders, trying to hold on to herself, her identity, even while he buried it under his rocking mass.

"I said, I came to see you." He moved forward, reached out. Gail almost stepped back until she saw his hand light upon the baby's head. "Ty seemed this small just yesterday," he said. "Look, I wanted to tell you, but I didn't want to get your hopes up if nothing came of it, but I been looking for Mase, puttin' the word out on the street about him since he skied out of here."

"Did you find out anything?"

"Maybe."

"I didn't know you were looking. You told me Mason was just being thoughtless, that he'd come home when he felt like it."

Dan Neighbors shrugged and tugged at an ear. "Yeah, well." He exhaled audibly. "I ain't looking for Mase for Mase's benefit," he said.

Gail said nothing, understanding more than ever lately why Dan found it difficult to relate to Mason.

"I got the name of a dude I'm told he drove out of town with. He's back, but Mase didn't come back with him. I'm gonna go over and talk with him, find out what he knows, and I thought you'd want to come along."

Her throat tightened. She hugged the baby closer. "Yes," she managed. "Who is he? The guy who left with Mason?"

"Lives over on Clark." Dan pulled a wrinkled piece of paper from his wallet and leaned toward the light. "Gamble. Ken Gamble."

The first lead since Mason left in September. Gail let herself drop onto her huge old sofa. She placed the baby on his stomach beside her. He seemed, she noted absently, willing to go back to sleep. Her mind felt muddied even as she pushed herself to think clearly. If this Gamble had returned without Mason, what did that mean? She didn't recall Mason ever mentioning a Ken Gamble. His name was not on the list of boys she regularly called hoping for word of her son. Had they intended to do something together? Were they friends? Where had they gone?

It seemed impossible that in moments she might know exactly where her son had gone. Perhaps she might be able to call him. This very evening she might hear his voice. Her mind flirted with things to say to him. What words would bring him back? Or, at least, make the separation not so painful. She realized then she never really believed it could happen. In her heart of hearts she'd already relegated Mason to that limbo where Lilly dwelled, lost to her and unknown.

Someone had to watch over the baby. Dan suggested Annie babysit, but Gail shook her head.

"Damn, it's after ten now..." Dan said.

Gail fumed. How could Jackie just leave a baby when no one had agreed to watch him? What if Dan had come over before the baby had cried?

Dan mentioned something about the lateness of the hour and that maybe they should wait until tomorrow evening to see Gamble. "We don't want to disturb him if he's gone to bed. Won't be in any mood to answer questions then," Dan said. His hands pushed deep into the pockets of his corduroy trousers. He posed opposite the coffee table, bent forward at the waist toward Gail, awaiting a reply.

She finally said, "We have to go tonight. I couldn't go through all of tomorrow waiting. I'd be a wreck."

Dan Neighbors smiled. He looked mean for a moment, something rare for him. "Not you, Gail."

Tyler showed up first. Gail thought she detected a barely perceptible smile on her youngest son at the sight of his parents together. They did not take the time to fully explain the situation to him. Gail said Tyler would have to watch Cole until Jackie returned and she shushed his quick protests by saying that they were going to follow up on some information Dan had on Mason.

She ignored the string of questions he peppered her with on her way to the door. She ran down the porch steps, pulling on her coat as she went.

Dan caught up to her. "Nothing may come of this."

She hurried to his car.

The drive took two minutes, which they spent in silence. Dan's Buick lumbered down Clark while he searched for the correct house number. In the middle of the block he brought the car to a slow stop, pulling over to the right side.

"Well, the lights are still on."

The house, in the dark, resembled its neighbors and the rest on down the row—tall, gabled, with a porch as long and wide as the front lawn. Light shone through two downstairs windows. One had a stained and tattered shade pulled three quarters of the way down and there seemed to be movement and the flickering light of a television behind it. The other window was completely naked. Any passerby could see what looked like a small bedroom with yellowed wallpaper cracking near the ceiling. A lamp with a flowered shade sat on a dark wood bureau and an unframed painting of a mountain landscape hung by a wire.

Gail climbed from the car. Dan said something but she chose not to hear.

At the door, Dan knocked and they waited. Gail did not feel the cold that caused Dan to rub his palms together and blow into them. She knocked until he grabbed her wrist and pulled her fist from the door.

"Be cool," he said.

She said, "You be cool; he's my son." She regretted that immediately, thought about apologizing, and was about to when the door opened a crack.

"Yes?" Half a face and a brass chain lock appeared. Behind the face, Gail saw several people in a dark room entranced around the blue television light.

"Ken Gamble?" Dan asked.

The face turned away from them. "Is Gamble here?"

Gail didn't hear a reply but the door closed then opened again. A little man in green pajamas retreated from them, looking shy with a hand over his mouth and the other holding the top of his pajama shirt closed. "Close the door quick," he said, uncovering his mouth. "I'll find him."

He disappeared around a banister and quickly up the stairs. Gail and Dan were left alone in a medium-sized front room. In the adjoining room, the television watchers did not look up to acknowledge their presence.

The foyer had a disagreeable stale odor, which probably filled the entire house. Junk cluttered the dull hardwood floor: a child's sneaker, a jacket, an assortment of clothespins, newspapers, two dead plants sitting in broken vases, and an armless, bald, black doll baby.

Gail picked up the doll, which still had a smile on its face.

Dan asked, "What are you doing?"

"I don't know." Tiny holes, from which its hair used to sprout, spotted the doll's scalp. She gently laid the doll back on the floor.

She looked at Dan, who gazed up the stairway. The opportunity to apologize for her remark on the porch seemed past, then she remembered she'd been short with him after church too. She did not trust herself or Dan when circumstance brought them together; she could never tell what he or she would say.

The little man came down the stairs looking sheepish. "He'll be down eventually," he said and scurried to his place among the dimly lit faces around the TV.

Just moments later, another man came downstairs, wearing jeans and a plaid robe. He was a heavy man, big from bones rather than fat and, Gail thought, probably younger than he looked. A thin dust of fuzz covered his head. As he stepped closer, she saw his veined eyes, pink from lack of sleep or drugs.

"I'm Dan, this is Gail." The two men shook hands. Gamble's grasp looked less than energetic.

Gail nodded to him. "You're Ken Gamble?"

He scratched at the back of his head. "Yeah. What do you need? I got to get up early." His robe was parted, revealing a massive, hairless chest. He was not as big or imposing as Dan, though, a fact Gail saw Gamble noticed right away.

The three of them, each with arms crossed, formed a triangle in the middle of the front room.

"You went out of town this summer past, early September, with Mason Reed. This is his mother and we're looking for him."

Surprise opened his red eyes for a quick second. "Word? Mase's mama. Is that so! Yeah, me and Mase and this dyke named Gina went..." His words trailed off. He looked from Dan to Gail. "You ain't heard from him at all?"

Dan started to reply but Gail cut him off.

"No," she said and glanced into the other room to see if anyone might be listening in. "No. And we'd appreciate anything you could tell us. Where is he? Is he all right?"

"I tell you one thing." Gamble's eyes turned to Dan. "He owed me money. More than fifty bucks. And no, ma'am, he ain't all right."

Gail felt frost around her heart. She moved closer to Dan. "What's wrong? Please..."

"He owes me at least fifty. Ripped me off."

Dan produced his wallet and handed Gamble thirty dollars. Gail realized she'd forgotten her handbag. Dan said, "I'll have to get back to you for the rest. Now, tell us. What happened and where is he?"

"I don't know." Gamble smiled just enough to tell Gail he enjoyed playing with her. She tried to relax, not to show him how anxious she was. "See, Mase loves the blow," he said putting two fingers to his nose. "He's fucked. He hit me, and he's taken up with some queer girl that don't want him for nothin' he might want her for. Them two took off. I figured, cool. 'Cause I don't need the trouble."

"Where were you when they left you?" Dan asked.

Gamble shrugged. "Upstate. Somewhere north of Indy. Him and the girl was doin' coke and herb the whole way. I told 'em, God damn you gonna have the state troopers on my ass. So we got into it, you see."

"This girl, you said her name was Gina. Do you know her? Does anyone else here know her?"

"No," Gamble said quickly and he glanced over at the group in the living room. "No. Hell, people in this cracker box don't know each other. She showed up with Mase."

"Where were you heading?"

"Detroit," Gamble answered. "But see, Mase started using the gas money for dope." He waved the thirty dollars in front of them. He waved it close to Dan's face and Dan pushed his hand away. "That girl was a bad influence I s'pose." He smiled at Dan. "You know how it is when you get pussy whipped. Dude loses all sense."

"I thought you said she went for girls," Dan said.

He shrugged again. "Maybe she's a switch hitter."

"She told you she likes girls? I mean, you said you didn't know her," Gail asked.

"I don't know how it came up, lady. Look, I'm wiped out and got to get up early." He stepped toward the door. Dan went to the door, but Gail had not moved. They both looked at her. "You know all I know now," Gamble said.

She did not want to leave. She turned toward the living room. "Excuse me in there," she called. "Do any of you in here know Mason, Mason Reed?"

The younger ones shook their heads. A couple of others said, "Naw."

Gamble looked impatient now. "One more question," Gail said and walked right up to him. "Did he say why he left? Why he was going to Detroit?"

"Yeah, he said he was lookin' for him." Gamble pointed to Dan. "He said he was goin' to find his old man."

Gail and Dan looked at each other as they stepped outside into the cold.

"Don't forget my twenty," Gamble said. "Are you gonna bring it by tomorrow?" He laughed then closed the door on them.

During the ride back, Gail replayed everything she'd just been told. None of it was anything she'd wanted to hear. And she still didn't know where Mason was. Looking for Pony? Why? Drugs, and strange girls, and stealing. She pictured him straggling along a stretch of highway in a drugged daze, and she recalled his eyes were no different than that Gamble's the last time she saw him.

"I don't believe that boy. I don't. You shouldn't have given him that money. That was dumb, Dan. I'll pay you back. But that was dumb."

"I'll tell you what was dumb: telling him we ain't heard from Mase at all so he could feel free to tell us anything that popped into his head."

The car stopped. It took Gail a moment to realize she was back home. She made no move to get out of the car. She watched her hands play with a loose button on her coat. "How many times did I tell him to stay away from them drugs. Blow is cocaine, right? God, what is he doing?"

"We don't know what's true, baby."

"We know he was hanging out with a guy like that Gamble. What do you think they were doing? Planning for college?" Gail pulled on the car door's latch. The dome light came on.

Dan leaned toward her, placed a hand over hers. "You gonna be all right?"

"I take everything out on you, don't I?"

He smiled.

His large hands completely enclosed hers. With his face near, she could smell the Bergamot oil he always put in his hair a little too thickly, and she could smell his maleness too, the scent of his skin. In the midst of all her turmoil over Mason, she had to fight back the crazy impulse to kiss Dan. She examined that very familiar face. "Do you believe Gamble?" she asked.

"I think we better take everything he says with a grain of salt. After all he don't know Mase well enough to know who his daddy is. He thought it was me, remember?"

Gail nodded and freed her hands from his. She figured Dan could believe anything of Mason. She wanted to make a statement of confidence in her eldest son, to say that he had his share of problems but wouldn't just take off on a drug binge, that her warnings had reached him, that in his core he was a good and thoughtful young man, and Gamble a boldfaced liar. At the least, she wanted to thank Dan for his help and concern. But she said none of this as she stepped from the car.

In that part of the morning or night that is very early or very late, Gail stopped wrestling with the bed sheets. After she found she could not will herself to sleep or ignore Ken Gamble's oily voice, she jumped from her bed, pulled on her robe without seeing it, and went downstairs to the kitchen.

She made herself a cup of coffee without turning on a light. She watched the heating element on the electric range glow a red spiral. She only took a few sips of her coffee. The kettle had not been left on long enough and the coffee was barely warm. Soon, she forgot she held a cup in her hand.

Leaning at the kitchen sink, she let her weight shift to her right leg, and as still as the shadows around her, gazed out the small window to her backyard of sycamore trees, one ash, and a spiny rose bush over near the broken brick fire pit, skeletal and ugly in late October. Like hair on the hide of a mangy dog, tufts of weeds, which refused to die even in the cold, sprouted here and there. Leaves had formed knee-deep drifts near the fence, and more came swirling down as Gail watched. Her mind drifted down like the leaves, and fell into a familiar pattern.

Lilly is twenty-five and today she is dressing baby Charlene—named for Gail's father—for a visit to Grandma Gail's. Lilly is an attentive mother; she never puts other concerns before her daughter's welfare. Getting Charlene dressed in the red plaid jumper Gail bought for her birthday turns into a game as Charlene tries to squirm from her mother's grasp and Lilly tickles the child. If anyone else was in the house—Lilly's husband has already left for the office—even if they were downstairs, they could hear the squeals of delight from the nursery and they would hear Lilly's warm laugh too, and they couldn't help but smile.

Lilly and Charlene arrive and Gail gives Lilly a strong, fierce embrace—she has always hugged her daughter that way. Always. "Mom, you act like you haven't seen me in ages," Lilly once said. Gail hopes she doesn't embarrass her daughter too much. But Lilly has come to understand a mother's love better now that she's a mother too. Gail feels a squeeze around her calves and looks down to see Charlene hugging her. "Oh, does my big, little girl want a hug too? We can't leave you out!" She hoists the one-year-old into the air, then hugs her to her breast. "You both look so good!"

Lilly is dressed smartly in a gray tailored woolen pantsuit set off with darker gray piping, and a festive red and green scarf. Her long, brown-red hair is swept back into a soft ponytail that cascades over her left shoulder. They have planned a quick brunch and then a three-generations Christmas shopping spree. Nothing too hectic or pressed. No crowd-fighting nor elbowing up to the bargain tables just yet. It will probably be a lot of window-shopping and gossiping.

Gail and Lilly are notorious gossipers when they get together. "Oh, Lilly, you do carry on so," Gail says. But the truth is she hangs on every word. They are closer than most mothers and daughters and this may be because only fourteen years separate them. They share the same codes and slang. Both dig Aretha Franklin, though Gail likes "Respect" while Lilly prefers "Freeway of Love." People mistake them for sisters constantly. Gail doesn't mind at all.

The air is crisp. The store windows are filled with eye-catching displays. Along the street, paper bells and garlands have been hung and speakers play Christmas music. On the corner a Salvation Army soldier will be ringing her bell near her red donations pot. So many things to point to and see again through Charlene's eyes.

First comes brunch. Lilly's nostrils widen. "Mmmm. Something smells delicious." Gail has fried fish and potatoes and remembered to save some milk for Charlene—Lilly won't let her have soda—before the boys drink it all.

At the table, Lilly asks about Ty and Gail tells her his chances of going to college look good and she wishes Lilly could have gotten free to hear him sing his solo at church the other Sunday. Lilly smiles; the pride she has in her brother is obvious. But in a second the smile drops, so quickly, Gail thinks perhaps Lilly has taken unexpectedly ill or felt a sudden stab of pain. "Lilly?"

"Lilly?" Gail whispered at the window.

Lilly turns her copper-brown eyes on Gail. They point like beams of light; they convict her. "Where is Mason, Mom? How is he doing? Is he just like Daddy?"

The fantasy burst noiselessly as a soap bubble, and just as irretrievable. Gail was actually surprised Lilly asked about Mason.

That had not happened before. Mason had not invaded that world. She was shocked by Lilly's accusing glare, as if Gail had something to do with his disappearance. The look lingered like a memory. Lilly's eyes were Mason's eyes.

Her hands pressed near her mouth. The forgotten cup of coffee dropped, splashing its contents on the counter and shattering in the sink. The noise startled her, though she did not move. Coffee ran formlessly along the counter, dripped off the counter's edge, and made tiny smacking sounds as it hit the floor. The fingers of both hands knotted together. She held them tightly against her lips as if praying.

MASON

Before Gamble attacked, Mason was already in the middle of a fight. It was Pony smiling that deafened him to Gamble's approach. The face that carried the sound and smell, encrusted with fear and shame. The smile vanished. Pony's face underwent an abrupt metamorphosis, turning hard and lean like a strap of leather. "What's with you? Don't tell me you're a sissy? I bet your mama done made a sissy of you. Get in there. Wish my old man set me up like this. Get in there, sissy." His breath was harsh from whiskey.

Pony's hand like a claw grabbed Mason's arm and shoved him forward. A single, dull light shone in the room whose doorway Mason took one hesitant step toward. He believed he could see something of the woman's nakedness then, while he hung at the doorway, petrified. The room had a musky, thick smell, the smell of the woman, her sweat and her sheets. She moved among the wilted sheets and the light played over her breasts and belly and brought an unnatural iridescence to her black skin. An arm, dangling a hand tipped with red nails, motioned for him.

Mason lay in the back seat of Gamble's car in front of Gina's place. He felt the pressure of his stiffness and pushed at the betraying member with his hand. On one level, he struggled with the fact that his memories had lives of their own, and could occupy his consciousness quite beyond his ability to master them. On another level he fought futilely for control over them.

He fought away the memory of that night, or rather it ebbed away without resolution. Others came from unexpected directions: Dan teaching Ty to ride his new ten-speed that had stood near the Christmas tree, the one Mason, as the oldest son, had foolishly thought would be his. Mason later stole the bike and sold it. He saw Mr. Martelli's hand twirling an ink pen like a majorette would a baton. Martelli, the high school guidance counselor, was clearly exasperated and Mason liked that. If you quit now, he told Mason, you'll never amount to a thing. He'd quit anyway, though Gail had threatened to kick him out of the house.

He wanted to analyze the pictures, to find out why those particular ones had resurfaced, but the process was too painful. In the cramped car, he turned his face to the back cushion, feeling small and hating almost everything about himself.

Even in the humid night, the noisy highway rumble carried, heard along with crickets screeching and the barking of a restless dog somewhere down the road. The car was uncomfortable. He'd chosen to sleep outside mainly because he worried Gamble would desert him for real.

"You tell and I'll shoot those dogs of yours, Miss Annie." The look on the old woman's face scared him because in that moment she was terrified of him. In that moment she saw Pony.

He did not react fast enough when the car door lock clicked— too much Pony, Gail, Annie, and Cole. The door was wide open before he knew it. An enveloping shadow fell over Mason, snuffing out all light completely. A heavy blow slammed on the top of his head just as he realized he'd been covered by a blanket. More blows struck his face and smashed his hands as he tried to pull at the blanket.

"Payback is a real mother, ain't it, Mase?"

Gamble dragged him from the car. His duffel, which had served as his pillow, came out with him. Mason managed to grasp one of Gamble's arms, but fists pummeled his stomach, sides, and face and he let go just to shield himself from the punches. The blows and kicks came from different directions. Jagged patches of white light flashed just behind his eyes. A vicious kick caught his right ear and something ruptured with a loud roar, like ocean waves breaking over rock, filling his head. His hands trembled over the damp grass and gravel beneath him. He tried to push himself up. The blanket seemed to weigh a ton. His legs wobbled under him.

"You look fucked up, Mase. Let me give you a hand, brother." Gamble wrapped an arm around Mason's neck and wrenched him upward.

Mason choked. He could get no air in his lungs and managed only to make a whiny gasp, which caused Gamble to laugh and tighten the grip. Gamble began to run, forcing Mason to stumble beside him. Hooded by the blanket, suffocating in Gamble's grip, Mason felt his consciousness letting go. A wild thought—okay, you die now—screamed over the roar in his head. His blind, pan-icked hands grabbed at Gamble, first getting nothing but blanket but then Gamble's belt, then his thighs, in an effort to stop him from running, but Gamble's legs were too powerful. Then Ma-son's right hand found Gamble's crotch. His fingers dug in, and with all the strength he could muster, he made a fist. Suddenly they were falling, tumbling on the ground and over each others' legs. Mason breathed again but he did not relinquish his grip. He heard screaming. There were other voices. Gamble was screaming in high-pitched, girlish shrieks.

"Let go, Mason, let go." Gina's voice slowly seeped in through his good ear. She was pulling him away from Gamble. "For God's sake...Mason!"

Mason could see again too. The blanket had twisted around his legs. Across black spears of grass, Gamble lay an arm's length away, tucked like a fetus and crippled in pain.

Gina slapped at Mason's arm. "Mason!"

Finally, he let go.

Gamble crawled away from him and collapsed in a ball. "Son of a bitch, son of a bitch, Jesus." He continued to moan even after Gina told him to shut up.

"Look at you," Gina said to Mason. She touched the side of his face. Her touch hurt and Mason winced. "Your eye and your lips..."

He pointed to his right ear.

"Oh, Mason, blood's coming out of it. Jesus, you fucking goofs." She asked him if he could stand and he nodded, but made no effort to rise. She kneeled over his chest, her face inches from his. Mason inhaled and exhaled with deliberation while taking mental inventory of all his wounds.

Gina whispered, "Something's wrong with you. Both of you. Gamble is an ass, but what's your excuse?" She stroked his hair. "The Oateses down the road are standing out on their porch, trying to figure what the hell's going on. The Mrs. has those big dildo-looking curlers in her hair; I can tell from here."

Gamble stood shakily. He did not look Mason's way. Gina asked him if he was okay, but he ignored her too. He staggered to his car, which was a surprising distance away. In seconds, the engine started, the tires spit gravel, and the car sped off with the rear passenger side door still open.

"Mase, don't look now, but I think you lost your ride."

A whine in his wounded ear sounded like air escaping from a punctured tire. Everything hurt and he did not want to move.

Gina spoke of getting him to a doctor and how far away the nearest one lived, and she carried on about how she knew something like this would happen. It had come as no surprise to Mason either.

"My bag," Mason said.

She looked around for it, brushing the hair from her face. "Do you see his duffel bag, Tully?"

"What the hell is going on? Who won? If the other brother doesn't come back, I guess you won, Mason. God damn! Grab 'em by the balls and their hearts and minds will follow, eh? What do you say?"

Mason turned his head toward the house, enduring the pain that effort caused. A silver circle gleamed under the porch roof: Carl Tullis. In another second, through a half-swollen left eye, Mason could make out Tullis's spokes like a spider web catching the starlight and the porch light from the Oates's house down the road. The spokes rotated, taking turns reflecting the brighter part of the light, and Tullis appeared to float out of the porch's shadow. This silhouette of him made no distinction between the man and his wheelchair. They were one entity, floating there.

"Come on back in, Gina. He's okay."

Gina did not answer him. "I see something down by the driveway, Mase. Bet it's your bag. I'll get it after we get you inside." Gina freed his legs from the blanket. "Stand up, silly."

He had to roll on his side first, and then onto his stomach and pull his knees under him. This was the toughest physical beating he'd ever taken. He stood. But he wobbled and his hands of their own accord grabbed at Gina's T-shirt, pulling on it to maintain his balance. He felt drunk, the same stupefying cloudiness, except it was as though he felt the drunken high and the ensuing hangover simultaneously. "I can't walk," he said.

"Hold on to me." Gina stepped close to him, put his right arm around her neck, and together they lurched toward the house. They did not try the stairs, but made their way up one of Tullis's ramps instead.

Tullis blocked their way for a moment. "What were they fighting over? You?"

"Go get his duffel bag. It's down by the driveway."

Gina helped Mason onto the hard, thin-cushioned sofa in the living room. Mason's dizziness lingered. His left eye had swollen completely shut now. He put a hand to his hurt ear and brought away blood, which ran down between his fingers and coated his palm. He held the hand up and away from himself, not wanting to get blood on anything.

"I'll get some soap and water," Gina said.

Tullis rolled into the room before Gina returned with Mason's duffel bag in his lap. "It's not very heavy, fella. You travel light."

Mason wanted Tullis to set the bag down, to put it beside the couch, to let go of it. He wanted to get up and pull it away from him.

The bag remained in Tullis's lap. He even rested an arm on it as he spoke. "You and Gina friends? You met in Indiana? Is that where she went?"

Mason coughed. He could have answered but did not want to and used his pain as an excuse not to. It was an odd time for those questions, similar to questions Tullis had already asked but more pointed, and Mason sensed answering them might somehow put Gina in an awkward spot. But Mason figured he wouldn't have answered anyway, Gina or not.

Tullis didn't look as if he expected an answer; maybe asking the questions had been all he wanted to do for now. His red bandanna, sweat-stained and dirty, was still wrapped tightly about his head, covering his hair like a do rag. He watched Mason as a child does a stranger in his home when the father is away. He didn't fear Mason or else he'd have disguised the fierce distrust in his eyes. "You'll have to tell us later why that brother was so pissed off at you."

Gina returned with a large bowl and towels. She cleaned his hand and gently daubed his ear. The water in the bowl clouded pink then red. She gently washed his face and Mason watched her eyes as she examined him. "Can you still hear out of it?" she asked snapping her fingers inches from the hurt ear.

"Think so," Mason said.

"Hell, Gina, he's got one good eye and one good ear left. No problem right, buddy?" Tullis moved closer, and put a hand on Gina's wrist. "Let's turn in, sugar heart. God, I missed you." His tongue poked between his lips for a moment. "You sure taught me a lesson."

"You said that already. And I said I didn't leave to teach you any lessons. Old dogs can't learn any new lessons anyway." Gina took the bowl from Mason's lap and set it on the coffee table. "Mason, sleep here. I'll bring you a pillow and blanket." Gina smiled at him. "And I'll try not to deliver the blanket the way Gamble did."

"My duffel..." Mason said and reached toward Tullis.

"Sure, buddy. We'll trade." Tullis pushed the bag off his lap and it dropped to the floor against the couch. He had not relinquished his hold on Gina's wrist and he quickly pulled her down onto his lap and encircled her waist with an arm.

"Hey!" Gina said, but she giggled.

Tullis kissed her on the neck and the side of her face. "Goddamn hair's in my way," he said. Still holding Gina, he backed the chair away and aimed it down the hall. "Sleep tight, buddy, see you in the mañana." They wheeled away with Gina kissing his face.

Carl Tullis was waiting in his front yard when Gamble pulled into the driveway with Gina. He and his wheelchair were parked next to a permanent wooden sign planted in the lawn, painted red, white, and blue, that read, "Give a Ramp, America!" He wore a camouflage military field jacket and the red bandanna. He had medium brown skin and a broad, perpetually flared nose. His black moustache covered his upper lip and his beard was uneven, sparse, and flecked with white. Even with the jacket, conspicuously out of place on the last days of summer, Tullis's powerful upper body was noticeable. He had wide shoulders and his chest stuck out like a bodybuilder's. That virility had been cinched off at the waist, however, and he sat embedded in the wood and chrome chair with fragile rods for legs. Judging by the disbelieving relief evident on his face, he had not anticipated Gina's return.

Gina stepped from the car first, having finally talked Mason into giving her the window seat many miles before. "Jesus, the clown has returned to the circus," she whispered. "Tully, if you say a god-damned word...so help me..." And she walked straight toward him.

Carl Tullis had not moved, and neither the tilt of his head nor the expression on his face had changed. He had remained frozen even as Gamble cut the engine and Gina stepped from the car, whispering to Mason and adjusting herself in her clothes, giving a pull to her bra strap through her T-shirt. He did not flinch when she called out to him. Tullis watched her approach, but did not look up to her as she stood over him.

Mason could not catch what Gina said to Tullis. Clearly, she did the talking; her hands moved rapidly in the air. After a minute, there was silence. Then, abruptly, Tullis wrapped his arms around her waist and butt, burying his face into her stomach. Tullis's shoulders shook.

"She got an old man?" Gamble asked. "I thought she was butch."

They heard Tullis's sobbing now. He held on to Gina with his face thrust below her navel for a long time. She patted the top of his head, the red kerchief, and gave a little embarrassed glance back toward Gamble and Mason.

Gamble asked, "What's 'give a ramp' mean?"

Tullis did not apologize for his tears nor make any move to wipe the damp tracks from his cheeks. He energetically helped unload the car, all smiles. Gina introduced everyone. Mason and Gamble were labeled her traveling companions. She called Tullis her guy. His smile dimmed a bit after he learned they would be hanging around all day and did not plan to leave until the next morning.

Gina did her best to stay near Mason or Gamble, not to be alone with Tullis for more than a moment, or so it appeared to Mason. She flitted in and out of the small, one-story house. She washed a sink full of dishes Tullis had allowed to accumulate, she did laundry, made a show of beginning to unpack her suitcases and boxes, but near the end of the day, she had gotten little if anything put away. She went with Gamble—a surprise to Mason—to pick up a pizza.

She'd said, "Tully, there ain't a thing in this refrigerator except beer of course, and a salad bar of various molds, fuzzy white ones and hairy green ones, and something stinks way bad."

Tullis asked for a beer and told her he'd taken to eating out while she was away. "Went by Willoughby's just to give him shit about not having a ramp. I won't go around to no goddamned back door. Just spend my bread somewhere else. Us nigs don't do the back door no more." He looked to Mason, for concurrence Mason supposed, so he nodded to him.

Gina shut the refrigerator door without retrieving a beer for Tullis, glaring at him. So much passed between them with a look or a shake of the head. Obviously, Gina's departure and return had resolved nothing between these two. Mason kept his peace, trying not to notice too much.

Gina and Gamble left on their errand. Tullis wheeled to the refrigerator and took out two beers, tossing one to Mason. Tullis negotiated that chair of his through and between anything in the house with ease. All of the floors had been covered with linoleum. The wheels turned almost silently, and Tullis could brake and pivot on a pin head. He moved so naturally that the chair appeared to glide of its own accord, covering a lot of distance with each deft downstroke of his arms.

Mason followed him out to the porch. The day had cooled off. He leaned against a porch support, a rough four-by-four in need of paint. Tullis's beer went quickly, and the rag-headed man crumpled his can.

They were in western Maryland, amongst its steep, old and stiff hills. Houses, most of them small and white, looking like polka dots on green cloth, nestled on tiny plots of flat space and along the gentler slopes. The yard in front of the porch stayed fairly level for twenty or twenty-five feet to the road, beyond which the ground dropped away so precipitously that the tops of evergreen trees and maples came up to the eye level of anyone standing on that road. The roads themselves wandered like water, zigging and zagging around hills and outcroppings of rock, seeking the downward path of least resistance. The road in front of them meandered by two neighboring houses of the same dollhouse clapboard before curving up to the left and out of sight. In that direction lay the highway, which had been carved from the white and yellow rock of the higher mountains. The sound of the highway was subtle, absorbed by the trees and the great hollow between the hills. Depending on the unpredictable turns of the wind, the sound could grow or diminish, and the air, too, sometimes clean and evergreen sweet, would stagnate or bring the odor of a distant mill in thin, pale yellow clouds.

"Are you from Indiana? The part down near Kentucky, right?" Tullis asked.

Mason did not look in Tullis's direction, pretending to watch the hills and the mountains behind them. He had nothing to say to this man, and could think of nothing he'd want to hear from him either. "I've been there," he said. From the corner of his eye, he could see Tullis measuring him, something Mason innately did with every man he met. It had not taken long to size up Tullis. The wheelchair spoke volumes, and loudly. Tullis, Mason concluded, was no threat to him. Yet, obediently, he submitted to the instinct that warned him not to be too forthcoming with this man. Don't run off at the mouth like you did with Gina, he told himself.

"I've been living up here for, Jesus, three years? Yeah. Me and Gina. I'd live higher up if I could." He pointed toward the blue shoulders of the mountains. "Up there. Live high. Gina loves it here too. The nights we just sit out here sippin' with Mister Jack Daniel and gazing at so many stars you'd think they were going to crowd out the night. And the mountains, they have their own noise. Gina turned me on to that. A deep, rock on rock earth noise. It has to be a silent time to hear it. No birds, no highway, silent." Tullis paused, then added, "Gina's a funny girl."

Mason glanced at Tullis.

"She doesn't say what she means. She's not deceitful, don't get me wrong. It's simply, her words and her ways don't match up. You have to be able to read her. And nobody can. That's been her downfall her entire life. Except me. I can read her."

Mason wondered about Tullis and Gina, together, as a pair. Parts that didn't seem to fit.

"Me?" Tullis said as if Mason had asked. "I'm just surviving on my hill. Let all the crazy shit go on below me. I'm above all that. Figuratively and literally. I came out here from California heading to New York. This is how far I got. Them hills are a snare, brother. Don't let them trap you. What kind of gig you and Gamble got lined up in DC? That's an asylum, Washington. The murder capital. One murder a day, minimum. No lie. Mostly over drugs, and hell, the mayor himself does coke. Lies to the people and they love him anyway. He gets out of jail and they make him a councilman. So what part of DC do you want?"

Mason thought about the question, but not the answer. His goal, he realized was not so far away. This moment not so far from the one that dangled like a carrot on a stick in front of him.

"Fine. What's the mystery here, brother?"

"Don't 'brother' me, man." Mason's hand slapped repetitively at his knee. This "rest up" had been Gina's idea, a break from the road before going on to Washington. Mason had been looking forward to the time when they would drop her and all her rattling junk off, but when she suggested Gamble and he stay over awhile with her, Mason had almost eagerly agreed.

Tullis opened the front door and wheeled back into the house. Mason's hand ceased its tapping, and he sat down at the top of Tullis's porch ramp. He stayed there until Gamble and Gina returned with the pizza. During that time, the scenery of humpbacked hills and towering, imperious trees, so different from his Midwest home, started to work on Mason. He began to take notice of it, and as he did, his mind no longer dwelled on his appointment in Washington. He forgot about Tullis's prying, and Gina and Gamble, and the largely untouched beer in his hand.

Several hours later, lying on the couch after his fight with Gamble, Mason was keenly aware of every aching part of his body. He tried to arrive at a compromise with his pain, pledging not to move or breathe too deeply in exchange for a duller edge on the hurt. He slowly allowed his muscles to relax, to let the couch, though hard and lumpy, support him. He exhaled audibly, from pain and from relief. He settled on his back. His long legs angled crookedly off the couch, putting his feet flat against the floor.

He waited for Gina to return with the promised blanket and aspirin. He thought she'd mentioned aspirin. The smell of dust rose from sofa cushions, and his own body odor hung persistently about him. He hadn't bathed in two days. A weak light and no wind came through the window behind the couch. At one point, he'd actually slipped back to sleep, but awoke in minutes without opening his eyes. In the dark, his right hand gingerly surveyed his face, familiarizing himself with the feel of the swollen tissue around his eyes and lips, everything sensitive to his probing.

He gave up on Gina returning. The night was too hot for a blanket anyway, in fact he didn't care if he ever saw another one. And he was surviving without the aspirin. The pain was his punishment. Not a punishment for anything he'd done to Gamble, who Mason had all but forgotten. He did not brood about revenge nor worry if Gamble would return. It was as if Gamble had served his purpose. This hurt was appropriate to Mason's quest. Mason reveled in it, savored it on a subconscious level, which he did not allow himself to question too deeply. Gamble's beating had made physical all the hurt Pony Reed, and Dan, and his mother had put him through. The disappointment and shame, the pointing fingers, the brow beatings and whippings Gail had administered manifested themselves in his broken blood vessels, torn skin, and angry bruises. He could feel it all.

He thought he heard Gina sometime during the night, and a bit later, Tullis. He couldn't be sure; his head was still filled with the sandy static from his ear. Gina's voice filtered through the darkness, not talking but moaning, soft, drawn out and rhythmic. Lovemaking was going on not so far from him. Not until then did Mason speculate on Tullis's abilities in that area. He strained to hear more, hoping he might learn some tidbit about the odd pair. No other sounds escaped from the small bedroom down the hall, yet Mason imagined he heard the rocking chorus of bedsprings and a fierce, teeth-strained grunting.

Leftover voices lingered in the chambers of his ears. Noises, whose ripples had fanned out lightyears ago, reached Mason lying as still as he possibly could on a couch in a tiny house in the folds of western Maryland. The sounds disoriented him and he could not distinguish the new from the memory. Pony and the woman, whose name Mason never learned, hissed and groaned behind the door. Mason waited. Mason, twelve years old, who had cussed at Gail that morning and told her he was old enough to go where he wanted—but didn't dare mention where he wanted to go was on a drive with Pony—waited in the cramped apartment with the red roses wallpaper listening to them, suppressing a smile, feeling awkward, yes, but pretending he was a man too, on a man's adventure. Then came the fear when Pony strutted out, stuffing in his shirttails, and announced it was Mason's turn.

And Mason, who wanted to show that damn Dan Neighbors he already had a father, stood in the doorway staring at a naked leg on the bed, bent, black-skinned with black threads of hair slicked against it.

"You ain't a sissy are you?"

When the woman's hands pulled at him and unzipped his fly, Mason had looked away, but caught himself reflected in the mirror above her bureau.

He did not know where he was. He sensed movement near him rather than hearing it. He smelled her skin and her weight settled next to him on the couch.

"Mase," she whispered. "How're you doing?"

"No!" Mason shouted, striking out at the darkness in front of him, feeling his fist connect with skin and bone.

"Damn it, Mason!" The lights came on. Gina stood over him, scowling and holding herself just above her left breast. "What did you do that for?"

The sudden light blinded him. Salty tears burned his bruised left eye. A single tear squeezed from the other, clearing his foggy picture of Gina, and running back to his ear. "I didn't mean to do that. I didn't mean to do that," he said.

"What's the matter with you?" Gina rubbed the spot where she'd been hit.

"I didn't mean to do that," Mason repeated. "I didn't... Turn off the light."

The angry lines on Gina's face curved down into an expression of concern. For a moment, she stood over him, saying nothing.

Mason crossed an arm in front of his face, enduring the discomfort to his black eye. He wanted Gina to go away, fearing at the same time that if she did, the memory would come back. "Turn out the fucking light," he said.

She glanced down the hallway toward the bedroom. "What's wrong?" she asked, stepping close again. She reached toward the lamp and then disappeared in the dark. "Hey, did you think I was Gamble?" She settled on the edge of the couch.

A minute or two passed with neither of them speaking. Mason could see her by starlight, though her hair hooded her face. The side of her thigh touched his side, touching and then not as he breathed.

"Tully is still asleep. Hear that snore? I thought we might have woke him."

Mason heard no snoring.

Gina rested a hand on his chest.

"What do you want?"

"A favor," she said. "I want you to hang around for a little while. Stay here with us." She whispered, close now, her breath warm in his face and smelling toothpasty. "It's Carl...I can't explain. I could just do with some support. Okay?"

Mason was confused; he had just heard them making love. "I don't know."

"Come on, goofy. You have to heal up these bruises anyway. Can't go into DC looking like a hit-and-run victim, and have people dialing nine-one-one every time they see you."

Mason did not know why he said, "All right, a day or so." Instantly, a sense of betrayal flooded him.

"Thanks, Mase. Now where's that pillow you made me drop? It's around here somewhere." She searched about on the floor. "Here it is. Lift your head."

When Mason lowered his head back, it sunk into a cushioned, comforting embrace.

She stood. "Better? See you in the morning."

"Gina?"

"Yeah?"

The delicate sound of his zipper as the woman pulled it slowly down. That was a new detail. He had not remembered it before. This memory did not diminish with time; it grew. Mason said, "I did not mean to hit you."

When he was eleven years of age, before the family moved from the tiny apartment on Judson Street to the huge boardinghouse on Gum Street and months before he first met Pony, Mason lost the art of sleeping through the night. After Gail had kissed Tyler and him goodnight and supervised their prayers, he'd lie awake tucked into the shelf of the bottom bunk, witnessing all the movement and whispers of the night. He could hear water swishing through the pipes in the wall after the toilet flushed in the apartment above. He could hear the television from the next-door apartment blaring Hollywood gunfire from TV shows Gail would not let him stay up to watch. He could hear steps in the hallways, chain locks sliding, doors opening, doors closing, the nail-tip scratching of mice, the bass thump footsteps and horse laughter of the big woman up-stairs. He could see the abstract patterns in pale silver and black that the window threw on the opposite wall of his bedroom. He could hear the shallow, even breathing of his younger half-brother. And he knew the moment Dan Neighbors arrived home from the second shift. There would be the slip of the key fitting into its lock and, if there was any moment Mason was likely to fall asleep, it would be then he would lie back and sleep.

If not, he could spot the brief breaks in the straight line of light under the door placing Gail and Dan in the kitchen. She would make Dan a bologna sandwich with ketchup, the way Dan liked, and they would talk about the house on Gum, which they dreamed of getting, for which they saved their nickels and dimes. Gail would get an envelope from a piece of junk mail and scratch figures on it, interest rates, points, and account balances.

Mason often saw the evidence of their kitchen councils the next morning on the table. He could tell without looking at the scraps of paper that the figures were not adding up the way his mother and stepfather hoped by the way they were short with one another in the mornings, quicker to have words. Tyler would not look up from his cereal, stirring the soggy mass in his bowl. And Mason, always conscious of being the only one at the table whose last name wasn't Neighbors, took to secretly returning his lunch money to the coffee can after school.

The boardinghouse had been for sale a long time. It was a fixer-upper, the realtor said as he took the family through. But Dan was just the man who could do it. As the slow tour progressed, Dan listened to the white man in the Totes hat intently. Gail looked to Dan or wandered from window to window. Mason and Ty ran through the high-ceilinged labyrinth from room to room, up stairs and down hallways.

"You could put a hundred apartments in here!" Tyler said. The day finally came when Dan uprooted the for-sale sign from the front yard and Tyler ran and jumped into his arms, and big Dan spun his son around and around. Mason watched from the porch.

The family rolled up their sleeves. To keep the house they would have to quickly fix up the extra bedrooms and rent them out. They scraped layers of old wallpaper, and painted, and chased each other around with wet brushes. They washed windows and handed Dan tools while he lay face up under sinks. The first evening there, they ate dinner on the dining room floor, sitting on blankets with buckets of fried chicken, cole slaw, and potatoes passed amongst them.

"Which wing do you want, Mason?" Dan asked.

Mason shrugged. "They're all the same," he said thinking Dan referred to the chicken.

"No, I mean the house, boy. You want the east wing or the west wing?" They all laughed. Dan reached over and grabbed Mason's ankle, literally pulling his leg.

"I want the attic," Ty said, "Or maybe just the third floor."

"I don't think we'll have any trouble getting boarders," Gail said. The house had a kitchenette on the second floor in the back, though it was in poor condition. Gail hoped to get a fair piece of change from renting it out along with the bedroom nearest it.

Gail's dream of a big, beautiful home for her family was coming true and Mason tried to help it along as much as anyone. He'd hurry home from school to assist Dan with his latest project before his stepfather had to head off to work. Mason used to bring school friends by to show off where he lived.

Those were the best times Mason could remember, yet he seldom thought of them. Maybe there was something too sweet, too unreal or too tender that made those first few months on Gum Street as painful in his memory as the days that haunted him the most. Over time he learned to set aside his memory of those days as if it were a fragile book that could not bear to be thumbed too often.

Instead, he would dwell on the day Dan Neighbors left him. *Just like my father,* he explained to Tyler at the time, before he discovered that not to be the case at all. He could not hear any of Gail and Dan's nocturnal arguing in the new house, so he had assumed it had ended along with life in the cramped apartment. Maybe he'd just been too excited and distracted to notice. Just before dusk one day, Mason was roaming the backyard. He kicked at the legs of the rusted red swing set that had stood in that yard for a decade, and decided to ask Dan to get rid of it just in case any of the guys accused him of playing on it.

Dan Neighbors walked down the back porch steps. "You could sand the rust off and brush on a coat of paint."

Mason shook his head without looking up. "I'm too old, Tyler too. We should take it down."

"Oh, yeah. Yeah. I know you too old for this kiddie swing. Thought maybe your mama might want to hang some plants from it or something. Women like to do things like that, you know. Pretty things up."

Dan paused for a moment there, and that's when Mason knew he had something more specific in mind to say to him. Mason tried to guess what new chore it might be, and didn't Dan realize he didn't mind the chores?

"Yeah, I know you getting up there in age. Getting tall, too."

From the house came the sound of Tyler crying. Mason heard him distinctly, but Dan did not turn.

"Since you getting big, I feel okay about leaving you some responsibilities. Look after things..."

Mason stared into Dan's face, but the big man's eyes looked over Mason's head. Mason knew that moment intimately. Like déjà vu, he knew what he would say and how Dan would reply. This had somehow been rehearsed. The back of Mason's head throbbed. "I could get a job, Dan," he said. "And I don't have to eat lunch. I been skipping it for a long time now."

Dan's eyes met his now. The man smiled down to him. "Is that why my daily coffee can count was always off? I thought I was losing my mind, boy."

"I could get a job," Mason repeated.

"It ain't money, Mase. Me and your mama ain't been getting along for a while now and if I stay longer I'm gonna mess up whatever we got left. She's got stuff she's got to work out and seem like she wants to do it alone. I'm thinking I may be able to come back one of these days. We'll see."

Dan reached out for Mason, but the boy slapped his arm away, stumbling in the process and falling to the ground. His fingers raked in loose dirt and rock, which he flung at Dan. "Save that shit for Tyler," he yelled, scrambling to his feet. "You ain't comin' back."

"Boy, you better watch who the hell you're talking to."

"What the fuck for? You don't live here. What the fuck you gonna do about it? Just go! Just go!"

Dan Neighbors stood there like a tree.

"Get!" Mason screamed, but he was the one to flee, racing across the backyard to the alleyway. He did not run far. A few houses away, he turned to see if Dan might not be chasing him. Maybe Dan wouldn't leave until he'd had the chance to give him a whack for cussing at him. But no one followed. Mason pushed his hands into his pockets and walked slowly around the block, looking down at the broken slabs of concrete that made up the sidewalks of his new neighborhood. Dan was gone by the time he returned home.

When Mason walked through the front door, Gail stood by the window in the foyer. A room for greeting people, Gail had explained to him their first day there. *If somebody funky and smelly stop by, you don't have to let 'em get any farther than here,* Dan had added, winking.

"Take a bath now and I'll let you stay up and watch a little television," Gail said quietly. She did not seem very upset. Maybe she looked a little rigid, a little uptight, Mason thought.

Mason wanted to know what had gone wrong. Hadn't they gotten the house? Wasn't a new boarder supposed to be moving in soon?

Gail's hand came up before he could speak. "Don't ask me any questions now, boy. Don't."

"Dan Neighbors stinks," Mason said and ran up the stairs.

He went by Tyler's open bedroom doorway. His younger brother, nearly four years his junior, lay facedown on his bed. He had a stuffed brown bear with a red T-shirt protectively snuggled in one arm. Tyler was much too old for stuffed animals and Mason had begun hiding the bear from him behind bathtubs and in the back of closets, but Tyler always located it. Here in the new house, Mason had once hidden the bear in a top cabinet in the second-floor kitchenette. Amazingly, boy and bear had reunited in just an hour.

Tyler sniffled, raising his head in Mason's direction. He wiped at his eyes, but his entire face was wet and drooly like a slobbering baby's.

"Boo hoo, boo hoo," Mason said. "What's your problem?"

"Daddy ain't going to live here anymore."

"Yeah? Well, welcome to the club. My daddy ain't never lived here. Big deal." Mason stepped into the room. His first thought was to take the stuffed toy from Tyler and hit him with it. Give him something to cry about, as Gail always said. Sometimes, Tyler made him sick.

Tyler sat up. The boy's hair was kinked into little black beads. He looked like Dan, almost as mahogany black. Tyler would eventually grow to be bigger, Mason knew already. But Tyler would never be tough. "Are we going to have to move back to Judson Street?" he asked.

"Tomorrow."

"Really?"

"You're a simp. You know that? Look, I don't know. Depends if 'Daddy' pays the bills or not. Probably we go back."

"How come he left us?"

"Got tired of your whining, I guess. Like I know." Mason walked to edge of the bed and picked up the bear. "I'm going to swat you with this upside your head for being such a crybaby."

"Don't." Tyler shielded his face behind a hand.

"Don't," Mason mimicked. "Don't."

"Why did your daddy leave?" Tyler asked.

Mason sat down on the bed. "I'm not going to hit you. I'm going to let Mr. Yogi here do it. First he's going to get in your face." Mason held the bear nose to nose with Tyler. "You gonna let ol' Smokey front you, Ty? Huh?" He pushed the bear at Tyler, who leaned back and, finally, with a thin smile, shoved the bear away.

"Tell me," Tyler said.

"Mama said my daddy don't like to be in one place for a long time. And she said he couldn't find no good job here."

"But Daddy has a good job, and he liked it here." More tears rolled down Tyler's cheeks.

"Lots of men book out. They just do." He wrapped an arm around his brother's shoulders. He pressed his forehead briefly to the side of Tyler's temple. "Go to sleep. And if you keep me up with your crying and sniffin', I'm going to come back in here and knock you unconscious."

Dan Neighbors came back the next day. He was working on some loose siding, sweating with nails in his mouth, by the time the boys arrived home from school. Tyler hugged him around the neck. "I want to take you boys out for a milkshake later, okay?" Dan said.

Mason did not understand what Dan's presence meant. He shook his head. "Is Mama here?" he asked.

"She's inside."

Tyler had taken the hammer from Dan's tool belt. "Show me how to do this," the boy said.

He left father and son on the porch. Mason wanted to ask Gail the questions he couldn't bring himself to ask his stepfather. He could not show himself to Dan that way, to unmask a care that Dan did not reciprocate.

Gail was in the living room sitting opposite a little, tan-skinned man in a brown, double-breasted suit.

"I would rather go month by month, you know what I'm saying?" The man rolled his head back and surveyed the ceiling. He had a square head and his hair had been cut scalp close.

"I can offer a six-month agreement, Mr. Claibourne," Gail said.

Hammering pounded just outside the living room window and Mr. Claibourne gazed in that direction. "Will a lot of construction be going on?" He stood and walked to the window. He pushed a curtain to the side with the back of a hand.

"There's some fixing up to do. We're still wallpapering, reworking some outlets in the other rooms, but, no. Things'll be quiet for the most part."

Mr. Claibourne looked back at Gail, looked at her a bit too long, Mason thought. The man scratched himself just under his chin.

Gail waited for his answer, to find out if she had her first boarder or not. The man seemed to be stretching the moment out, perhaps enjoying Gail's attention.

More hammering filled the space in the conversation, weak beats without the rhythm of force. That would be Tyler.

"Let me look the room over again," the man said.

"You do that, Mr. Claibourne. And take your time," Gail said.

He rushed up the steps. His shoes, Mason noticed, were very shiny.

For the first time Gail turned and spotted Mason just inside the living room. "He's going to take it. Just don't want to appear too eager about the whole thing. Can't say why the act. Ain't like I'm moving on the price a lead cent." This last bit was said in the general direction of the stairs, though not so loud for anyone upstairs to hear. Then, eyeing Mason, and maybe realizing he had more on his mind than the new boarder, she asked, "How'd my big man do in school today?" He was her big man and Tyler her little man.

"All right." Mason walked up to her. He looked down on her now as she sat. "Did Dan come back? Why is he here?"

"We'll be seeing plenty of Dan," Gail told Mason. "He still owns the house with us. There's a lot to be fixed. And he still cares about you boys."

Mason wasn't so certain as Gail sounded about Dan caring for both her sons. He asked, "Can he make us leave the house?"

The door opened and Tyler bounded into the living room. He pushed his way between Mason and Gail, greeting his mother by jumping up and down in front of her.

Dan stood in the doorway. Mason's eyes were already old enough to see this difference. Dan did not stroll right in. He did not drop his tool belt and say, "Somebody, anybody, get me a glass of water." In the space of one evening, after events known only to Gail and him, convention had changed. Dan Neighbors hesitated at the doorway before stepping in. His eyes momentarily snagged with Gail's.

Mason looked from him to her and back.

Tyler said, "We're going for milkshakes."

"Before dinner?" Gail asked Dan.

He answered with just a shrug. Big Dan looked tired. Finally he said, "I have to talk to them, Gail."

Mr. Claibourne came down the stairs. Dan and he nodded at each other.

"You coming, Mase?"

Mason looked at Mr. Claibourne, wishing he'd go away. "No."

"You can if you want to," Gail said.

"C'mon, Mase, we'll talk man to man. Things ain't so bad as you thinking."

But Mason had picked sides and wanted his allegiance clearly known, and also he felt funny about leaving his mother with a stranger in the house. He would become suspicious of every boarder who lived there.

"Suit yourself," Dan said, "I'm full up with the attitudes around here anyway." He stepped out of the house, letting the screen door go.

The new boarder wandered into the living room, pretending not to hear.

"I should go," Tyler said, but it was definitely a question asked of Gail.

"Of course you should," she said, and the boy followed his father at a skip. "You should too," she said to Mason, but did not wait for an answer before returning to her new boarder.

Mason went to the door in time to see his brother climb into the car. He reminded himself he could find out what Dan had to say from Tyler later. But Ty didn't hear everything most of the time. And with Dan, he only heard what his father wanted him to hear. Mason's curiosity almost bested him. Perhaps Dan might tell them what had gone wrong, because he knew his mother well enough to know he would never find out from her. Still, the impulse to call out to the car could not pry his set teeth apart. He turned his back as they drove away. In the living room, all smiles, his mother and the double-breasted Mr. Claibourne were shaking hands.

It did not seem fair that Tyler's father would go away and come back the very next day, and then, a couple of days later, back again, and not a week after that, stay the night and eat a bowl of cereal in his boxer shorts the next morning. Nor was it fair Tyler seemed to be always searching frantically for his jacket or his right sneaker because Dan waited downstairs to take him bowling or to a basketball game or to see Dan's sister in the country who "has chickens all over the place, and some real smelly pigs, and horses and Auntie Lynn lets me ride them." Dan would sometimes invite Mason along. At first, he asked every time, because Gail would've given him a hard time if he hadn't, Mason believed. But after a while the invitations stopped, and Mason could not say why this burned him even more.

Partially, he snubbed his stepfather's offerings out of loyalty to his mother. He elected to be on her side in this, even though understanding little of it, especially on those occasions when Gail and Dan talked as if everything was fine or on those mornings Dan's car sat beaded with dew in the driveway. He caught on finally that his loyalty went unnoticed. With her new job as a household administrator for the wealthy Hirsch family filling her weekdays (Gail, who'd only performed maid work previously, stretched the span of her boarding-house management experience on her résumé in order to get the job), and Gail's holy crusade to find the right church absorbing her weekends (a task she attacked with renewed vigor after Dan left her), she had little time for appreciating a son whose refusals of his stepfather meant less discretionary time for her.

The vacuum created behind her by her almost continual movement formed a gap for Mason to slither through. Mason thought this worked out just fine. He could stay out later, hang out with the older boys, do more fun things before hearing Gail's voice pealing from blocks away, calling him home. As his mother missed his gestures of loyalty to her, she also missed the notices the school mailed home reporting her eldest son's class misconduct or truancy. With Gail's preoccupations, Mason began to suspect why Dan had left: if for nothing else, to get her attention.

The paradox of Dan and Gail slid to a back burner, then boiled away altogether in the space of one evening. After the playground basketball game when Rick Franklin introduced him to his father, the renowned Pony Reed, who shoved Mason's face against the concrete wall of Doc's Liquor Store for interrupting his attempts at a pickup.

He did not know what to think of Pony Reed, yet somehow he succeeded in thinking of little else. Teachers tapped him on the shoulder, appearing from nowhere to tower above his desk in the middle of his daydreams, in which he and Pony somehow met again. "I've been gone too long, seeing the world, working in every continent from here to Africa, but I came back to make it all up to you." No. Even at his age, Mason was too much the pragmatist to believe he'd ever hear anything like that from the slick-looking hustler he'd met in front of Doc's. But how would Pony have reacted if he had known who Mason was? What if Mason went right up to him and introduced himself? What would Pony say? Mason spent long hours supplying the dialogue for that confrontation.

The greater part of a year comprised these hours when he could think of little else even when he tried, the year he lived "between." He coined this term himself to describe his place, his position on the grid, not aligned with Gail, definitely not with Dan, nor Rick and the other guys who scathingly teased him about Pony. Between the hoops of the playground blacktop, between the pews of Gail's foraging, between the comings and goings of nameless boarders, between the walls of his bedroom, he maneuvered, not trapped but possessing a passage, a trench in which to move undetected. While "between" he stole Tyler's bicycle—the shiny Christmas ten-speed Dan had run behind for blocks until Ty had pedaled up enough confidence. Gail had said she wanted the boys to share it, though Tyler rarely did. Months later, she had to warn Tyler not to leave the bike outside unlocked, but Ty seemed to forget a lot. Big brother Mason, with a one-sided smirk, accepted the responsibility of teaching Ty a lesson about his carelessness by hiding the bike in the garage behind large moving boxes.

Mason listened to music in his bedroom, the volume cranked just enough to bother the boarders, when Ty howled from the backyard.

"Mason! Mason! Have you got my bicycle?" Tyler hollered.

Mason went to the window. "Yeah, you dummy, I'm doing wheelies around my bed." He shut the window then, laughing to himself.

Gail charged into his bedroom five minutes later, arms crossed, with Tyler lagging behind like a kite's tail. "I don't want to believe you stole your own brother's bicycle," she said. But her tone and her diving eyebrows said she already believed it absolutely. She turned off his stereo. "Well?"

Mason had thought she would see. This was no different than the times he hid Tyler's silly teddy bear. Her attitude angered him. She said something about how he was forever torturing Ty when as his big brother he was supposed to be looking out for him. Mason summoned all the indignation he could muster, "I didn't steal his bike. How come you automatically think it was me? I don't know where it is, but you know where he probably left it. You the one always telling him not to leave it laying in the yard and he does it anyway."

She paused at that, unsure of herself now. "Did you leave it outside, Tyler?"

The boy looked trapped and confused.

"See?" Mason said. "But no, blame me."

"I told you, didn't I?" Gail said to Tyler whose tears massed along his lower eyelashes.

They both walked out of Mason's room. He turned his stereo back on, nodding his head to the beat, noting with a smile that no one had apologized for falsely accusing him. After all of this, he figured he'd really have to get rid of the bike, and he did so a day later when he rode it over to Jamal Jenkins's house and got twenty dollars for it.

On his way home from school one day with rain falling on his uncovered head, Mason heard Rick Franklin shouting for him to hold up. Tired of the older boy's teasing, Mason turned and knotted his fists, prepared to fight rather than walk away this time, knowing he would lose badly and wondering how bad it would hurt. He ignored the rain running down his face and neck, and waited.

Rick's feet slapped in shallow puddles, sending spray above his knees. "Hey," he said, stopping in front of Mason. He laughed, at the rain Mason supposed, and held his white palms upward.

The boys looked at each other through the shower for the moment. Rick seemed not to notice Mason's ready fists; he grinned. "We're gonna get up some full-court games, Saturday, noon. And I'ma want players on my side." He held out his hand and Mason slapped it, a loud smack sound coming from their wet hands.

"Cool," Mason said, recognizing an apology when he heard one.

Rick then said, "He's still in town, you know. Living with a friend in the projects off Dunbar Street. Don't know the number."

Mason tried not to react to the news.

Rick Franklin shrugged. "Well, thought you'd want to know. Gotta fly."

He watched Rick splashing down the street and then continued home, but when he came to Evans Avenue he turned south instead of north and turned left on Lincoln Avenue at the City Youth Center. Mason was wearing his basketball shoes, split near the soles from rough wear. Rain water had begun to soak through to his socks and by the time he made his way down Dunbar it felt like his feet were strapped to sponges.

The projects in town weren't the huge, towering stacks in Chicago or Detroit. But the stigma was the same. The two-story yellow-brick buildings arranged in barrack rows weren't built much differently than garden apartments on the other side of town.

Mason walked up and down the projects, across the bald yards and over the broken wine bottles. He slowly circled the buildings while people ran from their cars to their doorways. He wiped rain from his face, eyeing windows and doors without giving thought to what he expected to discover. When the skin on his fingers sagged like raisins and a chill braced him beneath his clothes, he finally trudged home. But he would return the next day, and the next, haunting the projects, casing them like a burglar.

He found him. By the time Mason could walk the route without looking up from the sidewalk, and no longer debated with himself the foolishness of his search while crossing the schoolyard, and had half forgotten why he strolled eight blocks out of his way to go down Dunbar Street, he found him.

He simply glanced up, and there sat his father on the steps of a first-floor apartment stoop. Blood surged through Mason's heart and he quickly looked away. Four doors away he chanced another look. Pony Reed folded a newspaper and blew out a plume of smoke while allowing the cigarette to dangle between his lips. His hair had been slicked back, shiny blue-black, reflecting the weak late-afternoon sunlight. The man seemed calm and, Mason thought, sure of himself, confident, as if he sat on the stoop not to get out of a small, hot apartment but as part of some plan. He was probably waiting for someone or...

He looked up.

Mason spun and started to jog across the street. He stopped in the middle of the street and turned back around. A car whooshed by him, its horn blaring. Pony Reed looked directly at him then; Mason could see his frown. The man returned to his paper, though, and Mason walked straight up to him, not scared, exactly, but anxious, expectant, tense, and certain he was forearmed for whatever happened.

Pony Reed's eyes flicked over the top edge on the newspaper and narrowed as Mason approached. He lowered the paper and blew another stream of smoke, this time holding the cigarette between two fingers.

With Pony sitting on the top step, his and Mason's faces were even. Pony's skin wrapped thinly over his cheekbones, which angled down to his narrow nose. He looked hard. He seemed capable of pointing his face as well as his eyes, jabbing with both. "Yeah?"

Mason searched for the resemblance, something familiar around the eyes or the width of the mouth, maybe the chin line, like the mimicry Tyler's youthful face performed with Dan's. "Do you remember me?" Mason asked.

Pony returned to his paper, or pretended to. "Maybe," he said. "What do you need, little man?"

"You bought a bottle of wine for me last year at Doc's." He waited to see recognition in Pony's eyes, recognition and what emotion might go along with it.

Pony only looked guarded and suspicious. "Okay, but you ain't getting another bottle out of me, little brother."

"Do you know Gail Wallington?"

Now the man looked at him truly, scrutinized him, and his cigarette fell from his mouth onto his newspaper. A thin line of smoke rose above the paper. "Shit," Pony said, coming to his feet and shaking the cigarette off the paper. He stepped it out and then picked up the butt. Not for a full second did he take his eyes off Mason. "Damn, burnt a hole through the sports section. Goddamn. Is your name...Jesus, Jesus..."

"No, it ain't Jesus." Mason started to walk away, waving a dismissing hand at Pony Reed.

"Wait a minute now. Damn, you just can't show up out of the blue and...hey, come back here. Hold up...Mason."

At the sound of his name, Mason turned to him again. Son and father faced each other, for the first time both knowing the identity of the other. And neither had a word to say. Mason remembered that this moment seemed to last a long time, each measuring the other, or maybe just thinking what should be said first.

Pony Reed smiled and he looked suddenly like a much nicer person. "Damn," he said, "a blast from the past, a very goddamn big blast."

"Guess so," Mason said and managed to smile too, though feeling awkward and thinking he should be very angry with this man.

"Lettie ain't gonna believe this. Hell, I don't believe it. Letitia!" Pony called over his back to the apartment door. "My girlfriend's place," he explained. "So, how's your mama? Is she an artist?"

Mason frowned.

"She always said she wanted to be an artist, didn't you know that?"

"She runs a boardinghouse on Gum Street."

"Yeah? Gum Street, that's in a nice part of town. That sounds good. C'mon. I'd say we got to catch each other up." Pony placed an arm about Mason's shoulders. Mason was grinning despite himself. Pony called, "Letitia!" just as a woman opened the door. She was small and dark with large, pretty eyes. "Lettie, this is my son."

Lettie grinned. She had teeth missing. "Bullshit," she said.

"No jazz," Pony said and squeezed Mason's shoulder. "And a good-looking kid he is."

She held the door open for them to come in. "I see. That's why I said bullshit." She laughed and Pony, shaking his newspaper at her, laughed too.

That first meeting had gone well, better than Mason thought it would. They sat at a small kitchen table, just the two of them. Lettie, who seemed a lot younger than Pony, hovered about, sometimes leaning against him hip to shoulder, to get a cigarette or to add to the slow conversation. Pony was funny. He asked Mason if he wanted some wine. "I know you drink it," he said.

Letitia gave Mason a Coke instead.

Pony didn't ask very many questions. He asked if Mason was in school and then told him to make certain he stayed. "I was good in school," Pony said. "Especially math. You good in math?"

Mason shook his head.

"Well, maybe you take after your mama there. How is she? She married?"

Mason told him Gail was married but separated, then regretted giving him that piece of information.

"Well, I hope she's doing good. She's a good woman," he said and slapped Letitia on her butt as she walked by him. "All my women are good, though."

Mason wondered if he should ask. Pony did not try to explain why he'd left. Couldn't he be like Dan and come back and visit? And he wouldn't have to come back as often as Dan did. Every now and then would have been okay. He wouldn't have to buy bicycles and tickets to basketball games, either. He could've just stopped by or written letters. *Didn't you ever think about me at all, all this time?* Pony had asked him something about the boardinghouse; Mason had missed the question. "I got to go," he said, abruptly standing. "I got to go." He moved quickly, aware that Pony followed him to the door, though he did not look back.

"Hey," Mason heard while on the apartment stoop. Pony stood in the doorway, a friendly smile on his face and his right hand extended. "Nice to meet you, little man."

Mason stared at this stranger's hand, his father's hand: clean, with long, tapering fingers and trimmed nails, which were tipped with white crescents and long for a man's. Dan kept his nails short. Mason leaped the two steps below, not allowing himself to look back, and ran two blocks down Dunbar before slowing to a walk. He thought, *so that was Pony Reed.*

He did not tell Gail about having met with Pony again. She had her secrets; this would be his. It turned out to be a short-lived secret, however. A week later Pony was there, in the front room of the boardinghouse, face to face with Gail.

Gail must have just arrived home from work. She still had her heels on, which were usually the first things she shed coming through the door. Her arms were crossed over her chest and her pocketbook, and her face was immobile.

Pony and Gail must have come through the door at the same time. Mason had heard it open only once. He and Tyler stopped on the stairs in the middle of a planned raid on the kitchen.

Tyler peeked between the rungs of the banister. "Who's he?"

"So what," Pony was saying, "you've been carrying a mad for ten years? That's pretty destructive. Didn't anybody ever tell you that?"

"Thirteen years," Gail said. "And I'm good for thirteen more."

"Imagine you are. Well, it ain't been too destructive; you looking very good. Still got your figure, and the finest legs in the Midwest. Look to be prosperous too," he said, glancing around the room.

"Looks can be deceiving. And I don't need any of this at this point in my life. Pony, what could you possibly want? Huh? There is not a thing here for you. Drum that into that rat head of yours."

Pony's mouth continued to smile, but his eyes did not. "I want to forget ancient history. I want—say, there's my little man now." Pony held a hand up in Mason's direction.

"Hey," Mason said and started down the stairs.

"That's your daddy?" Tyler asked. "Mason, is that your daddy?" He pulled on Mason's shirt.

"Boys, go back upstairs," Gail said.

Tyler retreated immediately. Mason held his spot near the bottom of the steps.

"I just want to visit my boy from time to time, baby," Pony said. "What problem you got with that?"

"Yeah, right. Too many to mention before the sun goes down. Look, Pony, you left—"

"So did Dan Neighbors," interrupted Mason.

Gail glanced back at Mason, a look more of surprise than anger on her face then. She said to Pony, "You know, I liked it much better when you were a mystery. When I had no idea where you were or what happened to you. Then I could picture you under the wheels of a semi-trailer or sitting in the electric chair someplace. But, damn, now I know you're alive, if not still brain-dead, and I want you the fuck out of my house right now."

Instead of heading to the door, Pony took a step forward. Mason came down the remaining stairs to stand next to his mother.

"People change, Gail. Apparently you don't. But most of us do," Pony said. "We'll be getting together again, all right, Mason?"

"No," Gail said.

Mason said, "Okay, yeah."

Pony backed to the door like a movie cowboy leaving a hostile saloon. He did not close the door after him.

Gail moved swiftly to the door and slammed it shut. "God damn it, Mason!" She whirled on him, her open hand bringing that momentum and the power of her hurt and rage into a vicious slap.

The blow staggered Mason and he covered the left side of his face with both his hands. The pain electrified his cheek. It twitched uncontrollably. But he took his hands away. He fought to look calm and unflustered. He couldn't bring himself to look her in the eyes, so he stared at her mouth, watched her top lip pulled thin over the top of her teeth.

"All your young, silly life I've tried to keep you in line. Giving you a swat when you needed it. Trying to get you to do right.

Worrying about where you were or what you were up to." Hair had fallen into her face. Her lips quivered. "All I got for it is a sore hand." Her left hand rubbed the palm of the right. "Go upstairs. No, you do what you want, I'll go."

Mason watched her climb the stairs. The side of his face pulsed.

His father's car, as long as a driveway, hugged the street as if trying to get intimate with the pavement beneath it. A light purple, like the sky at dusk, the streamlined Bonneville reflected ribbon-thin images of its surroundings like carnival mirrors or the back of a spoon. It seemed to shine even on rainy days, when a thousand jiggling beads of water massed on its hood. The porta-walled tires rolled slowly, and the engine hummed a monotone bass. The inside smelled like air freshener and cleanser over cigarette smoke. Big speakers were canted forward in the rear window, nestled in red shag carpet. Pony kept the carpeting shampooed and the seats slick with vinyl protectant. His left hand rested in his lap, holding lightly to the steering wheel, influencing it subtly with a push one way or the other with the pads of his fingers. He leaned to the right, propped on his elbow over the center console so that he could see right down the center of the hood, and that's where he seemed to fix his eyes even though nothing or no one on either sidewalk escaped his notice.

These rides with his father were not fun. The best part of going out with Pony ended the moment he let the screen door of the boardinghouse bang shut behind him. Watching Tyler watch him get ready was the highlight. "What's up? You thought you were the only one who had a daddy?" He'd grin, moving quickly, rifling through his drawers for a clean pair of socks, lacing up his sneakers, pushing change and his house key into his pockets, all to show his eagerness for the evening's events to begin. It galled him that most of the stories he came home with, which left Tyler with undisguised envy, were made up.

Gail would be scarce when Pony came to pick him up, by her design or Mason's timing, and that was just fine. He knew she was always mindful, maybe even apprehensive, when he spent the day or evening with his father. Pony and he seldom went anywhere.

Pony always had someone he wanted "to look up" or "have a word with." And these people were never to be found at a specific address; they were around. So the two of them cruised Lincoln Avenue and Dunbar and Judson, searching, it turned out, for whomever they happened to find. During the rides, Mason did not look at the town he'd lived in all his life, the streets whose every manhole cover and chuck hole and dead end he'd already blueprinted. He looked at Pony. He examined that right side of Pony's face presented to him, and tried to figure the importance of this man, not understanding his attraction to him. He studied him, hoping to discover information he desperately needed but that Pony could not impart. They did not have conversations. Pony would ask him questions every now and then or make quick speeches, things he had been thinking about so long, it seemed to Mason, that finally he would speak his thoughts aloud, and it also seemed as if he would have done this had Mason been with him or not.

"The black man don't have a chance. You understand that?" Pony said on more than one occasion. "We're the endangered species. They jam us in their overcrowded prisons and treat us like livestock. But that's traditional, a throwback from the slavery days. They still think we're chattel. You know that word? Chattel? It means, Mason, you ain't shit. But I ain't either. We're just niggers. We can't get ahead because they done made all the rules, they got things set up the way they want." Pony would look angry enough to spit, but Pony didn't spit, just fumed at the end of his dangling cigarette. "And the moment a brother tries to make something of himself by playing beyond the rules, he gets slapped into jail so fast his head spins for a month. God damn, but there ain't no way for a black man to be nothing. Say, look, there's Chill, just the nigger I been looking for." And Pony would, with deliberation, ease the Bonneville to the side of the street, his indignation seemingly vanished like wind while Mason rolled down the passenger side glass so that he could suffer between the laughing and joking, gossip and coded conversation that blew stale, smoky breath on either side of his face.

"I didn't know you had a boy," his friends would say.

"Oh, sure," Pony would answer.

They stopped by a McDonald's when Mason said he was hungry and Pony would hand him a twenty and let Mason get anything he wanted while he waited in the car. Once, the line was long and it took Mason a while to get his meal. He hurried back though, juggling his sack and drink, and jumped in the car. He asked Pony if he wanted his change back.

Pony stabbed a finger at him, his angry face pointed like a dart. "Don't you keep me waiting like this again, boy," he said, "Don't piss me off."

He would try to picture them together, as a family, like the way it once was with Dan, Gail, Tyler and himself. What if, he wondered, his parents had married and stayed together? Pony, and Gail, and Mason. He could not picture this.

It didn't help that Pony did not stay with one woman at one time, and Mason realized just what a large amount of luck had been involved in finding Pony in the first place that day in front of Letitia's. He seemed to live with two or three women simultaneously and date two or three others. Increasingly, their outings involved women.

This was the secret father and son shared: Pony's womanizing. Mason realized he had been honored with privileged information, and it was by keeping this secret that he could be close to Pony. Mason used to wonder how these women could all believe Pony lived with them when he didn't show up every night, or returned wearing different clothes than he'd had on when he left. The closest he ever came to solving that mystery was something Pony had said to him: "Women only want a piece of a man. If you are a real man, give them this, but take back that," he said, extending his right hand and withdrawing his left in illustration. "If they ever get all of you, they'll like that for a while, then get bored and lose respect for you. When they lose respect, it's over. Let 'em work to get you. You can keep that going forever."

Maybe a year into their relationship, Pony had learned he could trust Mason with secrets, that no details of his doings would find their way back to Gail or Letitia or any of the others, and Mason knew Pony liked this about him. He had earned his father's confidence, conveyed by an infectious smile and a furtive wink while in the presence of one of his several girlfriends. He began taking Mason around with him when he dropped by Sheryl's or Carmen's. Now the adventures were more exciting, tipped with an edge of danger. Mason felt grown up and important going out with Pony to visit these ladies. This was what men did.

Carmen had a daughter. Mason could not remember her name. He'd only met her one afternoon that slowly wound down to evening. She was three or four years older than Mason and the exact mirror image of her mother on a slightly smaller, thinner frame. They both had yellow-brown skin and black hair, bushy eyebrows resting above light-colored eyes, and overly fleshy, pouty lips, which looked seductive on both. Pony flirted with the daughter as well as the mother, but the girl was plainly uninterested and Pony's continued advances embarrassed Mason. Carmen found Pony's attentions toward her daughter funny, or maybe the gin and tonics she kept lifting made everything funny. Red lipstick prints decorated the edge of the glass she never set down for more than a moment.

Pony, sitting between them, squeezed first Carmen's shoulder and then the girl's. She would scowl and scoot another inch or two away from him, pushing her elbow into his ribs. "You two are sisters. Right? Y'all can't sit here and give me this mama-daughter line. Twin sisters! Am I right?"

Mason tried to catch the girl's eyes, offer an apologetic look, and roll his eyes to show he sympathized with her, but she would not acknowledge him. Telling her mother she was tired, she left the room. Mason could not help but watch her walk away, her shapely bottom wrapped in a tight, short skirt. Pony caught Mason staring and winked at him.

Pony began campaigning immediately, charged with his idea. He put his lips to Carmen's ear.

Giggling, she reflexively drew her shoulder up, in part as protection for her ear. "I don't know, honey." She took large gulps at her drink, her nose going into the glass each time. "She usually do what she want." Pony gave her a look Mason did not understand.

"Okay, okay, I'll ask." Carmen stood a little shakily, said something about new high heels, and disappeared down the same hallway her daughter had.

"Be cool now, Little Brother," Pony said. "Get you some of that tight pussy tonight. Wouldn't mind that myself. We'll see what kinda rap you have. Ain't gonna take much."

Mason's heart skipped when the blood surged up to his head. Outwardly, he grinned stupidly; he knew that's how he always looked when he tried to force a smile. The panic fluttered inside him. He was a virgin. He'd only felt up a girl once before. And he didn't know all he might be expected to do. He tried to get control of himself, remembering things the guys in the gang had talked about doing, wondering if they had been lying as much as he had been. His hands rapidly patted his knees.

It took a while to coax the girl from her room. They heard Carmen's raised voice from time to time. Pony winked at him and Mason would look down at his sneakers.

Both women finally reemerged. And Pony was right, they did look alike. The girl appeared to be a lot older than Mason, already grown. In her silence, she seemed even cooler and more knowledgeable. Now she studied Mason with an appraising gaze that chased his eyes away from her. She sat down on the couch opposite him as Pony stood. He took Carmen's offered hand.

"Well, now we're on a double date," she said and led Pony away, jogging back in a moment to recover her drink. "Don't you two do nothing I wouldn't do."

At the entrance to the hallway, Pony said, "That leaves a wide spectrum of activities." The two adults left them alone.

"Hey," Mason said lamely. She looked at him in cold disdain. Anything else he might have thought to say died en route from his brain to his mouth.

She reached across the cocktail table for the television's remote control. In a moment her attention appeared fixed to the TV tube.

Mason figured he ought to sit on the couch next to her. He could think up something to say, maybe about school, then try to get his arm around her. Pony made it all seem so easy. He put his hands on women as if they belonged there. Not that Mason particularly liked this girl. As he sat there planning his strategy, he realized in fact that she was too tall, too old, and acted too seditty for his taste. But he still felt the pressure, placed there by Pony, to try something.

He half-rose from his seat just as the girl said, "You can relax over there. I don't care what my mama say. You ain't g'ttin' a thing off me tonight."

He let his weight sink back into the chair, feeling very much relieved. He caught himself before almost saying thank you.

Pony didn't call for nearly two months after that, and trying to call Pony never did any good. Mason had to wonder if his absence was because of his disappointment in him that night at Carmen's, though Pony only casually told Mason he'd missed a great opportunity. "Didn't that man your mama married teach you anything?"

The next time they got together was on the occasion of Letitia's birthday, though Mason did not know it was her birthday, and apparently Pony had forgotten.

At nearly ten p.m., hours late, the Bonneville stopped and idled in front of the boardinghouse. Gail had told him an hour ago that it was too late for Mason to go anywhere. But she was watching television in her room with Tyler when Pony pulled up. Mason reasoned if she heard the front door opening, she would probably think it was just one of her boarders. He did not really want to go out that night, but feared turning Pony down might mean not seeing him again.

Letitia, angry to the bone, jumped into Pony's face as soon as he stepped through her doorway. She wore only a black slip. Her fists were anchored to her hips, and in a high-pitched cackle announced she would no longer put up with Pony's trifling ways, how he was always standing her up and taking her money. She did not notice Mason behind Pony, not for a while. "I been waitin' all damn evenin' for you. You promised you was gonna take me out for a birthday dinner. I should've known. You ain't ever gonna do nothin' for nobody else." She blocked his way into the room, defying him, her dark pupils alive and surrounded by liquid white.

She sniffed, then noticed Mason for the first time and said, "Hi," almost shyly with a quick gap-toothed smile while crossing her arms in front of her. Then she turned her eyes back on Pony. Her anger and resolve had not diminished. "Get out of my place, Pony Reed. I don't want your shit anymore."

"Shut up," Mason whispered under his breath. "Lettie, shut up." She did not seem frightened of Pony, but Mason was frightened for her. He tried to push around Pony to maneuver part way between Lettie and his father. She had become his favorite of his father's girlfriends, maybe because he'd met her first, or because she did not always act as if he were in the way as some of the others did. He had not asked himself why, or even thought he'd felt this way about her until that night.

Pony blocked Mason's maneuver with an arm. "Wait for me in the car, boy."

Mason looked to Lettie for some signal she was willing to back down—the only way, as he saw it, the situation might be defused. And he knew she knew that. But she stood her ground and did not look Mason's way again. He stepped backward to the doorway, helped by the firm pressure of Pony's hand on his chest.

"And don't be eavesdropping by the door either," Pony said and handed Mason the keys to the car. He didn't seem too upset. His face didn't have that pointed, focused look. "Don't look so worried, Little Brother, just goes to show you. Never forget a woman's birthday, there'll be hell to pay. I'm just gonna smooth things over with Miss Thing here. You wait in the car and I'll be there shortly."

"Ain't nothing to smooth out," Mason heard Lettie say as the door closed in his face.

Mason could hear her hollering the same declaration of independence she'd launched into when Pony first stepped through her doorway. The door did little to muffle her. Her voice carried across the stoop and the littered yard and into the car out front, until Mason shut the car door and for extra measure turned on the radio. The stream of chatter from the giant rear-window speakers annoyed him and he finally clicked the radio off. It seemed he waited a long time. He rolled down the window, but heard nothing then.

Some boys crossed the street in front of him. They all wore bomber jackets. They were laughing, enjoying each other's company, having a good time. He watched them until they rounded the corner of one of the project buildings. Opening the glove compartment, he found a vinyl slipcase containing invoices for work done on the car and the registration made out to William Collier Reed. (William Collier...he hadn't known that.) Besides the slipcase, the compartment held a neatly folded white towel, a bottle of Armor-All, and an ice scraper. Dan Neighbors's glove compartment was far more interesting, choked with receipts and bills and hastily scribbled forgotten notes, spare change, candy bar wrappers, maybe an issue of *Jet* magazine and always a pair of pliers or a screwdriver.

Now it felt as if he'd been waiting a long time. He thought of getting out of the car and just walking home, but feared angering Pony enough so he wouldn't see him anymore. As it stood, the outings had become less frequent already, dwindling down to barely once a month. Finally, he told himself he didn't care. He had to see how Lettie was doing, and thought to go around back of her apartment and peek in a window.

As he stepped from the car, Pony came walking briskly out of the apartment. "Get back in. We're booking. Get in the goddamn car."

Pony pulled his Pontiac from the curb. The tires squealed, something Pony never let happen before. His animated eyes looked as though they tried to see too much at once. He lit a cigarette and calmed down noticeably.

"Is Lettie okay now?" Mason asked.

Pony looked at him hard, already leaning near. His answer took a while to form. "Lettie is a bitch, boy, don't worry about her."

"I ain't," Mason said.

"We going to show you that procuring tail takes about as long as a sneeze," he said and then added, "and it's about as easy."

They drove in silence for several minutes. The headlights illuminated yards and porches and stragglers still on the streets as Pony turned corner after corner. If he had a specific destination in mind, he was having trouble locating it.

"Mama wants me home by eleven," Mason said, by now tired of the whole evening. Pony acted as if he hadn't heard.

Near downtown, not far from the courthouse, in the older part of town where the streets are narrow and all marked "One Way," they stopped at a four-story apartment building of white-painted brick. It stood alone on its corner of the block, snug against the sidewalk. The building that once stood next to it had been razed and the unpainted silhouette it left on the standing building looked like a great shadow with nothing to cast it.

On the sidewalk, Pony threw an arm around Mason's neck and yanked him close. This intimacy startled Mason. In the darkness, he could not see Pony clearly. Their foreheads touched and Pony pressed the contact. Pony's cologne clung to the inside of Mason's nasal passages. Mason scrunched his nose. "Father and son, on a mission together," Pony said. His eyes flicked to the building in front of them. "Like James Bond or Our Man Flint. The utmost secrecy will enable us to succeed, supplemented in no small measure by our indisputable good looks. You're lucky you took after me."

Except for their skin color, Mason had never noticed much resemblance to Pony, a fact he found disappointing because Dan and Tyler looked so much alike. But he agreed now, grinning and nodding, warmed and enthused by his father's arm draping his shoulders. The pair went into the building and up two flights of rickety stairs, each step worn and splintering in the middle.

The very first look he had at the woman is blurred in Mason's memory. Perhaps because standing on the landing in front of the door, his attention centered on Pony Reed. Pony knocked three or four times at the cheap, rattling door. Near the lock, the door appeared chewed where someone had taken a tire iron or crowbar to it. The woman let the door swing wide open and retreated from it. She was not one of Pony's regular girlfriends. In the middle of an apartment that was little more than a room with a kitchenette off to one side, she posed for both of them, hugging her arms across her belly. Her upper arms forced her sizeable breasts to thrust outward together. When she moved, her deep cleavage proudly went before her, clearing a path. She wore a loud lime jumpsuit, which hugged too tightly the roll at her hips. Under her lip, extending to her left cheek, she had a series of moles she'd attempted to cover with makeup. Mason couldn't recall, later, if he had noticed them then or when he was to get much closer to her. Her hair hung long and straight, an obvious wig, with bangs forming a roof over her sleepy eyes.

She swayed at the shoulders. "Betting on the Pony," she said and thought it clever enough to repeat. "Why did I know you'd show yourself here? Pony too bony." She liked saying his name, stretched it out on her tongue. "Who is this with you? Does Winston know you're here? He's your friend."

Mason heard his name mentioned. He heard Pony say, "The hell with Winston. Nothing this fine should be left behind." Pony stepped toward her and she stepped back.

Her eyes still looked half closed. "I don't think so, Pony." She wagged an index finger at him. "Winston's been good to me."

"Wait here, Little Brother," Pony said. He advanced and this time the woman did not step back. Instead she tensed up as Pony encircled her. One hand expanded across her bottom. He pressed himself to her, nibbling along her jaw line to her ear.

"Damn, I'm gonna get in a fix over this," she said, going limp against Pony as he nuzzled under her chin.

He swept her, clumsily because she did not seem to know what was going on, into her bedroom and the door shut behind them. As quick as a sneeze, Mason thought.

He stared at the closed bedroom door for a long moment, then scanned the rest of the tiny apartment, which reminded him remotely of the old apartment on Judson Street. A few sticks of press board furniture, including the sofa he sat down on, crowded a room with space for little else. The wallpaper, sporting giant bouquets of red roses, shrunk the room even more.

His eyes, like a compass needle to north, returned to the door. He knew what they would be doing behind it; he knew what men and women did. Boys his age in school claimed to have already had sex, but Mason knew most of them talked bull. Disconcerted at first over being abandoned, and over why he had been abandoned, Mason then began to think the entire situation quite funny. This was, after all, what men did: chase women, get laid. He promised himself that the next time they went to Carmen's, he would definitely try something with her daughter.

When the first squeak of a bedspring escaped from behind the door, Mason chuckled, swallowing the embarrassment he felt. The squeaks became more frequent. Gathering momentum, they became rhythmic and predictable. Then he heard the woman, first a slippery, lazy moan, sliding from under the door, and then a breathy gasp.

Mason covered his mouth with a hand, smiling broadly behind it. Damn, he thought. I don't believe this. He thought of how he would tell the guys at school.

Heavier grunting created a duet with the woman's moans, using the bedsprings for accompaniment. Pony's groans rolled through the door. Suddenly, Mason could find nothing funny in his situation. The throaty release of Pony's exertions jabbed at him. The noise hammered like an assault against him.

The deadline Gail had given him to be home had passed, and he wanted to go. Still, he did not move, but not because he couldn't find his way; he was intimate with almost every corner of town, and walking about late at night didn't concern him. He came to ask himself many times in the years since why he did not leave.

The gasps ended abruptly. Mason crossed to the door, listening into the trailing silence. "I got to get home," he said, his nervousness giving over to anger now.

The door opened with a popping sound around the doorway frame. Pony came out, stuffing his shirt into the waist of his slacks. Pushing the back of a hand against his mouth and nose, he leaned toward Mason. "What you doin'? Trying to hurry me up?"

Mason recalled Pony shoving his face against the liquor store wall. "No," he answered. He was not afraid of being hit; Gail had gotten him over any fear of that. But he could not cross Pony.

Sweat had beaded at Pony's hairline. "I done hooked you up, Little Brother," he said. His smile for a moment made him look like a boy. "She's nice and she's ready. Ready for you. Hell, I was just the warmup." Pony gripped him by the upper arm and steered him to the open doorway.

The bed was lengthwise, directly in front of them, with the headboard against the far wall. The woman lay naked. There was a dim light somewhere in the bedroom, and Mason could see the contrast of her dark skin and the white sheets that lapped over one leg, her crotch, and half her belly. The exposed leg, drawn up, she let hang open. Sweat slicked the heavy, black threads of hair against it. Her face was hidden in shadow, but her breasts and belly glistened as fleshy islands in the light.

"School's in session," she said.

Mason did not move though a raised hand, sporting fake, red nails, gestured for him.

"Well, get in there," Pony said, though he had not relinquished his grip on Mason's arm. "Wish my old man had set me up like this."

Mason looked up at Pony. The smile vanished, leaving only Pony's narrow-faced meanness.

"What's with you? Don't tell me you're a sissy? I bet your mama done made a sissy of you. Don't you embarrass me. No son of mine is a sissy. Get in there." Pony shoved him forward. "You're in for a time you'll always remember."

The door closed behind him. The smell of the woman, her sweat, and her sheets closed all around him. He managed only to stare at her nakedness, from her thigh to her hip to her stomach.

She rose out of the shadows. The wig was gone. A tight nap of short hair remained. She studied him from under her eyelids. As she sat up, her breasts drooped, not far, but they dangled, almost shapeless. "Hey, young stuff." Her voice was low. "What are you afraid of, huh? Come over here."

Mason wanted to tell her he was not afraid. He wanted to call her an ugly bitch of a whore. But nothing came from his mouth.

Her nakedness had transfixed him. He felt a tug on the waist of his pants. She had stepped half out of the bed in order to reach out and pull him close. Docilely, his feet consented. He could smell her skin now. Her lips were close to his eyes. He looked at the little, shaded brass lamp, the only source of light in the windowless room, and the mirror hanging over the bureau behind it. In the mirror his pants were being opened and his zipper pulled down. He could feel her fingers fumbling at him. That boy made a weak attempt to grab his pants as they fell down around his ankles. The woman's hands—for all he could see in the mirror were her hands, arms and head—loosened him from his constricting underwear and briefly played with him. She snickered. She pulled his sweatshirt over his head and in that blind moment, with his head covered, her lips closed around one of his nipples. His body shuddered. When the woman had undressed him completely, she pulled him into her bed. He was drawn after her, under her control.

The old mattress, abused over the years and soft as dough, enveloped him. The sheets were still damp and clingy.

The woman said nothing. She moved over him. Her hands manipulated him. Mason felt as if he were smothering, sandwiched between her skin and the sheets. Her breasts were in his hands one moment, then pooled on his chest. She inserted him. A thin line of breath snaked into his ear. The thick air, full of her scent, did not seem enough to sustain him. Each lungful seemed less than the one before. Then he smelled something that froze him, a scent that, once he'd noticed it, pervaded the bed and his nostrils: his father's cologne. It was there, riding him in waves just as the woman did.

He told her then to stop. "Get off of me," he gasped and pushed against her weight. He had to get free of the cloud he pulled into his lungs with each breath. Pony's cologne scalded his airways. He fought only to disentangle himself, he thought, but the woman began screaming his father's name over and over. Mason said, "I ain't Pony. I ain't Pony," as he fought to get free.

Abruptly, he was hurled backward from the bed. He landed hard on the floor, striking his head on something behind him.

Light streamed in from the living room and Pony stood next to the bed. "What the fuck do you think you're doing, boy?" Pony hollered.

The woman was clutching at her belly, "God damn it," she kept saying. Blood formed a trickle over her left eye and under her nose. The blood rounded her lips and dripped to the sheets.

"What's wrong with you?" Pony asked. "Did she do something to you?"

The woman said, "I didn't do nothin' to the little nigger."

Mason swept up his clothes in his arms and sprinted from the room, pursued by Pony, who kept asking for an explanation. Mason only glared at his father while he quickly dressed. He slipped into his sneakers without tying them. Finally, he said, "She's a smelly bitch," though it was Pony he wanted to call names.

He backed his way to the door while Pony watched him retreat without making a move to stop him. His father looked more perplexed than angry.

Mason slammed down the apartment building steps. He gulped in the chilly night air. Those clean breaths could not erase the odors that hung about him.

Pony's Bonneville sat at the curb and Mason ran up to it and kicked the passenger-side door several times. He stepped away, furious. Tears streamed down his face. He yanked a fistful of his shirt up to his nose. Everything reeked. He thought of the woman moving on him and his stomach tightened toward his spine. He thought he would vomit. He bent over, but nothing came out.

He walked two blocks up the street before he got his bearings. Down one avenue, he sighted an ornate column supporting a corner of the old courthouse. Using that landmark, he knew which direction to go, and a half-hour later was home.

He threw himself across his bed. He was pretending to sleep when Gail peeked in on him.

ANNIE

By November, there was still no word from Mason and the Mondays were increasingly hard to take. Mondays she missed Mason the most. In their hectic sprints to grab breakfast, take a shower, make a lunch, get the baby ready, and find textbooks or keys, Gail, Jaclyn, and Tyler left Annie in their wake. Everyone else had schedules, appointments, things that just had to get done, and they drained their coffee cups while pulling on their coats and hunting for their purses. Gail and Jaclyn fled to the bus stop, while young Ty hopped in a friend's car.

So soon the huge boardinghouse was empty, the high-ceilinged rooms quiet as mausoleums, except for the slow, foot-dragging steps and sometimes jerky movements of Annie Gant—one hundred two pounds, five feet one inch tall when as straight as her back allowed, and the survivor of eighty-nine years on this earth. Today, Annie decided to make up all the beds and maybe dust around a bit since lately Gail had let things go. Annie was certain Gail would appreciate the help.

She made up Tyler's bed first, and though her hands frequently trembled, she worked efficiently and meticulously. Her hands skimmed along, flattening the spread, and tucking the excess under the pillows. Tyler had a piece of sheet music on his desk. Annie brought it close to her face to get a good look at it. She could not read music. But she thought the tiny notes fit well. Neat and pert, they seemed to be hopping and dancing along the lines they'd been drawn against, some with little round feet and others with wings for heads. "La, la, lah, lah; la la lah," she sang, studying the notes as she did so as if reading. A finger traced the notes in the air. "La, la, lah." In a moment, thinking Tyler a remarkable boy, she returned the paper to the exact spot, as well as she remembered, that she'd picked it up from. She stooped for a pair of soiled socks on her way out of the room and placed them in the hamper near the bathroom.

In Gail's room, she made up the bed, but then sat on the edge of it for a brief rest. She thought back to an exchange she'd heard several nights ago between Gail and Reverend Wilson from Calvary. The osteoarthritis had locked up her knee again, and Annie lay awake suffering through it and heard the muted voices from a floor below. The reverend asked Gail about Annie, several questions Annie herself could've answered. They spoke about her as if she were not just upstairs, not within hearing, but already on that journey for which they contemplated the finances.

"Is she provided for when the time comes?" the reverend had asked Gail.

I have money enough, Annie thought. *Me and Joseph done saw to that.* The reverend's question did not scare her exactly. Annie had little cause to worry over how the laws of God and nature dictated people's lives. You are born, with love you grow, and you work, and if you are blessed you find someone to love, if you are blessed and lucky you give birth and life to others—and Annie and Joseph were never that lucky. Finally, when you had done what you were supposed to do, God lifted you up and gave you rest. A simple process, as Annie saw it, made complicated by fearful people. She did not fear death. For nearly nine decades, she had held vigil by enough bedsides to know it was nothing. What burned Annie about the reverend's question was not that he asked it, but that he asked it of her landlady, not of her.

Annie wanted dearly to know when, how, by whose decision had she become someone to be talked about, but not talked to? What did Gail say to Jaclyn? *We have to watch her like we watch Cole.* No! Annie's fists shook, all joints and veins. She saw them in the mirror over Gail's bureau and pressed her hands to her lap. The evolved face in the mirror would not show her anger, but she said aloud, "I'll go when I go. But I refuse to start over. I did not live this long just to be a baby again."

She nodded her head once in total agreement with what the reflection had said. With that she got to her feet; one more bed remained to be made, and she refused to let this be one of those days when she did not venture down the stairs at all. To hell with the leg. If it wanted to go now, let it. The rest of me will stay a bit longer. Now full of defiant energy, she proceeded down the stairs, her pack of canines nonexistent for the moment. She gripped the banister and let her right foot lead with each step.

Jackie's bed was in such chaos that Annie did not even attempt to make it up. Cole's toys got underfoot with each step. As she had done in Gail's room, the old woman sat down on the edge of the bed. She picked up a toy near her feet. It was a bright yellow school bus of molded plastic with soft, rubber tires. She smiled, delighted.

It was a wonderful toy! Inside the little bus, behind the smiling driver, sat rows of paired-off children with happy faces painted on their round heads. To Annie's joy, the children had been painted all different colors, white children with yellow and red hair and black children with brown and black hair, even yellow children grinning with narrow eyes. Annie remembered walking past the playground of the big brick school for the white children in order to reach the one-room house where colored children of all ages learned their letters, numbers, and the laws of the land.

Small George would ask his big sister, "Why can't we learn there? It's closer and they got swings."

Annie didn't remember if she answered Small George. She recalled seeing the white girls on the swings, though, their hair and pretty dresses trailing as they swept in arcs into the air. But now, look at this little toy! All children smiling and going to school together, Annie thought. If you just live long enough... Everything will be even better for Cole, she supposed. He won't even know what it took to get these different colors of paint on the same bus. He'll think all children going to the same school is the way it's supposed to be. Annie smiled. And he'll be right.

She did not get to see Cole much lately, at least not since Perry Sullivan had finally showed up. It had been Annie who'd answered the door to find him standing there with his back to the door, sporting the strangest haircut she'd ever seen, short as a soldier's on the side and as long as a lady's on top and in back. He turned to face the door and he looked surprised to see Annie.

"Yes?" Annie asked. She had not seen him before and did not know who he was. But afterward, when she knew, the resemblance to his baby boy was clear.

"Hi, ma'am. I'm Perry, here to see Jaclyn."

Annie let him in. He stood in the middle of the foyer with his hands dug deeply into his pockets. He looked about, and Annie glanced back at him, as if to make certain he would stay put, before going for Jackie.

Jackie lay across the bed on her stomach reading a magazine spread open on the floor. Cole beat against the rails of his playpen.

"Boy named Perry here to see you, child."

Jackie sat up quickly, craning to look around Annie. *He's here now?* She mouthed the words, disbelief on her face.

"He's the one, Jackie? Cole's papa?"

The girl brought her hands to the sides of her head. "Oh, God, my hair. Damn it. Now he shows up when I look like an old mop."

"Don't worry about your hair. You ain't seen his yet."

Jackie jumped to the bathroom. "Miss Annie, what did he say?" she whispered, frantic now. "It's matted! It's a kinky matted mess. I hate men, Miss Annie. I looked all over the damn tri-state for that—and he shows up now." She fought to pull a comb through her hair. She still whispered. "Tell him I'll be a minute. No, forget that. Just let him wait, damn it."

The little woman scurried from sink to closet and back. She pulled off her sweatshirt, tossing it over her back in Cole's direction. She pulled on a sweater. She put on a touch of lipstick, seeming to calm down a bit after that. Her lips pressed together, then made a kissy sound. "That's all the damage control I can do now."

"Child..." Annie reached out to touch Jackie's shoulder in order to get the distracted girl's attention, but Jackie moved by her too quickly. "Jackie," Annie said louder just as the girl was about to head down the hallway.

"What is it, Miss Annie?"

"Girl, you're a tried and true mess." Annie grasped Jackie's wrist.

Jackie touched at her hair again.

"Naw, I don't mean that. You keep your head about you. From what I know, you ain't oughtta be worrying what he's thinking. He oughtta be worrying what you thinking. You hear?"

A faint smile served as a reply. Jackie pulled her arm away.

"Child? Do you want to bring the baby? You should."

"No. You watch him for me, Miss Annie," she said, looking at the baby for the first time since Annie had entered the room.

Annie went to the playpen. "I think you too heavy for me to lift out of there," she said.

Cole eyed the hallway his mother had just disappeared down.

"Yeah, well, I want to know what's going on too," she told Cole. She tried to wait. A couple of minutes went by, during which she could barely hear the voices in the front room. When everything got quiet, Annie leaned over the playpen railing and dragged Cole over it and into her arms. Her breath came short and quick for a moment. "Like lugging a full pail of water, boy." She carried him with her to the front room.

Little Jackie was on her tiptoes, barely, almost lifted fully off the ground. Her face was pressed into Perry's. Their open mouths gobbled at one another. They certainly made up quick enough, Annie thought.

Perry eased Jackie back to the floor. "Okay, so I missed you too."

"I'm still mad at you," Jackie said. Her back was to Annie and Cole and she did not know they were there until she saw Perry looking past her. "Annie..." Jackie looked exasperated for a second. "Did you miss your son too?" she asked Perry. She crossed the room and took Cole from Annie's arms.

The white boy suddenly appeared very nervous. His eyebrows arched high and his hands tunneled back into his pockets as Jackie brought the baby to him. He pulled them out, with effort it seemed. "Oh, my, he's gotten so much bigger now. Look how big he is."

"We know," Jackie said. Cole cooed something unintelligible directed at his father.

Perry looked at Jackie then Annie, to whom he nodded, then eyed his son, running his fingers over Cole's forehead and sweeping the boy's hair to the side.

Jackie said, "He just jabbers and drools a lot."

"Can I?" Perry brought his hands up to take the baby from Jackie, who handed him over with more care than Annie had seen her use in a long time. Grinning, Perry lifted him toward the ceiling. "Hey, boy, you know I'm your daddy, don't you?"

"He looks more like a Sullivan than a Bell," Jackie said. "Favors your mom a bit."

"Yeah. Mother said she met you," Perry said and brought Cole back down. "Some meeting," he said.

"She thinks I'm stupid, don't she?"

Perry chuckled and shrugged. "Stocking footed on a cold night, peeping into garages? No, she just thinks you're boy crazy or a bad cat burglar. Jaclyn," he licked his lips quickly, "I told her everything."

"You did?"

"Everything. She wants to meet you again and definitely wants to see her grandson. I'm not hiding you two anymore."

Jackie threw her arms around his neck upon hearing that, squeezing the baby between the two of them.

Shaking her head, Annie left them alone. She could not feel happy for the girl then, nor now as she sat on the edge of her bed with Cole's little yellow bus in her hands. She could not say why she did not trust the reunion she had witnessed. It looked too easy. In her experience, a relationship or anything else that came easily only seemed so after someone had worked hard for it. And she did not think Perry and Jackie had worked hard yet.

Annie had told Gail about Jackie and Perry, but Gail had not shown much interest.

"It's not my place to tell that girl nothing, Annie," Gail had answered. "She's got to stumble until she falls. We all do."

Annie placed the bus on the floor and gave it a shove. It rolled until it collided with one of Jackie's house slippers. Her mind shifted from Jackie and Cole back to those long-ago walks to school and the lanky, long-armed shadow who hopped at her heels, the boy who attended school only so he could walk with Annie on the trips, the simple, nappy-headed boy in soiled coveralls, laughing and hunting rocks with Small George. "What did we call him, Small George?" Annie asked aloud. "Some silly name." His mother used to chase him helter-skelter about the field behind their shack, brandishing a raised switch. He'd run to Annie's mother for sanctuary.

"Hide me, Miss Dabney. In Jesus' name!"

Despite his many offenses, invariably Annie's mother would let him slip under her bed or down in the cellar. And the Dabneys would try to keep from laughing when his mother showed up shaking her switch and cursing up a streak. What was that nappy-headed boy's name?

Her hands trembled like scared birds in her lap. After all, this was the only job left to her: to keep alive in memory all those who had gone before. And that was everyone. Joseph, and Mama, and Daddy, and Small George and the nappy-headed boy and Mrs. Buckler—all gone. They had left Annie Gant with her memories. She solemnly owed it to them to remember, a charge to spare them from oblivion on earth until she could rejoin them in heaven.

Annie collected herself, stood, and moved through the quiet of the big house. She went to the windows in the living room and parted the curtains. If she stood to the far left side of the window and looked to the right down the block, she could see the old Buckler house. She wanted to go there, though in all practicality it lay a lifetime away at the end of a very long block. That last walk home from church a few weeks ago had scared Annie. Her leg had hurt her tremendously. She'd never felt so tired. Fortunately, cold and wet weather had forced them to get rides from friends the last two Sundays. Annie wondered if she had many more walks left in her.

More than fifty years had passed since she'd been in the Buckler house. She had thought her life could get no better than to work for the stormy Mrs. Buckler, the mister, and their three sons. Joseph Gant proved her wrong, but that had been a happy house and Annie always felt privileged to have been part of it. Herr Buckler died in 1958 and his dominating frau passed in 1970. Annie had been long out of touch with them by then. "We are going to pick out some beautiful fabric, Anna. Beautiful," Mrs. Buckler had said, "and together we will sew you the finest dresses so when the Gant boy comes back, *ja,* he must leave his heart!" The idea of visiting the Buckler house took on the form of a pilgrimage. "You're the only one I trust to care for my boys, Anna. *Ach!* I trust you more than I do the mister," she had said. The creases in Annie's face deepened, turning up around the eyes and mouth. There would be no one to offer her an arm to cling to should she falter, but she must go.

If all went well she would be back before Tyler came home to check on her at lunchtime. Now that her mind had been made up, she did not hesitate. She put on her rubber boots and long, black, wool coat, and a soft cloth hat that tied under her chin and resembled a bonnet to protect her head. She remembered to get her keys at the last minute. She stepped onto the porch and into a harsh, cold wind that gusted first one direction then the other. She had forgotten her gloves, but refused to go back in the house for them. Instead she slipped her hands into the deep pockets of her coat and began her adventure.

Her bravura fled her the moment her bonnet was nearly ripped from her head. She looked back at the boardinghouse; its fences on either side resembled waiting arms stretched to accept her return. She managed to tie the hat snugly back into place. Looking forward, she leaned into the gusts again. Her head bowed, she saw the chalky sidewalk cracked and broken by the same forces of weather that did not want her to complete her journey. Annie's dogs began to fall into file behind her.

No cars moved down the street. The people had gone to work, the children to school, leaving their neighborhood empty and dull. Halfway to her destination, she became nearly exhausted though her leg had held up well. She leaned against an icy cold lamppost and shielded her face from the wind. "Aren't you the silliest old woman?" she asked herself, her lips barely supple enough to form the words.

On the porch of the house she had stopped in front of stood a tall boy, a young man perhaps; Annie could not tell his age. He wore no coat, just a plaid shirt buttoned to the collar. He had a large round head made to seem all the larger by the misshapen bush of hair sprouting from it. His blank eyes watched Annie curiously in a way that at first frightened her.

"Could you help me, young man? I live just a few doors down..." The rest died on her raw lips because his expression had not changed, and Annie suspected his mind had gone. They eyed each other for a moment. Annie wanted to tell him to go inside before he caught his death from the cold, but doubted he'd understand.

Feeling more rested, she pushed away from the post. To her surprise, the wind had died down appreciably, so instead of heading back to the boardinghouse she continued her pilgrimage. The dogs had not come away with her, fading away ghost-like from her mind again.

This street used to be made of red clay bricks, which had been tarred over long ago. The yards used to be green and even and perfect, the houses painted and shingled and adorned with potted plants, and the white ladies used to stroll to each other's houses wearing wide-brimmed hats against the sun. Annie could look up now and see her destination. With each tiny step she remembered something more about the yards and the walks and the gardens of the old neighborhood. The colored help back then would steal a few seconds to meet each other across back fences and gossip over what the white folks were up to—their adulteries, abuses, and drinking— frailties more damning because of the white folks' extraordinary efforts to conceal them, even from themselves! Their lives could never be so neat and tidy as their front yards. Except, perhaps, those of the Bucklers, who were very much what they appeared to be. Maybe they lacked the imagination to act clandestinely, maybe they weren't bright enough to embrace options to their old world values and ethics, or maybe they were much that more adept at disguising impropriety—or, just maybe, as Annie had convinced herself through the years, they were genuine good hearts.

The pale green house had been a sunny, perky yellow back then, with real oaken window shutters. Mr. Buckler had screened in the side porch so even come dusk and the nervy mosquitoes, the family could sit in the cool evening air, feel the breezes, and watch the comings and goings of neighbors. They always invited Annie to join them. She would lean just inside the doorway and listen to Mr. Buckler's stories of Germany. On some evenings, the yellow-headed boys in their short britches would beg Annie for peach ice cream and she would send them out to the screened-in porch to wait for it, if only to get them out of her hair, while she turned the gears of the ice-cream maker. Ernest, Henry, and young William, good boys, Annie remembered and she added aloud, "Most of the time."

Finally she stood directly across the street from her destination. The house hardly resembled the one she'd worked in. The haughty spirit of Mrs. Buckler had been defeated at last by time, and the wooden frame of the house, without this critical support, sagged in on itself. The paint cracked, and in places the siding hung loose as old skin. She had no desire to go into the house. She could recall perfectly every room and shivered to think how the inside must look now. It had been a mistake to come here, to see the decay up close, to add these sad pictures to the album. The little woman raised her chin. She had fallen in love on the very porch at which she now gazed.

Young William had peeked from the window. Annie had pretended not to notice him. Joseph Gant faced her on the porch, his hat in hand, sporting a dark pinstriped suit and a blinding white shirt.

"Miss Dabney, is it the dress or yourself?" Joseph said. "One has dazzled me, and the other has taken my breath away."

Mrs. Buckler had said to act reserved and demure like a lady, but after Joseph said that all the frau's coaching was forgotten.

A long, dark Cadillac interposed itself between Annie and her reverie. Plumes of white exhaust blew over the car as it idled in front of the house. The tinted windows prevented her from seeing the driver well. She figured this was the current owner wondering why she stared at his property. Let him wonder, she thought. But then the door opened and an elderly white man with frothy white hair stepped out. He wore a suit but no tie and a long, navy blue coat. His attention was definitely directed towards Annie and even as he reached behind him and retrieved a cane from the car, he kept his eyes on her.

Annie's mouth opened. Something so familiar behind the wrinkled lines of the white-headed man's face pulled at her.

"Yes," the man said. "I knew it was you right away, immediately, I knew." He was close to her now, his smiling face a puzzle to Annie, a trick of time. "'Y'all get to bed. Don't let me have to go get y'all's mama,'" he mimicked her from long ago.

Annie walked to meet the man in the street, her arms raised in front of her. "Which one are you?" Annie asked.

"I am Henry Buckler, Miss Annie."

They hugged tightly. Annie could feel his arms through her thick coat. "Henry! Henry!"

"How wonderful. How wonderful. I get to set eyes on Annie again."

They looked at each other briefly and hugged again, swaying this time from side to side.

"I am crying," Henry said. Tears welled in his blue-gray eyes, but he smiled broadly. "I saw you. I could not believe it. I sat in the car and said, Henry you old fool, your mind is gone at last. Oh, Annie. How are you, Annie?"

Words failed her. They would not come out and she thought, *he must think me senile and crazy.* She brought a hand up and touched the side of his face. Finally, she managed, "This is a miracle."

"Not so much a miracle. I come by to see the old place too often. Just to hurt myself, I think. It slowly falls down, like us."

Annie told Henry she lived just down the street and he walked her around to the car's passenger side and drove her back to the boardinghouse. "Too cold for walking," he said.

Over coffee in the living room, they began to fill each other in on the past sixty years in just a couple of hours. Henry showed Annie pictures of his daughter and her husband and the five grandchildren and the one great-grandchild.

"Oh, my. The children look like you and your brothers did. The same eyes, the same faces."

"Yes, I think all things come around. You see it here. Such a circle." He told Annie that Ernest had passed on seven years ago, but William lived with family in Wisconsin.

Annie looked at Henry's face in wonder. She had washed that face, brushed that hair. She had fed him and put him to bed. "My daughter," Henry said standing, "she sends me for milk and I am gone three hours. She scolds me now, Annie. As if she is the parent. I must go." A look of chagrin drooped his face momentarily.

Annie understood. "You must come back soon, Henry. There's more I want to know."

His smile returned, conveying with it undeniable evidence of the boy she had reared. "Of course, and what if I bring some of my grandchildren with me? I want them to meet my Annie. I have told them much about you."

Annie's big grin must have been answer enough for him. He left, having to slip his hand from Annie's grasp.

Annie stood by the door for a long time. What a day. What a grand, great day! The walk had been scary, but she had managed it. Would have done it with ease if not for the wind. And what a blessing she had found at the end of her walk! She had figured the Buckler boys were scattered to the winds, never suspecting one may have returned to town.

Briefly, she recalled the boy on the porch a few doors down, the blank-faced boy without a coat who'd watched her struggle against the wind. His nappy hair reminded her of that other boy who used to follow her down the narrow lanes to school each day. We called him Cholo, Annie recalled with satisfaction; he would hide from a switching under Mama's bed.

JACKIE

Kei's red Volvo rattled to a stop in front of the house inches behind Dan Neighbors's Buick. Kei waved but didn't immediately get out of his car. Jackie nodded in return, preoccupied by greater concerns. From the porch, she gazed down the street in search of Perry's car. At his mother's feet, strapped in his car seat, Cole busily sucked on a fist. The front door squeaked behind them and Tyler came to stand next to Jackie, cradling books in his arms as always. Jackie gave him a quick glance, hoping he'd hurry on his way.

"Hey, you're going to be late to work," he said. "Is that Kei?" Tyler waved.

"Took off today," Jackie said.

"You can't have any vacation days left. You haven't been to work three days in a row this month."

"Ty, what do you want?" She was trying to ignore him, but he refused the hints. It annoyed her when someone brought up her job. "I called in sick, okay?"

"Oh, yeah, this is the big weekend. Cole meets his grandma. You and Perry go off for the weekend."

Jackie continued to gaze down the street, leaning out from the edge of the porch.

"Got something for you," he said. He set his books down next to Cole and pulled out his wallet. "Don't get excited; it's not cash." He produced a condom and pushed it in her hand.

Jackie shook her head. Looking at the plastic packet in her palm, she couldn't help but smile. "I didn't think you were getting around, Ty."

He shrugged, looking suddenly embarrassed. "Well, the boy scouts say, be prepared. And better safe than," he glanced down at Cole, "anyway, better safe." He then mumbled about forgetting something and dashed back into the house.

Kei came up the walk. "Jaclyn, Little J, Cole's mommy! How're we doing?"

"God, don't call me Cole's mama. What are you doing here?"

"You're joking, right?" He placed a fist to the side of his face as if holding a phone. "Oh, Kei, I'm freaked. I'm freaked. I don't want to see this woman again. She probably thinks I'm crazy. She caught me barefoot tiptoeing through her tulips—"

"I didn't say that." Jackie grinned.

Kei continued his impersonation. "And, Kei, everybody there's gonna be white. Real white. The refined white sugar type. They gonna look down their pointed noses at my black nigger's ass and—"

"Now, I know I didn't say all that." Jackie giggled.

"Yeah. You laughing now. You was crying last night. Things looking better now?" Kei sat on the porch next to Cole. "Who's books? I know you ain't reading no calculus." He poked Cole in the belly. The baby gurgled. "Nice dress. Glad you could finally decide. Pleats are a bit preppie though."

"Don't get that demon child started, Kei, unless you're the one who's gonna spend three hours trying to shut him up."

"Uh, uh. That reminds me though." He fished in his pocket and produced an unopened box of Trojans.

"Kei…"

"A new box. You probably already have some, but I find a new box makes a certain statement. It says you're smart and safe without clueing them in on how many rubbers you've gone through in recent history. Nothing's more tacky than being with someone for the first time and you take a 48-count box of rubbers from the nightstand and there's only two left."

"Is that all you people think I'm going to do this weekend?"

"Frankly, yes."

Tyler came running back out, letting the door slam behind him. Jackie quickly slipped the condoms into a jacket pocket.

Tyler asked, "Is he here yet? I'm going to be late to school."

"Then go on, boy. I don't want neither of y'all hanging around."

Kei said, "Hi, Ty. She's ashamed of us."

"I am, so go away!"

"No one's seen Mr. Perry Sullivan except Annie when he showed up again last Saturday," Tyler said, ignoring Jackie.

Dan Neighbors appeared from around the side of the house. He wiped his hands on a rag and smiled at the three on the porch. "Too cold to have that baby outside," Dan said.

In her anxiousness to be away, Jackie had stepped out into the November cold too early, forgetting about Cole. She resented being reminded of what a bad mother she'd turned out to be. She'd bundled Cole tightly, though, in a lined jumpsuit and two blankets. Only his face and one hand was exposed. His nose looked like a pale red berry. "He's okay," she said.

"Hey, Dad," Tyler said. "You missed Mama. She's gone to work."

Dan did not acknowledge that piece of information. "Jackie's big weekend," he said, joining the group.

"Aren't you supposed to be fixing something? And it's just a date. Who told you anyway? Who's the big mouth around here?"

"You," Tyler and Kei answered together.

Dan climbed two porch steps. Still standing two steps below Jackie, he had to bend to put his lips at her ear. A hand lightly held her arm. "Ty told me about your big weekend," he whispered. "I'm puttin' something in your pocket. Cole's too young to be a big brother." He straightened up, smiling, seemingly pleased with himself.

Jackie eyed him suspiciously, slipped a hand in the pocket and felt a ribbon of about six to eight condoms. "I'm going to meet his family, not screw them!" she said.

The men gave her innocent, bewildered looks before breaking into laughter.

"There's some silly niggers around here."

"Here comes a white Toyota," Kei said. "Don't sweat this, Little J. This ain't nothing but a thing."

"Carry my bag to the walk for me, Ty," Jackie asked, but Dan held his son back.

"Naw," he said. "Perry can come pick it up for you." Dan crossed his arms across his chest. Kei did likewise and Tyler followed suit.

Jackie rolled her eyes while picking up Cole by the car seat handle. He was alert. He did not seem too cold, but Jackie tucked his blankets tighter around him. "Go away. You'll scare him off," she said. Dan, Tyler, and Kei stood like sentries around her.

Perry hesitated at the front gate before coming up the walk. He nodded, but only Jackie answered.

"Hey," she said. "We're ready. These are friends of mine with nothing better to do. That's Dan, that's Kei, this is Tyler. Guys, this is Perry, my fella and Cole's old man."

There was some nodding and grunting, the kind of greeting men do when they're acting tough. Tyler said, "How's it going," in a voice much lower than his own.

Kei said, "Heard a lot about you. We were wondering when we'd get a chance to meet."

"Don't let them bother you, Perry. They are probably the three most harmless men on earth."

Perry didn't seem bothered or intimidated. He obviously understood the accusation in Kei's remark; it just didn't worry him.

Jackie slid her suitcase forward with her free hand and Perry yanked it up. "Mostly Cole's things," she said. She shouldered the baby bag.

"Nice meeting you guys," Perry said.

Jackie followed him to his car. She looked back at her three friends. Apparently, they were going to keep up the stony, tough act until Perry and she drove away. She felt funny and self-conscious walking away from them with Perry, understanding that the ease she enjoyed with them wouldn't be present where she was headed.

Kei called, "I remember where the Sullivans live. I can pick you up, Little J."

At the car, Perry said, "That one is precious isn't he? A real flaming fruit." He took Cole from her and strapped him in the back seat.

"He knows who he is, and he likes himself. He's my friend." Perry didn't reply.

During the ride, Jackie tried to relax. After all, everything was going as hoped. Perry wasn't trying to hide Cole and her away nor pretend they didn't exist. Other girls never saw their babies' fathers and had to fend for themselves. To Jackie that was the scariest prospect of all: to be in this alone. The night she had snatched Cole from the floor when he almost ruined her best dress replayed itself in a continuous loop in her mind. For one second she'd teetered. It could've gone either way. She could've killed him. Her heart still jumped when she thought of how close she'd come to disaster. She did not know how she'd been able to stop herself. Something of a miracle, she thought. Suddenly she said, "I'm scared."

"You're scared?" Perry said quickly. "I'm terrified. You don't know this woman. My mother is a take charge, whatever-I-say-goes type."

Jackie turned in her seat to face Perry. They hadn't been think-ing about the same things, but Perry's words burst from him the way people get chatty after doing coke.

"I mean, Jackie, she told me which college I would be attending, what major to take up. Though let's be fair," he held up an index finger briefly, then clamped the hand back to the steering wheel. "She did let me choose between Business Admin and Finance. To say the family is matriarchal is an understatement. She's always in control. And I had to inform her she was a grandmother! She hadn't even picked my wife out yet! Damn, but we screwed with her plans and good." He paused. "God, she took it well though. Very calm."

"She did?"

"So cool it freaked me. The calm before the hurricane. She said, I see. I told her twice because I naturally assumed she didn't hear me right the first time. I told her everything. She's eager to meet you, again."

"Why'd you decide to finally tell her? I mean, you waited for so long." Jackie was instantly angry with herself. That question she had promised herself not to ask.

He glanced her way. Then he looked into the rearview mirror, maybe eyeing Cole. "Look, I don't know. I thought I explained to you."

Perry was getting visibly upset. She had not wanted to anger him. Not now. "It's all right," she said.

"Look, I don't know," he said again. "I told her because she asked about you. She has a way of asking... The FBI could use her. She wanted to know about the 'little barefoot snooper.'"

"That's what she called me? A little barefoot snooper?"

"In the nicest sense," he answered.

Dimly, Jackie caught his attempt at humor. "Then you never planned to say a thing, did you? This all came out because she caught me looking for you, which I shouldn't have had to do. Sounds like you ain't planned to do a thing about me and Cole. See, you don't play me that way, see. I don't want to meet your old lady anyway. You can turn around at the next light and take us home."

The next traffic light came and fell behind them without Perry turning the steering wheel or making a reply. Jackie didn't know if she was relieved or not. Unsure of how she should feel, she only knew she wanted to hold on to this weekend, see it through, and give themselves a chance to work things out. How Perry had told his family about her was disappointing, but at least he had told when he might've come up with a lie. She blew air through her rounded lips. Getting on him now won't help things, she reminded herself.

Perry's neighborhood amazed her. How could people be worth so much, have so much? Lawns stretched far in front of their respective ivy-cloaked estates. Trees rose from perfectly round mulch islands. Evergreen shrubs paraded uniformly between houses and along walkways, used as fencing for privacy. Jackie said, "You live in a park." All of this made up Perry Sullivan, this and so much more she couldn't see. His life had been carefully landscaped, while hers was a dropped seed sprouting where it fell. His mother had insisted he attend Purdue; Jackie's mother had insisted Jackie leave home when her boyfriend showed more interest in Jackie than her.

The car turned into the Sullivan driveway. Perry parked behind a Mercedes.

Jackie asked suddenly, "Think your mom will want a paternity test?"

"She mentioned it. I certainly don't need one. Don't worry about that." Now trying to smile, Perry said, "Look, we're going to both feel better after this is over with. They see the baby, a quick brunch, then an even quicker getaway."

Jackie nodded. "Stay with me." They drew deep breaths, exhaled loudly, and opened the car doors.

The house had polished, reflective hardwood floors and plush area rugs. The sofas and chairs looked elegant but not inviting, nothing you'd want to melt into after a long day at the office. The walls were white. The rooms might have been smaller than at Gail's, the ceiling definitely was lower, yet they appeared airier and brighter.

Perry's parents and an aunt from his mother's side entered the living room from the opposite end after Perry announced his return. Jackie carried Cole in the car seat, grasping the handle tightly with both hands. They approached each other cautiously, like strange cats crossing each other's path. The three of them halted in sync. Jackie made it a point to keep her gaze level during that first, awkward moment. *Don't take no shit,* she told herself.

"Nice introductions, Perry. We really have done a splendid job with your upbringing," Mrs. Sullivan said.

"Sorry," Perry said; his head briefly bowed. He looked more uncomfortable than Jackie. He made the introductions. "This is Jaclyn Bell," he told them—not, Jackie noted, "my girlfriend Jaclyn." "My mother, Mrs. Frances Sullivan, my dad, Mr. Robert Sullivan—"

"Bob," Mr. Sullivan said.

"...and my aunt, Mrs. Angela Rossovich."

They shook hands. Jackie felt Mrs. Sullivan briefly squeeze her hand. She had guessed her to be in her fifties, but now figured the late forties to be more accurate. She had probably been beautiful in her day and that beauty had evolved into a mature attractiveness. Her eyes, the same blue-gray as Perry's, looked hard. She smiled but her eyes did not.

Mr. Sullivan stepped up next. His silver hair sprouted thinly. He wore it brushed back and his scalp shined through. "Hello and welcome," he said. He wasn't smiling so much, yet his face seemed more open than the women's.

Jackie tried to smile. "This is Cole Sullivan." The name snagged them good. Angela Rossovich looked amused. Mr. Sullivan looked stricken with heartburn. Jackie set the car seat on a thin, straight-backed chair. She unwrapped Cole from his blankets and freed him from the hooded jumpsuit. She lifted him up and the trio crowded around. Perry stood away, looking lost.

Any concerns as to paternity must've choked right in their throats. The family resemblance was startlingly clear.

"Oh, Bob!" Now Mrs. Sullivan's eyes lit up.

Jackie thought, *well that's one battle I won't have to fight.* Frances Sullivan scooped the boy from her arms.

In the breakfast nook—a glassed-in porch is how Jackie would've described it—everyone sat around the table with dishes partially emptied to one degree or another in front of them. The nook, situated just off the kitchen, had a glass ceiling overhead that allowed sun to beam down, making it greenhouse warm. Cole had never received so much attention; he sucked it up, removing pressure from Jackie. They asked her several questions, though. She couldn't tell if they had forced themselves to act pleasant or not. She told herself she might be overly suspicious. Angela Rossovich had served the meal. Evidently, the servants were given the day off for this occasion. While her sister had fried the omelets and placed the platters on the table, Frances Sullivan had asked Jackie about her job, where she lived, who babysat while she worked, and did she have good medical insurance. Jackie didn't like the questions at all, assuming criticism in them somehow, but she supposed as Cole's grandparents they had the right to know those things.

Frances Sullivan held Cole the entire time, letting him stand, with her arm for support, in her lap. She kissed his cheeks. "He's so soft," she said. "He's a charmer, don't you think, Angie?"

"Yes."

Jackie wondered if Cole would've been a charmer if his complexion had been more like hers rather than his father's.

"What are your plans for the immediate future?" Frances Sullivan asked at the end of the brunch. "What do you see happening next?"

Bob Sullivan watched Jackie. She took the linen napkin from her lap. "I do a day at a time right now," she said, and this didn't seem like an answer to them; their faces still waited. "Perry and I haven't had time to discuss our plans."

Now they all looked to Perry, who ran a hand across the back of his neck and forked up another piece of his omelet.

"Well," Mrs. Sullivan said, "You two need time to discuss the options, so you are going to leave the baby with us and that will give you time to...well give you time away."

Jackie grinned. "I thought Cole was coming with us?" Jackie asked Perry. He had not spent much time with his son. If the Sullivans were willing to watch Cole, it meant more time for Perry and her to be together. "I don't know what to say."

"Nothing to say, dear. Now, I want you and Perry to begin your weekend, and Cole can stay here with his Grandmother Frances."

Perry said, "I told you who was in charge."

Mrs. Sullivan flashed her eyes at Perry. "You two need some time alone."

Jackie nodded under the pressure of the older woman's persistent smile. "A weekend without the baby is too nice a present not to snatch up."

"Good," Frances Sullivan said, exiting the room. "We're all agreed."

They drove through a countryside of rusty-colored trees and weathered gray barns. The fields stretched away from the road brown or yellow, or totally empty. Perry kept his foot on the accelerator and the speedometer wiggled around eighty miles an hour the entire trip. Jackie had kicked off her sensible low heel pumps and sat Indian style in the bucket seat. She did not ask where they headed; she thought she didn't care. The day had become nothing short of exquisite. Cole and she had been accepted by the Sullivan family— graciously, under the circumstances. Not that she fully trusted them, but it had turned out okay. Gail Neighbors had prophesied gloom and doom. Just because Gail had given up on getting her man, she tried to get Jackie to give up too. Obviously, Gail didn't want anybody happy in that monster house of hers. No wonder Dan left her. No wonder Mason left her too. Maybe now it was Jackie's turn. Perry and she could get a place, a cute little apartment for families just starting out. That was the likely next step. And marriage! Now that his family had met her...She felt she had done fine. She didn't care what they thought of her, really, but it was important to Perry, and she thought she'd carried it off. The navy skirt with the pleats had been the right choice. She'd looked smart and together. And except for getting whiny toward the end, Cole had behaved better than ever.

"I want to move out of that tired boardinghouse," she said. "My landlady gets on my last nerve. She's one of these church-going-think-she-knows-it-all nig—folks. Always telling people what to do." Jackie waited for Perry to respond, but he said nothing. "See, she was all right when I first moved in. But we stay out of each other's way nowadays. She used to watch Cole and..." Perry wasn't listening. "...and let me go to bed with both her sons at once. We'd do a six ninety-nine kind of a thing." No reaction.

Jackie scooted over to sit partially on the console between the seats. Perry glanced down at it, briefly scowling.

"I ain't gonna break it," she said. "I don't weigh enough." She placed a hand at the back of his neck, felt the cords beneath his skin. "You driving the car and you ain't even here." She peeked around to see if other cars were near. Perry would soon be overtaking slower cars in front, but she only grinned. An audience would only make it more fun. "I know how to relax you." With one hand, she straightened his fly and with the other, unzipped it.

"Jackie."

"Now you'll pay attention to me." She fished into the folds of his briefs and freed his penis.

"Jackie..."

She lowered her head. "Mama said not to talk with my mouth full."

The Inn-on-the-Knoll looked like Gail Neighbors's boarding-house—enough to make Jackie frown.

"It's a bed and breakfast," Perry tried to explain.

"I thought we'd go to Six Flags in St. Louis or up to Indianapolis or something. This ain't much different than where I live, Perry," she said.

He waited for her to follow him up the winding flagstone walk. "Come on, give it a chance. They have a lake in back and stables."

Everything was country inside, that rustic, homespun look Jackie hated. The wallpaper had large patterns of birds and flowers. A painted wooden plaque depicted geese wearing aprons and galoshes. The furniture was heavy wood with dark, varnished knot-holes. Dried flowers and cattails leaned from clay vases. Pumpkins and striped yellow-green squash decorated table tops. If not for the desk in the front room, it would have looked like anyone's home. Behind the desk hung a framed cross-stitch of a dog flushing quail.

"Have you been here before?" Jackie asked.

Perry said, "You're not supposed to ask that." Then he added, "Yes."

His first genuine smile of the day he gave to the thirtysome-thing woman in jeans who checked them in.

"We have two rooms available for you to choose from, Mr. Sullivan," she said. "One overlooks the lake, the other, a part of the Hoosier National Forest. So what'll it be? Fish or fowl?" She held up a room key in either hand.

"Fish," Perry answered.

The woman led them up the stairs and down a narrow hallway to their room. She opened the door and handed the key to Jackie with a bright professional smile. "Dinner tonight is pot roast, any time before nine. Temperature's gonna drop tonight. My husband would rather guests be too warm than too cold, so don't be surprised if you have to close off a vent before he melts you. Enjoy your stay."

"They serve dinner," Jackie said, closing the door after the woman.

"Brunch too," Perry said.

"Brunch," Jackie said. "I never heard the word til you came along. Think it's a white thing?"

"I think it's a people-who-don't-have-to-get-up-early thing." He set the suitcases at the foot of the bed, then flopped backward onto it. He groaned as if exhausted.

"What is there to do in this hillbilly hotel? Besides the obvious." She leaned over him and slowly lowered her weight onto him.

Face to face, they examined each other. Jackie liked Perry's long eyelashes, and she loved his boyish mouth; he could look so devilish with a smile. She kissed him lightly, tracing over his upper lip with the tip of her tongue. He responded, covering her mouth with his.

"I don't think straight around you, Jackie," he said. "Did you know that?"

"Yeah, most guys don't. Hey," she kissed him again. "Look what I got." She dug into her jacket pockets and displayed the condoms over his face. "New fashion for the nineties. You can have a safety headband." She put a ribbon of condoms across his forehead. "With the new box, I think we got about thirty-three cock cozies here. Goodbye gifts from my friends. You might have to run out for more before brunch."

"Great. Where were your friends about seventeen or eighteen months ago? This mess might have been avoided."

"What mess *haven't* you avoided, Perry? Hmm?" Jackie pushed herself off him. A helpless part of her warned that she was about to run off at the mouth. "You've avoided the dirty diapers, the slobber that goes everywhere, getting pissed in the face when you change him. You done avoided that mess. And hunting for babysitters and getting up ten times through the night, and falling asleep at work, and the screaming and hollering that drives me up the goddamned wall." Even as she spoke she realized she was saying too much too fast. She stood and turned partially away from Perry, aware her eyes were filling with tears.

"Can you lower your voice?" Perry said. "You probably manage to out-holler the baby."

Jackie kicked once at Perry's dangling legs. He sat up. "No, I can't lower my voice!"

Perry said, "Jesus."

"I'm trying to explain!" And she repeated herself, lowering her voice, "I'm trying to explain what it's like, raising a kid by yourself, and you can't explain it to someone who ain't done it. You can't. He takes all the space, that little boy, all the time. I got to feed him, or change him, or watch him, or hold him, and it's all on his schedule. He takes it all, drains me dry. No time for nothing, not to see nobody, or do nothing. He wears you out, and if you manage to get some sleep he wakes you up. Teethin' or spittin' up or just twisted his blanket, or dropped his toy out the crib and can't get it. I wish we'd been more careful too! Damn me if I don't. Drains me. I lose myself. And I'm afraid cause I think I want to hurt him sometime. Really just..." She held her fists up to her mouth. "I get scared." The tears did not fall until she blinked her eyes.

Perry rubbed a hand through his hair.

"I been wantin' to get away for a long time now. Get out and do something fun. Get out of that boardinghouse. And you take me to another house just like it. So you can hide me away, and fuck me."

Perry stood and went straight to the door.

"Where are you going?" Jackie asked.

"You want to know what mess I wanted to avoid? This mess!" he said. He jerked the door open and slammed it closed behind him.

Jackie followed him out to the hallway. "Perry, damn it!"

He pushed past a couple coming toward him. They looked behind them at Perry, then eyed Jackie.

"Who you lookin' at?" Jackie said and returned to her room.

She kicked the suitcases, pulled off her shoes, and flung them across the room. "God damn it. God damn it," she said, stomping about. She hurried to the window to see if she might spot Perry going to his car, but the parking lot could not be seen from there, just the dreary gray lake they'd driven seventy miles to see. "Damn it!" She was aware that she trembled, that her heart raced, and that she wanted to find Perry, but didn't trust herself to say the right things. "Oh, fuck it," she said and took off her jacket and skirt. In her half-slip and blouse, the little woman curled into a large and, she thought, ugly chair by the window. It was very comfortable. She looked toward the lake. The wind scraped foam caps from its surface. Cattails and bobbing reeds ringed it and two gray wooden docks pierced it from the near shore. There was nothing there to see or appreciate. Why had he brought her here?

She did not know what had happened. One minute they had been kissing and joking, and the next she was jumping down his throat and he was storming out. She wondered why she had to say everything on her mind. Why had she voiced every grievance she'd promised herself not to bring up the second they were in the room? She tried to formulate her thoughts so she could know clearly what to say to Perry when he returned. She sat for an hour giving herself suggestions and dismissing them before falling into a fitful sleep in which she could hear faintly, as if from an ocean away, Cole crying.

Hours later, Perry nudged her awake. "Let's go get something to eat," he said.

Jackie dressed in jeans and a peach blouse. She teased at her hair a little bit and followed Perry down to the dining room. She couldn't remember any of the things she had figured to say and Perry wasn't speaking either. With the dining room all to themselves, they had a quiet dinner of pot roast and carrots and thickly sliced chocolate cake for dessert. He commented that he thought the food was good, and Jackie quickly nodded her agreement. She smiled over a bite of the rich cake, and Perry smiled back. He said something about the beams in the ceiling and the fireplace, and Jackie said, "Yes," and smiled again.

"Perry," she said when again in their room. She had remembered a point she'd wanted to make, which was that she wasn't usually a nag and didn't like being bitchy. But it sounded too much like the apology she didn't want to give.

"Don't worry about it," he said, making it seem as if he'd extracted the apology from her anyway.

They took turns in the bathroom. Jackie had brought only the silk lace nightgown that hid nothing. She hoped they would cuddle up in bed, talk things out, then make love.

Perry sat at the foot of the bed in his boxers. He looked at the palms of his hands at first. "I didn't plan this well. I guess. But I didn't plan any of this. I mean about us, and Cole and my mother, and the future. I haven't planned a fucking thing about my own life yet. And I didn't bring you here to screw you." He looked up at her then. "I brought you here to tell you something," he said.

Jackie was suddenly very frightened of what he'd say next. She walked up to him and stood between his knees. Her fingers brushed over the blond hairs on his legs. "You don't have to say nothing," she said. "I've said too much already. Talk doesn't always mean something. Like this morning, I was just tired, Perry. Babies cry when they get tired sometimes." She laid a hand on his chest, gently pinched a nipple between her index finger and thumb, and felt him shudder from the touch.

"Stop it, Jackie," he said.

"You stop it," she said. She stepped closer to him so that one of her legs rubbed the crotch of his boxers. She kissed the top of his head. Behind her, she raised her nightgown over her buttocks, brought one of his hands to an exposed cheek and pressed his fingers between her. She kissed his forehead and her tongue spread over an eyebrow.

"No," he said, but his hand squeezed her butt.

She straightened up, held his head against her chest. Suddenly she was lifted into the air in a quick spinning motion, an arm's length over Perry who twisted around and slammed her down on the mattress. The movement was so quick it almost took her breath away. She giggled, thinking he played, believing he only wanted to get her quickly onto the bed, but then saw the fixed stiffness in his face, his eyes hard like his mother's.

"Stop it," he said again. And he jerked his hands from her, showing his palms like a basketball player professing not to have committed the foul. "Just stop it. I need to think. You think I brought you here to hide you away? Or just to screw?" He bit at his thumbnail a second. "It wasn't even my idea to come here exactly," he said, taking the hand away.

Jackie had not seen him like this before. Not ever. He looked timid and scared. Not scared of her, but of something, the room or what it held with them in it. He seemed on the verge of panic. This boy she'd always associated with fun and ease, who seemed as though his whole life was avoiding problems like gliding over tree tops, now looked as if he might leap to the door again at any moment. His white skin betrayed him so easily, draining from a balloon red to a pale chalk. He said it again, "It wasn't even my idea. I didn't know what to do."

Jackie pulled her nightgown down from around her waist and sat up. Perry couldn't keep his eyes on her. The fear Jackie saw in them kept her from getting angry, kept her quiet.

"Mother told me to bring you here. But," he held up a palm, "I thought it a good idea. We used to have family horseback rides up here. Mandatory attendance. Like everything else." He grinned while shaking his head. "Jackie, I stayed up at school not to avoid you and the baby exactly, but to avoid Mrs. Frances Sullivan, the woman who keeps one of my arms pinned to my back." His voice had a nervous tremble in it. "I haven't been free. I haven't made my own decisions. She makes them. When do I get to be free? You've been on your own. I never have. You and I aren't anything alike, really. And it's not just race. You know I don't care about that. It's everything, really. You and me, we were just supposed to have fun." He took a step back. One hand pulled the fingers of the other. His quavering voice sounded like begging. "I am not getting tied down now. Sorry. There can't be a me and you. Can't. Sorry, okay?" He finished all the lines and arguments he had no doubt neatly prepared yet nervously jumbled together.

"What about Cole?" Jackie asked quietly. Now she admitted she always knew it would be this way. Either because she was black and he was white, or he was rich and she was poor, or he was educated and she was not, or he wanted to be free and she was part of a trap, it would play out as she'd truly known all along it must. She thought it funny, that knowing all that lessened the hurt not one bit. "What about Cole?"

"Cole's our son."

"We could take things one day at a time," she said, not certain what she meant by it.

"Just go to bed, please? Please?" The face he showed her pleaded, looking tight and on edge. "We can leave in the morning. Please, just go to sleep, please?"

Jackie scooted to one side of the bed. Neither of them got under the sheets. He turned off the light. The light in the bathroom had been left on, putting his face in silhouette. After an hour, maybe two, of lying in the silence, Jackie moved toward Perry. She didn't know if he'd fallen asleep. She eased her body against his.

"That wouldn't change anything," Perry said.

Monday morning, Jackie was running late. She had neglected her laundry. By the time her ride blew her horn the second time, Cole and she had on the cleanest of their dirty clothes. First stop was the babysitter's to drop off Cole.

CeCe Greene, twenty-six years old with no children of her own, sat for five kids all under four years of age and made it look easy, as far as Jackie could tell. But five kids for eight or nine hours couldn't be as tough as one for a lifetime. When Jackie held Cole out for CeCe to take, the babysitter frowned.

"I'm running late," Jackie said.

CeCe touched two fingers to Cole's forehead. "Girl, your baby is feverish. Bet he's got that flu going around. All the school-aged kids are dropping like hail."

Jackie felt the side of her baby's cheek; it did feel a little warm. She felt embarrassed she hadn't noticed. Cole looked at her, his eyes half closed. "Have you got something here for it? Some children's medicine?"

"Uh-uh. I start dispensing medicine and the police will put me under the jail. You going to have to take him on home, or better yet to the doctor."

From the street, Jackie's ride tapped her horn twice.

"CeCe, I got to get to work. Take him for now. I can't miss any more work." She held Cole out for the woman who took a step back.

"Can't risk the other babies catching it, Little J. Can't."

"CeCe, I can't miss no more work." The car horn sounded again. Jackie hollered for her friend to wait another minute. "Please," she pleaded to CeCe, but the babysitter only looked to be getting angry.

"You don't want him spending the day here if he's getting sick, Little J."

"God damn it!" Jackie exploded. "What a funky bitch you are." She spun about and scurried back to the car.

"You skinny shit! Learn to take care of your kid," CeCe shouted after her.

Her ride was angry about having to take Jackie and Cole back home. "Now I'm going to be late for work too," she said. When Jackie stepped from the car, the driver reminded her, "And you owe me for two weeks gas money."

Jackie returned Cole to his crib. He began to cry almost immediately. She gave him a dropper of medicine left over from the last time he'd gotten ill, but only one more dose remained. "You sick, boy?" She felt around his face. Yes, he was hot. How had she missed it? She pulled up a chair next to the crib. Guilt kept her by his side throughout most of the day.

She had to call in to work the next day also. Her boss, Mrs. Tremaine, had heard the my-baby's-sick excuse too often in the past and had very little compassion left.

"Can't somebody else watch him, Miss Bell?" Her boss had said the last time she called in. "We are falling behind here. The other girls are trying to cover for you and it's not fair to them."

She briefly thought about asking Gail or Miss Annie for help. But Gail and Jackie had been on the outs ever since she had left Cole alone that night to go searching for Perry. Plus Gail had made her leery of trusting Annie with the baby for more than a second at a time.

Her phone call to Perry was very unsatisfying. "Maybe I can get over there to see him," he said. "I'm job hunting. I've got interviews."

"He's doing better, but I still couldn't go to work today. He'd like to see his daddy," Jackie said. But Perry didn't stop by.

Cole cried all day, it seemed, so much that Jackie couldn't even think. She remembered calling CeCe Greene a bitch, and wondered if she'd made the woman too mad to ever babysit for her again. Her anger at Gail and Perry grew. Cole's crying persisted. Miss Annie called something from upstairs. "I've got him, Miss Annie," Jackie answered. Jackie pressed her hands over her ears. She wondered if she should have gone to the doctor for more medicine. Then she thought, through Cole's screams, that it would have been a good idea to make Perry go get it. Then he would have to come over.

He'd asked her, "When do I get to be free?"

Perry had pushed her away at the inn when she had thrown herself at him. She had curled up on her side of the bed, feigning sleep, waiting for his hands to squeeze her shoulder, for his arms to slip around her waist, for him to pull her to him, whisper that everything would be all right, and slide over her.

"Damn it, boy!" Jackie leaped to the crib. She rocked it violently, so violently the casters came off the floor in turns, front then back. She was trying to startle him into silence. "Shut up, shut up!" She shook it again and again. The baby was jostled to the far side of the crib and struck his head on the wood slats. Then he was still.

Cole did not move. Neither did Jackie. She didn't know what had happened, how she came to be at the crib or why the baby lay awkwardly on his side against the rails with his head wedged in a corner. The confusion lasted maybe two seconds, feeling like two minutes. When her mind unstuck, an overwhelming horror clutched her. Cole wasn't moving! She dropped the crib's side rail. She reached for him, saw her hands hesitate over his little form, then lifted him. Cole shrieked. Red-faced and frightened, he wailed with his mouth gaping wide.

"Damn, boy." In her relief, Jackie was smiling while patting Cole on the back. He clung tightly to his mother with a fist full of T-shirt. "We scared each other that time." On the top of his head a long, narrow bruise began to show, shaped like a crib slat.

Wednesday she called Mrs. Sullivan. The woman agreed to help her; in fact, she seemed eager. Perry came out to pick up Cole.

"I need some money," she said to him, and she did; there might not be love, but there had to be money. Jackie saw no reason to fear asking for it now.

He looked pained and subdued. Mostly, he tried not looking her way at all. "Here." He emptied his wallet in front of her, handing over nearly sixty dollars. "I'll see you get more. We'll work something out."

She nodded.

He said nothing more, simply walked out with Cole in the car seat.

When he left, Jackie thought she should've had him wait and give her a ride to work. Then it occurred to her she should've already been dressed to go. But she hadn't done either of those things and felt incapable of organizing herself or entertaining more than one thought at a time. She dressed quickly, chased down a bus which nearly drove past her, and, by eleven o'clock, was sitting before her computer. At eleven-twenty, Mrs. Tremaine called Jackie into her office. By eleven-thirty, Jackie was fired.

To make certain Jackie didn't walk out with anything belonging to the firm, Mrs. Tremaine and another manager stood over her as she emptied her desk of personal effects: three issues of *Essence* magazine, a framed picture of Cole, an extra pair of panty hose, and various junk. She shoved it all into her purse. The other girls in the office sneaked glances at her from under their bowed heads. Embarrassment flushed Jackie, making her hot.

"Motherfuckers," Jackie said. She stuffed her handbag. "Act like I can help it if my kid is sick." She overturned a file, by accident the first time, but then emptied another and another, letting the loose paperwork cascade over the desk and onto the floor.

"You're not hurting me by doing that. The time it takes to reorganize those files will come out of your last paycheck," Mrs. Tremaine said.

The man next to her swallowed nervously.

"Bitch," Jackie said. "I had to stay with my kid!" Though two heads shorter, Jackie faced off against Mrs. Tremaine. She pressed close to the woman and could smell her scented talcum powder and perspiration. "You tight-assed, cracker-lipped *bitch*."

Mrs. Tremaine's eyes blinked rapidly and her lips twitched.

"Enough of this," the man said. He pushed an arm between the two women.

"Fuck off," Jackie said, but she did step back. She stared fiercely at Mrs. Tremaine.

The woman said, "Thank you for making me feel better about my decision, Miss Bell." She turned and went back to her office.

Jackie glared at the man whose stern face didn't match his nervous eyes. From around terminals and filing cabinets, all eyes watched her unabashedly now. She was aware she could end the awkwardness by just walking out the door, but the finality of it kept her there, frustrated that her only power to affect the situation was to prolong it. Even as Jackie had cursed her, her boss had been in total control.

"It's okay, Little J," someone said, "ain't nothing."

"Just fuck it," Jackie said and dismissed the man in front of her with a wave. Dry-eyed, nostrils a bit flared, she strode from the office.

She boarded the wrong bus and sat with her face toward the window. The tears, forbidden to emerge while she'd been in the office, slipped from the corners of her eyes. When she finally realized she didn't recognize the storefronts and buildings the bus passed, she pulled the cord and stood rocking in the aisle until the bus stopped.

She waited at another stop, one with a protective overhang and wind barrier. The temperature had dropped all day and now a chilling wind swept between the buildings.

A hugely obese woman sat lazily on the bench with her legs splayed out in front of her. She wore tube socks, the only partially clean item on her. Within the Plexiglas wind blind, she smelled. Jackie would not sit next to her.

A man in a long, black, tattered, and soiled coat hustled inside the wind blind. A red knit cap perched on his head like a crown. He said to Jackie, "Gone bitter to bitter ain't it?" He smiled; between each tooth, brown matter had caked up. He dropped next to the fat woman, saying, "Couldn't uh, find it." He seemed to eye the fat woman cautiously, then slipped a hand under her coat and sweater and settled it over one of her large breasts. His hand rhythmically squeezed and unsqueezed the breast.

The woman didn't appear to notice. She looked up with lidded eyes at Jackie and smiled. The red-capped man pushed his face into the woman's swelled cleavage. He looked like a mosquito feeding upon her.

Jackie fled the bus stop. She took haven in the doorway of a shoe store for a minute before deciding to walk the entire distance to the boardinghouse. She held close her pocketbook, almost as she would her baby, plump with the items from her desk.

Miss Annie had guests: a well-dressed old white man, a couple in their thirties or forties, and three children were in the living room with Annie when Jackie walked by. Annie looked very happy. Everyone in the room smiled. The smallest child, sporting blond pigtails, accepted a cookie from Annie.

Annie looked up at Jackie and frowned. "Is everything all right, girl?" she asked. "Where's Cole? I haven't seen him in a while."

"Cole's at his daddy's," Jackie said. "Everything's cool." She nodded to the guests but didn't stay for introductions.

Finally in her room, her fingers and toes tingling from the long cold walk, Jackie released a whine not unlike Cole's. She dropped her purse and coat, kicked off her shoes, and threw herself across the bed. She wanted to call Kei, but he would still be at work. She picked up the phone to call Perry, then thought better of it. What would he think about her getting fired? At any rate, she didn't think it would make her feel any better to talk to him.

Though it was only afternoon, she felt suddenly very sleepy. She wondered how much unemployment insurance would pay her. It wouldn't be enough. The image of the gritty-toothed man snuggling at the fat woman came back as she began to drift in and out of consciousness. "Bitter to bitter." Isn't that what he'd said? Yes, she concluded bitter to bitter sounded just about right. She hadn't slept well for several days, but now slept heavily.

Night had fallen by the time she awoke. Moonlight came in her window. The room held shadows, dark twins of furniture, lamps and scattered clothes against the walls and floor, and a cozy, conspicuous silence. Lying with her face half immersed in her pillow, she immediately identified the silence; it was the sound of no one crying for her.

She called the Sullivans and spoke briefly with Perry's father.

"Cole is a well-behaved little boy," he said.

"Must be an act," Jackie said. "He's lying to you."

Mrs. Sullivan got on the phone. "Jaclyn, we took Cole to a pediatrician, a wonderful doctor, really. He gave us something for his cold. Hope that's all right?"

Jackie remembered the bruise on Cole's head, wondering what the doctor had made of that. "Thank you. Yes. He was just about over it though."

The line fell briefly silent. "We've enjoyed having him. He reminds me of Perry as a baby."

"Is Perry there?" Jackie asked. "I really need to talk to him."

"Certainly," Mrs. Sullivan said. Jackie heard the receiver set down on the other end. After nearly a minute, she heard "…just left." It sounded like Perry's voice from across the room; Jackie felt sure it was Perry. "Jaclyn," Mrs. Sullivan said, "I thought he was here, but I'm afraid he's stepped out. Is there a message?"

He probably stood right next to her. "Mrs. Sullivan, I was wondering if you'd keep Cole another day. It would help me out a lot, plus I don't have a ride lined up to get out there." Jackie found herself fighting back a sudden desire to cry. She wanted to demand Perry get on the phone. "And…and Perry's already made one trip out here today."

"That's no problem, Jaclyn. We're more than happy to keep him. It's nice having his energy in this house. We'll keep him as long as you like," Frances Sullivan said.

"I'll pick him up tomorrow," Jackie said.

After hanging up, she crawled from the bed. Her office clothes were wrinkled and twisted. Her arms and legs seemed heavy. She did not feel rested. Everything had come down on her now. "Oh, man," she said. "Sonovabitch, Perry, oh." She shuffled from her bedroom. Her feet were cold. She sniffled, tasting a tear that had fallen into a corner of her lips.

Light from the kitchen spread down the dark front hallway. The smell of ham cooking on the stove and the sound of its sizzle in the skillet ranged down the hall too. The little black and white portable TV Gail kept in there was on and Jackie heard its buzzy, quick voices and canned laughter. She heard Annie's soft laugh too. Annie and Gail often prepared meals together. Annie would come down to peel potatoes or help set the table. She would be there now trying to find something to do.

Gail crossed quickly in the light from refrigerator to range.

Jackie remained in the darkness. She crossed her arms subconsciously against the draft in the front room. In this huge house, the kitchen lay at its heart, warmer and brighter than the other rooms. Jackie took a step toward that heart, then hesitated. The hallway looked like a tunnel, a dark vein. "Screw it," she said.

Returning to her room, she climbed back in the bed. She called Kei. No one answered. She let the phone ring maybe twenty-five times.

Kei picked up Jackie after he got off work the next day and they drove to the Sullivans'. He'd already heard from a friend of a friend of Jackie's firing.

Jackie wore faded jeans and her white leather jacket. She hadn't done her hair and knew she probably looked ratty.

"You're black, Little J. You should've known your baby wasn't allowed to get sick. Though sometimes your baby was sick when he wasn't the least bit sick." He smiled; she didn't. He quickly added, "But they didn't know that. You ever notice blacks can't get away with dirt the way whites can? They can't. Not that whites are sneakier or anything. Although I believe they are. It's just that everybody is already suspicious of a nigger from the get-go. He tries something and they pounce. Confirms what they suspected all along. Blacks have to remember that." He went on with such comments about her firing and what she should do but Jackie didn't listen. Kei's philosophy couldn't help her now. Eventually, he asked how her weekend with Perry went. "You ain't said nothing about it so I imagine it wasn't all you'd hoped."

"No, it wasn't all I'd hoped," she mimicked.

"Well? Bad fight? Or bad sex? In the dating game, bad fight is preferable to bad sex, by the way."

Jackie didn't answer.

"Okay, what did Mr. Sullivan say? Did he call you a fighting name?"

"Dumped," she said.

"You or him?"

"Me," she said.

"Oh, shit, Little J, I'm sorry. It's been a bad run of days for you, hasn't it? What did you do? I mean, why'd he dump you?"

She shrugged. "Had a baby. I guess."

Kei pulled up to the Sullivan's. Perry's car was not in the driveway, of course, and Jackie couldn't say if this disappointed her or not.

"They told me Cole behaved," she told Kei. "He'll turn back into a screaming monster soon's he lays eyes on me. He hates me. Not even a year old and he already hates his mother. I didn't hate my mother til I was ten."

Kei looked as if he wanted to say something but changed his mind. He finally said, "I'll wait here."

A black woman in a clean white uniform answered the door.

"Hi. Is Mrs. Sullivan here?" Jackie asked.

"Girl, is that your baby?" the woman asked.

Jackie nodded. "Yes."

"I seen Mrs. Sullivan runnin' around doting on that baby. I *thought* there was somethin' in him. I said, that baby's got a bit in him from somewhere. Come on in. Come on in."

The woman escorted Jackie as far as the living room, then disappeared to locate Mrs. Sullivan.

Mrs. Sullivan appeared without Cole. She wore dark slacks and a light gray cashmere sweater. "Cole's with Mr. Sullivan in the den, Jaclyn. Did I tell you, by the way, I like the name you chose, Cole? Is that a family name?"

"I just like it. You know, like Natalie Cole."

"Oh. I see. I love Nat King Cole, too. That voice, it's like silk for your ears," she said. "We have a surprise for you. Tell me, how are you fixed for baby things? Crib, bassinette, diaper pail, blankets, stroller?"

"I have all that stuff." She didn't have everything she could have used, but some part of her warned her not to admit it. There was something about the way Mrs. Sullivan stood, the way she held her shoulders and head, that convinced Jackie she had been a fool to think she and Perry would ever be together.

"Good. That's good. Come on," she gave Jackie's upper arm a squeeze and a gentle tug. "I want to show you something."

"My ride is waiting on me," Jackie said.

"I won't keep you a minute or two," Frances Sullivan said. "Speaking of names, I'm glad you named him Sullivan. That was the right thing to do."

She wiggled a finger and showed her perfect, too-even-to-be-natural teeth.

"Ah, Jaclyn, I need a friend. We've been working around here. Well, Debbie and Mr. Sullivan have been doing all the work. I've been playing peek-a-boo with Cole, who doesn't seem to tire of that game, by the way."

Jackie followed her up the stairs, noting the framed art on the wall, the softness of the runner, the glossiness of the wood, the height of the ceiling. She made a conscious effort to not look like she was looking.

She felt tired when she got to the second floor. She was tiring herself out, thinking of Perry, pushing away the impossibilities and seeing nothing left to the future she had once envisioned. Jackie stopped.

Frances Sullivan continued, saying something that Jackie didn't make out. Jackie wondered where the den was so she could find her boy.

"Well, come see," Frances said.

She sensed a trap. It was a funny thing to think, but she was wary as she walked past Mrs. Sullivan and into a nursery. There was a crib and changing table, a chest of drawers, a cushiony upholstered rocking chair, a day bed opposite the crib, and bookshelves with board books and kiddy books on them and stuffed animals peering down. It was a bright white room with one blue wall.

"A lot of this was Perry's. Then we bought a few things. I told Mr. Sullivan that I want to freshen up the paint." She watched for Jackie's reaction.

Jackie glanced her way and then pretended to be looking at the blue checked curtains. Everything in the room looked so nice. A prince could grow up here. Perry had.

"You see? We're ready to babysit any time you need us."

"Oh, that's great, Mrs. Sullivan. Really? I may have to take you up on that. I can't afford babysitters these days."

"It must be hard."

Jackie finally looked the woman's way. There was a smile for her there, but she couldn't read it, and she knew she couldn't trust it.

"I lost my job," she said, surprising herself with the admission.

"Oh. Sorry to hear it. You work with computers, don't you?"

"Yeah. For a kitchen supply wholesaler." The woman already didn't think much of her, no need to hold anything back now.

Mrs. Sullivan sat down on the day bed and crossed her legs.

"I don't know what I'm going to do."

"That's tough. It's tough being a single mom. Let alone looking for new employment."

Jackie felt sure the woman would offer her some money. If she could just get enough to get Gail off her back and tide her and Cole over until she found another job.

"Any leads?"

Jackie shook her head.

"I know how we can help. We can take Cole for you. Look, you've got to update your résumé, get it out there, follow up on leads…you need a bit of breathing time, right?"

Jackie nodded. She wanted to sit down in the rocker, but did not.

"We have this lovely room. And we're both retired, or semi-retired," she laughed, "I don't want to sound too old, empty-nesters with lots of time on our hands. Cole already loves it here."

"I'm sure he does."

"Look, I know Perry should be helping you. And I'm sure he'll do his fair share." She shook her head. "He's a good boy, a good young man. Maturity does not arrive for all of us at the same time. Even if it's thrust upon them."

Jackie wondered if she meant her…the thrusting.

"Let's do this. Let's get Jackie the time she needs to sort things through, huh?" She looked excited. She brought her knees together and slapped them with her hands.

Jackie tried to think. She had lost Perry. She was trying to find a way to hope that things could still turn around.

"Okay," she said. "It's a very nice offer."

"You know, so that if the baby were to get sick…is he up on his shots? Do you have insurance? What with losing your job?"

"I don't—"

"I'll tell you what. We will get some papers worked up. Giving Mr. Sullivan and me some authority so we can take him to the doctor, authorize treatments just in case, that sort of thing."

"Um, I guess so."

"Great." She clapped. "Am I being pushy? It's just, you and Perry need time…he's not much of a catch right now. But you hang in there."

"You think so?"

"I see he likes you."

"You do?"

She made a face, a dip of the eyebrows that said, of course.

Mrs. Sullivan's sister leaned in the doorway and looked at them sitting there, and said, "You see, Jackie, the benefit of having the keen inability to throw anything away?"

Frances Sullivan laughed. "I've tried to tell them you never know when something might come in handy again."

"So baby Perry slept in this crib?"

"When I could get him to go to sleep, yes."

"Must be like father, like son, because I have a hard time getting Cole to go to sleep, too."

"Angie, we are going to help this young lady out. I'm going to get Mr. Sullivan to wake up those lawyers of his and get some papers drawn up. We'll get Cole on our health insurance plan and get something for Jackie to sign."

"Oh?"

"We will be co-guardians or something. I don't know the legal terms."

The sister laughed lightly and glanced at Jackie.

Jackie saw the sisters looking at one another. The entire time Mrs. Sullivan had been talking, Jackie had felt the insult, had known what the woman was really offering; how stupid did the woman think she was?

"Sounds terrific!" the sister said.

Jackie crossed her arms, holding on to her shoulders. "My ride is waiting on me," she said, having just remembered. "I'd best collect Cole now."

Mrs. Sullivan appeared to ignore the tone in Jackie's voice. "Yes, let's see where our precious is," she said.

Cole wore a Pamper and a dirty T-shirt with snaps at the shoulder. He sat on the bed with his mother near the footboard playing with a doll that had one silk sleeve, one corduroy sleeve, and a denim chest. Cole examined it studiously like a little scientist. He distracted Jackie from the newspaper want ads, those small-print boxes offering small chances, which she had spread out in front of her. She'd been looking at them for the past hour without really seeing them. She couldn't concentrate. She thought of Perry and his mother's offer. Cole could be a Sullivan, but she could not.

"Hey, Miss." Gail Neighbors startled her. She stood in the doorway, obviously angry. She held a torn envelope in her hand.

"What now?" Jackie said.

"This now," Gail said shaking the envelope. "You are not going to treat me this way." She pulled a letter and a check from the envelope and let the envelope fall to the floor. "This is your rent check.

This is the letter from the bank to me informing me my account is overdrawn and that this check bounces higher than a basketball."

"Oh, shit," Jackie said. She grabbed her handbag that sat on the floor by the bed and dug out her checkbook.

Gail said, "You just don't give a damn, do you? I don't get it. You make a mess of your life and now you're going to mess with mine by destroying my good credit. You don't understand how important credit is in this world, do you?"

"Gail," Jackie opened her checkbook ledger. She hadn't kept up with the math. The truth was she didn't know how much money was in her account. "I'll make it good," she said.

"I know you'd better. Shouldn't be bad in the first place. I've got bills to pay too. You don't have your head on straight, Miss. Leaving this baby alone, skipping work just to chase after that boy. You better get your priorities straight 'cause he's the one who's going to suffer." She pointed to Cole.

"Get off my back! I'll get your money. The rest of my business ain't none of your business."

The shouting scared Cole. He started whimpering, holding his hands in front of his face.

"I want my money and soon!"

"All right."

"I'll need cash to take to the bank."

"Okay, damn it. You're making the baby cry."

Gail took a deep breath, glancing at Cole. "When did you start caring about that?" she asked. She stepped to the bed, tore the bad check in half and dropped it in front of Jackie.

"Get out of my room," Jackie said, but Gail was already on her way out.

Jackie knocked her handbag and checkbook off the bed with a sweep of her arm. With a second sweep in the opposite direction, she sent the newspapers and the bad check floating to the floor. "Damn it!" she shouted.

Cole gaped at her.

She grabbed him up quickly and held him against her. She let herself fall back so that she lay diagonally across the unmade bed with Cole on top of her. "Boy, your mother is falling apart." Cole's little hands grabbed for her bottom lip. She let him pull it before turning her face from his grasp.

"So when do we tell her I lost my job?"

After a bit of squirming, Cole fell asleep with his head at Jackie's chest and his fat legs on either side of her stomach. The winter sun, slanting in the window as it did, warmed the both of them. The baby had grown too heavy to lay atop his small mother, but she endured it, grateful for any time with her son that was quiet and restful. The bruise she'd given him made a short blue-purple line on his scalp. His breathing was rapid and raspy. She stroked the infinite softness at the back of his neck, that dimpled spot in the middle. He must weigh fifteen to twenty pounds, she guessed. He probably had lost two or three pounds in the last few days from his bout with flu.

She had too much to think about, so she tried not to think of anything. She only wanted to enjoy the warm light and this brief time-out that held nothing in it, no demands, no responsibilities. Jackie stared at the ceiling, which was high up in this old house and noticeably warped. The light fixture of milk-colored glass had dark specks at its middle where moths and camel flies lay dead and dry after having been seduced. Cole stirred. Jackie held her breath. Tiny fingers brushed her neck, then curled into rest. Tears on either side of her face trickled into her ears. She whispered to the sleeping infant, "You'll have a better life with them."

GINA

Gina Manara trudged uphill along the gravelly road leading to the little house she rented with her boyfriend. From this high up, the ranges of dark purple mountains looked like a forbidding wall sealing her in, or the world out. The air was already brisk, smelling of wet pine, car exhaust, musty loam, and the undergrowth that lined the roadway. The hardy vines, which could grow between rock, and the scruffy, black-green scrub pines waved and nodded like a cheering crowd whenever a car sped by, then settled down as the parade left them.

The thought of another winter up here on the rim of eastern America almost crippled her. Yet like the old folks, she could feel it coming; a taste in the air or the furtiveness of the wind as it moved around and through you with more purpose now gave away winter's approach. The oldsters had taught her to heed these sorts of subtle alarms. "Rain today," they might say and know it with far more surety than just an educated guess. Something to do with living high up in the hills, she supposed, being that much closer to the schemes and machinations of the heavens.

The snow could fall for days, hush this entire world, and remain on the ground for endless lingering months. The hills became an ocean of the purest white waves. The little houses became tiny, imperiled ships bobbing on the current. Gray smoke, twirling up from the chimneys until the wind dispersed it, marked the only signs of life on the bitterest days, the days when even the children and their sleds did not venture outside. On days like those, she could count the houses in the surrounding area by the plumes of smoke, even the houses obscured by the hills or stands of pines. Gina knew and feared that overwhelming isolation, feeling cut off completely from the world beyond the snow-laden hills.

Mr. Oates's pickup came up from behind her and matched her pace. Mr. Oates tried to talk without rolling the passenger side window down. He had big bumpy features resembling the hills he'd lived in all his life. He had a wide mouth, and his efforts to talk through the glass and over the rough groaning of the truck engine looked comical. Gina smiled. She refrained from giggling, afraid Mr. Oates would misinterpret her. He was asking if she wanted a ride. Mr. Oates's offer surprised her. She declined with a shake of her head, then realized that had been a mistake. She had pushed away an olive branch by spurning an opportunity to socialize. Mr. Oates shifted gears and the truck jumped up the steep road. Her neighbors, the Oateses and the rest, all but ignored Gina and Carl these days. Tully claimed the cold shoulders were because of his wheelchair; Gina did not believe that. The fight between Gamble and Mason did not help things, nor the fact that Mason remained. The neighbors did not understand his presence.

She switched the plastic sack of groceries from her right hand to her left. She didn't dwell long on her slight of Mr. Oates. She was thinking she did not want to spend another winter on this hill. It was probably true she'd been thinking that since her return. What a goof! She had gotten away, all the way back home, only to turn around and come back.

The hill grew steep where she walked now. On the narrow shoulder of the road, dirt and tiny, grainy rock crackled under foot. She had to look down frequently to avoid stepping on the larger rocks that might turn her ankle. She was in good shape, and used to find these walks invigorating, but this time she could not shake the feeling of dread hanging over her. It had nothing to do with the approaching winter; it had everything to do with Carl Tullis.

Love is a state of mind. She had heard that in a Fleetwood Mac song. If that were true, Gina wondered, why can't I just change my mind?

Gina had given up on him, exonerated herself of responsibility for him at last, and gone home. And every day she was back in Indiana, she'd felt like a deserter and a coward. Her fear was she would return to the little house on the hill and find Carl Tullis dead.

This fear was well founded. He had said he would kill himself. On two or three occasions, flatly and matter-of-factly, as others might say "the Pirates dropped another one," he would say, "I'm going to have to finish this off soon." That was his coded way of saying it so Gina and he could pretend she did not understand what he meant. One afternoon, when the piss bag from his catheter overspilled onto his lap and the seat of his chair, he had said, "I can't live this way. Not me. I can't." He had been very embarrassed by the spill, though they had been alone in the backyard at the time.

Other people in wheelchairs learned to redefine themselves in time, discover their new limitations and then challenge them. Tully dreamed of steel beasts. He said he'd dreamed his chair was alive, that the wheels were actually huge eyes and the seat was the thing's mouth. The beast promised to carry Tully around and not to eat him. "But then I learned the beast is full of guile, and gets hungrier every day." Tully sat in the maw of the beast.

"Uh-huh. That's what he said? How come you're the one being chewed to death?" Maxy, the woman who for all practical purposes was Gina's mother, had asked her that. Gina had not answered.

She loved Tully. He had seemed the wisest, deepest, most sensual man she'd ever met. He could see through and around anything, had a considered opinion on any topic and never feared to state it. And the sex they used to enjoy. Few men had found her appealing, what with her scarred face. Tully had told her she was beautiful, physically beautiful, sexy even, and he'd meant it. He had loved her with such a fierceness the memory of it made her shudder. In California, they sometimes raced from classes to their apartment, kissing each other and pulling at one another's clothes as they went. Down the long hallway of the apartment building Gina would often be stripped to the waist or worse before getting to their door. Passersby would gawk or shake their heads. Gina didn't care. Inside, they rarely made it to the bed. Tully would pin her to a wall or the door; taking his surges against the wall would somehow hurt and feel delicious at the same time. The memories of those days in California could sustain her always, she told herself; it was enough good sex to last a lifetime. It would have to.

Still a little ways off, she could see Tully's sign now, "Give a Ramp, America," throwing a thin shadow across the yard. He wanted more businesses to grant access to handicapped people, build ramps, widen aisles and doorways, lower water fountains— as if he would ever come down off his hill and go anywhere. Mason crossed the yard to the road and headed toward her.

"Hey," she shouted. His hand came up lazily in reply. She wondered where he might be going. Sometimes he and Tully went down the road to the truck stop or to the Trailblazer Inn for drinks, but Mason never went down there alone. "Where you heading?" she called.

He did not answer until he stood an arm's length in front of her. "Right to about here," he said and relieved her of the groceries.

"Damn. Manners. I had no way of seeing that coming."

Mason smiled, or almost did, and fell into step beside her. That was just like him, to try not to smile. He seemed—and Gina had searched for the right word a long time—guarded. He acted as if he held a deep secret, something he could confide to no one. For some reason he held himself in check, tried always to curb himself. Yet he made frequent slips. He'd forget himself and begin talking about the time his family went to a storefront church, or how he helped his stepfather do carpentry work in his family's boarding-house, or how he'd sit up with one of the boarders, an old lady he called Miss Annie, and listen to her talk about the people she once knew. He was a phony, Gina had concluded. He pretended to be a loner when in reality it seemed he craved company. Gina sensed he was up to something. The act wasn't just show. He was up to something involving his father in Washington. That much he'd let slip on their way here when they'd stopped at the roadside grill in Ohio. Also, he'd talk about any member of his family, when in the rare talkative mood, but never his father. And when Tully would ask him what he planned to do in DC, Mason shrugged, or said, "Just see what's there."

He walked next to her, holding back his long-legged strides in order to stay with her, and said nothing.

Gina liked having him around. He was something to add to the mix of her and Tully. He was tall. Gina barely came up to his shoulder. And she thought he had pretty brown skin, and restless eyes a shade darker. He fidgeted a lot, like a large dog in a small yard. He tapped a hand on a leg when sitting out on the porch, or patted a fist against an open palm anytime he had to wait. Gina figured his coming down the road to greet her stemmed more from his impatience than from courtesy. Better, he would think, to go to her than wait for her to come up the road. His bruises had healed. Gina wondered how long she would be able to keep him on the hill.

"Are you going to ask me how my day was?" Gina watched him, but he stared straight ahead. He had small ears, a bit too small, but he had a strong jaw line.

"Naw," he said.

She stopped, but he kept walking, forcing her to jog to catch up with him. "You don't give a damn what kind of day I had, Mason?"

"Now, I didn't say all that."

"Sounded like it."

Now he smiled her way. "Gina, you work in a town that's nothing more than an exit ramp off the highway, sweating in a grocery bake shop, selling nasty donuts to old white folks who look at you without saying thank you, count their pennies, and hope you didn't put your black hands on their powdered jelly roll. The question isn't how your day went, but what can we do to turn it around?"

Gina grabbed hold of the sleeve of his jacket, lightly, at the elbow. "The old men around here pay extra if I touch their donuts. What have you done to turn my dismal day around?"

"I cooked."

Gina was about to flick her hair to the side to make sure Mason saw the look of mock astonishment on her face, but then she remembered her pocked cheeks, as she always did, and let her dark hair hang like a protective curtain. "Did you?"

"Beans and franks."

Gina laughed. Mason looked at her as if nothing was funny. "Beanie weanies? Well, that certainly uplifts my day, Mase. I done died and gone to heaven."

"I use brown sugar, and bake it with strips of bacon on top."

Gina kept laughing. She stopped walking again. This time Mason waited for her. She covered her face with one hand and laughed behind it.

"It's good," Mason was saying.

She snorted. "I'm sure it is."

The three of them sat on the porch in the evening after dinner. The shadows of the taller mountains fell to the east. The sun had found a niche to settle in between two far hills. The sky blazed with color, red across the horizon and higher up a pastel purple. A large flock of small birds, looking like black darts, banked together in an amazing display of unanimity and dropped into the trees across the road, where they screeched and chirped noisily.

"Wonder what all those birds are shouting about?" Gina asked. She sat propped against a wheel of Tully's chair. Gently, he stroked her hair. Mason sat in front of them, his legs dangling down the ramp.

"Nothing except where to find the next worm," Tullis said. "Food and mating calls is all they chirp about, the ornithologists would tell us." Tullis's fingers caressed Gina's cheek. She caught his fingers and held them. They felt dry and calloused.

She said, "And speaking of worms... That was a great meal, Mason."

Mason leaned back to look at her. "And how was your day, Gina?"

"Simply fantastic." She and Mason grinned at each other.

Tullis asked, "What was so great about it?" And when Gina only shrugged against the spokes of his wheel, he said, "I could use another beer."

"Me too," Gina said. She let go of his hand and jumped to her feet. She asked Mason if he wanted another one. He shook the can in his hand, then nodded.

Just as she let the screen door close, she heard Tully ask loudly, "Mase, you still planning on heading out this weekend?" She hovered just inside the darkness of the living room, listening for the answer. He had not mentioned leaving this weekend to her. Then Gina realized Tully had asked that question for her benefit. He'd waited until she left but was still within earshot. He would be listening to hear her steps to the kitchen and she hurried to the refrigerator.

The surprise should have been that Mason had stayed at all, let alone two months. Still, she felt caught off guard, even though each morning she'd quickly peek into the living room to discover if his bunched form with sprawled legs still filled the sofa, and when she came home in the evening, if he was not about, she checked to see if his duffel bag still sat at the side of the sofa. She cradled three cold beers against her side while trying rapidly to think of what she should do.

The chain on the screen door rattled while she stared blankly into the refrigerator. Tully wheeled into the kitchen. His chair drew up next to her, between the kitchen table and the refrigerator, blocking her way out.

He looked up at her. His eyes searched wide open. "What else do you want?" he asked.

She did not understand. "What do you mean?"

"In the fridge. Looking for a snack?" He pushed the door closed when Gina shook her head. He wore a yellow sweatshirt with the sleeves raggedly cut. His muscular arms erupted from the sides of the jersey. His hands clamped on her waist. "You've been preoccupied ever since you came back here. Looking over the next hill."

She said, "No," not really certain of what she was denying.

"I know it's a good thing you've been doing. Trying to save that young brother. But if he wants to go down to DC and find trouble, there ain't a thing you can do about it." He let a hand slide behind her, over her butt. "I think he wants trouble. But there is a brother you can save. You can save me, Gina." He stretched his neck, tilted his face toward her while reaching for her upper arm. His lips parted.

She leaned to him, said, "Mind the beers," because he pulled on the arm cradling them, and gave him the kiss he wanted. The bristles of his beard scratched. His lips pressed hard against her mouth as his tongue passed over her lips.

He whispered, "My nepenthe."

She pulled up, smiling. "There's no such thing. Take your brewski." She dropped a can in his lap. "I better get Mason his." Then she asked, "What did he say? Is he going?" She tried to push him and the chair just far enough back to get by, but he slapped a hand on a wheel.

"You can't avoid me by keeping him here."

Gina tried not to show any reaction to that beyond shaking her head.

"It's true."

"Tully, try to think of someone besides yourself. I know it'll be taxing for you, but give it a shot."

"Most of the time, I only think of you. I only want what's best for you. You should know that." He held her upper arm, trying to pull her down for another kiss.

"I know you don't keep me on this hill for my benefit." She pushed at the chair with her leg and managed to squeeze by him.

He let his hand slide from her arm. "I want you to wait up tonight." His back was to her now and he did not turn around. He missed the hesitancy on her face.

"Silly, we'll go back together—"

"No." Only his head turned, just a bit toward his shoulder.

Maybe he saw her from the very corner of his eye and so she smiled, not wanting to argue, wanting to just go back to the porch and see the remainder of the sunset. "Sure, baby," she said.

Dusk fell, deepening the shadows in the valleys. One by one, lights from surrounding houses and those below spotted the hills. Gina had not given much attention to the sunset. Tully had rolled to one end of the porch and begun a harangue about the sound of the highway, how it never quits, how the hum and rumble of it backdropped everything. He spoke interminably. Mason didn't seem to mind, but Gina couldn't tell if he listened or not.

"Think of how many people must be on that road for the noise to never end. How many pass by each minute, the sound of one flowing hot after the sound of the other, so tight you can't discern between them," Tully said. "At least not from here."

Mason shifted, leaning his back against a porch support, his legs still stretched in front of him. Gina sat cross-legged on the other side of the ramp, trying not to listen to Tully but, in doing so, hearing every distracting word.

He said, "Where are they going? Sixty, seventy, eighty miles an hour. With no better idea of why they are going than you do, Mason." He paused after this little jab.

Mason glanced briefly his way. He began tapping a hand to the side of his leg.

Tullis kept going. "We've become migrants. As migratory as those birds we saw, but a lot less efficient. Everyone zips here and there after greener pastures. It's like they think they'll find happiness growing somewhere, a plant found in a specific region or climate. No one puts down roots, builds communities, invests time. It's all fast food. No production, just quick service, hell, no service except self-service. The if-it-absolutely-positively-has-to-get-there-overnight mentality. No wonder the Japanese are rubbing our noses in it. People should keep their sorry, never-satisfied asses at home."

Mason leaned toward Gina. "Did that make any sense?"

She did not answer. "The people aren't afraid," she said and had time in the silence following to regret opening her mouth. But it was clear where his diatribe against driving and highways would lead: to the accident that had cut him in half.

"What's that supposed to mean?" Tully asked.

"Look. Is all this shit about me staying put?" Mason asked.

"No, Mase. Tully doesn't expend that much energy for someone else's benefit."

"Good. I don't have to tell him to shut the fuck up."

A truck rattled by. The driver appeared to slow down long enough to read Tully's sign before winding away downhill. When the sound of the truck disappeared, only the highway back-drop Tully had railed against remained.

With a quick shove he sent his chair gliding across the porch to Gina. "You didn't tell me what you meant. 'The people aren't afraid.'"

She stood and opened the door. "I'm going to see what's on TV," she said.

"Bring us out some more beer," Tully said.

"Fuck you," she said.

Tully chuckled. "Guess that means no beer." His voice carried inside quite clearly through the screen door along with weak light and a chilly breeze. She curled up on the couch and looked around for the remote, but since it wasn't near at hand she chose instead to sit alone in the dark.

A tear rolled down to her mouth, where the tip of her tongue caught it. She tasted its saltiness. Her hands, nearly of their own volition, played in her hair, and she held her elbows tight in front of her face. *Why did you come back, Gina?* she asked herself. *Why did you think leaving him would scare him off this hill?* That hadn't been the plan. The plan had been just to leave, to abandon him to this place, let him sit in the mouth of the beast alone.

"Well, you've heard, brother, what DC is like on the news. Gotta have a plan, man."

"I just want to get it over with. The trip I mean."

"See, it's just like I said, people going every which way for no reason at all." Tullis's voice was heavier than Mason's, and smoother. He was calm now.

"No. It ain't like that. I know what I'm up to," Mason's voice replied, but he did sound unsure, Gina thought.

"Nothing personal, but everyone thinks they know what they're up to. Most don't. They bounce along reacting to whatever the world sets in front of them."

"What do you care, man?" Mason's voice rose on edge quickly. "You'll be ear-to-ear teeth when I book out."

Tully's voice said, "Our Italian-African-American friend in there won't be so pleased. And she'll take it out on me when you're gone. You're her puppy. She thinks of you as a stray. She told me so herself."

God damn him. Gina's fingers dug into her hair. She had said that to Tully once, but hadn't meant it as he'd put it.

Mason's voice came back softly and Gina had to strain to hear it. "I can't relax. I been here months and I figured this is what I needed maybe, time out. But..." After a pause, he said, "Don't matter much. Nothing does."

The men did not speak for several minutes. Gina's mind turned on Mason's words. They had leaked from him like a confession. The interstate hum filled the silence from the porch. Tears ran over Gina's lips and chin; she didn't know if they fell for her or for Mason. She felt unhinged. Sitting in shadows, she felt a common sadness for everyone, for Mason, obviously lost, and for Tully, crippled and afraid of the world, and for everyone else who was heartbroken or disillusioned, or who felt trapped or helpless.

She had missed Tully's beginning, but now she heard, "...on my way to New York. Driving this old '74 Javelin, another extinct species. I was going to meet Gina there. We were going to finish school in the east. Meet the challenges of the Big Apple."

Oh, yes, Tully, Gina thought, as she pressed the tears from her eyes with the palm of a hand, *tell your story, let's not let the moment belong to someone else's pain.*

"I don't believe we had a plan, Mason. Gina had gone there on vacation with some girlfriends, loved it and we decided to do it. Soho, the village, Manhattan... I wanted to see it all. Radio City."

"How'd y'all end up here?"

"How did I end up here? My folks used to live nearby. This used to be the last place I wanted to be when I left for California after high school. They live in Hagerstown now. Just far enough away. We don't speak much, but they do send money. Anyway, I never did see Greenwich Village. Never did walk down 42nd Street. I got into a car accident on a stretch of interstate in Pennsylvania. Smashed into a car in an intersection, one of those bus/wagon things."

Mason's voice said, "I figured you got hurt in Vietnam or some-place."

Tully's laughter followed. "Yeah, well that's the army jacket I wear. Scares people; they don't ask stupid questions." He continued, "The wagon rolled on its side and my Javelin flipped completely over. Never saw it til I hit it, I swear. Made the whole thing seem unreal because it happened so damn fast and I never saw it. This was late into the night on a deserted little byway—"

"Hold up, man." Mason's voice was on edge again. Gina leaned forward from her vantage spot. "I don't want to hear your story. I mean it. Go wheel down to the Trailblazer where you got everybody thinking you're some kind of war hero. Tell it to them. I ain't volunteered to get unloaded on."

Gina grinned, biting her lower lip. She wished she could see Tully's face.

"Your problem is you think all this crap matters," Mason said. "Well, don't look now, brother, but it don't matter a stack of shit. If you go or stay, who the fuck cares? You're a nothing nigger just like me." Footsteps sounded on the ramp.

No reply came from Tullis. Gina rose from the couch. In the darkness, she shook a fist in the direction of the front porch, before heading down the hallway.

She went in the bathroom, used the toilet, then stood in front of the medicine cabinet mirror while putting paste on her toothbrush. The sad feeling hadn't gone exactly, but she did not give herself over to it. She saw a mischievous smile on her face in the mirror. How many times had she listened to Tully's accident story and wished she'd told him, I don't want to hear it? That seemed inspired! She wished she'd said it just once.

By now she knew the story as well as Tully did. He had made her feel it over the years, suffer it along with him: the tumbling nightmares in which the steering wheel came to life and spun out of his hands. He had jerked at the squealing of tires, the rupturing metal, the glass bursting, showering like hail, the rapid, rolling confusion and lack of control like falling into a kaleidoscope—the panicky, horrible abruptness of it all.

And when the earth had settled down to its natural axis again, the real fear had begun. Flat on his back among shards of stabbing glass, the wait, the helplessness that started and would never really go away. The dread that his entire world had changed but not knowing how. A red taillight from the car or the minivan glowed nearby, reflected a hundred times in scattered fragments of glass. He could feel the slick greasiness of blood. At first, lying on the pavement, he'd managed to stay calm, but as no help arrived, as no sirens were heard, a flighty wildness took over. The scary smell of gas filled his nose. And the hot metal of the cars ticked like a time bomb. He attempted to move, he slapped at the car, pushed at the road, and the pain rushed in. He screamed. And then suddenly stopped. Somehow intermingled with his screaming he had heard it: the weak, plaintive cry from the minivan not far away. It was a child's cry, a soft, raspy whine, full of hurt. It did not understand. "Little baby? Hold on, little baby. They are coming to get to us." The whining persisted. Time stopped. But the crying went on. He couldn't see the child. It must've been in terrible pain. "Little baby? Oh, God! Is someone here?" He tried to turn his head. Something cut at the back of his neck. "Won't someone help us? There's a baby here." The crying continued mindlessly, on and on. To Tully's horror, he wished it would stop. "Someone? Please, hold on, little baby. They're gonna come for you. They haven't forgotten you." Yet he thought the world had forgotten them, like trash flung on the street. Finally his wish came true: a cruel quiet. "Baby?"

Gina finished brushing her teeth and her hair, the long, thick, tangled product of her mixed heritage. She went into the bedroom, undressed except for her underpants, and pulled on a light, pink nightgown. Then she remembered Tully had asked her to wait up for him. She bit at her left thumbnail for a moment, looking like a perplexed young girl, then pulled her panties off. She climbed into the middle of the bed.

During Tully's hospital stay, a couple of days after the accident, he'd received an after-hours visitor, the woman who'd driven the minivan. She had suffered a concussion in the accident and hadn't regained consciousness until reaching the hospital. "She still had scars on her face and bandages around her head," Tully had told Gina. "She handed me a framed picture. A photo of a bright-eyed toddler with a pink-gummed smile. 'That's Susan,' she said, 'my baby girl. You killed her, you drunken son of a bitch,' she said, and her hate gave her shakes."

They had accused him of being a drunk driver. He denied it and they could never prove it. "I just didn't see them," he said. "If I was drunk it was from lack of sleep. I hadn't been drinking."

Tully said he had cried, and fumbled through an apology. He didn't remember what he said, and doubted the woman heard him. "She said, 'Have they told you what your prognosis is yet?' And I slowly shook my head. I had been badgering my doctor about it, but they had told me they weren't certain yet, that I'd have to wait for the results of more tests. She smiled—she fucking smiled, but I don't blame her. I don't. She said, 'I heard the doctors discussing your case this morning; you are going to be paralyzed for life. For life, you son of a bitch.' That was how I found out. I cried. I think I screamed. The woman walked out. At the doorway she told me I could keep the picture."

Gina lay still in bed. He still had the girl's photo. It was somewhere around here; Gina recalled seeing it. *Aw, Mason,* she thought, *Maybe you should've listened to Tully's story.*

The sound of Tully's rubber wheels over the hall's linoleum signaled his approach. Gina stiffened, though she tried to relax into her pillow and into the mattress. She closed her eyes most of the way, feigning sleep, waiting. From under her eyelashes, out of the corner of an eye, she saw him waiting too from the doorway. This was the only variable in the game, the only bit of suspense for Gina, because on occasion he would back up and retreat out to the porch or, more likely, to the kitchen to get a bottle and drown himself with it. If he wheeled in, the rest of the play followed the script. He coasted to the bed and she closed her eyes completely.

For a while he would only look, checking to see if her eyes were really closed and watching the rise and fall of her chest. His eyes would follow the contours of her body. She had peeped before as he indulged this voyeurism. Then his hands joined his eyes, gently flowing over her breasts and stomach, pausing to squeeze the vital, useful muscles of her calves and thighs.

Gina disassociated herself from the game. It was for him. She remembered California. They sprinted across the campus lawn. She pulled his T-shirt over his head. They laughed breathlessly.

Finally, Tullis began his climb. His arms pulled him from the chair. He grunted. Gina felt the mattress dip for his added weight. She was not allowed to move. Not allowed to help. He huffed and puffed in strains of exertion that must have been partly faked. His elbows shoveled him forward and he pulled that dead half, the un-cooperative weight of him along, moving not like a man at all. Gina would not look as he made his ascent. He maneuvered between her legs, grasped them by the ankles and controlled them, lifted them up and apart. His hands ran up her thighs, bunching the fabric of her nightgown before them. He pushed the hem past her waist, nib-bling and licking at her inner thighs all the while, biting sometimes, and Gina sucked in her breath at the tiny pearls of pain his teeth produced. Small dots of blood would blossom there and an edgy, warm, needle-like hurt. A rhythm started somewhere in her body. Her shoulders dug into the mattress. Her weight was supported by the back of her neck as the small of her back raised. His spread fingers cupped her buttocks as his nibbling climbed higher into her inner thighs. Bruises from his grip would mark her for days. A feather-thin gasp came from behind her teeth. Now her hands were permitted to move. Roughly, she grabbed the back of his head, clawed into his hair, and held him in place.

Well into the lost part of the night, Gina stole from the bed and Tully's side. She did not put on the nightgown she'd discarded earlier, merely held it against her in front as she slipped from the bedroom. She tiptoed down the short hall to the living room to check on Mason. It only took a moment.

GAIL

She awakened in the gloom of the bedroom with a start that for a second constricted her lungs. "My baby," she said. The words came out as little more than a coarse, worn whisper dissipating only inches from her face. Her throat could no longer form words over the rough and raw tissues of her voice box. So she listened. Her fingers dug into the spread collected at her waist. A car, maybe a truck by the heaviness of the sound, drove by on the road out front. Wind blew through the vineyards out back. That was different; the air had been so stagnant here. She listened for the cries of the baby. Only the wind could be heard, mimicking a cry in a way, and the fading sound of the truck some distance away now. She tried to move. The pain between her legs reawakened, crackled to vividness, causing her to moan and move her thighs farther apart, wanting nothing to touch anything else down there. A hand slipped under her chin, massaged her throat. She had not wanted to sleep. Had promised herself to remain alert and listen for clues. Now voices came, growing closer and rising in anger. "I don't give a damn what you had to handle. And you, you ain't family. You shut up." She recognized his voice.

"This is my house, joker." And that would be Alice Durkee. Steps marched hard down the hall, toward the bedroom door, and it burst inward. "Baby Girl?" The round man with the round head filling the doorway was her father. Her arms and hands reached for him. She tried to say, "Daddy."

"What they done to you?" His bulk crashed into her, his arms locking her to his soft chest. He turned his head away from her for a second for the benefit of the women who hung back out of the doorway, saying again, "What they done to you?" He turned his bulging eyes back on Gail. His down-turned eyebrows looked like wreaths over his eyes. Sweat slicked his brow, formed rivulets in the worried furrows across his forehead.

Gail tried to speak. She had to tell him what had happened. She touched her stomach. "My baby, they took it," she said.

"You done had a baby, child? When? How come you can't talk too good? Where's this baby? Does your mama got it?"

Gail nodded to the last question. "Been hollerin' for it," she said. "They done took her." Tears flowed and her nose ran. Both hands closed around her stomach. The last place she had seen the baby was upon her stomach, where Alice Durkee had laid the newborn as soon as she'd come out, wet and wrinkled with delicate, minute fingers grasping at the air. "Daddy, find my baby." Gail gripped her father's shirt and buried her face in his chest, smelling his sweat, feeling his heat.

He patted her head. "Shh, shh, now. We gonna get that baby. You can believe that. I'm gonna have some police down here quick. Nora, where's this child's baby?"

"If police come, you'd be the first one they'd take, Charlie," Nora Wallington said from the doorway.

"The girl's distraught," Alice Durkee said. "Her baby didn't survive. It was born dead."

Gail held her stomach. The haunt pressed against her, that small weight that had briefly rested there. Lillian in the first minutes of her life had rested there and Gail could feel the weight, the movement of her, hear her crying, informing the world that she was a living, breathing, integral part of it.

For a moment she could see her father's eyes, so big they seemed to be squeezing from their sockets. He was making a promise to her with his eyes. *I will find your little girl,* they promised. A bump and a knock sounded in the hallway. "Daddy?" Gail asked, but already he had disappeared from her bedside. The heavy sweat and skin smell of him vanished and the mattress recovered from the sag of his mass. Gail awakened at the bump and the knock to find herself sitting up in bed holding her stomach. She rubbed a hand across her belly.

The clock on her bed stand stated six exactly in glowing LED numerals. She supposed she'd slept sometime during the night, but had no notion of when or for how long. It didn't matter. Her body had been trained over the years to awaken at six a.m. no matter what, even if it was Saturday and she did not have to get to work.

She heard the noise again, a knock as if something heavy had hit a wall or a door someplace down the upstairs hallway, near Mason's room. She did not get up to investigate. Over the years she had owned the seventy-year-old house, it had groaned its settling sighs nearly every day. It had its own forces at work within its walls and flooring, much like the fault lines under California. She listened to what it had to say, but paid little attention to it.

She was thinking of the lie Alice Durkee told her father. Lillian had not died. But the lie had given Charlie Wallington, gambler and loan shark, reason to pause. If the baby was dead, no good reason existed to involve the police. Gail had heard him, before Alice Durkee ushered him from her house, demand to see the baby's body. How would they have lied their way out of that? It didn't matter. Two days later the situation had brought on the heart attack that killed him. Though he had not been around much of her childhood, Gail remembered her father dearly. He had flown to her bedside when she'd needed him most.

The noise bumped and knocked again, more deliberate than the settlings of an old beam, and Gail slipped from her bed. She went to her door, then on second thought retrieved her robe from the back of a chair before venturing out of the bedroom.

She determined the sound had come from the little kitchenette on the second floor, a narrow room held together by successive bad coats of paint—white in the fifties, pink in the early sixties, and a loud, sun yellow in the seventies, each layer so sloppily applied into hinges and corners that it never completely hid the evidence of the previous coat. The room had one skinny, dusty window at its far end, over the sink. Painted shut, of course. They'd never really gotten the kitchen back to fully functioning order. The sink, fridge, and stove took turns breaking down.

She stepped toward the kitchenette cautiously, her mind fully in the present; her eyes instinctively searched for something she could heft as a weapon. She passed a little stand in the hallway, quickly unplugged the ceramic lamp, and pulled off its shade. She held the lamp by the neck and tiptoed forward.

Dan lay under the kitchen sink, his torso and legs stretching out into the room. He made grunting sounds along with the clink of a wrench against metal pipe. He fished around the edge of the cabinet doorway with his left hand, seeking a way to brace himself to best exert his strength against a stubborn fitting.

Gail adjusted her robe around her without relinquishing her lamp. A hand moved to check her hair, but she pulled it down. She didn't speak for a full minute, but rather simply watched one of his legs rock back and forth with extra energy between the moments when he marshaled himself for another try at the pipe. This all seemed so familiar—frighteningly so, as if she had not made it all the way back to the present from her dreamed reminiscences of twenty-five years ago. She had come up eight years short, stuck in some trick of time. She and Dan had just bought the place and spent their every free minute hammering, painting, and scraping it into shape. How natural it would be for her to say to him, "How many eggs do you want?" or "You want bacon or sausage this morning?"

Gail would usually be the first one awake. Sometimes she'd put her feet to his back and try to shove him from the bed. "Up and at 'em!" she'd say. Now and then he would get up, scratching and yawning broadly. Most of the time, he'd fight back, grabbing her legs. It was always more fun when he fought back. Finally, either way, he'd go to whatever project they'd abandoned the day before and growl for her to bring him coffee. She would rush it to him. He always wanted too much sugar. "Keeps me sweet for you," he'd say, so she made it the way he wanted. Sometimes she'd find something to do in another room, but he didn't like that much. He wanted to talk, to explain how he planned to fix a door or something, or he'd insist he needed help just to keep her near. He liked the audience. At least, he liked her for an audience.

Gail wondered if she might not still be asleep. Like Scrooge she was being visited by a queue of haunts from her past. First her father had returned to her bedside, and now Dan was performing early-morning chores in their house.

"How many eggs do you want?" she asked to test the dream.

Dan's head jerked upward. The thump it made against the bottom of the sink sounded painful. "Oh, shit."

"Sorry," Gail said, but she smiled.

Dan scooted from under the sink. He rubbed the crown of his forehead. He looked at her a moment before saying, "Hey."

"Hey."

"How did you know?" he asked. "That's just what I needed. I can hardly see a damn thing under here."

Gail looked at the lamp in her hands.

"Sit it there." He pointed to a spot next to him and near his toolbox. "We must be on the same wavelength, like they say."

Gail did not move except to turn the lamp right side up. "I don't think we are. What are you doing here?"

"What's it look like? Knockin' this old kitchen back in order. I'm thinkin' we don't have to redo the cabinets, just the doors and handles. It'll work." And then he grinned and said, "Three."

Gail frowned, then realized he'd answered her question about the eggs. *Great,* she thought, *now I'm cooking for him again.* She placed the lamp at his side. The cord barely reached the outlet next to the sink. "If you bump it, it'll fall over," she warned.

He stared at her.

"What?" Gail knew she probably looked a mess. Her hair was always flattened to the right side of her head when she rose from bed.

"We're still young," he said. "You're still in your thirties. A thirtysomething, as they say."

"I haven't been young since I was fourteen," Gail said and tied the belt of her robe.

He seemed at a loss briefly, then said, "We're going to need the extra money the kitchenette and the room next to it can bring in with Ty going to college. Can't count on a full scholarship. Boy is smart, though, gets his smarts from me, don't you think?"

"Yes, and his good looks too. Don't forget that."

Dan grinned. "Sure. But I didn't want to say and have you feeling bad. You must've contributed something; the kid does get cranky now and then."

"Stick your head back under the sink so I can slam the cabinet door on it, please." Dan laughed and Gail felt herself smiling.

He sat up and examined his fingernails. "I'm putting in a new trap, and washers," he said.

"Good," Gail said. "Better ten years late than never. I'll bring your breakfast." She turned back toward him before getting to the door and noticed he'd been watching her walk away. "I wanted to thank you for helping to look for Mason." Gail met his eyes. "It means a lot to me. I know he's an adult, supposed to be, but I think about Lillian, you know, and I think I'll never—"

"He'll show, Gail. Problem is it'll be on his schedule. You know how hardheaded he is. He'll run out of money or options and come straggling back."

Gail's arms crossed in front of her. "I'm going to shake him so hard when he comes back his teeth will fall on his feet. Or maybe I'll choke him." Briefly, her hands formed a circle in front of her as if she had someone by the throat. "I'll choke..." Gail remembered the last time she'd seen him. His red eyes glared at her and his hand locked with all his strength on her wrist, trapping veins and flesh against her bone, bruising her skin. He'd said, "I don't take a hit so easy anymore." She had been afraid of him, the boy she'd raised. "If you had seen him the last time I did," Gail said. "You might not be so sure he's going to come home. I think I pushed him out the door, Dan. I told him he was just like his father." Her breath came quicker.

Dan looked down at the tool in his hands. "Did you ever find out what they fell out about? Him and Pony? I know for a little while there, Pony used to come by and pick him up. Then, nothin'."

Gail shook her head. "Uh-uh. Guess I assumed he finally figured out what kind of man Pony was. I should have done more to keep them two apart."

"You did the right thing. You let him find out on his own. Try-ing to interfere woulda just made him want to hang out with Pony more. Don't you think? Those two ain't seen each other in years and years, right?

"Pony left town. None too soon. That had to be eight or nine years ago." Gail went back to Dan's side and squatted down on the backs of her calves. Her errand to fix breakfast had been forgotten. Right now, Dan seemed willing to listen and Gail wanted to talk. "I don't think any of us did right by Mason. He got ignored when Tyler was born. Even back then he started cutting up to get attention. Everything seems so connected. You do something wrong and you don't get a lot of chances to fix it. Remember the Christmas you got Ty that new ten-speed? I let you talk me into that one. I shouldn't have allowed it. I think that hurt Mason bad. It's twenty-twenty we shouldn't have done that. You said, 'Why should both boys suffer because money is tight?' Because they's brothers. They should have went without together because they were brothers."

"So it's my fault. I tried to do right by my son. But this is all my fault now."

"Oh, no, baby. I ain't saying that at all." Gail reached out, held Dan's right forearm, and let the hand linger. "I didn't mean...it was just as much me." This wasn't doing any good. She had wanted to defend Mason, not attack Dan. She'd wanted to tell him every-thing that had happened had a reason, everything connected to something else and could be traced back from one event to the next. Plus, she somehow had believed that if she shared her thoughts about Mason and Lillian, she could be closer to Dan. "I'll get your breakfast," she said, and quickly retreated.

Her hair brushed back and tucked behind her ears, and wear-ing matching sweat top and pants, Gail returned with a full tray of breakfast. He seemed not to have made much progress while she'd been gone. She'd made herself a little something too and remem-bered Tabasco for his eggs, a touch for which he smiled broadly. The sun had finally come in strongly and they ate on the cold floor together, mostly to the sound of forks scraping on plates.

"Did I tell you I've been living alone for more than a month now?"

Gail looked up from her plate to see Dan pretending not to be intently eyeing her. She sipped her coffee.

"Yeah," he said, "That didn't last too long. She wasn't the girl for me. I told her it'd be for the best." Dan's fork chased the last piece of egg across his plate. "She didn't mean nothin'."

Men always say that, Gail thought. How can it not mean anything? Dan looked uncomfortable. Finally, she said, "Well, I have to get my day started. Lots of errands and chores to catch up on." For a second, Dan looked disappointed by her reaction to his news, or Gail supposed she only imagined he did.

"All right, but I need someone to hold the new pipe up while I fit it in place. I'm having a dickens of a time with it."

Gail collected his plate. "You want me to send Ty in?"

"Naw, it won't take a second. Come here." He retrieved his monkey wrench and shoved himself back under the sink. "You'll have to squeeze in here too," she heard him say, and he moved to one side, making a pitifully small opening for her.

"Dan, I'll get Ty."

"Won't take a sec," he said.

Gail rolled her eyes, exhaled, and stuck her head under the sink. "Dan, I can't see a thing under here. And it smells. Or is that you?"

"Your eyes will adjust," he said. "Your nose will too. Now hold this."

She had to push her arms between her and Dan to get them under the sink and she squirmed deeper into the dark hole, pressing against Dan's stomach, then his chest. The lamp did no good with both of them blocking its light. "I can't see shit," she said, but she could feel Dan's breath against her left cheek and eye. She remembered now how unusually deep the space under this sink was. Dan had her right hand now and pushed the cool pipe into it.

"Gonna need that right here," he said and guided her hand along the rough bottom of the sink.

"Here?" she asked.

"No, up," he said, and it seemed he pressed tighter against her than he had to. "Don't move. I'll just tighten this bad boy right down."

Gail held the elbow joint over her head. Her arm grew tired. Something, maybe the cabinet latch, stabbed her in the back. "Dan," she said.

"Just a sec. Hold it still." He was tightening the ring over it now and Gail had to grip the pipe hard so it wouldn't move with the ring.

"Is that it?" she asked when she felt no more force against the pipe.

"Let me check."

She waited. His chest breathed against hers. She felt something brushing against her neck.

"Let me check," he repeated and his mouth was near her ear.

Something brushed over her cheek.

"Are there bugs under here?"

"Could be," he said and kissed her on the mouth. It was not a gentle kiss. At first, his mouth covered hers. He held the back of her head in the crook of an arm. He sucked in on her top lip and ran his tongue under it. Passively, Gail allowed him to continue, then responded with movements of her own. But when a hand covered one of her breasts, she knocked it away and wiggled herself from under the sink. She slammed the cabinet door on him but he didn't even notice. He followed her out. She got to her feet while he remained sitting on the floor, looking boyishly mischievous, despite his white-haired temples.

"I hope you enjoyed that more than I did," she said. "You don't get it, do you, Dan? Too much time has passed for us. What did you think, we'd start kissing and everything would be rosy again? Negro, please. You waited way too long. I used to think we'd..." Gail shrugged. "It's gone. Got it?" She noticed he'd left grease from his hands on her sweatshirt. She wagged a finger at him. "And the next time you bring your sorry butt around here, keep your hands on your goddamn monkey wrench and off me."

She left him and the breakfast dishes, she realized, behind and stormed down the hallway.

Tyler had just emerged from his bedroom and he grinned at Gail. "What that on your shirt?" He pointed.

"Grease. I leaned against a dirty—"

"It looks like a handprint, Mom," Tyler said.

"Have you cleaned your room up yet?"

"Yes."

"Well, go get it done. Why do I always have to ask twice?" Gail went into her room and pulled the sweatshirt over her head. Two fingers and the palm of Dan's dirty hands showed distinctly on the shirt. Always was a good kisser, she reflected, behind her closed door.

Gail had the receiver trapped between her right shoulder and cheek. She listened to the rings; it was all part of this perfunctory exercise. Next to the phone, on a stand that stood in a small alcove off the living room, lay open her pocket-sized spiral notebook with a dozen or more names and phone numbers written in it. Some of the names had more than twenty checks next to them, some neatly entered, others stabbed onto the paper like little daggers. Mason's friends and acquaintances had checks for each time they failed to duck her calls. "Naw, he never said a word to me, Miz Neighbors. Yeah, I been asking around like you told me." Some had given to hanging up at the sound of her voice—those who really hadn't run with Mason, or those whose compassion could not extend to a mother searching for a wayward son. She, having grown as tired of the calls as they, took the hang-ups and rudeness in stride. Although today, she had new information. Perhaps someone on the list knew Ken Gamble or knew someone who knew him.

Before picking up the phone, Gail recalled the details of her conversation with Gamble. What could she reasonably believe of his story? She hesitated to trust any of it. Gamble had seemed cocky, nasty, and useless. Useless, Gail decided, because he looked as if for all his days on earth he'd never been of much use or help to anyone but himself. The idea that Mason and he could be friends did not sit well. It made her feel as if she hadn't really known her son at all, that he had gotten away from her long before he left.

"Hello."

"Hello. I'd like to speak to Cindy Reese, please."

"This is Cindy. Mrs. Neighbors? I haven't heard anything, Mrs. Neighbors. Like I said, he ain't gonna call me."

"I understand. But I have a lead I want to check with you. I know he left town with a boy named Ken Gamble. A big, kinda stocky guy. Real short hair."

"Gamble? No. I ain't heard of him, I don't think. I got to go, Mrs. Neighbors."

"Yes, Cindy. Thank you for your time. If you hear—" A monotone buzz hummed from the receiver; Cindy knew the rest of the routine already.

The fourth call put her in contact with Jamal Jenkins, the first person who knew or had heard of Ken Gamble.

"Actually, my brother knows him, but he don't live here anymore and where he stays ain't got a phone. He lives with his girlfriend and her mama, and he's got a baby by both of them. Believe that."

"Gamble?"

"No, my brother. Gamble and him, they... well, they hang out. You know. Neither one worth a shit. Scuse me, Miss Neighbors."

"Did you hear anything about where Gamble went last September? He left town with Mason and a girl. I think they were going to Detroit."

"I don't know nothin' about that. I heard he was going to DC. But I don't know about Mason goin' along."

"Could you ask your brother, Jamal?"

"I suppose. I'll have to see. We don't talk much."

The remainder of the calls proved less useful and the familiar frustration burned in Gail as she flicked the last check mark in her notebook. She allowed herself to calm down while making breakfast for the second time, this time for Annie and Tyler. The burner in the furnace ignited with a whoosh; soon the vents were exhaling their dry heat into the kitchen, though the floor remained cold even though she wore slippers. She pondered what Jenkins had told her about Gamble going to DC and not Detroit. The possibility presented itself that what Gamble had told her bore not the slightest resemblance to the truth. And then there was the curious thing he'd said to Dan, "Mason said he was going to look for you." By that he'd probably meant Pony, mistaking Dan for Mason's father. Mason looking for Pony? That worried Gail very much.

Out front, the engine of Dan's Buick raced to a pitch before settling into an uneasy idle.

Annie came down for breakfast, followed by Ty.

"Is there orange juice?" Tyler asked.

Annie said, "I'll get it for you."

Gail walked hesitantly to the front door and looked out to see Dan load his tools into the car's trunk, shut it on the third try, and climb back behind the wheel. White exhaust obscured him and half the car.

Absently, her left hand traced over her lips. The presence of his kisses, the pressure, the sharpness, still lingered. She had wanted to ask him if he might again take her around to Gamble's. Perhaps, if she were cleverer than she'd been at the first confrontation, she might catch Gamble in a lie, or even exact the truth from him. Dan's Buick pulled away from the curb, giving her an odd feeling of relief. After all these years, what could he have been thinking? Certainly, the years must have engineered on him what they had on her: dissipated regrets, healed wounds, cooled passions.

Not yet sorted, the mail from yesterday lay in a short stack on the little secretary in the foyer. One envelope from the bank caught her attention and she sliced it open with a thumbnail. She peeked into the envelope, not drawing the letter out. "Notice of Insufficient Funds" it proclaimed, stapled along with a check in Jackie's handwriting.

This was the last thing she needed now. Her credit could be ruined just when she'd need to apply for tuition loans for Tyler. Jackie and Cole were sitting on the bed with the newspaper spread out between them when Gail stepped in. She hadn't bothered to knock and noticed the slightly surprised look on Jackie's face. Later, Gail would not be able to recall word for word what she said to Jackie, but she made it clear she would not allow Jackie to drag her down with her. "You don't have your head on straight, Miss. You abandon your baby. You traipse off after some boy who won't give you the time of day... I need this money! You straighten up your act or this one," she pointed to Cole, "this one is the one who's going to suffer." She stepped up to the bed and tore the bad check in half right in Jackie's face.

"Get out of my room," Jackie shouted.

Gail was already walking out. She said more to herself than she had to Jackie: "Now I have to figure out how many of my checks are going to bounce because she bounced one on me." Monday she could call a few of her creditors, warn them, maybe straighten this mess out in advance.

By the afternoon, Gail finally decided on a return trip to the house where Ken Gamble lived. She'd also decided not to ask Dan to go with her, though she'd lifted the phone up twice during the day. He had made it impossible for her to ask anything of him.

Gail brushed her hair in her mirror. She noticed how long it had grown, and how the ends were splitting. She noticed, too, how her oval face had gotten thinner; the bones in her cheeks now lifted up, leaving shallow valleys between them and her jaw line. Dark swaths spread just under the puffy bags beneath her eyes. The overall effect made her eyes appear more deeply set and her face more gaunt than it had since she'd last taken a long look in a mirror, instead of just a rushing-out-the-door glance. She wondered when this had happened to her. Her fingers lightly followed the shadow between her eyes and nose. Except for them, she acknowledged, her face might look better than before. Had Dan Neighbors noticed the change? She fought a brush through her hair, tugging it through the ends. "We're still young," he'd said. Gail held the brush at her neck and stared eye to eye with her reflection, searching for what youth he might have seen.

Annie stood at the bottom of the stairs when she came down, and Gail thought the older woman looked younger today; rethinking, she figured "younger" maybe wasn't quite the right word. Annie's eyes, lighter than Gail's, were wide open, and the crow's feet flowing to them seemed less deep. Sunlight from the front door and front windows reflected on her metal-gray hair. Annie seemed to have collected the small winter light around her. "Lively" was the word that came to Gail's mind; Annie awaited her, a hand on the banister, bright and vigorous.

"I am having guests over in a few minutes," Annie said. "I told you about them. The man I raised, and his family. Last time they came by you were out. Are you about to leave?"

"Yes, I have to go now."

"I wanted you to meet them. The Bucklers, from—"

"Can't, Annie," Gail interrupted. "I have a lead about Mason. You understand?" She patted Annie's shoulder.

"Oh? Yes, honey. You go on." Annie stepped away from her. "Tell me what you find out."

Gail moved toward the door.

"I worry about the boy too," Annie said after her.

Surprising herself with how easily she remembered the way, Gail strode rapidly to Gamble's. Her march kept her warm, burning the anxiety that kept her mind in constant agitation. The row houses on Gamble's block looked much the same. The colors varied, and the care the owners took with their properties varied too. Maybe the house Gamble lived in appeared more neglected than most. Gail climbed the steps and rapped briskly on the door. It never occurred to her Gamble might not be home. She had set in her mind what she would say, how she'd eye him levelly and demand the truth. The door did not move. "Please, Lord," she whispered and knocked again. That terse whisper was the closest she'd come to a prayer in a long time, and it had only slipped out with her exhalation, without forethought.

A few nights ago, her mind reeling with thoughts of Mason and Lillian, she had crawled from her bed directly to her knees, intending to pray. Her request would be to find both children, for all her offspring to be restored to her. In the time it took for two breaths, and without clasping hands, Gail pushed herself up and rolled back under the sheets; that prayer had already been whispered and shouted a thousand times. He already knew the words.

She raised her hand to knock again and struck only air as the door opened widely. A large, very black woman stood in front of Gail, looking annoyed.

"I need to see Ken Gamble, please. It's urgent."

The woman's face knotted in a definite look of disdain. "It always is," she said. "Don't let the cold in." She went to the foot of the stairs and called Gamble. "Someone to see you." Then she said to Gail, "Go on up. It'll take forever if you wait on him. You're a bit old, ain't you?" She walked away on flat, broad, bare feet.

Gail placed a hand on the loose handrail, which creaked under her touch. It occurred to her she might have been able to ask Dan to come along after all. She headed up. The temperature rose with each step. Gail felt her skin moistening under her clothes. The air on the second floor was suffocating and nearly refused to be drawn into her lungs. She pushed her coat off her neck and back to the hills of her shoulders.

Three doors, two partly opened, waited for her. He'll be behind the closed one, she thought, but peeked into the other two to make certain. The first bedroom was empty and bare. The second room reeked of medicine, Lysol, and alcohol. A thin little man in worn pajamas lay sprawled in the bed. He slept.

She knocked on the third door. "Ken Gamble?" Reluctantly, she took off her coat, thinking she'd hate to have to pay these people's heating bill. She said again, "Ken Gamble?"

"What?" came from behind the door.

"I need to talk to you. It's Gail Neighbors, Mason's mother."

"Fuck off."

"I've got the rest of your money," she said.

Laughter. "Slip it under the door." Gail didn't respond. "All right. Come in."

She had to put her weight against the door to open it. It was warped and stuck at the top. Gamble lay on his back near the head of his bed with his thick, broad feet braced against the wall. He wore only boxers, white or off-white, or just so soiled. The fly of his boxers gaped open, showing a black nest. His body looked like a black trunk with a navel and nipples and to one end a widely smiling head.

The smell of him clogged the room. A brown shade pulled all the way down effectively blocked out the only light, except for a rent in its middle that described a jagged tear.

"Close the door," he said.

"I can't breathe in here," she said. Gail flicked the light switch on her left twice to no effect. Looking about for some source of light, she saw under the nightstand lamp a spoon with its handle bent. The surface of the nightstand was spotted with black smudges and spent matches. On the floor nearly under the stand lay two syringes, very sleek and mean-looking. At the other end of the bed, amongst a pile of sheets and pillows, were sprinkled here and there vials of crack—tiny, clear tubes with red stoppers.

He saw her looking at them. "I don't smoke the shit myself. I ain't that stupid. I just need a little side money. You got mine? It's fifty."

Gail held herself in the room, reminding herself to breathe and to ignore Gamble's stink. Her face grew stern. "You just do the horse for yourself," she said. "And it's twenty dollars."

His feet tapped against the wall. "Oh, lady, lady. I think its fifty now." His feet pounded a beat. Gail imagined she could see the wall bowing in. "And 'sides, I done told you everything. Didn't I tell you that?"

"You didn't tell me what you were going to do in DC. Sell that crack?"

"Yeah, maybe I was..." He laughed and grinned at Gail. "Did I say DC?"

"You just did."

"Oh, you slick, huh? Tryin' to out-slick me." He swung his feet around and sat up quickly. The move startled Gail and she took a step backwards. "Mase got a good-lookin' mama," he said. "You want some of this, Mase's mama?" He rubbed his crotch slowly. His feet slid under him and one hand braced at the edge of the bed. He looked as if he were about to lunge at her. His tongue flattened over his bottom lip. "You give it up and I'll tell you what you want to know."

He was about to try something. Gail knew it. "Fuck yourself," she said, "It's all you'll probably get."

He leaped toward her, reaching out with a grasping hand.

Gail jumped back, but he had grabbed the sleeve of her sweater. "Fuck off," she said and struck his arm with her fist. His grip broke not because of her blow but because he'd stumbled jumping away from the bed. He hit the floor with a thud. Gail did not look back. Clutching her coat, she ran down the stairs.

The big woman hustled to her. "What's going on up there?"

Gail's heart hammered inside. She breathed the freer downstairs air. "You've got a junkie pusher living up there," she said to the woman.

"Hell, that's why I thought you 'needed' to see him."

"He tried to grab me."

"Call the cops on him. Let them take his ass away."

Gail looked up the stairs.

"He ain't gonna follow you down here," the big woman said. "Come on, I'll get you some water."

Gail followed her into the kitchen, where she poured chilled water from the refrigerator into a plastic mug for Gail.

"Is he your son?" Gail asked and thanked her for the water.

"Hell, no. I'd have to hang my head in shame everyday if I'd brought that into the world. What you want to truck with him for?"

"You weren't here the last time I came by?"

"Not if you came at night. I mostly work nights."

Gail sipped the water. It tasted funny. "He and my son went to DC this September past—"

"Yeah. Mason, right? They carried my Gina back home. He been staying at her place ever since. You want the phone number?"

MASON

Above them, the narrow, rocky knob of the mountain poked into a low and lazy cloud. Above the knob and the cloud flew a hawk, not seen but heard, piercing the shrouded sky with a high, phantom-like call that seemed to slice through the mist from all directions. Something urgent in its cry made them crane their heads around to look for it.

Gina had told Mason she could give him a tour of the entire town from one spot. She led him to this place of gray and yellow rocks and squat, scruffy pines growing amongst the slope's cracks and crevices. Touching his arm, she'd held him from charging farther up the stone incline; because of the cloud, they could climb no higher and still be able to see the view below.

He hid his gratitude. Pride alone had allowed him to match strides with her over the shifting, crumbling slope. He could hear himself breathing, his lungs working very hard for very little. As she had warned, he felt overheated. He pulled off his jacket, but she prevented him from removing Tullis's borrowed sweater.

She said, "It's still cold. You just don't know it."

Below, little presented itself to him to justify the effort: the roofs of houses; treetops everywhere; and a section of the highway, with the darts and flashes upon it reflecting the sun from across the valley as they followed the road's contours.

"Look east," Gina said, "that dark band, that's rain still miles and miles from here, but coming. From high up, I've seen bad storms rolling in, like walls...no, like that old horror movie, The Blob, sucking in whole mountains as it moves."

Mason briefly glimpsed the dark line Gina spoke of; it looked like part of the distant mountain range. Finally, his lungs regained rhythm. Standing slightly behind and to the left of her, he gazed at Gina. He'd been mistaken, he concluded. He had thought the traces of old scars on her cheeks marred what might have been a beautiful face. Yet, she was beautiful. Not despite her mottled skin, but because of it. Her face had character and strength, and commanded his eyes to remain on her longer than he felt comfortable watching. With her light-colored eyes and rope-like hair, she looked exotic, singular. She turned her head and caught him looking.

Gina seemed to regard him warily. "Are you watching the view?" she asked.

"Yes," he said, not taking his eyes from her. He did not think about closing the distance between them; he simply walked up to her. He did not consciously choose to raise a hand to her face. But he felt on the pads of his fingertips the marvelous soft, firm texture of her skin.

She turned her face to the side. A curtain of dark hair fell in between them. She did not step away.

He tilted her chin up toward his face, wondering if she would stop him, wondering if she would turn away. He kissed her, softly. Her eyes remained as open, as his did his. He kissed her again. Her response forced his mouth open, and it seemed that all he could do, staring at her eye to eye, was drink in her mouth as avidly as possible.

Her hands slipped around his waist and climbed up his back as her body leaned into his. He staggered backward slightly on the slope. Tiny rocks rolled away at their feet, and, neither wanting to relinquish the kiss, they both went down. He caught the weight of both of them on his right knee and right hand, jamming his wrist badly in the process. A gasp went from her mouth to his as her eyes closed and opened, her tongue squirming. He was able to ease them slowly to the ground at last, taking the weight off his painful wrist. Something hard and sharp stabbed him in the left buttocks. He tried shifting away from it and they both went sliding down the stone face of the mountain with the dust and small rocks.

The kiss broken, Gina called out his name. "Oh, shit, you goofy," she added.

They didn't tumble far. The mountainside was not that steep. Mason caught a small, half-dead but still pliant pine, and Gina caught him. She began pulling herself up even with him by grabbing handfuls of his pants.

"Hey, let go before you pull me down," Mason said.

"What? You want me to fall?"

"Sorry, babe. It's every man and woman for themselves."

She whacked him on his butt. "Avalanche," she said when they were again face to face.

Mason needlessly held on to the little tree. With his free hand, he swept her hair back and gingerly brushed white dust from her face. "Were you hurt?" he asked. "How far did we fall?" He looked up the slope where his jacket lay two yards away at the spot where they'd stood.

"I think I fell all the way," she said and touched her lips to his, and they found that same kiss again. Mason held on to her and the little tree.

They lay there a long time, faces so close he could feel a tickle from her eyelashes. Gina said his eyes looked fierce normally, but not now, she said, now they looked as soft as chocolate or pebbles under a clear stream. They blamed each other for the fall. Mason said she couldn't stand and kiss at the same time. He kissed her marked cheeks. He found the courage to tell her she was beautiful, and she didn't turn her face away. They heard the hawk cry again and this time spotted him, quick and effortless against the white sky.

Time escaped them completely. The short autumn day had nearly spent itself, and the curtain of approaching sleet and rain would finish it.

Gina sat up abruptly and began dusting herself off. Mason reached over to brush dust from the leg of her pants. She moved her leg just out of his reach. "I can manage," she said.

He shoved himself from the mountain crust as if doing a pushup, stood, and retrieved his jacket from up the slope. Side by side, they moved slowly down the mountain. Neither spoke. The wind was strong and cold. Mason's lips and nose began to burn slightly, a tingle at the edges. With the lesser light, it took longer to go down the slope than up. Proper footing became more important. He pretended this kept him from making conversation, supposing she did not want to talk either. Once or twice, and briefly, she lay a hand on his shoulder or arm for support while stepping over treacherous rolling gravel, but long before they regained the tree line, she kept her distance from him. Under the trees, out of the wind yet colder, they walked on soft, needle-strewn ground and made better time. They walked several feet apart, and Mason lost sight of her frequently as dark pine trunks and tangled shrubs passed between them. He caught her glancing his way from time to time from behind her hair. The looks were nothing like those she'd given him on the mountain, nothing like she'd given him before. Maybe she remembered a man waited for her back at home, the one who could not take walks into the mountains with her. Maybe she remembered Mason would be leaving tomorrow, that they would probably never see each other again.

The desire to leave was no longer clear cut. Momentum had swept him from his mother's porch months ago, but it had gradually slackened ever since. Mason had grown angry with himself. For so long his course had been plain, if not the finish. He saw himself in control. He saw panic on Pony's face. The gun hovered between them and Mason's view of Pony bobbed at the end of the barrel. He would scare Pony, have him blabber apologies, and then...and then they would see. Suffocating under white sheets like the thin clouds above, and under black flesh like the great legs of the pines, he could smell Pony's cologne thick in his nose.

They broke from under the trees. The roof of Carl and Gina's place came into view, along with the road and the lights of neighboring houses. Gina had turned to face Mason, waiting for him to catch up. He could not make out her face, which was hooded by her hair. Mason halted feet from her, holding his arms like luggage straps across his chest.

The silhouette of Gina asked, "Are you still leaving in the morning?"

"Yes."

"Fuck you." Arms, coat, and hair swung in arcs behind her as she spun about, aiming directly for her home.

Carl Tullis waited in the backyard. Gina marched right by him, ignoring whatever he'd said. He asked Mason, "What's pissed her off?"

Mason forced his eyes from the wheels of Tully's chair to the man's face. "Guess I didn't fully appreciate the mountain view," he said.

"That's my sweater," Tully said.

Lights came on in the house. Gina could be heard moving around loudly in the kitchen, running water, slamming kitchen cabinets. The light threw an elongated shadow of Tullis from his chair perch across the backyard.

"She said it was okay."

"Yeah, no problem." Mason tried to walk by him, but Tullis put an opened hand against Mason's chest. "Hold up," he said.

"Man, it's cold out here. And it's about to snow."

"Rain, more than likely," Tullis said. "The temperature's been rising a bit. I want to talk to you."

Mason breathed out. "It wears me out to talk to you people."

The back door light came on. Gina leaned half out the doorway. Her face looked yellow in the light. "Did you eat yet, Tully?"

His eyes stayed on Mason. "Don't fix me anything. I'm heading out in a few minutes."

She asked where, but Tullis didn't answer. "What about you, Mason? I'm having the salmon patties. Or maybe you're not sure what you want?" she asked with sarcasm.

Now Tullis looked from Mason to Gina and back to Mason. His shoulders straightened against the chair back. "Be nice, Gina," he said. "It's our guest's last night here."

The door slammed and the light went out.

"Damn, Mason, what did you do?"

"What do you want to talk about?"

Tullis's hands shoved down on his wheels and the chair jumped forward. He cut a half circle around Mason, who turned to face him again. "Hell, me, of course. The half of me that's left." He wheeled another half circle, returning to his original spot. Mason turned again.

Gina was at the window, her face down. She must have been washing something at the sink.

Tullis said, "A buddy of mine, um, Conklin, is coming over in his van to pick me up in a little while. He has a modified van with a lift and hand controls. Conk's a crip too. The only damn thing we've got in common. He really is a vet. I think he suspects I'm not, but I pretend for him. Think he likes that." Tullis looked nervous, or cold. He'd slid his hands into his armpits. "We make each other miserable—misery loves company—and we get pretty shit-faced too. And I usually end up spending the night on his floor."

Mason shuffled, tapped a hand on a fist.

"Could you go sit on the ramp? I'm breaking my neck looking up at you." He shoved his head to the side by pressing a flat hand against his ear, and Mason heard his neck pop. Tullis smiled at the sound.

The short ramp led from the back door to a bald spot in the yard. Narrow ruts from when the ground had been softer showed the different directions in which Tullis and his chair had rolled off. Mason sat down in the middle of the ramp. From there, he could no longer see Gina at the window. The men's eyes were level now.

Mason made up his mind to give Tullis only a minute to say what he wanted to say. Never possessing much patience, he had none when it came to Tullis.

"I want to talk about me, of course," Tullis said again. "Mase, I'm...I'm half dead meat, you know. Feels like being perched on rubber." He pushed the tips of his fingers into his thighs. "I can touch my legs but the feeling is one-sided; you know, like touching someone else altogether. Part of me is alien to the other. It pisses and shits without my consent. That's worse than not being able to walk. I swear it is."

Mason got the notion, something in Tullis's face, that he'd had a few beers already.

"And if you been wondering, I don't get hard-ons anymore. Worst of all."

"What do you want, Tullis?"

"God damn, brother, give me a fucking minute will you? Think if you couldn't get it up..." He glanced up at the door and lowered his voice. "What if you weren't really a man anymore? That's what it comes down to, manhood. How you are with a woman defines what you are as a man. Do you see that, Mason?" Tullis leaned forward.

Mason wasn't sure what he was getting at, but he didn't like it. He wanted to hit Tullis.

"I used to have dreams. Not dreams really. Delusions. I used to have these delusions. I'd be in bed lying next to Gina; she'd be asleep. And I'm on my back or side or something and roll over on my stomach. And that's when I would feel it. A raging hard-on. Throbbing! Like the first time your first girlfriend let you feel her up. When the blood is all the way up and it almost hurts. I mean, I felt the head of it pushing into the mattress when I tried to turn over. I felt my PJ bottoms stretched to cover it. And I said, *oh my God!* I screamed it. I got excited and I woke up Gina and told her I had a goddamned fire hydrant in my drawers.

"Mason, she grinned big time. I'll never forget. I see her even in the dark. Her eyes light up. She squealed. Kissed me like she ain't done in a long time and threw back the sheets. And there ain't a thing happening down there. Not a fucking thing. She touches it, but I don't feel her touch it. Her face closes back in. She squeezed my shoulder and told me I dreamed it. But I felt it and I knew it was real, and I guess, at the time, I thought, maybe it just didn't last long. So a few days later, it happens again! The return of the raging bull. I shook her awake. Her back was to me and she mumbled about how it was just a dream. But I felt the stiffness, like a horn, so I grab her hand and put it down there. She told me to quit playing. Playing. Jesus." Tullis shrugged in his chair. "I told her I was sorry.

"After that, whenever it happened I didn't bother her. I just let the phantom dick have his tease. I don't peek under the covers; that breaks the spell. I just lay still, pretend I'm jerking off. It hasn't happened in a while, anyway." Tullis blew into his hands. His breath vapor rose through his fingers. "What gets me the most is that first time it happened. The look on Gina's face, her eyes. She was really psyched up big time. The impossibility of the whole thing didn't occur to her. We've talked about it—well, sort of. I mean, I guess I knew she was suffering too. Maybe I didn't know how much, or maybe I didn't care."

Mason's impulse to hit him had faded. He no longer wanted to walk away from him, either. He said, "Maybe."

Tullis said nothing else for a while. He looked down at his lap.

Mason supposed he should feel sorry for Tullis now, not jealous, not disgusted. "We should go in, man," he said. "It's getting late."

The man in the wheelchair raised his head and regarded Mason with glistening eyes. "Do me a favor. I know you like Gina. You wouldn't have stayed here so long if you weren't hot for her." Tullis wringed his hands. His eyes dropped to his lap again. "Jesus," he said.

Mason came to his feet. Now standing partway up the ramp, he towered over Carl Tullis. "Just what are you asking, Tullis?"

"Just what you think. What you want, anyway."

"You're ill, man. What are you, her pimp now? Do I pay her or you? First off, brother, if we wanted to get something going we wouldn't need your permission. And the next thing, if you really worry about Gina's sex life, then kick her ass off this hill." Mason shook his head. "I ought to kick your ass."

"Yeah?" Tullis smiled. "But kicking my ass wouldn't be fair, would it? One against point-five. I'm going to spend the night on Conk's floor." He backed his chair up and wheeled around the house.

Mason went inside. The kitchen felt almost too warm. Gina was at the stove. He pulled off his jacket and sweater. When Gina asked him where Tullis had gone, Mason told her he was waiting out front for his ride. "Somebody named Conk," he said.

Just as they sat down at the little kitchen table, they heard the van in the driveway and the motor of the lift raising Tullis. Gina scooted her chair back and hurried outside. In a couple of minutes, the van had driven away and she'd returned. They ate in silence until Gina cleaned her plate and Mason had gotten bored with his food. He chased the corn around with his fork.

"Tully said he left a bottle of wine in the fridge for us to celebrate your departure. Guess somebody's glad you're leaving."

Mason said, "And you wanted two boyfriends living in the same house."

"A feminist Mormon doctrine." She smiled, but looked serious when she added, "I could've handled it." She began clearing the table. She said, "Both buses come early. The first heads west, Pittsburgh first, I think. The second comes not quite a half hour later, Hagerstown, Rockville, and DC. Neither one stays more than a second."

"Okay," Mason said to the information, and allowed her to take his plate away.

Gina wore a sloppy dark sweatshirt that read "California" on the front. The neck of the shirt had been stretched or cut to allow one smooth yellow-brown shoulder to be exposed. The shoulder seemed to have avoided all the blemishes of Gina's teen years. Mason thought it looked like the caramel frosting his mother used to pour over cakes. He remembered kissing Gina. The memories felt older than just an hour or two.

She dumped the dishes in the sink without giving them a second thought. "I don't want to be mad at you on your last night here. Let's watch TV and drink the wine." She grabbed the bottle from the refrigerator and Mason followed her into the living room with two glasses.

"I know why he left the wine." Mason took the bottle of Cold Duck from her and pushed out the plastic stopper with his thumbs.

They sat on the sofa that had served as his bed since early September.

"Why?" she asked, holding the glasses.

"He wants me to jump your bones."

Gina smirked. The space between her eyebrows wrinkled. "You think that? Just because he left us a bottle of wine?" She handed Mason a glass, which he placed on the table in front of him.

"No. I think that because I heard it straight from the horse's ass. He gave me his permission in the backyard just now."

"Bullshit." But her eyes said she believed Mason. "Did you tell him we kissed on the mountain? You told him, didn't you?"

He shook his head. He sipped the sweet, bubbly wine.

"Hey, goofy, what did you say to him? 'Sure, no problem, I done already started on her on the mountain top?' That's why he went with Conklin. You said yes."

"This is good," Mason said, and poured more Cold Duck in his glass. "That's some generous boyfriend you have there. I mean for giving us the wine." Now Mason smiled. "And about you I told him, no way in hell. Not a chance. Not for all the malt liquor in Milwaukee."

"Oh," Gina said.

Mason found the remote control near at hand between the sofa cushions and turned on the TV. He flipped rapidly through the channels. He settled on a sitcom, but didn't pay it any attention. Gina and he worked their way down the bottle.

"Why would Tully say something like that? What did he say exactly? That sonovabitch."

Mason absently scratched through his hair. He settled back on the couch. He hated the couch, he realized; he hadn't thought of how uncomfortable it made him until just then. "He said he couldn't do the job, so would I be kind enough to give it a knock. That's the edited for television version. He said he knows him being paralyzed must be rough on you too."

Gina drained her glass and refilled it. "That must be the most unselfish, stupid, male chauvinist crapola—but unselfish—thing he's ever done."

"No it ain't," Mason said quickly. "He wasn't thinking about you, girlfriend. He was just trying to move people around like checker pieces, mess with our minds. Which he's doing a good job of. He's got his hands on the remote control." Mason used the remote to flip channels. "Just like that."

She scooted farther from Mason. "Why would he?"

"Keep you thinking about him. I shouldn't've told you what he said, maybe then we'd have done it."

"In your dreams with your hands down your pants," Gina said. "Tully was thinking of me. He's just not used to thinking about anybody but himself. He's not good at it."

"Fine." Mason waved a limp hand at her. "Write your own fairy tale. You wanted me to hang around for support. Well, you seem to have everything answered now. So I can get the hell free of here."

Gina stood. "You can go right now, 'cause ain't nothing else happening between us." She stepped over the coffee table. Her leg brushed the empty, green wine bottle and it wobbled without falling over. "I'm going to bed."

"Gina," Mason said to her back. "Gina!"

She kept walking, which he told himself was fine; he had not known what to say anyway.

Mason worked the remote again, popping by each station, looking at but not seeing the bright images in front of him. He put the bottle to his lips and tilted his head back, though he knew they had already emptied the bottle. He thought about the mountain climb with Gina. He remembered the clouds masking the peaks, and the cry of the hawk, and the quiver of Gina's tongue over his lips. Pony had not been there. He had not felt suffocated, even as she lay close by. He had not shrunk; he had expanded through Gina, through the mountain, and the hawk. For a while Pony had not found his way there. Remembering this, something surged under his ribs, an agitation, an exhilaration, and he jumped to his feet unable to contain it. Not knowing what to do, how to release the feeling or to hold on to it, he stood dumbfounded, alone in the living room in front of the shifting television spotlight.

Rain pounded on the roof and the walls and the glass of the windows. Not snow but rain, just as Tullis had predicted, and it drove away the sound of the highway for the first time since he'd been there. Then the drumming amplified from within the house. Gina had turned on the shower. She would be sticking a hand past the plastic curtain to test the water's temperature. The water spray struck the porcelain tub bottom like the rain on the roof over his head. The sound came intermittently. She would be stepping into the spray, one long, smooth leg first, and then the rest of her. The water hit the tub heavily at times as she moved in and around the spray. She would be letting it flow over her. Mason listened. The water was all around him too. He yanked off his T-shirt. He raised his face to the ceiling and closed his eyes as if letting the surge from the shower head strike him.

And then he was moving. He bumped the coffee table. As on the mountain, he moved toward her without thought. The knob of the bathroom door turned in his hands. Steam rolled toward him. Her form turned slowly behind the translucent shower curtain. Mason stepped to the curtain. He heard her hum, not a tune, but just from the contentedness the warm water gave her. His hand grabbed the edge of the curtain and flung it back. The plastic hooks banged each other on the pole.

She shrieked his name, attempted to cover herself with an arm and her washcloth. She screamed for him to get out.

Her hair looked like a dark liquid, a black wine, spilling from her head down the contours of her neck and shoulders, flowing over her back. Water splattered, beaded up, and ran over her freshly scrubbed skin. She seemed to glow a soft gold.

She grabbed for the shower curtain, reaching with the arm that had concealed her breasts. She tried to pull it between them, but Mason blocked it easily. She snarled. The soaked washcloth swung up, slapping Mason a stinging blow to the side of his face. The tip of the cloth had caught the outside corner of his eye. Mason touched the eye. His fingers came away with just water.

Gina said, "Now get the hell—"

Mason grabbed her by the upper arm, his fingers encircling it like a band. He pulled her from the shower. Her feet had no traction when she tried to pull away from him and she had to step over the lip of the tub quickly to avoid stumbling. His arms encircled her wet, slippery body.

"Mason, stop."

Holding her to him, his chest now wet against her, he caught her towel from the far end of the curtain rod. "Shh," he whispered. "Shh." He placed a hand at the small of her back to hold her tightly against him. With the towel, he dabbed gently between her shoulder blades, and then patted slowly down the shallow valley of her spine. "Shh, it's just us here," he whispered. He kissed the shoulder her sweatshirt had left bare in the kitchen. He licked it, sucked the water from it. Now he kissed the water from her neck, drinking her, pushing his face into her soaking hair. With both hands, for she no longer tried to step away, he drew the towel over her buttocks and then slowly up her back.

He heard his name whispered near his ear like a soft breath, like the steam roiling around them. She kissed at him under his chin. Moving gingerly, he toweled off her shoulders as if dusting a priceless artifact. Mason stroked her hair with the towel. He brought the towel around her front, leaving her hair to drape over one shoulder. He kissed the water from her breasts and between her breasts. Gina held on to his neck and shoulders, submitting to his caressing attention. He kneeled in front of her, dabbing, and kissing and drinking her in.

"Hey," she said. She smiled down at him. Her nipples stood erect. She shivered and each pore pimpled with goose bumps. The steam had dissipated. The shower had exhausted the hot water. "You goof." Her voice was no more than the breath it took to speak. "That's not going to get dry, so turn off the shower and take me to bed."

Mason moved quickly to turn off the shower. He kept his eyes on her, her beautiful nakedness, while his hand felt blindly over the tiles for the spigot. The shower off, he could hear water coursing in the drain and the rain still hammering madly outside. He grabbed her up.

In the hallway she cried, "Oh, it's cold out here. I'm freezing!"

Mason thought to say, *I'll warm you up,* but the connection between his brain and his voice box didn't work. He laid her on the bed.

"God! One of the only days I make up the bed," she said. She dug under the covers and held them open for Mason. "No, wait." She unbuttoned his pants and pulled down the zipper.

He heard the quick zipper sound distinctly and felt her hands fussing down there. He slapped her hands away and stepped back.

"What's wrong?" Gina asked. "Mason?"

He stood in the shadows, out of Gina's reach, and fought his confusion. He couldn't seem to get a breath; something, he thought, pressed against his chest.

The light on the bed stand came on. "Mase?" Gina looked at him with concern. She was beautiful, and she waited for him.

"I just...I just want to say you're beautiful."

Gina grinned.

Now, he squirmed from his jeans and briefs and slid under the covers Gina extended over him.

They simply held each other at first. Mason needed the time to understand what was happening, to breathe and not feel suffocated. He hovered over her; her skin was still damp and hot. He examined her eyes and nose and mouth. Her full lips looked tender.

"I don't mind when you stare at my face," she said. They kissed. "It's been a long time since I..." Her hands touched him, pulled on him.

The thrill made Mason shudder as if he were a frightened little boy. "Me too," he said.

Mason was glad the light was on; he needed to see her, to know it was Gina who moved next to him. They measured each other and grew confident and felt safe. The wet friction ignited Mason. He grunted at her ear, and heard her moans that seemed to burst from her throat without breath behind them. Gina rocked fiercely against him, turned her head to the side, her mouth open, and gasped into her pillow.

They cuddled tight and sticky to one another. Mason didn't think he would catch his breath ever again. He loved the sensation of the rise and fall of her chest against him. He listened to the rain, feeling quiet and complete, charged and calm.

"It's not like this…" Gina began, then restarted. "It's not the same at all."

He wanted her to be quiet. He let two fingers glide over one of her breasts, still marveling over its soft resiliency. He remained silent.

"I know you feel you have to leave. I could go with you. I could," she said.

Mason exhaled. His moment was slipping away to whatever came next.

"Maybe if you told me why…tell me what you plan to do. I think you owe me that much. What's so important? I know it has to do with your father."

It startled him she knew even that much.

"You let it slip once," she answered his question before he asked. "At the diner in Ohio, I think. And I don't forget anything."

"You're going to make me talk now, aren't you? Shouldn't we just smoke cigarettes or something?"

She raised up. Her hair tickled his chest. The lamplight reflected in her eyes, and her lips appeared a bit swollen from their kissing. "Please," she said. "And I know something else. I know it's not a good thing. If it was, you'd talk about it. And your eyes wouldn't look so hard most of the time. They're not pretty when they're like that. Please."

"God. Okay," he said. "Pretty, huh?" She lowered herself back into his embrace. He didn't speak right away. He wanted to say it right because he wouldn't be telling only her, he'd be telling himself too. Aloud or silently, it was something he had managed to avoid: putting it all in words. He couldn't tell her of the confrontation he envisioned with Pony and himself and the gun. "He's this low, mean, mean-spirited man. He thinks everybody else is too, so he treats them that way. And, I guess you should know, some people think I'm just like him. I got all mixed up with him, and stirred up with…" he paused. "Check this," he said. "I ain't seen him in years and sometimes I still smell his cologne. That's fucked, ain't it?" Mason's eyes teared suddenly, and he wiped them quickly with the tip of a pillowcase.

"My daddy, they call him Pony. Did I tell you that already? Pony. Don't know why. He had this gap-toothed girlfriend, one of dozens, believe me, named Lettie. I remember she was my favorite. She was nice, not too pretty...Anyway, one day we come over her place and she's highly pissed off. Pony had missed her birthday or something. She calls him names, shouting this and that, and says she ain't gonna put up with his trifling ways any more. And they were trifling. I was scared for her because she was standing up to him. He sent me to wait in the car while he beat the shit out of her. I kinda knew what was going on, but I didn't. It's hard to explain, and I've never tried to before."

"How old were you?" Gina asked.

"I don't know, twelve? Thirteen? Next day, or so, I went to see her. Her face was all swollen. One side bigger, skin all puffed out, one eye closed and the sickest green purple color. And she had to breathe out of her mouth. I asked her why she'd fronted Pony. We both knew what he'd do. So I asked her why she'd asked for the beating."

Gina asked, "What did she say?"

"She said, 'I knew he'd get after me good but I had to bring it to an ending. Had to pay the price,' she said. She said, 'He been chewing me up, had to get him to spit me out before he swallowed.'"

Lightning brightened the window. Mason wondered what Gina was thinking about. Had she understood? He had tried to make sense. He took her silence as his answer; she at least understood as much as he'd told her. It made him feel closer to her. He squeezed one of her shoulders, and felt her kiss his chest in reply. He did not want to let her go. He wondered if she'd really meant it when she'd said she could go away with him.

"Mason, " Gina began.

More lightning flashed, just outside it seemed. This time an explosive crack came with it. Two things happened at once. Something thumped like a hard-swung sledgehammer into the wall above them; the vibration of the impact went through the bed and him in a wave. And the window burst into shards flying at them like the rain and the wind that whipped into the room behind the glass.

Gina screamed. The shock made Mason holler out, too. Just above the headboard, he saw a gaping hole in the wall. This had not been a lightning strike. The report had been a gunshot. He rolled off the side of the bed farthest from the window taking Gina with him. He felt a glass shard cut him on his ribs.

"What! What!" Gina cried.

He held her to the floor.

ANNIE

Gail said she had a lead on Mason. She looked anxious and animated, but tired too. Weeks ago, Annie had thought Gail had all but written Mason off, but when she saw Gail's face, she knew she had been very wrong.

Annie said, "Let me know what you find out. I miss the boy too." But she doubted Gail heard her as she hustled out the front door.

As soon as Gail left, a thumping and bumping knocked on the walls and floor. Tyler couldn't have been causing that noise. Unless he was making music, he was normally a quiet boy. Besides he'd gone out in the morning, hours ago. Dan Neighbors had been here. Annie had spotted his car in the driveway, but he'd left before breakfast. Only Jackie remained, and her baby, Cole. Annie and Jackie had last talked days ago when the baby's father had showed up at the front door. Annie wondered how Jackie and her boyfriend were getting along: not well, she suspected. She knocked at Jackie's closed bedroom door. Dresser drawers scooted with dry squeaks and their handles rattled.

"Who is it?"

"Annie."

The door opened. "As long as Gail's not with you," Jackie said. She wore only a T-shirt and panties as far as Annie could tell. She moved from the doorway and back to her open bureau, where she pulled clothes out by the armload and hurled them onto the bed. Cole watched from a playpen in the corner. The room had been turned inside out. Boxes had been pulled from closet shelves, clothes were heaped everywhere, and drawers had been pulled completely from the chest and sat one tilting over another as haphazard as a car wreck.

"Well, Miss Annie, this is it. I'm pulling a Mason on this damn house. Hasta luego." Jackie switched clothes from one pile to another. She worked swiftly, but Annie couldn't discern any progress.

"What are you doing, child? Are you moving?"

"That's what I said. I'm tired of Gail jumping in my face, 'where's my money'," she mimicked, "'The rent's due. How could you leave Cole? You ain't gonna ruin my credit!' That's all she gives a shit about."

Annie walked into the room, around a pile of shoes. Jackie bumped her while turning to the closet.

"Excuse me, Miss Annie," she said. She was breathless. She hugged a section of clothes from the closet, lifted them in mass from the pole, and staggered to the bed with them. "God, I've got a lot of stuff."

Annie supported herself on the edge of the bed and picked up a lacy purple slip from the floor. Such indulgences, she thought; she'd never worn such frivolous things. "Where—"

Jackie almost bumped into Annie again. They were both small women. Annie was actually a bit taller than Jackie. Jackie put her hands on Annie's shoulders. "I wasn't going to skip saying goodbye, Miss Annie. But I've got to haul my butt. Kei and some girlfriends are coming by any minute to help me. I'm moving in with a couple of the girls. And I got to get all these things stuffed in boxes." She wrestled more clothes from the closet, leaving a trail of hangers.

"These girls know what they getting into with that one?" Annie watched Cole pull on the netting of the playpen walls.

Jackie had stooped to gather up the hangers. She stopped for a second and glanced at Cole. Then her eyes met Annie's and she looked away. "They won't complain," she said.

Jackie's friends arrived a minute later, and Annie was politely herded from the room and out of their way. She climbed the long staircase to her bedroom to sit in the room's only chair, a straight-backed armchair that had been in Joseph's and her home. Absently, she massaged her left knee. It had begun to petrify. It hurt. Sarrie trotted into the room, leading the others, who bunched around and nipped at one another in order to get closer to Annie. "Stop this nonsense," Annie told them. "General, stop." She wished Gail would return, or Tyler. Jackie ran past Annie's room a couple of times, bringing empty cardboard boxes down from the attic. Annie heard the front door opening and closing as the girls made trip after trip. They laughed. They squealed over something, sounding like kids roughhousing in the yard. Something was very wrong. "Sarrie, where's Gail got off to?"

A car's engine cut in front of the house. Annie went to the window, hoping to spot Gail. The white boy with the funny hair stepped from a small white car, Cole's father.

"Jackie!" she called. "Oh, Jackie!" Annie stood in her doorway.

The baby started crying.

Her arthritic leg became excruciating. With a small gasp, she returned to her chair. "Jackie," she called. Sarrie rested her long snout with its ancient whiskers in Annie's lap. "What's that girl up to?" she asked.

"Here we come, Miss Annie," She heard from the stairs. Jackie walked into the bedroom carrying Cole on her hip. "He wants to say goodbye, too. Don't you, boy? I asked his daddy to hold him for a minute and he started bawling. What a kid," Jackie said.

Annie reached out, and Jackie placed Cole in her lap. Annie hugged the baby.

Jackie looked around. "I'm going to miss your dogs too, Miss Annie. They's so well-behaved. Never kept me up howling or nothing. All housebroken and everything." Jackie grinned.

"Your friends sound as young as you, child," Annie told Jackie. "They won't put up with Cole after a week. You'll see. Stay here and work things out with Gail. Talk to her. It will be okay."

"Don't worry about Cole. He's going to have it better than all of us. His daddy's parents are going to be taking care of him."

Annie felt panic. "What do you mean, child?"

From downstairs a male voice called, "Jackie, everyone's waiting. Let's get a move on."

"I'm taking him to live with his grandparents in a ritzy neigh-borhood. No drugs, no punks and winos..." And Jackie answered the call, "Coming!"

"Jackie?" Annie could not believe her ears. The dogs were gone again. Annie, who'd never had a child of her own, felt suddenly numb. "No, girl. You ain't giving your child away?"

Jackie reached for the baby. "They are his family too. They have money. They got their lawyers out on a Saturday just so I can sign the papers."

Annie tightened her grip on Cole, who began to squirm.

"Miss Annie, I can't handle him, okay? He cries all the time. He needs me all the time. See, I know I ain't no fit mother. You want him tossed into a wall one day?" Tears welled in Jackie's eyes. "I almost did that already."

Cole reached for Jackie.

Annie could not remember feeling so weak. She wished she could lock this girl in the house until she came to her senses. "Don't do this, Jaclyn. It will weigh you down your whole life. It'll weigh him down too."

For a moment they were actually tugging at the baby between them.

The father called out again. There was the whine of a boy in his voice.

Annie felt Cole's chubby legs slide from her fingers. "You being a fool, girl," she whispered.

Jackie wiped at her eyes with her free hand. "Thanks for every-thing, Miss Annie," she said. "Bye."

Annie watched her run out the door. Her feet pounded rapidly on the stairs. "Jackie!" Annie called. By the time Annie had pushed herself from the chair and struggled to the head of the stairs, the front door had opened with a slight creak. She called out to Jackie and started down the stairs. She heard the door shut. She tried to take the next steps in a hurry and her leg gave out on her. Each step rushed up to batter her brittle body. She tumbled down the entire first case of stairs to the landing. She hit heavily and something snapped; bones somewhere in her chest had given way. With one arm trapped beneath her, Annie lay on her stomach. For a while she couldn't get oriented, didn't know if she faced up the stairs or down, didn't know where her limbs were exactly. For a terrifying moment, she had no control of her body, no sensation. Then the pain sprang to sharp, biting life. Her face pressed into the worn fibers of carpet. A spot of blood formed an almost perfect circle at her mouth. Pain seared her lungs with each breath. Something under her breasts, her own bones, stabbed her. She shut her eyes tightly against the pain. Her cheeks twitched and her lips trembled. *Where is everybody,* she thought in her fear, *they done all left me.*

She lay on the landing for what seemed like a very long time. She found that if she breathed shallowly the pain lessened. Her mind calmed. The woman who'd for months suffered her arthritis in silence began to cope with this greater pain, too. She managed to free the arm trapped beneath her. The moment she propped herself up on her elbows, she felt better. "Lord, what you do," she whispered. Annie dragged herself to the next set of steps. There was no going back up. Slowly bringing her legs around in front of her, she was able to sit up and place her feet on the second step below. The exertion left her dazed. She leaned against the wall. One hand gripped the handrail just above her head.

On the floor below, her loyal dogs waited. Massed in a pack of red, black, and white canine fur, they paced and shuffled at the foot of the stairs. A few let out impatient, restless whines. *I'm coming,* she told them without speaking, *do y'all need to be let out?*

Her father had kept dogs, as many as nine at one time. They were strays who'd learned that the family in the split-log cabin with the split-log outhouse would feed any dog that didn't try to take a bite at them. Her daddy would try to hunt with the dogs, with little success. They were wet-tongued playmates to Annie that pounced on her clean skirts with dirty paws. Mostly they were loyal guardians, arranged about the cabin at night, barking at strangers and gophers, howling at the evil spirits borne on the wind. These sentries, long forgotten through most of Annie's adulthood, and recalled only during these last years, used to keep vigil over her, ensuring a little girl's sleep went inviolate.

One step at a time, Annie scooted down the stairs to them. With her feet on the floor, leaning a shoulder and her head against the balustrade, she rested.

The front door opened with a crack and startled her. She brought a hand to her mouth and came away with a bright smear of blood and dry flecks. She wiped the blood on her skirt, then tucked the stain from view by folding it under. She sat up as straight as she could. The broken bones raked her inside.

"Hey, who's home?" Gail called. "Ty? Annie? I've got news!"

"Here, Gail," Annie said. She dared not lean around the banister to glance Gail's way. "Did you bring Mason home?" That question slipped out like a whisper.

Gail came to the staircase. She smiled broadly, looking down at Annie. "Annie, I know where Mason is! He's in Maryland. I have his number! I'm just about to call him now. I can't believe it. I've got his number right here. I had a long talk with this woman named Maxine." As Gail spoke she rummaged through her purse. She pulled out a yellow slip of paper and held it up in front of her as if it were a trophy. "I told myself all the way home, be cool, Gail. I almost ran the whole way. People looking at me like I was a crazy woman. Told myself not to bitch at him. I don't want to fuss. He ain't done a thing wrong. I...I just want to tell him to come home. Gotta get to a phone." Gail started to walk away.

"Gail," Annie said. "Wait, Gail." Every word took an effort Annie fought not to show.

Gail said something about needing to make her phone call first.

"No," Annie said. "Jackie's done left."

"What?" Gail marched away and returned in a moment with a sheet of paper in her hands. "It says, don't worry you'll get the rent money. No prior notice, nothing. Maybe this is for the better."

"The girl's gone to give her baby away," Annie said. "She said she couldn't raise him. Said she was going to give him to the daddy's parents, and she was moving in with some girlfriends."

Gail covered the lower half of her face with a hand. "She told you this? When did all this happen?"

There was a knock at the front door.

"Just now," Annie replied. She didn't think she could hold on much longer. Something inside seared.

"The fool," Gail said and went to answer the second knock.

Annie heard another voice.

"What can she be thinking?" she heard Gail say. "Do you know where the Sullivans live?"

Gail came back to the steps. "Annie, Kei's here. He's a friend of Jackie's and knows where Perry lives. We're going." Gail frowned. "Are you all right? Why are you sitting here?"

Annie waved a hand. "Girl, I been running up and down these stairs, trying to talk sense to that girl. Wore me out. I'll just sit here a bit."

"Well, if you're sure you're okay?"

Annie smiled and nodded.

Gail and Kei left. The door shut behind them. The car started and Annie heard it driven away. She leaned against the banister. On this short autumn day, the late afternoon shadows began to fill the corners of the room and the spaces behind the furniture. Annie sat very still. She was trying to remember if the Bucklers had said they would come by today or tomorrow. She didn't know. The dogs climbed the stairs and surrounded her protectively. Sarrie rested her head in Annie's lap. The others settled on the steps above her and at her feet. The snouts of some rested on the backs of others. They all eyed her, their big, dark eyes full of concern and sympathy for their beloved friend, watching her, guarding her. They waited with her.

The pain eased at last, she stands on the Bucklers' porch at twilight, a cool, late spring evening. Joseph Gant has a bouquet of flowers, yellows and reds and pink-tinged whites with dark eyes that he has picked himself. She recognizes some as coming from the gardens of the Bucklers' neighbors. Joseph is a caution. He is wearing his dark suit with the thin white stripes, and the same heavy-soled boots he works in, his only pair, but they've been polished enough so that light from the kitchen window gleams on the toes. Annie wears a flowery print dress she and the Frau made. It almost perfectly matches the flowers Joseph carries. He tells her she is beautiful tonight. Annie spreads the skirt of the dress for Joseph to see and knows she grins far too widely. She is also aware this fledgling courtship has witnesses. From the same window that casts light on Joseph's polished boots peek the Buckler boys. She pretends not to notice them, hoping Joseph doesn't, but their faces are crowded together in one corner beneath the raised curtain. Annie knows the boys resent Joseph because he may take her from them, but she knows, too, they love her enough to be happy for her.

GAIL

Minutes ago, nothing could have kept her from getting to the phone and dialing Gina Manara's number. Gail had burst through her front doorway excited and agitated, anxious to call her son, nettled by something close to fear over what he might say, how he might accuse her, yet in minutes, she tore from the house again, buffeted by an entirely new set of emotions. It had not been a decision, simply a reaction to grab the strange boy, Kei, by the arm and run with him to his car. Bewildered by her own haste, she could see in the sidelong glances Jackie's friend gave her that she confused him too.

I don't owe her anything, Gail thought, and then corrected herself. *Why do I owe her?* She had taken to the young girl initially when she appeared one day with a baby in her arms, looking for a room to rent. Gail had felt sorry for her. They had put it to a vote, Ty, Mason, Annie, and herself, on whether they would be willing to endure the crying of a baby who'd not yet learned to sleep through the night. The vote had been unanimous. Not that she didn't still have affection for Jackie; she did. Over time, she had distanced herself from the girl just as—and this new notion startled her—she had distanced herself from Dan. Too busy praying about the past to live in the present, Dan once said of her.

"Where do the Sullivans live?" she asked Kei. She saw his earrings and oddly cut hair, but made no comment, even to herself. He answered; she nodded, and said, "Step on the gas."

He smiled and did, and they zigzagged down the highway from one lane to the next.

"Ms. Neighbors," Kei said, "I don't know if you've thought about this, but isn't there a grace period or something? Won't Miss Thing have time to change her mind? And besides, it's Saturday. You can't make anything like adoption official on a Saturday. Can you?"

"Probably not," Gail answered, but suspected her haste was not entirely rational. After today, she might not see Jackie again. The girl would be out of her influence, thus losing Gail the chance to talk her out of it, and the act would have been done. Jackie would have handed over her baby, relinquished her responsibilities to Cole, even if she later changed her mind. People shouldn't always know what they are capable of; as Gail saw it, there was something about such an act that could never entirely be undone. Gail feared that the more time went by, the harder the decision would be to break, the way poured concrete grew in time to be hard as stone.

Those reasons all seemed good and defensible, but they had occurred to Gail only after they'd gotten on the highway. They were explanations she'd hoped to fool herself with.

It seemed like a long time before they exited the highway and turned into a tree-lined neighborhood of expansive yards, brick wall fences, and curving drives.

Kei drove slowly, searching for the Sullivans' house. Bare poplars lined either side of the street, all so close in size and equidistant from each other that they looked artificial in their perfect orderliness. Driving between them reminded her of walking down the aisle between church pews. She recalled one particular walk, the last time her mother and she attended service together. The pews at New Life Baptist, the church they had belonged to, always shined with a layer of polish that Gail and her friends could slide on. With just a little shove, and holding their patent leather shoes off the floor, they'd glide over the pews on their underpants, giggling and getting glared at as they went.

When she returned from Alice Durkee's house, she no longer slid along the pews. She sat with her friends, but she did not giggle at the fat ladies who sat up front, nor did she run for cold Cokes and hot tamales after the service. She placed all her money in the silver offering plate and passed it on with a prayer. To those who noted the change in the teenager, Nora Wallington explained how Gail's father had recently died. And though he wasn't much as fathers go, "I guess she misses him some."

All eyes had turned the last time Gail walked down the center aisle of New Life Baptist Church. The young reverend Clay Hammond had barely begun his sermon when she stood and pushed past the knees of the other worshipers who sat between her and the aisle without asking their pardon. She started from far in the back where her friends always sat. Reverend Hammond's sing-song oratory continued, something about Joshua and Daniel, and faith and mustard seeds, if Gail recalled correctly. She did not look up at first; she eyed the wine-red carpet and her own glistening shoes. The aisle seemed so long, at least the length of a block. She felt the eyes turn in her direction, heard the soft rustle of Sunday finery as people shifted in the pews for a look. The reverend's voice faltered as he finally noticed her. The time in the service allotted for testimony and public repentance, or for accepting Jesus Christ as your personal savior, had not yet come. Gail heard one of her friends trying to call her back in a loud whisper. Gail held her head up midway in her journey. The reverend's wide sleeves, like black wings, dropped to his side. Hammond's perplexity was clear. Maybe something in the young girl's face caused the last sentence in his head to dribble out, each word a drop, until he silently watched too. Finally Nora Wallington, whose attention had been focused on the reverend, turned her head, the last to do so. Gail saw the puzzlement on Nora's face and saw her mouth form her name. Gail glared at her. Her mother's puzzlement turned to anger.

"What is it, child?" the reverend asked. "Have you come to re-dedicate your life to Christ? Can I get an amen from the faithful?"

"No," Gail said, and most of the amens died in people's throats.

Nora Wallington stood. "She's distraught. Her father died recently," Nora explained to those around her.

Heads turned from Gail to Nora and back.

Nora moved toward Gail. "Let me collect her," she said.

"Don't come near me," Gail said, pointing a finger at her mother to hold her in place.

She rotated slowly at her spot just before the altar, where silver trays crowded with tiny glasses containing shots of the blood of Christ sat on white linen. On one side of the church, Nora stood in the Mother's Board pew next to elderly matrons dressed in cleanest white with hanging dewlapped skin and expressions ranging from stern to confused. Still turning toward the front of the church, seeking a friendly face, she confronted the New Life Gospel Jubilee Choir in their rustling blue shiny robes. Faces she'd known for years appeared as strangers just then, altered by expectation and embarrassment. Gail turned to the young reverend draped in flowing black. His mouth opened, but he said nothing. She turned back to the congregation, the side where the dark-suited deacons sat up front, arms crossed with well-thumbed Bibles wedged in them.

The fourteen-year-old girl with two plastic red barrettes shaped like bows in her hair, patent leather shoes with straps across the top and flat heels, a member of the Youth of New Life Baptist, had fixed every man and woman in place on a Sunday morning already hot and damp, the AC not working quite right, and the paddle fans, cardboard funeral home ads stapled to tongue depressors, working rapidly under their sweaty chins. In front of all of them—her mother, her mother's pastor boyfriend, entire families, her friends—she sought one face not necessarily sympathetic but not accusing, not put out, and settled on an old woman in a bell-shaped green hat whom she did not know but whose memory reminded her now of Annie. She said to that woman, "You said if I love Jesus...I do. You told me...you told me if I knocked, the door would be opened." Gail saw frowns and people craning their ears toward her. She shouted, pushing each word from deep in her belly, "You told me knock and the door shall be opened! I'm praying crazy," she hollered. Her hands clasped and wagged in front of her. "I'm praying my mama will tell me where my baby is. I prayed for my daddy to help me, but he died. Tell me how I'm praying wrong!"

The congregation murmured collectively. No one had known of her pregnancy, or of the cover-up. Eyes rolled to Nora now, amused, surprised, judgmental. A scandal would be something almost tangible they could take home from the Sunday service.

Gail said, "I know I sinned, but I repented." Her vision was so blurred with tears she could barely see. Nora was moving toward her. "I repented about not wanting the baby at first. I want her now. Mama, who'd you give my baby to?"

A member of the Mother's Board asked, "Where's the baby now, Nora?"

People waited on Nora, less amused. Clay Hammond looked to Nora.

"She's depressed and she's still ill," Nora said. "We were going to bring it back. I was going to say it was mine." Nora returned Hammond's gaze. "But there was no baby. It was stillborn."

Shouts came from every pew. "Oh, honey," the woman in the bell-shaped hat said.

"No, I saw her," Gail shouted. "A girl. She had a full head of hair already. I saw that."

"Where's this girl's baby, Sister Wallington?" someone asked.

Someone else grabbed Nora's wrist, which she yanked from his grasp.

"They were shamed of me and didn't want anybody to know," Gail said. She turned a pointing finger on Clay Hammond. "He knew all about it."

Reverend Hammond's face opened in a look of pure shock. She did not know what he knew. His surprise seemed so genuine Gail doubted her accusation, but she knew it would hurt her mother. Innocent or not, Hammond saw his career at New Life end that day.

Nora was in the aisle now. "Gail, let's go home."

"Mama, I want my baby!" she screamed. "I told Jesus I'm sorry. I want her!" As Nora wrapped her arms around her shoulders, Gail tried shrugging her off, and said one last time to her, "I prayed. I want her now."

Kei pulled partially into a driveway behind a line of cars. He cut the engine. "You're not going to change her mind. You know that, right?"

"Are you coming?"

"Oh, this will definitely be worth the price of admission."

Gail led the way to the door with Kei trailing a step or two behind. She rapped hard on the door.

"Jackie wants to start over. She feels cheated, I think," Kei said. "She tried to make things work, but this Perry was no help. And, well...she's Jackie...Little J. Girlfriend used to step out at two a.m. to party."

A black woman Gail vaguely recognized opened the door. She smiled, then eyed Kei with quick condemnation. "I know you," she said to Gail. "Come in. Come in. You hired me for a party at the Hirsches last year. Judie Garvey. I'm always available, you know."

"You did a good job, Judie. I'll keep you in mind," Gail said. "We're looking for Jaclyn Bell. A little woman." Gail held a hand out at shoulder height. "And her baby."

Judie's face glowed with instant excitement. "Yeah," she said. "There's a lot buzzing around here today. Lawyers and everything. Perry done fathered that girl's baby, didn't he?"

Gail stepped past the woman. "Where are they, Judie?" The woman motioned with an arm and Gail moved swiftly by, not waiting for her to take the lead. "Jackie!" she called. "Jackie Bell!" Gail felt blood rushing up inside her. She crossed the living room in a trot, not noticing, at first, that Judie Garvey had not followed. Gail's agitation increased. "Where?" she asked. *This one will not get away,* she thought.

"No. This direction, ma'am." Judie pointed down a hallway. "The library," she said. She and Kei let Gail jog past them.

"Jackie!" Gail called. "Jackie, stop." She peeked in doorway after doorway, not waiting for her guide. "Jackie Bell!"

"Gail?" she heard Jackie's voice.

She turned a corner and stepped into a crowded room. In the library lined with bookshelves and old books, Jackie sat on a green leather couch next to a white woman who held Cole on her lap. Everyone looked up: Jackie, the woman with Cole, a man next to her, a young man with punk-cut hair standing off to himself, a man sitting behind a large desk with two others hovering over him.

"Jackie, what in God's name do you think you're doing?" Gail asked.

"Is this your mother, Jackie?" the woman with Cole asked.

"No. No, Mrs. Sullivan, she ain't."

Gail stepped farther into the room. Jackie's and her eyes were locked.

"Well, could you wait, Miss?" the man on the couch said. "We're taking care of an important family matter here."

"Kei?" Jackie said.

He answered from behind Gail, "Hey."

"Jackie, we have to talk now," Gail said. "Come on with us."

"Who is this?" Mrs. Sullivan asked.

"Just my ex-landlady," Jackie said. "Kei, what did you bring her here for?"

"I think she made me," Kei said.

The man on the couch, Mr. Sullivan, Gail supposed, stood. "Miss, you'll have to wait in the living room."

Gail ignored him. "You can't give your baby away. You mustn't. Let's talk about it. Come on."

Jackie snickered, but she was frowning. "You need my rent money that bad, Gail? That's all you're worried about, right? Your credit rating? Girl, get away from me."

Gail wanted to turn and walk out. She looked at the huddled lawyers, not in suits on Saturday but in open-collared dress shirts. They seemed indifferent, or merely irritated at the intrusion. The boy off to the side glanced about nervously; his eyes finally settled on his feet. Gail said, "You haven't been the greatest mother in the world, Jackie. Hell, no one is. But I thought you loved Cole. I know you do. When he gets old enough, you gonna tell him, I loved you, but I gave you up because you cramped my style?"

"Go to hell."

"That's it. Get her out of here, Bob."

Bob Sullivan reached for Gail's arm.

"I'll knock you so hard you'll rattle for a month."

"It's my house..." Bob Sullivan's voice waned.

Jackie jumped to her feet. She glanced at Cole, and said to Gail, "I can't do what you did. All right? I know you raised two boys almost by yourself. But everybody ain't like you, Gail. I can't do it. I tried to tell you before. He takes more than I have. He's always crying for something. You know how he is. I'm afraid I'll—" Jackie took a breath. The tiny woman's lip quivered. "I can't do it alone and he, that cowardly shit," she pointed to Perry, who looked distressed, "ain't about to help me."

Gail stepped around Bob Sullivan to stand near Mrs. Sullivan and Cole. She wanted to say this right. Too much was at stake. She touched the top of the boy's head and Mrs. Sullivan scooted back on the sofa, taking the baby just out of Gail's reach. "You said you couldn't do what I did," Gail said. "But that's just what you're about to do. Only person I've told this to is Dan, but I had my first baby when I was fourteen. I had a girl, and I gave her up, Jackie. I was scared. More scared than you. That baby growing in me terrified me. I thought it wanted to take me over, you know, like you said. But then I realized too late that all she wanted was to be born, to be my daughter, to love me and for me to love her." Gail shook her head slowly. Don't cry in front of these people, fool, she told herself.

"Jackie, you give him away and you'll regret it every day forever. I know. You'll feel like you've betrayed him. You won't get over it. It won't feel better tomorrow, or next week, or ten years from now. Some people have to give up their babies. I understand that. But I didn't have to, if my mother had stood with me. And you don't, either."

"Look, whoever you are." Mrs. Sullivan held Cole tightly. "You're missing the point. Jackie wants Cole to have the best opportunities and education. What's best for the baby is the point. Jackie is doing the right thing."

"You want to give him those things? You still can," Gail said to Frances Sullivan, "Unless you're planning to forget he's your grandson if he's not living here?"

Jackie rapidly shook her head. "You ain't listening. I said I couldn't do it alone."

"That's what I'm here to tell you, girl. You don't have to. I want—" Gail's heart raced. She hadn't known she would say this. "I want to take care of both of you. We'll raise the boy together. Me and you, and Annie and Tyler. You won't have to pay rent if you don't have it. I'll look out for you, you look out for him."

"Gail." Jackie's eyes were flooded.

"Okay?" The tears Gail had fought against fell anyway. "I need a daughter."

"Keep your baby, homegirl," Kei said.

"Keep him, Jackie," Perry said.

"Perry, shut up," Mrs. Sullivan said.

"Don't give him up," Kei said.

Mrs. Sullivan turned to her husband. "Bob," she said.

"Don't Bob me. What can I do?"

Jackie fell into Gail. Gail wrapped her arms about the little woman, hugged her as fiercely as if she hadn't seen her in twenty-five years.

Perry took Cole from Mrs. Sullivan. He kissed the baby on the forehead. "We're going to want a lot of visits," he said.

Jackie nodded, loosening more tears, and took her baby.

They were quiet on the way home. Jackie and Cole rode in the back. Gail wet her lips with her tongue. The enormity of the commitment she'd just made hit her. She would not only be seeing to the rearing of the baby, but the mother as well. She feared that if she lingered on the effort and responsibility she faced it would feel overwhelming, and at a time when her own boys were finally grown. In Kei's canted passenger side rearview mirror she saw herself resting her head against the glass. She smiled wryly. Now where was this youth Dan had glimpsed this morning?

"Gail?" Jackie said. "I forgot to tell you. I got fired from my job."

MASON

Wind and rain gusted in like the spray of ocean waves. The shade slapped frantically at the wall and ceiling. Gina tried to get up, but he held her to the floor.

"Somebody just shot at us through the window," he said. He peeked over the bed trying to see out the window; he could see nothing. Rain drummed on the side of Gina's bureau. He reached up quickly, trying to stay as low as possible, and turned over the bed stand lamp. He felt for the switch and turned the light out. A piece of glass fell from the window and shattered.

"What was that?" Gina asked in a whisper. "Who's out there?"

"I want you to stay here. I'm going to find out, but I bet it's Gamble. I'm going to fry his ass this time."

Mason tried to crawl over Gina but she held on to him. "What if he gets in?"

"Don't worry, stay put. He ain't pissed at you. It's me he wants."

"That's supposed to make me feel relieved or something? Get to the phone. Dial nine-one-one."

"He wants a piece of me. Well, I got something for him." Mason scrambled lizard-like on hands and knees into the hallway. He heard Gina calling after him in loud whispers. He crawled over the linoleum in the utter darkness, feeling vulnerable in his nakedness, and thinking only of getting to his duffel bag and his gun. Just head and shoulders into the small living room, he had to stop for a piercing pain cutting into his lower right ribs. In the dark he could not see the wound. A bit of wetness trickled from the spot where he removed a toothpick sized splinter of glass that had punctured him when he rolled off the bed.

Mason crawled into the living room and crouched near a chair, looking toward the door and then the windows. The dark was not so absolute in the living room, where light from the Oates's porch lessened it. After a few moments, when nothing moved at or passed by the windows except splattering rain, Mason dashed to the sofa. On his knees again, he crawled to where he had kept his duffel bag tucked away on the floor against the wall since the first day he'd come to the little house. A noise, a small click and tap, came from the back of the house. Mason fished through his bag for his handgun.

"Mase, I hear something," Gina called.

He didn't answer her. Mason turned the bag upside down and shook out the contents, his clothes—more than he'd started out with, and all pressed and folded for his departure by Gina—tumbled into a pile. He scattered the pile, pressing his hands into the mass. "Damn. Damn it," he hissed.

He definitely heard noises now, but could not place them. He resisted the temptation to turn on the light, fearing it would make him an easy target for the prowler outside. The idea of running from Gamble irked him, but he wondered if he shouldn't just grab Gina and make a run to a neighbor's house. He made one more blind hunt for the gun, then grabbed a pair of jeans from the pile.

The back door slammed. Still naked, Mason leaped up, headed toward the kitchen, and fell over the coffee table. The empty bottle of Cold Duck rolled near his right hand and he grasped it by the neck. Gina screamed and another gunshot went off, this time in the house.

Mason dashed into the kitchen calling her name. Lightning flashed through the glass of the back door. "Gina!" he shouted. Mason ran back down the hallway, almost slipping on the wet linoleum floor, completing his circle of the house and returning to the bedroom.

"Mason, stay back," Gina said. Her voice came from the far side of the room.

"Get your ass in here, lover," Tullis said. "And turn on the light. You guys like to do it with the light on, anyway."

Mason stepped into the room. The burnt powder odor of a discharged gun hung inside the doorway. His feet stepped on pieces of glass but none of it cut him. He found the lamp he had upset earlier, righted it, and pressed the switch. Gina stood at the window holding a soaked sheet tightly against her. Her hair blew up and out like the shade. The window had a huge gaping hole surrounded by intricate cracks like a mosaic. On the same side of the room as Mason, but parked in the other corner, sat Tullis, soaked through and through, holding Mason's gun sideways and straight out in front of him as an extension of his fist. He blinked at the light and droplets fell from his lashes. His army jacket was sopping wet, as was his red bandanna. And the rain in his beard looked like tiny lights. Tullis's eyes looked over Mason's nakedness. Then he glanced up and Mason eye's followed. In addition to the hole in the wall over the bed, another hole had been put in the ceiling. A hand-sized section of plaster dangled. The gun pointed somewhere between Mason and Gina, closer to her maybe.

Mason still held the bottle in his right hand. He held it slightly behind his leg, though Tullis must've seen it.

Tullis's top lip curled over his teeth. He sucked the water from his moustache. He gaped at Gina mostly, yet his eyes flicked regularly to Mason.

Mason could not afford to look Gina's way. He eyed Tullis and the gun, his gun, held by Carl Tullis, who controlled the situation, dictated the events, just as Mason had wanted to do. "What the fuck do you think you're doing, man?" Mason asked.

Tullis shuddered, his wet tires squeaked on the linoleum. "She was trying to climb out the window when I came in, Mason."

Now Mason glanced quickly at Gina. She shivered from the rain and the cold. Hair blew across her face. He couldn't tell if she looked frightened, but he thought she must be because she wasn't saying anything.

"Mason, Mason, Mason." Carl Tullis still held the gun rigidly forward. "You took me up on my offer, damn but quick. God damn! Whoo, weee." Water dripped from Tullis; he looked as if he were melting into the chair. "Gina, did our Mr. Moody Guest tell you what we talked about this evening? Bet he didn't."

Gina said, "The Oateses have probably called the cops by now. After those gunshots." She sniffed, held herself by gripping her shoulders. "Tully?"

"Right. With all the rain and thunder. I don't think so."

"Tully? I want to put on some clothes."

Carl Tullis answered back with a snarl, "You shouldn't have taken them off!"

Mason said, "When you put that gun down, I'm going to beat the shit out of you, crippled or not."

"Shut up, Mason," Gina said. She shivered in the blow of the elements. The soaked sheet, clinging to her body like a wet T-shirt, gave her no protection.

"Step away from the window, Gina. Put your robe on. He ain't going to hurt you."

Gina didn't move.

Tullis switched the gun to his left hand, still holding it out like a salute. He shivered too. "You weren't supposed to really do it," he said. "Damn. I mean, I wanted you to. I told Mason it was okay with me if you two got it on, right? But, Gina, this dumb, young punk…" For the first time, Tullis aimed the gun directly at Mason.

Mason stared at Tullis's eyes. If Tullis was going to shoot, his eyes would warn him. Mason braced himself, but the stubby barrel swung away to the middle of the room.

Tullis switched gun hands again. This time he held the gun closer in. "You remember California, Gina? I can't for the life of me think why we ever wanted to leave. Remember how we used to race across campus after classes? Couldn't wait to get home."

Her whole frame trembling, Gina moved forward. She dragged her robe from the foot of the bed, slipped it on. She said, "I remember it all." The soaked sheet dropped to the floor.

"No you don't. If you did you wouldn't climb into my bed with him, God damn it."

"It was your idea, man," Mason said.

"Shut up," Gina said again. She had overcome her fear. She took another step toward Tullis, now just six or seven feet from her. "It wasn't like that. He told me what you said." She shook her head, then pushed the wet ropes of hair from her face. "We weren't going to do anything but watch TV. But then…I don't know." She shrugged. "I don't know."

Tullis tapped the armrest of his wheelchair. "I thought this happened to both of us. You said we were in it together. That's what you said at the hospital."

"My teeth are chattering," Gina said. "Oh, Tully…I'm sorry. It didn't happen to both of us. I don't think I can share all of that with you. But I've been here for you, haven't I? Haven't I? You tell me. Why did you think to send Mason to me? Why did you want us to sleep together? Huh?"

"I don't know," he said. His gun hand dropped to his lap. Nothing else was said for a long minute. The rain slacked off and the wind too. The shade quit its struggle. A huge puddle had formed on the floor from the window side of the room to peek out from under the bed near Mason and the doorway.

Mason said, "I'm going to go put some clothes on."

"No!" Tullis brought the gun up and fired. Mason dropped the wine bottle. His hands covered his head. In the small room, the explosion slammed Mason's eardrums.

Gina screamed.

"You ain't going nowhere," Tullis said.

The room filled with the sulfurous smell. The bullet had punched another hole in the wall, this one small and neat, just a foot from where Mason's head had been.

"God damn it, Tully!" Gina said.

"Next shot, I'll shoot your dick off. She'll have no reason to love you then." He waved the gun in Gina's direction.

"I'm not afraid of you," she said.

Tullis's free hand pulled the bandanna from his head. His wet hair clung to the shape of his skull. "That's the problem. Why should you?" In a quick motion, Tullis shoved the gun against his right temple, pushing it hard against his head as if he wanted to drive the barrel through skin and bone. The chair rolled back and bumped the closet door behind him. He quaked from the waist up. Spit came from his mouth. "I love you, Gina," he said through his teeth.

"Tully! Don't. Please, don't!" Gina's hands reached out helplessly, but she didn't move from her spot.

Mason stepped forward quickly. His foot slapped into the puddled water and sent the forgotten wine bottle skittering toward Tullis's chair.

"Stay back," Tullis said. The features of his face were pulled into lines. His head vibrated. His fingers tightened on the trigger.

Mason swept at the gun just as it made a dry, quiet click over an empty cylinder. He knocked the gun from Tullis's grasp. It bounded off the wall and dropped in a puddle at the chair's wheels.

"It was my gun," Mason said. "Only had three bullets."

His face covered by his hands, Tullis slumped forward and fell from his chair. Mason just missed catching him. Gina dropped immediately by Tullis's side, whispering and petting his head. He lay in a curled heap in his soaked field jacket with his small, thin legs trailing behind, looking like a tadpole, all body and underdeveloped legs. He cried loudly.

Gina glanced up at Mason. Hair hung in front of her face, nearly obscuring her eyes.

"I'm going to put some clothes on," Mason said. He hesitated over the gun for a second before leaving it there on the floor.

Mason dressed in the living room without turning on a light. He wore the clothes he would leave in. After repacking his bag, he dropped onto the sofa and stretched his legs across the coffee table, though he did not feel relaxed at all. His own reaction to Tullis had surprised him. He'd been startled, especially with the third shot close to his head, but mostly Mason had not been frightened, and he figured he should have been. A point-five man, as Tullis called himself, was certainly as dangerous with a gun as anyone else. Tullis had sought to control the situation, force Gina and him to listen, yet nothing profound had transpired. Carl Tullis could have killed or not killed, but he couldn't change what Mason thought about him. Even when Tullis turned the gun on himself, Mason had no sympathy for him. The gun had not increased Tullis's stature, it had not given him dominion. The gun could not increase nor convince, only take away.

Light began to show at the windows. Mason had not slept but figured he would get enough rest on the bus. He had let his mind roam where it would and not pulled back when thoughts of Pony Reed and Lettie entered, or the image of himself squeezing Gail's wrist as hard as he could. He thought of Tyler, and Miss Annie, and baby Cole and his tiny, grabby fingers.

He did not return to the back of the house to check on Gina. She would call if she needed help. Noises and talk came from down the hall, but he tuned them out. Finally, with the morning peeking in, and the night's rain dripping and draining outside, Gina walked into the living room dressed in white sweats, her hair tied behind her except for stray wisps framing her face.

She did not sit on the sofa with him immediately. "I changed the sheets because of the glass and put him to bed," she said. "Swept up the glass, mopped the floor. I used some heavy plastic and duct tape on the window. Fat lot of help there. He's asleep. He apologized." It seemed she was waiting for a comment, but Mason said nothing. "And before you ask, I've hidden your pistol. You won't find it and I'm not telling you where it is. Later I'm going to bury it somewhere."

"Sit down," Mason said.

"You don't care?"

"Sounds like it wouldn't matter if I did."

She said, "It wouldn't," and sat down next to him, legs tucked under her.

Mason turned toward her. She was as beautiful as she had been yesterday on the mountain. He touched her knee lightly with his index finger and skimmed it along her leg until he reached her hand, which rested in her lap. Their fingers entwined on contact. "I'm never forgetting last night," Mason said.

"Who could?"

"I ain't talking about Tullis."

Gina said, "I know."

"Then you remember you said you might come away with me. Well, you started to say it."

"I know I did, but well, you see I can't, at least not now. Carl needs me."

"He always will, like a tick sucking on the back of your neck. You're doing just what he hoped. I think he pretended the whole thing. First to make you feel guilty for being with me. And then so you can feel sorry for him all over again. For legs that don't work, he sure is getting a lot of mileage out of them."

Gina pulled her hand from Mason's. "I don't see how you can say that," she said. "He was drunk and distraught. And what if he'd gotten more bullets for that pistol? From Conklin or somebody? You could have gotten him killed rushing up to him like that."

"He knew he'd emptied the gun. He don't want to die any more than anybody else. Staged the whole thing right from when he said to me outside, go give her what I can't."

"What for?"

265

"Like I said, to guilt you. So you could feel sorry for him. Like you do. And so you'd stay. Like you will."

"Bullshit. Danny Glover don't act that well."

"Mighty funny he didn't turn the gun on himself until he'd fired three times."

"You're wrong."

Mason shrugged. "I've been wrong before." He planted his feet on the floor. *It's time to walk,* he thought, and he felt certain of that. "You like all this anyway." He waved a hand in the air. "You like playing the put-upon refugee in the mountains."

"Oh, you've got everybody figured out now. How smart you've become. If anyone's the refugee it's you, running away from home like a little boy." Gina's face looked as if she regretted saying that, but she didn't apologize, only looked down, tugging on the draw-string of her sweats.

The pair sat silently. Mason fought the impulse to stand and throw his duffel over his shoulder. Wind shook the outside of the house. Mason realized he had nothing to say to her. He wasn't certain he'd want her to come along even if she'd offered.

"I guess we're going to argue up to the end," Gina said.

"Least you ain't spanking me with a fly-swatter," Mason said. "Did I tell you you're beautiful?" he asked. She nodded. "Did you believe me?" She nodded again and smiled. "Good," he said and stood and picked up his duffel.

"I'd walk you to the bus stop, but..." She pointed with a thumb to the back of the house where Tullis slept it off. "You still going to DC?"

"Maybe. Probably not." Mason went to the door, turned the knob and leaned halfway into the damp, bracing cold.

"When I ironed your clothes, I put my name and number on a piece of paper in every pocket you own," Gina said.

Mason fished in one pocket and then another, producing a small square slip of paper each time. He laughed.

"They have both this number and Maxine's number back home on them. When I do leave this place, you'll find me there." Gina raised her open mouth to Mason and he kissed her softly.

As he walked across the soggy front yard, Mason adjusted the bag over his right shoulder and straightened his back. After the stuffy little house, the rush of the cold air invigorated him. When he got to the road he looked back. Gina stood framed by the doorway, a hand to her mouth. He waved, but she did not.

He made a point of surveying the angles and lines of the mountains and the woolly mass of tall pines as he went. He would not be by this way again. Rainwater from the night's deluge dripped off every limb and roof. At one side of the road, a rocky gully channeled the runoff, which coursed like a miniature river. He followed the rushing water until it fell away over a rocky slope. Mason and the road kept to a steadier decline.

The small hamlet of stores and gas stations at the bottom of the hill was completely deserted this early Sunday morning. He seemed to have what little was there all to himself. He went unhurriedly across a wet and oily street. Somewhere in the distance, a woman called, the first evidence he was not alone. Mason heard the faint voice drift just under the wind and the sound of the highway that was far above him now. The voice caused him to stop in the middle of the street. He tried to make out the name she called. He did not hear the voice again, though he strained to listen. He assumed he'd heard some trick of the gusty winds. Perhaps the way the wind coursed over, around, and over the small buildings, like the runoff, or ran along the wet rooftops into creaking gutters and downspouts, had allowed it to mimic a human voice, something it could never duplicate. Mason thought of Gina and Carl Tullis on their hill. Not only they, but also all the other souls around here, seemed so isolated. Some trait of this area lent itself to loneliness; maybe the mountains made people smaller. He continued to the bus stop, but in another moment clearly heard, "Coming, Mama," in reply to the phantom call he'd heard earlier. Then Mason heard or imagined the rapid slaps of footfalls on wet pavement. He envisioned a mother waiting on a back porch somewhere, dishtowel in hand or maybe a spoon from something she'd been stirring on the stove. The frown on her face will ease into a smile when she sees her boy run into the yard. She'll say, 'why ain't your jacket zipped up,' or 'get inside and wash up, breakfast is on the table.' The boy will grumble at the interruption to his play, but he is hungry and doesn't really mind. Mason realized something he'd forgotten: Gail had always called him in.

GAIL

The comb's teeth raked her scalp and that felt tingling good this morning. Her hair was clean and damp. Jackie used the comb to isolate a section, then used a brush to bring the hair in line. She then rubbed on oily conditioner, before rolling the hair taut over the pink sponge curlers so tightly that Gail felt her hair was still being pulled even after Jackie had moved on to the next section. Gail sipped her coffee.

Jackie said, "This wild tangle of yours ain't been tamed in a long time. Hold your head still."

"I have to drink my coffee," Gail said. "Don't know why we had to do this today anyway. And—ouch!"

"Well, hold still. If we'd waited any longer you'd have been sporting dreadlocks."

Cole, on a blanket in front of them, let out a wet, gurgling laugh.

"Oh, you think that's funny, Mister?" Gail said.

They were in the kitchen; Tyler was upstairs. Gail took another sip from her cup and submitted to Jackie's less than gentle care. The kitchen's warmth felt good, especially with the windows sparkling with frost. A pot of beans and ham simmered on the stove, adding its aroma to the coziness.

"You know, Gail, your head is shaped nice for corn rows…"

"Forget it. I don't have that kind of confidence."

Cole pulled on the ears of his favorite stuffed dog. He appeared quite content amusing himself and spying up at Gail and Jackie every now and then to make sure they were near at hand.

This moment contained a quality that allowed Gail to experience it and consider it at the same time—Jackie fussing over her hair, Cole sitting happily, the contrast of the iced windows and a bubbling pot. It seemed she had lived this before, or something so nearly this that it echoed like déjà vu. Her coffee cup fantasies. Her haunts and worries, and the losses of her past, could not ruin what she had and what surrounded her in this present. Gail figured she owed today to Miss Annie Gant. Gail risked another sip of coffee and got her head tugged back because of it, and silently thanked the old woman.

When they had returned from the Sullivans', they discovered that the lock on the front door had been smashed. Jackie called for her friend Kei to go see who was inside, but he rapidly shook his head and Gail marched in after flicking on the light switch just inside the door.

A teenaged white boy sat in the living room studying the pin-up in a Jet magazine. He jumped to his feet when he saw them. "My grandpa is Henry Buckler. There's been an accident," he sounded rehearsed and nervous. On the way to the hospital, he told Gail his family had come to pick up Miss Annie, but no one answered the door. "It was my little sister who spotted somebody lying at the bottom of the stairs," the boy said. "We broke your front window to get in. Mom called an ambulance and the fire department. The firemen had to bust your door cause the lock takes a key even from the inside, and we couldn't find it."

At the hospital, Henry Buckler's daughter, Cathy, told Gail and Jackie that Annie had passed away. Jackie cried while hugging her baby.

"Were you close?" Cathy asked.

"Should have been closer," Gail answered.

Cathy said, "My father adored her. I hope he doesn't take it too hard. He said she was his second mother. I sent him home. He seemed okay. She never came to, but my father is convinced she knew he was with her at the end. He seems happy for that, that he could be with her."

It wasn't until days later, when Ty noticed the dark blood spot on the stair's middle landing, that Gail realized Annie had already fallen the last time she'd talked to her. Gail remembered how she had appeared tired and out of breath. *I should have seen to her,* Gail thought, *but I was in such a damned hurry.* Then Gail thought, it must have been some feat for Annie to hold herself together long enough to send Gail after Jackie and Cole.

Gail didn't know why the old woman would make such a sacrifice, or if even she'd known what would be the full cost of her act. She tended to think that the woman who petted invisible dogs had known full well what she was doing. That was the gift of this moment in the kitchen, and all such moments that would follow. What next evolved under this roof in the relationship of Gail to Jackie and Cole, and the relationship of Jackie to her son, were the gifts of Annie Gant.

Gail had sat through that Saturday night in Annie's room, in her old straight-backed chair. She had sat there breathing in Annie's scent from the bed, the closet, and the powder on the bureau, and she held the image of Annie's face before her in her mind. Over and over she reviewed their last terse conversation, and began, even then, to find the truth of it. She remonstrated with herself for not having brought Annie closer. And she gazed about the room, picturing Annie moving slowly through her days, and wondered how lonely she must have been in this house when everyone else had left for work or school. Gail looked around at the floor and said, "You guys are gonna miss her, huh?"

Not until Sunday morning did Gail remember the phone number of Gina Manara. She took Annie's chair with her when she went to her room to make the call. She snatched up the receiver, but held it under her chin so long the phone beeped at her. She hung up, picked it up deliberately, and dialed the number. With each ring her anxiousness grew.

"Hello," a woman's voice greeted.

"Yes, hello, my name's Gail Neighbors. May I speak to Mason Reed, please?" Silence followed and a sinking feeling caused Gail's shoulders to slump. "Hello?"

"Hi. Is this Mason's mother?"

"Yes. Is this Gina? I got your number from Maxine."

"Oh, damn. You just missed him, Mrs. Neighbors."

"Do you know when he'll be back?"

"No," Gina said, "That's just it. He left maybe an hour ago. He's not coming back. I'm sorry. You just missed him."

"I see." Gail blew air from her mouth and tilted her face upward. She cursed softly to herself.

"What?"

"I said, I see. Do you know where he went? I need to talk to him."

"No, I don't know."

"Please. It's important."

"I really—"

"I won't hassle him or anything."

"I really don't know. Really."

Neither woman spoke. *Just missed him*, Gail thought. *If I'd just called when I first got the number.* With a hand over the mouthpiece she whispered, "I don't believe this!"

"Mrs. Neighbors, your son and I became pretty good friends, I think. He only talks when the mood hits him and even then he doesn't say a lot. But he's okay, you know? I mean, he wasn't when I met him. He was in a hurry, stressed out and gloomy, but I don't think he left that way. He's not as angry. I figure you two might have been having a hard time with each other…"

"We had…" Gail began, then decided she did not want to confide in this stranger on the phone, even if she did seem polite and concerned.

"I was just trying to say, I think he's okay with it now. I don't think you have to worry so much about him."

"Mothers always have to worry."

"Guess so," Gina said. "He'll show up soon."

Gail tried to decide if this girl was being patronizing, and if she really spoke the truth. She wondered how close Mason and she had gotten. "His father was like this. Leave and stay away years. Not caring what anybody else went through."

"He's nothing like his father, Mrs. Neighbors," Gina said.

Gail said quickly, "I know. I know that. I just meant…"

"Mrs. Neighbors—"

"Gail, please."

"Gail, I'm certain he's going to come back to one of us or both. Let's you and me make a pact. The one who hears from him first will call the other, okay?"

"Yes," Gail said, "Okay."

"We'll keep in contact. Any day we'll hear. I'm sure."

"If he calls you, Gina, tell him, tell him," Gail hesitated. The message was important and she did not know this girl. But she let the awkwardness go. She said, "Tell him I believe in him."

That had been a few days ago and she had not heard from Gina or Mason. Yet many times she went over what the girl had said and allowed herself to take a portion of comfort from it. There had been a lot to keep busy with and to think about since then—the funeral, and moving Jackie and Cole back in, and Gail had talked to Mr. Hirsch, her boss's husband, about a computer operator job for Jackie at his firm. He'd said, "Well, I'll give her an interview. No promises."

While Jackie rolled another curler in place, Gail asked, "What time is your appointment tomorrow?"

"Not til eleven. Hope I know the software he uses."

"Well, tell him you'll learn it quick if you don't. I'm taking Cole with me. I have a friend who's going to come by and watch him."

"Thanks, Gail." Jackie started humming. She interrupted herself long enough to say, "Mmm, you're going to look fly."

Gail thought she heard a noise coming from up the hall, maybe at the front door. "Shh, you hear something?"

Jackie answered, "No, I don't hear a thing," and began humming even louder than before.

"Someone's at the door, I tell you."

"Let me peek." Jackie took a step to the left, still holding a lock of Gail's hair, and leaned out in order to look down the hall. "Nothing," she said.

Then Gail distinctly heard the door open.

"That's Ty," Jackie said.

But Gail knew Ty was upstairs and her heart took a bloodless beat. More hope than she believed herself capable of filled her in the instant. Jackie tried to hold her down in the seat and Gail slapped her hands away from her head. She heard Ty pounding rapidly down the stairs.

The door swung open just as Gail reached the foyer at a run. Dan Neighbors stepped in carrying two suitcases.

Disappointment made her face fall. Dan's lips tightened over his bright smile when he saw her expression.

That's right, Gail thought, *he wouldn't have a key to the new lock, but Dan does because he installed it.* "What are you doing here? And what are those?" Gail wagged an index finger at the suitcases.

"Hey, Dad," Tyler said.

Dan looked to Jackie, who shrugged and said, "Hey, I couldn't keep her back there. You're too damn noisy."

"What the hell is going on here?" Gail looked from Dan to Jackie to Ty, and they all looked like reprimanded children. "Shut the door, Ty. I'm not heating the neighborhood."

Jackie sprinted back to the kitchen and retrieved Cole.

"Well," Gail demanded.

"Mama, you're always saying we should think about taking in another boarder, and now we need one more than ever," Ty said. His smile looked infuriatingly identical to Dan's.

"Gail, we'll be consolidating our money, honey," Dan said.

"Don't honey me. What makes everyone think I want you under the same roof with me?"

Ty said, "The other day I caught you two in the little kitchen upstairs. I didn't say anything, but it looked awful cozy."

Jackie laughed. "Go on, Gail."

"You didn't catch us doing anything," Gail said. "We were working on the plumbing."

"Exactly what I thought," Ty said. Now everyone but Gail was laughing.

"This is my house," Gail began.

"We took a vote, Gail," Jackie said. "You said I was family now, so it's two to one. Dan's in."

Dan set his bags down and stepped close to Gail. "I saw your face when I first came in," he said quietly. "If you really think it's a bad idea, I'll turn around right now."

Gail could smell his aftershave and the pomade in his hair. She looked into that familiar face with the burgeoning springs of white at the temples. She threw her hands up, trying to show more exasperation than she felt. "I'm sure you're going to do whatever you want, Dan."

Dan winked. "There's more boxes in the car, Ty," he said. He climbed the stairs with the suitcases. "Hey, nice do," he said over a shoulder.

Gail touched a hand to her head, half-covered in pink sponges. "Get used to it," she said. Turning to Jackie, she said, "Let's finish up," and took Cole from the girl's arms.

Acknowledgments

Because I wasn't alone even while by myself writing this, I'd like to thank Betty Tully, Fran Moshos, John L.F. Hopkins, Ned Kraft, and Vera Caccioppoli—renegade writers and diligent readers. I thank Bettina Bennett, Regina Bennett, Oscar Bennett Sr. and Pamela Bennett for lending me encouragement and faith. Thanks to Doug Seibold of Agate Publishing for aiding me with enthusiasm and uncanny insight. And thanks to Dan Lazar of Writers House for supporting me with caring advice and helpful kindnesses.